I0694034

ARMOUR OF GOD

A Novel

Gods. Grifters. Lovers. Saints.

Steven A. Coulter

Other books by this author:

Passageway 2 (published 2024)
Passageway (published 2024
Copperhead (published 2023)
Copperhead 2 (published 2024)
Rising Son, The Chronicles of Spartak (Book 1) (published 2017)
Freedom's Hope, The Chronicles of Spartak (Book 2) (published 2018)

Dedication

ONE HUNDRED YEARS AGO high school teacher John Thomas Scopes was tried and found guilty of violating a Tennessee law which made it illegal to teach human evolution in any state funded school. In a trial that drew intense national media attention, William Jennings Bryan, a three-time presidential candidate, argued for the prosecution and famed trial lawyer Clarence Darrow served the defense. The verdict was eventually overturned on a technicality. A 1960 movie, "Inherit the Wind," was made about it, starring two famous actors: Fredric March and Spencer Tracy.

Could it happen again? Is it happening now?

This book is dedicated to the memory of John Scopes and scientists everywhere.

Special Acknowledgments

This novel has a long history of people who believed in it and helped me reach the finish line. This is a partial list and I am grateful.

Dr. Barbara O'Connor, Emeritus Professor, Sacramento State University (who survived numerous early versions, offering advice and encouragement); Gerry J. Hill, Emeritus Professor of Biology, Carleton College, Northfield, Minnesota (when we were AIDS hotline volunteers at Project Inform); Brother Joseph (a believer in the inerrancy of the Bible); Marina Parisinou (an agnostic); Katherine V. Forrest, editor, advisor and an icon in lesbian literature; Dennis Myers, journalist extraordinaire, Reno, Nevada (U.S. Army buddy who died before this was published, a tragic loss. He loved the idea of him being the chief spokesman for the president); Ray Nelson (an artist who read an early version and said to keep going); Loa Semrau (longtime friend who endured early chapters and offered gentle and inspired advice); John Carini, my barber for 30 years had many ideas and was pleased his last name would be attached to the Cardinal's secretary. Unfortunately, he died before it was finished.); Lambda Literary Writer's Retreat where I took a version of this to the 2008 workshop, not an easy fit for authors exploring the queer experience but it was empowering being with such talented writers in a supportive environment.

And Greg McIntyre, husband and my evermore, who offered endless encouragement.

"The Bible satisfies me, it is enough."
–Matthew Harrison Brady, played by Fredric March in 1960 film, *Inherit the Wind*

"It frightens me to imagine the state of learning in this world if everyone had your driving curiosity."
–Henry Drummond, played by Spencer Tracy in *Inherit the Wind*

"…if there was no Adam, there is no need for Jesus."
–*Answers in Genesis*, an apologetics ministry

"I don't want to believe. I want to know."
–Carl Sagan, Astronomer

"I believe alien life is quite common in the universe, although intelligent life is less so. Some say it has yet to appear on planet Earth."
–attributed to Stephen Hawking, theoretical physicist, cosmologist & author

"I don't really care if they're watching. Maybe the show starts early."
–Daniel to Saito in *Armour of God*

1.

Plaza Shopping Center, San Jose, California

It was a glorious, goosebump giddy day, the sun playing peek-a-boo with broken clouds sprinting ahead of a storm. It was like when she first rode her bike hands free, the wind roaring approval in her ears, her heart pounding with pride and purpose. Nearly sixteen, she was now primed to change the world.

Thousands were converging on a bookstore in a San Jose shopping center, most of the parking lot roped off in anticipation, parents carrying and pulling along their children, a large contingent of young adults, likely college and high school students giving high-fives and laughing, cell phones capturing their role in this happening, some sending live video and commentary to friends. There were scattered police cars and a handful of pickets carrying signs she couldn't read at this distance. Four television news crews were here, microwave towers extended while a helicopter from a local station hovered overhead capturing the scene. And here she was, a nobody about to make history.

Her lips moved in whispers, thoughts too personal or dangerous to share.

"You will know my name."

Ruth Ann Ryan was the luckiest girl in her church, personally chosen by her pastor for a sacred mission. Friends who knew the plan called her a 9/11-style heroine, a First Responder for Christ, a true Christian soldier, as in the hymn, marching to war.

Her mom was next to her, reaching down from heaven, and it gave her strength, the confidence to do the unexpected, to vanquish low expectations, to be a leader, shedding her cocoon and taking flight. Other girls in the congregation, the pretty ones, the popular clique, were not even asked.

As she struggled with the vest, nearly a fourth of her body weight, the canvas straps bit into her shoulders. She tried to adjust the harness under her coat, hoping no one would notice. *Kinda silly worrying about such things when you're about to die.*

Daniel Duboce got to Harvey's Books a little early. These events were less about selling books than meeting people, opening minds, letting them see he was real, judge his sincerity. Some focused on the issues, most were there for his celebrity. Sometimes it seemed people had cell phones instead of faces.

His head of security, the dashingly handsome, Romaldo Vega, black hair with some silver at the temples, always dressed immaculately in a dark suit and tie, had the three armor-plated SUV's pull behind the shop and three guards stepped out, checking the alley entrance, and meeting two other guards who had arrived earlier, before Daniel exited the vehicle. He stepped through the back door into a storage room.

The shop owner, Bill Gueldner, seemed a bit flustered when they shook hands. He wore a tweed sports jacket just slightly smaller than his stomach and a warm *'Oh Gosh'* smile. "We're at capacity," he said, giggling, running fingers through his long gray hair. "We had two hundred people in line when we opened three hours ago. I've never seen book sales like this! Such a joy! I ordered eight hundred copies of your work and many times that number of buyers are here." He took out his phone and shrugged sheepishly. "Could we do a selfie?"

"I hope they all don't want each book autographed," Daniel said, forcing himself to smile, handing the phone to a surprised Vega.

"Squeeze in tight gentlemen." The phone clicked and Vega handed it back without checking the photo. "We're examining the crowd. No obvious problems. It should be safe or as safe as it can be when millions see you as Satan and the rest of the planet fantasizes on your celebrity, face, physique, and certain body parts."

Daniel's laugh at the teasing ended in a sigh. "I'm so lucky." He turned to the shop owner. "Can we set up some speakers and a microphone outside? I want to talk to the parking lot crowd after we finish in here."

"I think we can," Guelder said. "The sporting goods store next door has a portable set for use in softball games. I'll text the manager. Give me a few minutes." The man turned and started giving his employees instructions. He turned back, "Please don't forget those who got here early."

"I won't." Daniel emerged from the back room unannounced into the crowd inside. There was a shriek from a woman and a standing ovation as he walked into the crowd.

He made a few comments and then took questions, signing books as he worked through the main aisle. A small group of Boy Scouts in uniform stepped up to him, grinning. "Hi, Justyn," he said to one red haired boy with freckles. "Great to see you and the troop again." They all did a Scout salute and he returned it.

"Mr. Duboce…can we get a photo?" the boy asked, his voice breaking. He looked down in embarrassment. Daniel hugged the almost teenager and took his phone, squatting as the boys surrounded him. *"Books!"* They all smiled. They'd met nearly a year ago when Daniel spoke to their Tiberon scout troop and did a display of medieval swordplay, a favorite hobby.

The boys examined their photo, letting out a squeal as Daniel continued his step-stop through the store. Thirty minutes later the store owner signaled him.

"I want to spend time outside," Daniel told him, "and if I missed anyone, I'll come back to this room to finish signing and answering questions. Plus, selfies." There was laughter. "You're welcome to join me."

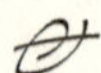

She spotted her target, Daniel Duboce, sixty yards ahead, coming out of the bookstore, wearing a blue knit shirt showing off his biceps and trim waist. Some claimed he was good-looking—the famous were always fawned over by the media, always beautiful even if they weren't—but she had the power to see him as he really was. The man was here for a book lecture, mentioned in the news. Reports claimed five thousand people were here. He was forced to come outside since the shop was small, making her mission easier.

Maybe Jesus brought the crowd to flush him from his sanctuary.

Duboce leaped onto the back of a pickup and was handed a microphone to address the crowd. She would make the evening news.

Ruth Ann started to laugh and then stopped, remembering her purpose on this special morning, a day that would end heroically across from an ugly flat-roofed Safeway supermarket. She had always been the odd kid, the one never asked to dance.

"Not anymore!"

The sky was overcast, increasingly unsettled, clouds racing. A sunburst flashed on Duboce like a klieg light in the movies. On cue, the man lifted both arms toward heaven and the crowd screamed his name, surging forward, hungry and desperate, packing together, making it hard to move.

Why was Jesus making it so difficult?

The crowd thickened and Duboce disappeared. She stepped to the right, searching. There he was, between the shifting heads.

"God, please help me!"

She dodged between two slow moving couples; her elbow caught against an old man. She staggered, bumping into a gray-haired woman, knocking her sideways.

"Slow down, girl!" the old lady snapped. "We all wanna get close!"

"I'm sorry."

The vest made her top heavy, thrusting her onto the balls of her feet if she moved too fast, tripping out of control.

"I can do this. I must."

She avoided a group of young men, some without shirts, two holding hands. Of course, people like them would be here. She knew what they were and what the Bible said. Duboce was one of them.

When Reverend McConnell gave her a final blessing, her heart pounding, she kissed the cross to seal her pledge. "Nothing is more important than faith," he had said. It was true and Christianity was in crisis. "Millions are questioning the divinity of Jesus," he warned, his face ashen, squeezing her hand, begging for her help. "And it's not just the liberals and perverts. Good people are confused. Duboce must be stopped."

She remembered earlier times and the pastor's dimpled grin she had loved all her life.

How could I say no?

When they were strapping on the vest earlier, she was trembling at first, a little scared. She didn't want to screw up. A balding man from the congregation, an old friend, Jonas Swift, said she looked beautiful, filled with the light of God. Sally Moss, a real beautician, had combed her brown hair, flowing to her shoulders, slipping on a blue headband to match her eyes. Today her acne was better, a relief on her last day of life before meeting with angels.

Will I have pimples in heaven?

Daniel switched on his hand-held mic, standing in the back of a Ford pickup in front of the store.

Those in front seemed taken aback by his sudden appearance, followed by assorted shouts and clapping. Moments later, many surged tighter toward him, held back ten feet by several policemen and two of Vega's armed guards. He noticed a half dozen police cars, lights flashing, parked on either side of the crowd, waiting if there was trouble.

He enjoyed the applause and whistles, frequent offers of marriage from women and men or something less complicated and graphic and many holding up copies of his book, either in solidarity or just looking for his signature. To the left, at some distance, two score of protestors stood silently, faces pinched, with signs calling him *"Christ Hater," "Liar," "Fake News,"* or *"Deviant,"* among other things. These people —men, women, and children— did not make eye contact and their posture and clothing were dignified. Critics were not often so stoic.

The secret ceremony blessing her mission had been wondrous. A boy from church, who sat with the popular girls at school, kissed her cheek before letting his lips slide across hers, pushing his tongue inside. He'd touched the side of her face. She felt heat. Ron Burrows, seventeen, tan and lanky with curly blond hair. Reverend McConnell insisted he do it and had left them alone for the task. She snorted and blushed, remembering her fantasies, wanting more, leaving hungry.

Too many images. Her head was bursting. Stay focused. Stop shaking.

Mommy. Help me…

Ruth Ann was closing in. He had the most famous face in the world, in every newspaper. The paparazzi followed him everywhere and tabloids once caught photos with his shirt off—a perfect, smooth physique except for the scar on his chest; a video of it seemed everywhere, looping endlessly.

How many times have I watched it? Some called him a hero, a new prophet. But she knew him for what he was: a Dark Angel, a homosexual, and Jesus wanted him dead. God's Kingdom must rise and was counting on her. The ball-bearing shrapnel vest was supposed to be lethal to thirty yards, but no guarantees. She wanted to be closer than five, just to make sure; there would be no retakes.

Keep moving. Almost there.

Ruth unbuttoned the mid-section of her jacket, reached inside, and gripped the dead-man's switch. She punched the safety release button. Just a few more feet. It was armed. If she was shot and let go, it would explode.

Will I be close enough to kill him?

She wedged further into the crowd. Ron Burrows' beautiful face filled her head. Her breath caught, remembering the time she hid in the bushes and watched him swimming in the river during church summer camp, the moon shining on his naked butt. Her hand felt slippery.

Focus.

Ruth Ann jerked her head back. A tall man, coming out of nowhere, pushed between a couple and stopped directly in front of her, staring into her eyes, snapping her fantasy. His hand thrust inside her jacket and encircled the pressure switch, clamping her moist palm against the metal.

She staggered, losing her balance. He grabbed her shoulder; she could feel his strength. He was beautiful with black curly hair, a touch of silver at the temples, and perfect skin. He wore an elegant dark suit. Hard fingers now gripped the back of her neck, pulling her close. It felt like a passionate embrace, their lips close enough to kiss.

"I am Gabriel, Archangel of God," he said with a deep, reassuring voice. His touch was electric, his accent exotic, the power rumbling through her. "You have a new mission." He pushed her backward through the crowd.

"NO! I've sworn an oath!"

"You are released from it."

"But Reverend McConnell will be angry."

"He will understand. We must talk in private."

His green eyes were hypnotic. She thought she noticed men in black moving people out of the way but he kept her face directed at his, inches apart. His breath was sweet and hot. Her hand ached yet she felt light headed, a little dizzy.

Could he really be an angel?

The Bible said angels were beautiful. He was the handsomest man she'd ever seen—better than any movie star! And she knew not all angels had wings on Earth.

Was it possible?

Inside a concrete stairwell next to the grocery store, he stopped. The thick glass door closed behind them. They were alone. He released her neck but continued his tight grip on the switch.

She gasped, her eyes widening as, one by one, he unbuttoned her jacket, inspected the vest, and wrapped both hands around hers and the switch as if they were praying. He asked questions; Ruth Ann felt proud telling him her story. She was the first recruit in her church to step forward and offer her life. The righteous would praise her name.

"Others will follow if I fail."

"Reverend McConnell is mistaken," Gabriel said, his tone unequivocal and righteous, like a thunderbolt. "God sent me from heaven to intervene."

She listened, not believing it, but fear was building in her gut as he explained the message on the granules from space and the purpose of the new God. He seemed so certain. She felt confused, adrift from her church. It wasn't possible!

But what if he is an angel?

Gabriel stared at her, unblinking. The only sounds were the muffled shouts of the crowd in the distance. He released her hands. "You will serve an important purpose," he whispered, touching her cheek with an open palm, kissing her forehead. "Go with God." He pivoted, exiting the enclosed stairwell, and closed the glass door behind him.

She stood motionless, replaying his words and those of her pastor, feeling increasingly bewildered. It'd seemed so simple. With her free hand, she pulled a cell phone from a pocket and punched the minister's number. It went to voice mail.

"*Reverend McConnell,*" she said haltingly, "*Help me! Archangel Gabriel stands before me...he...he came to me as...as I walked through the crowd. He said...he said you're wrong about Daniel Duboce and that he's... he's coming for you.*"

Through the glass wall she could see Gabriel standing outside. "*He's watching me. What do I do?*"

Gabriel nodded respectfully, so refined. She glanced briefly at her phone, biting her lip. When she looked up, he was gone.

Acid punched into her throat, flooding her mouth.

Daniel Duboce is the chosen of God?

The church was her life. What else did she have? She thought of Ron Burrows in the river, turning over on his back.

"I LOVE YOU, JESUS!" she shouted in exultation as she lifted her arms high overhead. The flash of light and the sudden warmth were what she expected entering the gates of heaven.

2.

The modified Boeing jetliner lifted above the clouds and banked right, leveling at forty thousand feet, headed west. Washington, D.C. was far behind.

Dr. Yoshita Wada undid his seat belt, moved to the center of the sofa, and smiled at the fresh-faced young man coming down the aisle, setting down a celadon tea service, an open bowl of hot water and, of course, a bamboo whisk. Tradition was important. The man also left two newspapers; print was so much better than online versions. He thanked the man who then hurried to the only other passenger, his boss at the Japanese Space Agency. Protocol required the senior official be served first but Wada knew his face was more familiar. He was used to the attention but preferred the solitude of his research.

He took a spoonful of the vibrant green *matcha* powder, dropped it into the cup and added water just shy of boiling. He picked up the whisk, dipped it into the warm water, shook it once briskly over a napkin and then into the teacup, stirring in a W-pattern for one minute. The tea foamed thick and astonishingly bright because of its quality; for the emperor tea leaves had been forced to overproduce chlorophyll, giving the finest robust tint and taste. He inhaled the earthy scent and took a sip. How he loved this bitter constant in his life.

He rubbed his eyes and considered the purpose of this unfortunate trip. In simplest terms, it was about rubble plucked from a rock as it orbited the Sun and passed between Earth and Mars yet it was now entwined in a celestial knot of politics and fear.

The interior of the plane was theatrical yet appropriate for the emperor, the last person to use it. The decoration was normally swapped between trappings for the prime minister and His Imperial Majesty. This trip was an unexpected one and there had not been time to change into a more frugal décor befitting a head of state not a god. There were rich draperies on every wall depicting scenes of ancient Japanese glory. Where he was, there were four small sofas and tables, more like a home interior than any plane or palace he had seen.

He picked up yesterday's *Asahi Shimbun*, one of his favorite papers. Nothing of great interest. He glanced at the *New York Times* and set down his teacup. It was a double headline across the entire page above the fold. Was there a war?

22 State Legislatures Pass Identical Resolutions Urging President Walton Declare America "God's Kingdom"

The article explained that legislators were demanding that a Christian religious figure should be appointed to serve as God's representative on earth and inform all levels of government on God's wishes. Wada shook his head. This would help explain the reaction to his White House meeting with the president. Talk about bad timing. His lips curled in amusement.

He hadn't expected it to go well. Jeremiah Walton, the photo-perfect Jesus-on-his-sleeve American president, and two senior aides who said little but glared and grumbled with disgust when they did ask questions, never mentioning what was going on behind the scenes.

One aide was a short bald man, perhaps a cousin of Middle

Earth's Gollum, who gloated with his privilege when he sat next to the president on a settee. He was some sort of political strategist. There was a general named Beauregard, a big man, head of National Intelligence or some such title, a war hero according to the president, with a horrific scar on his pockmarked face and a sour demeanor.

The tall silver-haired president had been polite, asked probing questions, more insightful than Wada would have expected from a politician, and ended with a plea for more time to consider the revelation. He was obviously calculating the fallout, which meant there was no doubt on the outcome. Surprisingly, Walton was known as a man who actually liked to read widely, including books, a curious intellectual with a large vocabulary, unlike the prime minister, his own boss, or one of Walton's infamous recent predecessors. Sometimes Walton even accurately quoted ideas from literature, not just the Bible.

The two men had shaken hands with gentle nods before Wada returned to the airport.

Imagine if he had told them everything?

He set the celadon cup into the armrest holder, remembering the wonder he felt as a boy discovering the hidden world in a drop of water and dedicating his life to science. The space-dust was like that in some ways, the sense of awe and humility, the marvel of the infinitesimal from the beginning of time. Yet this discovery was more primal, melding religious dogma and science. Perhaps, if he wanted to be astronomically hyperbolic, truly triumphant, it was like birthing a new sun or, maybe, given human nature, sucking reason, science, and faith into a black hole. He smiled at his own mental embroidery, but this was no hollow and ignorant shout by a thoughtless politician. Grandiose terms seemed preening and peacock but not incorrect. He had to think in laymen's terms to tell the story.

He glanced at his cane, hooked under a strap on the cushion beside him, the curved silver handle in the shape of *Misago*, the magnificent western Osprey, sometimes called a "fish falcon," or "fish hawk" in Korea, with a white head and belly, also the name of the ambitious space program that had consumed much of his life over the past decade. It was a gift from his late wife long ago and a source of comfort and remembrance. He ran fingers over the finely detailed folded wings, the golden eyes and the fierce beak holding a small round ivory ball.

The president had recognized the name of the space venture because of publicity on the wealth in minerals discovered but did not know its details. He had been given no advance information when the prime minister had called days ago, promising word of an astonishing discovery in space. Wada had made a power point presentation on a large screen in a room near the Oval Office, the three men watching him closely.

When the *Misago* capsule had reached the edge of the asteroid belt, Wada had explained, it launched a swarm of mini bots conducting fly-bys scouting for mining treasure. For months they hunted prime targets before a surprise finding—the giant asteroid *1620 Geographos* with a mean-diameter of 2.5 kilometers—seemed to contain rare earth metals in abundance and, importantly, moisture, almost as valuable as the platinum and rhodium. It hid riches it was not supposed to have and that was what made space exploration so much fun and dangerous.

The minerals were called rare-earth for a reason and finding their hideout offered wealth and power to those able to lay claim and extract it. Water could recharge power cells and be recombined with oxygen to produce fuel, a key to exploration further into the solar system. The Japanese Space Agency, the prime minister and the media were ecstatic at the discovery and had staged the mission with coverage comparable to a World Soccer Cup final with Japan or the first Japanese moon landing, with weeks of buildup, knowing it could end in failure but willing to take the risk. On prime time television, viewers in Japan and scientists from around the world watched *Misago* launch a robotic rock harvester with Wada providing expert commentary. It glided to the surface, hovered, then touched down on the rough, low gravity rock and planted a small flag of the Rising Sun, Japan staking a claim in the heavens. Millions shouted in jubilation, mostly the young, often drunk, pouring into the streets of Tokyo, blocking traffic, thrilled their country was blowing off decades of lethargy, making history. The robot drilled into the surface, holding on, digging, crushing, collecting a bellyful of regolith before lifting off, returning to the capsule, and beginning the long journey back to Japan.

Yet the real treasure, Wada had explained to the president, hidden at the edge of scientific understanding, was neither mineral nor water. It was biology. He laughed now, thinking about the arrogant bald advisor spilling coffee on his crotch. The general jumped in his seat and farted, not that anyone would comment.

Wada prepared another cup of matcha, leaned back, and crossed his legs. Would the discovery, if it went public, provide a new light for humanity to follow or invite darkness? He recalled a poem by a hard-drinking long-ago Welsh poet about the end of life and the death of his father; how appropriate it was in understanding this potentially lethal discovery, risking social upheaval.

"*Rage, rage,*" Dylan Thomas had written, "*against the dying of the light.*"

Did humanity want to know what it didn't know? Was this a black hole snuffing starlight or a revelation from *Amaterasu*, the Shinto goddess of the sun?

He had read some stories about the *Kingdom Movement* in America, to ditch democracy and appoint someone to be the sole recipient and interpreter of messages from God. Then that person would give the president, Congress and all the states their marching orders. So much for democracy and pluralism. How did theocracy work for Iran or Afghanistan? How did it work for Japan in World War II, the Emperor supposedly the descendent of *Amaterasu*? Clearly, the big man forgot to talk with the goddess. Humans could be ridiculous and America was now center stage in this ongoing folly.

Wada sighed and shook his head. He had just given the American leaders proof their Christian god likely did not exist and the Bible had gotten it wrong on its depiction of creation. The person doing the listening, according to the article, would be called

The Prophet or *The Light*. The discovery in space now meant the *Light* might be dark from day one.

Following the article was an analysis by reporter Daniel Duboce. Wada grinned, knowing the man from his visit to Japan last year when he was working on an in-depth story on the Japanese Space Agency. A good man. Duboce labeled the *Movement "a naked power grab, trashing democracy."* Polls showed massive opposition by the public, he wrote, but among registered voters it was popular. Duboce pointed out that decades of relentless gerrymandering, forceful intimidation, and restrictive qualifications meant only about twenty percent of adult Americans were registered and allowed to vote.

He put the newspaper down and picked up his teacup, going back to his thoughts on *Misago*. Whatever it was, the discovery posited an almost holy conundrum, a biological godhead riddle, equal parts rapture and poison. Every secret it revealed seemed to multiply the uncertainty; burn-out preceded exultation. Should science, logically, to preserve itself from the hurricane, accept the comforting embrace of silence?

Or maybe he was just an aging samurai guarding his feudal secret, a silly old astronomer full of himself and periodically obsessed with old Japanese *kaiju* movies—pure oxygen when reality was often so suffocating. Maybe in this remake, *Gigan*, the cyborg space monster, could play the lead, coming after *Godzilla* who was protecting humans for reasons known only to the screenwriter. And who was the author of this new adventure featuring regolith from an asteroid? For now, the research would remain tightly held, his staff sworn to secrecy.

3.

Chofu-City, Tokyo

Saito struggled to maintain his demeanor. Wada had asked him here as a professional colleague, not as a family friend. It was easier to believe new scientific discoveries when they conformed to your pre-existing belief system, not obliterated it. But the action on the screen mimicked the findings in the report.

The old scientist watched him, his stare at times intense, hopeful, or playful. How he loved this man, Dr. Yoshito Wada, teacher, scientist, philosopher, grandfather of his closest friend. Yoshito was his hero. And if you believed polls, he was one of Japan's most famous and admired men, a regular on talk shows, offering inspired insights on science. He was Japan's Carl Sagan or Neil deGrasse Tyson, with long steel-grey hair combed back and held neatly in place, as always, at the nape of his neck with a black elastic cord and a small jade carving of an orca, a gift from his late wife, Akina.

This discovery was more than unexpected. Clearly it was impossible, lethal to both faith and science. It was hard to comprehend in one reading, with the complex detail, a cornucopia of startling results, the testing, the implications, and the stunning hypothesis.

Yoshito reached for his cane, wrapping both hands around the silver Osprey handle as he leaned forward and scooted his wheeled office chair closer, like a schoolboy.

"Reaction?"

"I'm floundering, not something easy to admit. Asteroids have been sampled and studied for years with some rudimentary mining on a few. I remember Japan's second Hyabusa venture bringing back grains from the asteroid Ryugu, 190 million miles from Earth, in 2022. NASA delivered a tire size capsule into the Utah desert in 2024, taken from the asteroid Apophis. How could there be something this startling?"

"Maybe we can think this through together." He wore a grin as he leaned forward. "How about something less exotic?" Wada's eyes were impish. "Do you remember when NASA's Stardust brought back tiny grains from the comet tail of Wild-2 in 2006?"

Saito hesitated before replying, feeling like he had just swallowed a syrupy ice cone on a summer day. "I do," he answered, remembering articles at university on the excitement in the space community. "You assisted that project. They found glycine, as I recall, an amino acid, which many believe was able to create the first protein-like strands—precursors of life."

"You're amazing."

Saito reached over and touched his arm and squeezed.

Tio Ito was leaning against the wall nearby, a woman he also admired; they exchanged a knowing glance. She was in her mid-fifties, with the energy of someone half that age. There had been similar findings since then from other probes. NASA and JAXA often worked together sharing information. She never was one who liked to sit, always in motion, ignoring a chair beside her.

"What we see now is the next step, perhaps the final one," Tio said, her voice compelling in its excitement. "It's as if we're watching the missing chemical link, something we have theorized about since Darwin but never seen or understood before."

Saito stared first at the screen, over to her, then back to Wada, biting his lower lip. Scientists didn't talk like this.

"When we found the anomalies," Tio said, excitement overcoming her normally calm demeanor, words tumbling faster, "the cubes, shapes outside of nature, we knew we had entered a new scientific frontier. In my mind, day and night, I see the shapes—discoveries—from all angles, impervious, mocking, beckoning. Scientific research is not for those with short attention spans or lack of courage."

"Agreed," Wada said, smiling.

"I wondered if we would ever penetrate the outer shell," Tio remarked wistfully. "We needed to explore a thousand options, some beyond rationality. We did, using a mix of compounds: hydrogen, oxygen, carbon, nitrogen, phosphorus and sulfur."

"The mythical primordial soup." Saito's voice trembled with awe.

"Indeed." Tio glanced out the window at the night sky, the quarter moon high above the horizon.

Wada's eyes glistened as he spoke: "Inside was an unusual mix of chemical elements, some we identified, some still unknown, wrapped in a common protein shell, encased in a second shell, made from a never-before-seen material, apparently designed to protect the contents from the extreme temperatures and radiation of space."

Saito nodded, hoping he wasn't crazy if he believed this analysis, that personal feelings might outweigh science. "Make sure I understand the short version. Nestled among ordinary bits of pulverized rock, you found something beyond nature, perhaps from outside our solar system, something manufactured, from the beginning of time."

"Exactly. But by whom or what?" Wada's eyes were wide with excitement.

"*Man or God?*" Saito and Tio whispered simultaneously, followed by a quick burst of laughter and shaking of heads. Saito continued, "We're scientists and our world must remain factual, not supernatural. I'm not comfortable putting some god at the front end of evolution."

"What would Darwin think?" Tio asked. "Are man or God the only options? There is so much we do not yet understand."

Charles Darwin. This event might have given him some comfort considering the way he was pilloried by both ministers and scientists. "Without celestial trumpets, can people of faith or even scientists accept this?" A chorus of angels seemed unlikely to back this case. Many people, particularly in the West and Middle East, were so obsessed with religion and a rigid set of beliefs that this could be toxic. The three book-based religions—Christianity, Judaism, and Islam—would take it the hardest. Some eastern religions might be more flexible. The scientific community would be shaken but engaged, curiosity part of their DNA. It was the politicians and charlatans who were the problem, exploiting faith for votes and power. And those who would fear a blank eternity.

Wada offered a cryptic but grandfatherly shrug.

Yes, Saito thought, he was like a grandfather, one he had adopted, wise and humble. Funny too. Saito grinned, luxuriating in this mental burn. A lesser man, and the discovery would invite chaos. He exchanged glances with Tio, knowing they shared similar views and affection.

They were silent, listening to the quiet before Tio began again. "Here's another mystery—we could only dissolve a small percentage of the granules. Most remain inert and impermeable, their secrets hidden. We have no idea why. Yet."

"I'll bet you have a hypothesis."

Wada nodded in affirmation.

Movement amid the particles on the screen. "They continue to reproduce." They watched and counted together, losing track of time, touching the images, and laughing as the numbers rose: sixteen, thirty-two, sixty-four. Wada obviously never got tired of this, a boy finding wonder.

Another image stabbed Saito's calm. Dero Ozawa, the empty-headed, pig-faced JAXA president. "Your boss is an arrogant… foolish…" Wada shook his head but he continued: "What about religious fanatics? You could be in danger."

Wada raised an open palm. "Ozawa knows, unfortunately. As does the prime minister. Cordial would not be how I would describe our initial conversations; by the end I pretended to humbly acquiesce and stop research. The stakes are too great for us to be bullied by uninquisitive minds. We've been careful to contain it within the broader space community," he said, trying to sound reassuring, "sending out samples of the unexceptional material to those here at JAXA outside our circle and to our scientific brothers at NASA."

"Our statements to the press," Tio said, "focus on the minerals, gold and the fortune to come to Japan once full-scale mining commences. Greed is always a useful deflection."

"But the reason for our meeting tonight is my discussion with the prime minister about a face-to-face meeting I had a few days ago with the American president. It did not go well with either man, given Mr. Walton's dogmatic religious views and our need for help from the U.S. Navy."

"If you were so careful, how did your boss find out?" Saito waited for his response.

"One of my team turned traitor, apparently frightened by the findings and seeking reward, perhaps promotion and status through betrayal. The scientist whom I believe leaked the information was found murdered this week, a staged suicide from my view. I had to identify the body and talked with the detective. My assumption is he was selling it to an outsider. I have no idea who that might be. The police are simply baffled. Perhaps best they do not examine what we are about here."

Saito was speechless, reaching out and touching Wada's arm, reaching to Tio and interlocking fingers. "Please, please be cautious."

The two scientists shrugged.

Saito continued: "If the discovery leaks to the public?"

"A media *tsunami*." Wada's incendiary few words were stated almost matter of fact. "Scientists have protocols for dealing with complex and controversial issues. Government and media often resort to hiding the truth or exploiting it. Sacred cows, as they say in America, must be protected. And what is more sacred, more unassailable than Christianity and its entrenched bureaucracy and power in politics? Reason and logic are often beyond the purview of faith."

"Aren't you being too cynical?" A silly question, Saito scolded himself. He had the same view. How could one be too cynical about politics? Yet that was the easy view, a cheap one, disregarding the sense of service and human advancement as central motivators to many government workers enduring conflict, complexity, and often tediousness in public life.

"The pressure will be intense to discredit the research," Wada said, touching the silver handle of his cane to his chin. "All three of us have lived in the United States. Will Christians turn the other cheek if Jesus is stripped of his divinity? Nothing seems less likely. The country is being run by Christian nationalists and there are rumors the president will announce that future elections are pointless because God has made his selection."

"Yes," Saito responded, "I've seen the speculation. When a religion takes charge in a democracy, elections can get eliminated. Look at Iran long ago."

Wada nodded. "The implications for both governments, ours and theirs, will be staggering. Science itself could become a target, pilloried and accused of espousing fake news." He laughed at the term created by charlatans. "Truth, real truth, must be suppressed, I conjecture, because the disruption to cherished institutions would be too great. Powerful people do not easily give up a source of control."

Wada hung his cane over one arm, stood and offered his hands to both colleagues. "Come. I want to show you something."

They walked to a nearby elevator and rode down two floors. Saito pressed his elbow against Tio's, a comfortable gesture between longtime friends.

Wada was bubbling. "I want humanity to see the wonder in the discovery, a breakthrough on our existence. I want humanity to feel excitement and hope, not fear. Somehow there must be a way."

They exited the elevator and stopped in front of a glass wall, the *Misago* cargo pod on the other side. "As I looked into this chamber and the robotic arms came to life at my touch," he whispered, "I imagined the canister sitting in the lap of the Hindu god *Ganesha*, Lord of the Beginnings, with six arms wrapped around the tiny golden box from heaven."

"Prescient," Saito acknowledged, "considering what you found and with a flair for the dramatic. What do you need me to do?"

"Officially I'm finalizing steps to hide the discovery…" he said with a wicked grin, "…but I believe the value of truth, if revealed correctly, trumps fear of political backlash or imploding traditions. I would like you to be an invisible part of the team if you're amenable, reaching out to your army of contacts, those you trust, perhaps even stepping forward publicly in certain forums if conditions warrant."

"As I will be doing," Tio injected. "Perhaps we can share our lists and develop an outreach plan."

"Yes," Saito agreed.

"I'm asking a lot of both of you. Tonight, Saito, if you are disposed, I'll give you encrypted files of my research, sample particles and coded laboratory notes. You're a scientist but also an outsider to this agency and removed from immediate suspicion." His voice caught. "This is not without risk."

"I'll do it." There was no other possible response.

"Do you remember the American journalist from the *New York Times* who visited us last year to glean insights on cost effective space exploration?"

"Daniel Duboce?"

"Mizuki told me…" He grinned. "My granddaughter said you thought he was, what was the word…*scorching*."

"I will have to speak to her about revealing secrets." Saito laughed. "Indeed. We discussed his finer points at some length over *saki* as well as some of her interests that I will never divulge." His face wore an impish grin as he tilted his head and pictured the man. "Remember, you asked me to serve as his tour guide outside the agency." Duboce seemed to have inherited the best physical aspects of his Italian mother and Czech father. Handsome, tall, athletic, endowed, and insatiable in bed. "He was…

what is the right word…*intellectual.*" He offered a loopy grin, feeling embarrassed, knowing they knew, and anxious to project the professionalism that was the core of his life. He was bisexual as they both knew, and his time with Duboce had turned physical, starting with Zinfandel at a romantic restaurant, followed by fingers rubbing together, looks exchanged and then a fast walk to his nearby hotel room, no words necessary, intentions obvious as they stripped seductively and Daniel led him to the queen-sized bed. Now, given the intoxicating scope and power of the discovery, nothing should distract from its being effectively brought into the light. Science before sex, he told himself, wondering if he could keep that pact.

Wada pressed a finger to his lips as if to keep from grinning and nodded. "Yes, smart indeed and you both seemed to engage. This could be useful."

"Please share your thinking."

"We may not need personal chemistry to succeed. Or maybe it would be useful. You both have the skills we need to flourish, and the fight will be in America, not Japan, at least the first phase. You and Tio each have special strengths depending on the audience. I have announced internally that we are shifting the *Misago* focus to larger scale mining even as a handful of scientists will continue research in secret." The crinkles around his eyes tightened. "There are advantages to having a political appointee boss who has no understanding of science or management. Daniel Duboce could be an influential and canny ally in a fight, indeed he might take it public with our assistance."

"Why Duboce? Any reporter would jump at this, not that I'm objecting to your choice." He did not want to abuse the trust between them, mixing physical pleasure with a political agenda.

"He's custom made for this. Few have the competence and depth of character to manage such a story in the public interest. Most would sensationalize rather than inform. Remember his background—I talked at length with him as a guest at my home in Takayama—it meshes well with the discovery. He once studied to be a priest then quit for some reason and wrote three books on religious history. He began his newspaper career at the San Francisco *Beacon* where his godfather is now publisher." He offered a knowing smile before continuing.

"Duboce will likely understand the full dimensions, be able to give context, is uncommonly articulate and self-deprecating, useful attributes. Humility when announcing a discovery that challenges the accepted existence of a god is…disarming. His article on JAXA became a major data source in congressional debate on NASA funding. When I asked him his views on religion, he told me: *'I am disillusioned with organized religion and agnostic about God.'* Perfect symmetry for the discovery. Obviously, you know him already from your time together on his assignment here."

Wada was guessing correctly but Saito didn't want to disclose intimate secrets. What happened between them was private and he wanted to move the discussion away from the sexual fantasy he had on this special American. "You seem to infer an unlikely pairing with a divorced father who has a young son. He knows my attraction to him, but perhaps you see things I do not. You are, after all, the famous Dr. Wada." Saito leaned forward, picked up Wada's hand, remembering the recent loss of his friend's wife. "My heart is with Akina, forever a lovely and remarkable woman. And with you."

An hour later, Saito pulled up his hood as the trio walked out of the JAXA lab and headed toward the Metro station. A black cotton bag was casually looped over his shoulder; inside was a softcover valise. He would study the material, keep it safe, and prepare to travel.

4.

Angel Island, San Francisco Bay

"Help me remember! Is our topic today agriculture in the Middle Ages or knights in armor?" Daniel spread his arms wide and grinned at the forty Scouts, dads and moms sitting cross-legged on the crest of Angel Island in the middle of San Francisco Bay—Alcatraz and San Francisco behind them, San Quentin prison far in the distance. A dozen struggled to stay seated, raising their arms and shouting: "Me! Me!"

He pointed to a girl with a dramatic set of braces.

"Knights!"

"Excellent. So, we are going back in history, over a thousand years. Another question might be useful. What is history?"

There were no raised arms this time. He pointed to an Eagle Scout he'd talked with earlier. "Diego, what do you think?"

"Oh. History is what happened in the past."

"Very good. We know that mostly because someone wrote it down. If they didn't, we wouldn't know. Sometimes there are different accounts of history, not always the same. So, what you think you know may not always be accurate."

They watched him, patiently enduring his message—in a

squirming pre-teen way—suffering through the boring stuff while anticipating what was to come.

"Great stories, even if repeated for centuries," he said, touching the wireless mike clipped to his knit shirt collar to make sure it was working, "aren't always true. People can hijack history for their own needs. Always check your sources."

A scoutmaster from Tiburon, Jeff Brian, a former college roommate, had asked him to do a lecture on medieval history when he was back in town and, what he really wanted, a demonstration on ancient armaments and combat. The boys—and it was mostly boys in this newly configured Scout troop—loved to see a good fight with legendary weapons. Such opportunities came often, likely because he didn't charge a fee, had some museum-worthy costumes, and he accepted as many invitations as he could. His purpose was to help young people think critically but he was under no illusions about why he got the invitations.

Daniel had flown out from New York three days earlier, staying at his grandparents' vacant flat near Buena Vista Park, and had arranged to be on Angel Island with his martial arts partner on this foggy day. The two were members of a medieval knight's group and were frequent visitors at Renaissance Fairs. He loved this city, his hometown, finally rebounding after a period of decline. He had friends to visit and needed to do interviews here on a story about the new mayor, a talented and dynamic transgender man. After that, he'd start a six-month sabbatical to finish his fourth non-fiction book on religion and science. Most important, he'd visit his godfather, Bruiser Bloomingdale, long time publisher of the *San Francisco Beacon*. He loved this man, a mentor all his life, and like a father. His real name was Carroll and it had got him into endless fights in school. So he became a tough guy. The nickname Bruiser fit; few risked calling him Carroll given his prowess in street fights.

"Let's talk about Robin Hood and a guy known as *good* King Richard," Daniel said, his arms wide. "Who wants to tell me about the myth?" Always start with something they know then give the real story, unraveling fact from fable. Nearly all the boys and girls and a couple of the dads raised their hands. He then answered questions and gave details they had never heard about life, politics, and gallantry in the Middle Ages.

He talked about Richard's brutal exploits during the Crusades and how the legendary Muslim general Saladin once sent the ailing King one of his physicians to offer care, an uncommon act of chivalry in any age. Muslim medicine at that time far surpassed anything in medieval Europe, still in the grips of the Dark Ages. Fact was that Richard, the greatest warrior in Christendom, likely had a long-standing sexual relationship with Philip Augustus when he was Dauphin of France and later King, an irony of history. The term homosexual wouldn't be coined for a few hundred years. But best not to go there with this audience.

"You mean Muslims were sometimes good guys during the Crusades?" asked a young Tenderfoot with a sunburned nose slathered in zinc oxide.

"That's right!" He explained that chivalry—embodied in legends of the Knights of the Round Table—was mostly myth. "But that's enough learning for one day, let's get on to the fun part." The Scouts grinned and nudged each other as Daniel picked up a heavy quilted jacket with a large red Christian cross at the center of the chest and put it on.

"Time for a demonstration. Are you ready?"

"*YES!*" came the thunderous response, spooking a group of seagulls into flight.

A few feet away, another man started morphing into a knight. "This is Josh Winthrop, my combat partner," Daniel said. "We've done this often and have hopefully perfected what we call our combat choreography."

"*Yeah!*" a boy hollered.

"What we're wearing is something King Richard may have worn." Daniel explained, nodding to the boy, speaking to him. "It's called a *gambeson,* a thick wool coat that medieval knights often wore under their armor." He and Josh pulled out gleaming squares of chain mail armor, draped them over their tunics and tied them down with leather sword belts slung low on the hips.

"Josh and I'll be using replica fifteenth century Knights Templar swords."

"You look right outta the movies!" a girl gushed.

Daniel pulled up his chainmail hood and lifted a silver helmet. "We'll go back to the eleventh century—early medieval times—for our head gear. They're conical to deflect blows and the nose guard was reasonably effective at protecting the face." His triangular shield had a red lion; Josh's, a black eagle.

They bowed to the audience, faced each other and bowed again. Daniel moved first, flashing his sword overhead and hitting Josh's shield with a crunch that ricocheted across the island. The Scouts yelled and winced, leaning forward and back as the action progressed.

The two knights parried back and forth aggressively—pounding, taunting, twirling, yelling, leaping and falling—kicking up a thick cloud of dust. The audience alternated between screams and laughter, some jumping up and then being pulled back down if they blocked the view of someone behind them.

After fifteen minutes of non-stop swordplay, Daniel hit Josh's shield and in a show-stopping finale, ducked down as the man's sword swung close over Daniel's head, leapt up, catching the sword from the side and knocking it from Josh's hand. He grabbed him around the neck, pushed him to the ground, then pointed his sword at his throat.

"Yield or die!"

The Scouts were wide-eyed and silent before erupting in screams and applause, all on their feet, as the knights stood and bowed, an arm over each other's shoulders. Daniel slipped his sword into its sheath and took off his helmet, setting it at his feet, the chainmail hood still in place.

"He looks like Ivanhoe," one boy screamed to his friends.

"No, Lancelot!" came the urgent group rebuttal.

Daniel wiped the sweat off his face with a towel. "Now you know how it's done. You can see that I'm old and worn out. Who'd like to face me in combat?"

The crowd was silent and looked dumbfounded. Several

laughed and glanced anywhere but at him. Daniel pulled out his sword with a flourish, clanged it against his shield, and caught the eye of a startled red-haired boy recommended earlier by the Scoutmaster.

"The boy's painfully shy," he'd told him. "He lacks self-confidence but this could be a real boost to his ego."

"How about you, Justyn?"

The eleven-year-old's face flushed crimson, hiding his abundant freckles. His friends looked surprised but applauded, perhaps relieved, and pulled out their cell phones to record the fight. Pushing long reddish-blond hair from over his eyes, the boy stepped awkwardly out in front of the group, nervous but with a fixed smile. Daniel helped him with a smaller sized thick coat, chainmail, and helmet. He knew the boy was vulnerable in front of his schoolmates.

"Wow, this stuff's really heavy," Justyn joked, adjusting the helmet, apprehensively looking at all the phones aimed at him.

"This is a replica of the swords Josh and I just used." He held up the long tan colored sword to the crowd. "Some fighters call it a *waster*. In Japan it might be called a *Bokken*. It's a replica made of wood. Rattan in this case to lessen the risk of damage. So, a safety precaution but much like the real thing." He handed this sword to Justyn and picked up another. He demonstrated various techniques on slashing, parrying, jabbing and the use of a shield and practiced the moves with his young pupil.

"Okay," Daniel finally challenged, scrunching his face but barely hiding his grin, raising his wooden sword, "You are now a knight and we are in hand-to-hand combat. *Do your best!*"

The boy made some unwieldy swings as the Scouts screamed commands, and Daniel gave him pointers that everyone could hear. He repeated the process for several rounds. Then, covering his mike, he whispered a conspiracy. Justyn's eyes widened.

The young man charged forward, swinging his sword wildly and Daniel backed up, pleased with his ferocity, taking several blows on his shield in dramatic fashion.

Watching the boy, Daniel nodded almost imperceptibly, left

one thigh exposed and Justyn connected with his wooden sword. Daniel collapsed with a scream. The boy stood over him, his mouth agape, looking confused about what he should do next. Bouncing up quickly, Daniel put a hand on the young man's shoulder.

"I give you Sir Justyn, a valiant and victorious knight!" he shouted to the audience, his arm raised skyward. *"Give him a hand for his bravery. A born swordsman!"*

The crowd applauded, whistled, whooped, and checked their recordings. Justyn raised his sword and shield in triumph, grinning, obviously exhilarated and perhaps relieved.

"Thanks," he whispered.

Daniel touched his shoulder. "Well played. You're a natural."

As he was finishing his lecture, Daniel noticed a man behind the group, leaning casually under one of the few trees near the summit, his face hidden in shadow. When their eyes connected, the stranger stepped forward, removed a baseball cap, and slipped off his overshirt, revealing a Captain America long sleeved tee stretched tight over a muscular frame. No question about his identity. Dr. Hideo Saito.

5.

Sanmachi Suji District, Takayama, Japan

Wada took an early train to his ancestral home in Takayama, midway between Osaka and Tokyo in the mountains of central Japan. Today was a time to savor his culture and the ghosts and glories from history and his own life, a moment to remember his values as a man before jumping into the darkness in pursuit of the light. He also knew he needed to contain his own hubris.

He walked with a steady pace through the old section of the city, stopping when some landmark or quiet nook rekindled memories of family, beauty, and tradition. He slowed passing through the gates of a Buddhist temple toward a cemetery, his eyes fixed on a small stone monument containing the remains of his late wife. He was here to say goodbye in preparation for what was ahead. He hoped his own bones would one day rest next to hers. Maybe soon.

Akina had died at home, surrounded by family. He could still smell the *osenko* incense sticks that burned constantly for the thirty-five-day period of mourning. Tradition was important. Somehow, he had managed to be with her much of the time, meeting his duties for the Buddhist rituals even as the *Misago* project seemed increasingly chaotic. Politicians in panic.

"This is the beginning of the Takayama Festival, my Akina. May you be with the *kami* being honored today. At least the good ones." He grinned, imagining her spirit floating above him. "The air is thick with the fragrance of plum blossom. A little early this year." He touched the green and blue silk vest he wore, made by her many years ago from her old kimonos. "It's hardly typical Japanese style," she had said when presenting the surprise gift, "but it will make you look more festive on special occasions and it means something beautiful I once wore will now be close to you." Wada closed his eyes, relishing the memory.

The scientist left the temple, walking along a narrow path in the woods. He was surprised to see a rare green orchid growing where it shouldn't and stooped down.

"*Kumagaisou*," he said, his finger stroking the leaves. "A samurai's helmet."

His eyes dampened again as he raised the silver cane in a salute to her memory. "*Misago!*" He remembered the day she gave him the antique walking stick following the accident on the International Space Station decades ago that damaged his right leg and left him with a limp. The cane was a bit flamboyant but she loved it. As did he. It became his signature at JAXA and when the new mission was named, the obvious choice was, *Misago*—the *Osprey*.

Ahead were the familiar tall orange posts and black crossbeams of her favorite Shinto temple, one of many holy places in Sanmuchi Suji, the ancient heart of Takayama. He slowed as he approached the beloved pair of stone *komainu* lions watching in silence as they had for nearly a thousand years. A dozen yards further he stood before the purification fountain. He lifted a ladle of fresh water to wash his hands and then poured some into his cupped palm to ceremonially rinse his mouth.

At the offering hall, he tossed a coin into the box, bowed deeply twice, clapped his hands twice, bowed again and hit a small gong to draw the kami's attention before he knelt and prayed. He rose and took a slip of paper, an *omikuji*, from the shrine to see what it predicted for the future. "*Daikichi*," it read. "Great good luck." He tied the paper to a tree branch, an act to make it come true, or so the priests claimed. He loved the custom without regard to its veracity.

The scientist entered the narrow streets filling with locals and tourists on this, the first day of the Shinto festival, one of the country's three great celebrations each year. He heard musicians practicing on their drums, flutes and even a stringed biwa. There would be numerous decorated *kasahokos*—floats with musicians in elegant costumes and scores of priests, attendants and brightly dressed children. Wada stopped under an elaborately carved wooden archway and watched as the participants lined up on this bright spring day. The *kasahokos* were being pulled into place.

Young lovers kissed in the distance. One was the handsome son of a local merchant, the other the daughter of a Shinto priest. She was lovely in an elaborate old white kimono as befitted her status as a temple *miko*, a priest's assistant. She saw Wada and turned to him, giggling and red-faced, then waved at her old friend before scurrying away to find her place in the parade lineup. Her boyfriend grinned and bowed with respect for one of the city's most prominent and distinguished citizens. Wada returned the greeting to this young man he had known since birth. The man skipped boyishly into the crowd and disappeared.

"We were like that once, Akina…"

A teenager with an American flag on his t-shirt brushed him as he darted past. Wada let his mind drift back to his meeting with Jeremiah Walton.

"We need time," the president had stated, "to discuss this with our political and religious colleagues." His tone suggested it wasn't a request. Wada had suppressed his anger then; now he had nothing to hold him back. "I may need a samurai's helmet for the path I have chosen," he murmured. He brought a hand to his chin and smiled. "Akina, is the orchid an omen?"

Wada passed a dozen men in white robes, two long square-cut wooden poles on their shoulders supporting a Shinto shrine of intricately carved panels and latticed windows. Their orange sashes and headbands matched the thick orange ropes that hung and swayed from the roof and draped down the corners, ending in elaborate tassels. Lanterns were tied at the ends of the roof supports, swinging back and forth. Inside were invisible sacred spirits floating silently and watching those who honored them.

His mind drifted. The first argument with the prime minister had been ugly. They had raised their voices. He'd called the man a coward. How far would they go to silence him? How far would he go? He only wanted to continue research in secret. Now there seemed only one logical option.

The parade began to move. He hurried ahead through the business district filled with two-story wooden structures, unchanged in centuries and advertised as the lost Japan. His family had maintained a residence here for generations, an old merchants' home built in the *Edo* period two centuries before. Thick and twisted wisteria vines in full purple foliage covered the sides of the bay windows and wrapped around the dark timbers facing the street. Wada loved the feel of this ancient city and relished the contrast between his roots here and his career as a space scientist.

He stepped inside, slid the door closed and hung his bag on a wooden hook. The sounds of gurgling water, part of an indoor lily pond, mixed with the ancient rhythms of the thirteen-string *koto* playing on his sound system. He stood quietly for a moment, enjoying the combined melodies of nature and man. Then his mind returned to his current obsession.

Who were these holy men who wielded such power in America?

He paused to kneel and pick up a tiny intricately carved mythical figurine of a turtle and dragon that must have fallen from a shelf, one of his favorite *netsuke* treasures, perhaps dislodged by his housekeeper. He slipped it into a pocket and smiled in satisfaction.

But his legs trembled as he inched into the bedroom and looked at her pillows. Forty-nine years of marriage, they had not quite reached fifty. That day, when he lost her, was the most painful in his life. He pondered the western fixation with the rule of three: his wife dead; scientific proof of a creator, perhaps or perhaps not a divine; and what next?

He stepped into the bathroom and removed a syringe and elastic cord from a drawer. He wrapped the cord around his bicep, made a fist, swiped an alcohol pad over the veins inside his elbow and stuck in the needle, slowly drawing a vial of blood. He put the equipment in a bag to be disposed of in a trash container on the street. The vial he wrapped in a towel and set on the corner of a table near the front entrance.

In the early evening, he pulled his already packed suitcase from a storage space and added items from the duffle bag. His work and honor required that he join true believers elsewhere. Arrangements had been made. He texted a one-word message to a trusted neighbor: "Stardust." The man would come by, trash the office area as if there had been a scuffle, leave deposits of his blood in strategic places and call police about witnessing a possible kidnapping or murder. Wada had earlier left a bloody handprint near the front door. Some media attention involving a missing scientist might be a useful distraction.

A lone figure wheeled a suitcase through busy streets, his face obscured by a grey fedora worn low on his forehead. Groups of tourists, still pouring into this popular holiday destination, ignored him. He blended in with the crowd. He smiled as he thought about renting phones and securing credit cards in the names of ancient Japanese heroes and politicians. Secrecy needed extra precautions.

He crossed a nearby bridge over the Miyagawa River and boarded a train.

In his pocket, he felt a tiny ivory carving of a mythical pairing of turtle and dragon, a guardian spirit, a valuable and ancient specialty of local artists in this mountain city and it gave him comfort. Leaning back in his seat, Wada rested his chin on his open palm, gazing tranquilly out the window at his beloved city as the train slowly pulled out of Takayama Station.

6.

Angel Island, San Francisco Bay

As the children headed to the barbecue pit, Daniel walked over to his visitor. A large canvas shoulder bag lay on the ground beside Saito, a shirt folded over an arm. The smirk on his lips morphed into a grin.

"Sir Daniel. A great look." He glanced up and down the knight, approvingly.

"*Saito!* What a wonderful surprise." He held his helmet under one arm, his chainmail hood still in place.

Each started to lean forward to hug but pulled back, uncertain of the protocol when a sweaty twelfth century English knight encounters a rakish twenty-first century Japanese scientist.

"Come here," Saito said with a laugh, wrapping his arms around Daniel, pulling him tight for a chaste kiss on his cheek. "Daniel, you were wonderful with the boy. I got choked up seeing his joy. You gave him a fine and generous gift."

Daniel stepped back and pushed the hood off his head, sweat trickling down his cheek. "Thanks. I wanted to improve his self-confidence. What're you doing in California?"

Saito had a touch of gold in his brown eyes, a warm smile,

a man quick to laugh, yet could handle himself, a trait Daniel admired. On occasion Daniel got a sexual reaction when he did heavy physical activity so he was pleased his gambeson went nearly to his knees, not wanting to give the wrong impression. Or the right impression.

"I left a message on your cell phone and didn't hear back," Saito said. "The *Times* office said you were on sabbatical in San Francisco. You mentioned you had a family home here. It was easy to find. A woman in the downstairs unit told me where you were."

"You met Woesha Jones?" He smiled; pleased Saito was here. "I'm amazed she told you anything."

Woesha was his closest friend in San Francisco, fond of scolding him regularly about not getting over his divorce: "You're a good father and you'll find another woman," she'd told him. "Maybe one with more to love." She knew he was bisexual, mostly pointing out women but sometimes men she thought might make good lovers.

"Yes. She looked at me closely," Saito continued, almost giggling, then said, 'Do you have an older brother who's single?'"

Daniel laughed again. "How is Dr. Ito?"

"Still an integral and inspiring member of the *Misago* team. Of any team."

"Agreed. An impressive woman and scientist. I enjoyed our time together in Tokyo."

"My apologies if I interrupted your lecture," Saito said. "I lived in the Bay Area when I was going to Cal and came here because I need to discuss something of extreme importance. It's imperative we talk in private. Time is crucial."

"This seems private enough," Daniel responded looking around the deserted hilltop.

"Dr. Wada asked me to contact you if something happened to him. He has disappeared. It's very complicated to explain and this is too public. There are documents you need to see."

Daniel stared, not sure how to respond.

"I carry material that puts me in legal danger in Japan and

perhaps here in America. That gives you a sense of the urgency, risks and importance."

"We'll go to my grandparent's place." Daniel was stunned. He liked Wada; more than that, he admired him. The story he'd written about JAXA was popular, drawing hundreds of detailed comments on the *Times* web page and discussed in congressional hearings on the NASA budget.

Daniel excused himself, cleaned up and changed clothes. A group of Scouts walked them to the ferry dock, including his new sparring partner, Justyn. Josh agreed to take the equipment back to the city.

"Do you think I could learn medieval swordsmanship, Mr. Duboce? Would you teach me?" The boy looked so hopeful that he could only offer one response.

"Absolutely." He took out his wallet and handed him a card. "Call me Daniel. This has my personal cell number and email. If I don't answer, text and I'll get back to you. I'll also talk to Josh. He could also give you some training. I'm on a break from my job in New York and will be here for the next six months. I look forward to it." They shook hands before the boy wrapped his arms around him.

"Thanks, Mr. Duboce." The boy grinned as Daniel walked up the plank to the boat and turned, waved and smiled back at the boy.

The Blue and Gold ferry turned its bow toward Fisherman's Wharf across the bay. Leaning against the upper deck rail, they watched the red-orange Golden Gate Bridge in the distance. Saito kept his bag strapped over his shoulder, clutched tight to his side.

A dozen seagulls followed, gliding on the wind just behind the American flag on the stern. Daniel thought about his son, now living in Los Angeles with his mother, and how much he missed him. He took out his cell and checked that he had service. He texted Garrett that he was in San Francisco and did he have any free time later in the week. Sometimes ex-wife Trudy allowed an unscheduled visit.

They exited the gangplank at the Embarcadero pier, walked past Ghirardelli Square, up to the cable car turnaround and hopped on one of the iconic old vehicles, riding up the hill to the end of the line at Powell and Market.

"Are we going to your apartment!?" Saito asked.

"I was thinking we could reconnect there. Is that what you want as well?"

"It is what I want. But before that marvelous distraction, we need to talk quietly about why I am here. It is important."

They jumped onto a green vintage streetcar on Market Street headed west toward his home near Buena Vista Park. It stopped for a signal in front of the Orpheum Theatre.

The marquee read *Mother Teresa—The Musical.* A poster showed a diva-like nun singing to buff, bare-chested men in loincloths.

"Insane! This show I must visit," Saito said, taking a quick photograph.

"The world is certifiable," Daniel agreed, glancing at the huge granite-clad building next door, and feeling a sudden sense of inspiration. "Let's get out here." He stepped onto the street before Saito could respond. "Maybe the best place to be alone is in a crowd of strangers focused on their own pursuits."

"What?" Saito leaped off the car and sprinted to catch up.

Daniel glanced at the ornate gold and black dome of City Hall across the plaza as he touched Saito's back, guiding him around to the more dramatic front entrance of the block-long building. "This is one of my favorite places," he said, hoping to lift their spirits, "our charmingly schizophrenic Main Library. One side is modern, the other sort of minimalist nineteenth century."

Entering, they walked onto a wide bridge. He pointed up at the soaring vertical space and down at hundreds of people exploring the book stacks on the lower level and grinned. "Surely, Saito, you can share your secret here surrounded by the wisdom of humanity's greatest thinkers. Hopefully, it's not so complex that I'll need their assistance. But it's a good backup."

The young scientist shook his head and they strolled toward the light-filled atrium, putting his hand on Daniel's shoulder. Two young men on a grand adventure.

7.

Apostolic Palace, Rome

The phone message had been succinct—a crisis unlike anything the church had ever seen. The man who sent it never exaggerated. But he'd offered no details, saying only that he'd be here in under an hour.

For the cardinal, his visit was a welcome break in his otherwise tedious daily routine. He held yet another report from an informant at one of the Catholic universities in the United States. Some clergymen and nuns continued to stray from the official doctrines of the church. He muttered, "So many details to consider, so many false teachings…"

Since Cardinal Diego Martinez was responsible for maintaining the orthodoxy of the faith, the arbiter of moral questions for the Vatican, such reports came to him each week from all over the world. They bored him. He twisted his heavy gold ring embossed with a crucifix and engraved with the papal seal, a symbol of his office, and gazed around him.

He sometimes felt like an object in a museum in his office with its twenty-foot ceiling and gilded oak leaf crown molding, his eighteenth-century Italian desk, the patterned silk drapes, thick and purple, hanging under matching valances and kept open with heavy golden ropes and tassels. Behind them, dense sheer panels covered the windows, keeping out the sun and prying eyes. These days, even in the Vatican, you couldn't be too protected. His walnut-paneled walls held a dozen paintings by medieval and Renaissance masters and their dramatically lighted subjects were all members of the clergy. Some had been murdered for their sins, others made into saints. Where would he fit?

Martinez knew he was seen by many as a striking figure, even in the simple black robe he generally wore in his office, intentionally modest for the number two man in the Vatican hierarchy. He was tall and thin with a smooth brown face set off by short-cropped white hair. His nose was prominent and narrow. "A Roman nose, even if I'm Hispanic," he once joked to his aide. At sixty-five, he was well known for his political skill and concern about others, particularly the poor in Third World countries.

Father Guido Alito entered unannounced from a side door as he often did from his adjacent office. He was a serious and pleasant Italian who, at fifty-eight, maintained his trim physique and combed his thinning black hair forward. The priest was the cardinal's trusted, long-time confidant. Alito looked concerned. He sat in a nearby chair, his routine when bringing in news.

"Your Eminence, an armed incident is underway at the Church of the Nativity in Bethlehem," the priest said. "A group of renegade gunmen have taken refuge there and are being pursued by troops from the Palestinian government. I knew you would have a personal interest."

"What?" The cardinal put aside the report, alarmed yet pleased for the distraction. An incident at that very church had changed his life...

Church of the Nativity, Bethlehem

As a young monsignor from Argentina, Diego Martinez had been visiting the Church of the Nativity, one of the oldest continually operating churches in the world. Construction had started when Constantine I was Roman Emperor in 325 A.D.

Like Christianity itself, the building was split. The main section was a basilica, a large hall with colonnades that divided the space, and was controlled by the Greek Orthodox Church. The Roman Catholic Church managed the adjoining modern Gothic revival style building, the Church of St. Catherine. Other faiths also had their tiny fiefdoms in the building. Underneath the basilica was the Grotto of the Nativity, said to enshrine the birthplace of Jesus, one of the holiest sites in Christendom.

As part of an ecumenical program, Diego was meeting with two Maronite Christians from Lebanon and a French priest. Overwhelmed and inspired, they left the Grotto in prayerful silence and headed back up the ancient stone staircase.

Three armed gunmen, their faces hidden by *keffiyeh*-checkered headscarves, stepped from an alcove. With guns pointed at the cleric's heads, they tied their hands behind their backs and looped ropes around their necks. Pulled like cattle, the four tripped and fell repeatedly as they were kicked and dragged into a nearby alleyway.

Tourists blocked their path. A woman screamed and grabbed her child. A gunman fired his weapon in the air, scattering the crowd like pigeons.

The clergymen were pushed into a waiting van, blindfolded and driven through twisting streets then dragged into a building. With an automatic weapon jammed into his ear, Martinez and his companions were eventually shoved into a room that smelled of stale urine and feces. Their blindfolds were removed. There were no windows and only one door.

Diego soon discovered that the sole target of this kidnapping was Michel Bizri, one of the clerics who was part of the Maronite faction in the latest Lebanese civil war. Alliances had shifted rapidly and unpredictably during the fighting and nearly every participant had been allied with and subsequently betrayed by every other party at least once.

As Bizri told the others his identity, the four men found themselves held at gunpoint while their Muslim captors plotted their deaths in some public and spectacular fashion. Guilt by association, Bizri explained in doleful regret.

The rope around Martinez's wrists cut deep. He lost feeling in his hands. Presumably a search for them was underway but the prisoners suspected it would be very difficult to locate the hideout.

One of the gunmen left and returned carrying pita bread and a pail of savory meat. With him was a remarkably handsome and elegantly dressed stranger. He appeared to know the kidnappers or at least have their respect.

The dark-skinned man laughed when he saw the prisoners, apparently congratulating the gunmen on their work. He spoke in Arabic but was in western dress, wearing a loose-fitting dark suit and open shirt. His ethnicity was hard to judge, perhaps Arab.

The stranger turned and kneeled by the captives as if inspecting them. He spoke briefly and gruffly in French, "Trust me. I'm here to help." The dignified man exuded a muscular confidence despite his apparent youth, although his age was hard to determine.

The gunmen watched, obviously reassured by his tone even if they didn't understand the language.

The man stood and appeared to make an offer, perhaps a ransom, for their release. The leader immediately waved his arm with contempt, spitting on the ground. The guards watched passively.

As the stranger tried to persuade him, the leader grew increasingly agitated, clearly rattled. He lifted the barrel of his rifle, aimed it at the priests and screamed he would kill them now.

The other kidnappers looked amused, waiting for the executions. The clergymen hunched over, closed their eyes, and prepared to meet their creator.

There was a single shot, deafening in the confined, thick-walled, windowless space. When Diego opened his eyes, he was shocked to see blood and spatter from the side of the leader's head oozing down the rough dirty white wall behind. The man's face was frozen in shock as he tumbled face down to the concrete floor, the side of his skull missing.

The stranger stood there without moving, a large caliber pistol in his hand, his face rigid and hard. He said nothing, letting the other gunmen take in the situation.

Not their fight, they gestured. But as the man turned away from them, one of the gunmen clicked off the safety on his weapon. The stranger fired a single shot into the man's forehead and did the same to the other gunman, barely looking up. The high-powered cartridges slammed both men back against the wall and they dropped in tandem to their knees leaving blood, bone, and hair on the wall behind, then slowly folded over as if in prayer.

The man turned to the prisoners, signaling silence as he listened for anyone approaching, attracted by the gunshots. He tucked his handgun back into a holster strapped to his chest under his coat.

As he watched the doorway, the man bent over and pulled up his left pant leg, unsnapping an unusual looking knife from a holster on his calf. Martinez knew about the weapon, a *navaja* from the Andalusia region in southern Spain, popular with rogues and nobility centuries past, its hinged handle seeming to be carved ivory and silver that wrapped around and covered the steel blade in an intricate pattern. In a fluid motion, the stranger flipped it open, cut their ropes, snapped the knife closed and slipped it back in its hiding place.

Pistol in hand but concealed at his side, he led them into the street. A few twisting blocks away, he took them into a busy café, seated them at a table, calmly ordered tea for everyone and placed a call from a telephone brought to their table. The four clerics, Martinez included, were visibly shaking.

The man spoke briefly and hung up. "You are safe here," he said, his tone reassuring. "A car from the French consulate will be along in a few minutes. I apologize for any inconvenience and ask you not to think less of the Palestinian people because of this incident." He added, "It was an unfortunate end to the standoff. The men were fools. It would be best to keep this incident secret."

They agreed.

When the black armor-plated limousine arrived a half hour later, the stranger helped them in.

"If I may inquire, what is your name, sir?" Diego asked.

"Romaldo Vega."

And that had been the beginning. Over the years, Vega had come in and out of Diego's life many times when he needed someone with exceptional talents. As he rose in the church, Diego always offered resources to Vega for his work. But the man always refused. Indeed, Vega had often provided generous financial backing for humanitarian crises of interest to the church. And always anonymously.

The cardinal never insisted on the details of the results of the man's assignments. It had suited them both. Vega's assistance, he admitted to no one, had helped immeasurably in his rise in the church hierarchy.

A tap on the door brought the cardinal back to the present. His longtime secretary, Carlotta Carini, entered the room. A conservative middle-aged woman with immaculate grooming and style, she was dressed today in a dark blue suit, her hair in a neat bun. One of the few women in a secretarial role in the Vatican, she knew the secrets of the church bureaucracy and the needs of her boss. Carlotta seemed giddy with excitement. It could only mean one thing.

"Mr. Vega is here to see you, sir."

"Of course."

She stepped aside, closely watching the man as he entered. He nodded to her respectfully. "Thank you, Carlotta."

She blushed and looked down. "You are very welcome, Mr. Vega." The secretary slowly backed out of the room and closed the door.

Vega crossed to the cardinal who stood, smiled, and extended his hand. Vega took his fingers, raised them to his lips and kissed the ring, saying simply, "Your Eminence." He bowed to the other standing figure. "Father Alito."

Martinez smiled. "Please, have a seat my friend." He graciously gestured toward a chair by his desk. "What is the emergency?"

"You need to know of a discovery in space by the Japanese," Vega said. "It is being held in secret by scientists who mistrust their own government but rumors have been leaking. It has profound implications for people of faith. According to my sources, the American president has been briefed."

"Please tell me."

"It is, if I may use the term, a God paradox. It offers physical evidence of what we already know is divine truth. Yet, even as it offers certainty, it has the potential to disintegrate the very fabric of everything we believe is holy."

As Vega explained what he knew, the cardinal became increasingly grim. Father Alito began to tremble.

The cardinal twisted his ring as he contemplated the implications. He was charged with protecting the faith. How far should he go? He needed to brief the pope and talk to other cardinals, always an ordeal with topics far less difficult than this.

"Adding to this complexity," Vega said, "is the fact that the head scientist is missing, perhaps dead. I am investigating it now and will let you know my findings." He rose with an easy grace, nodding to the two men. "Your Eminence, Father Alito."

And he was gone.

8.

Main Library, San Francisco

Daniel and Saito walked through the book stacks on the third floor and found an open study carrel and sat down by a window overlooking the granite façade of the Asian Art Museum next door.

"Thank you for agreeing to meet with me, Daniel."

"Of course. I'm more than delighted to reconnect. What's the urgency?"

"I'm sorry I couldn't be more specific earlier. This isn't simple." He removed his black baseball cap with a gold logo and set it on the table.

"What's the secret of your hat?" Daniel picked it up, curious about what appeared to be the letter G imposed over Y.

"The Yomiuri Giants. Arguably Japan's most popular baseball team."

"You play as I recall." He set it back down.

Saito smiled. "Yes, minor league. Hmmm. That may be an overstatement. Neighborhood teams. I also coach kids."

"Commendable. My son loves baseball."

Saito leaned forward, elbows on the table, hands clasped in front of his chin. "I've known details of Dr. Wada's discovery for only a short time. He said he needed to talk to someone outside the agency, a scientist, whom he could trust. He gave me this package and I haven't talked to him since. He asked me to give it to you in person." His voice rose a notch higher, his words gaining speed, almost breathless. "He said he was planning to disappear and go undercover so he could operate in secrecy. That was his intention. But it's also possible he was kidnapped. I've lost contact."

"Please! Slow down," Daniel said holding up both palms. "What's this about?"

"Sorry." Taking a breath, slowing his speech. "You need to read it for yourself. He felt you would know what to do. My advice is to study the material and safeguard it if you are not ready to act. Yoshito put the pursuit of truth above his own safety and career. Now he entrusts you—us—with his findings. His work has been halted for political reasons. Once you read this, you will understand the danger he may be in. The danger we could all face."

He looked at the scientist. "Why me?"

"You're a well-known journalist for a major American newspaper respected throughout the world and you know many people in important institutions. He felt a connection with you and believes you're an honest man with good instincts. I do too. He's convinced you'll understand the scope of the issues as would few others. You know the real world as well as the spiritual. Practically, he also thinks you'll not be an immediate target, giving us time to prepare."

Saito focused on his eyes. "I've read the documents, seen the research specimens and was able to ask questions. I'm *staggered* by the implications. But I don't know what to do, particularly here in America. I suspect you will. He believes some people would do anything to get this package and keep it private."

Daniel's mouth felt dry as Saito bent over to open his large shoulder bag on the floor. He carefully pulled out a valise roughly fourteen inches square and six inches thick. It was covered in thick black micro-fiber with a wide brass zipper on three sides. Using both hands, he lifted it with care, placed it on the table and slid it across.

"Great caution is required. You need to understand the contents. It will take time for the implications to sink in, as you Americans say. It's in English. Dr. Wada was very careful in his planning."

It felt like a giant dictionary with a shock-absorbent cover to protect it. He clicked the lock, slowly unzipped the valise, and opened it on the desk. One side held several memory sticks, a folder with photographs and a handwritten letter to him on JAXA stationary signed by Dr. Wada.

Mr. Duboce, Daniel—
My apologies for communicating in this fashion but
circumstances make a more traditional approach
impossible. Several months ago, in Takayama, I
mentioned there was something I wanted to share
someday that might change your views on God.
This is that day.
Yoshito Wada

Daniel read the note twice. The other side of the suitcase held an elongated box strapped in place. He loosened the buckle and lifted out the wooden container. Inside was a well-crafted, heavy metal-like canister about the size of a small thermos. He unscrewed the finely machined top and saw extensive padding and thin glass rods. He put it back and lifted out the folder and set it aside. Next, he picked up the first wand.

"Really? The new Toshiba memory wand is called Kenobi?" He smiled. As civilization collapsed, humor was good. "I've not seen a wand-Kenobi before."

"Yeah. Some of their engineers are a little retro. Hold it six inches from the port, a green light will indicate connection, and hit download. I'll go visit your rare books while you read."

"Lots of treasures in here. The Chinese American Center's

around the corner and, across the floor is the remarkable Hormel LGBTQ+ Center." He began to explore.

Bible Museum, Clarksville, Indiana

Reverend Adam Wright was grateful this trip had been scheduled months ago, before yesterday's raucous meeting with the president about this obviously fraudulent discovery in space. He and three members of the board of the Congress of Conservative Christians had been summoned. Two were with him today on the sprawling grounds of the Bible Museum of Creation in southern Indiana. This place was a dramatic reaffirmation of faith, surrounded by the Garden of Eden in all its glory, a short walk from Jericho with Moses and the Burning Bush around the corner. He continued his stroll back through time, away from those who would seek to slur the truth of creation.

Board members were livid that the president hadn't implemented his campaign pledge, given privately to the Board and others, to declare America an earthly *Kingdom of God.* Christian nationalists controlled nearly all levers of power: government, key businesses, much of the media, a majority of state governments, many school boards and, through the president, the military. Heavily armed militias in nearly all states were ready to do their part. If Walton announced his intention to implement it and appoint a religious leader, opponents would file suit and the U.S. Supreme Court would expedite a hearing. Six justices were ready to declare this consistent with the Founders' intent. Future elections, it was assumed by many, would no longer be necessary since God would be in charge. At least three members of the CCC board saw themselves as the Prophet who would interpret God's will.

If Walton had acted during his inauguration, then this *Misago* nonsense wouldn't matter. Could it be an impediment? Why now? President Walton kept demurring, saying the time wasn't right.

Wright counted backward, always a good way to reduce his stress. He was in this perfect location with a group of schoolboys. He needed to be calm and authoritative, the teaching role he relished.

"This is Noah's Ark," he said, both arms lifted to heaven, an exuberant Christian tour guide as he led a group toward the large wooden structure ahead.

"Nice boat," Reverend James Robinson responded with a wink. The octogenarian minister, an icon of conservative Protestant Christianity and a leading proponent of Christian nationalism, took a sip of coffee from an embossed mug. "Too many steps, Adam. I'll go chat with Eve in the Garden." He wore an impish grin as he ambled down the path toward a row of palm trees, a total change in personality from his angry demeanor at the *Misago* briefing. Adam hoped it was as simple as just rejecting the discovery and accepting the president's promise to implement his campaign pledge.

Robinson was not shy in letting the president know he expected to be the Prophet. The man's signature long white hair, rising high and thick on his head and running to his shoulders Andrew Jackson-style, went perfectly with his beak nose and nickname— the American Eagle of Christianity. Easy to see why he was a star on the Christian Broadcasting Association network. Image was important, Robinson often rambled. It helped sell the message. That was what it was all about. Getting out the truth about God and saving souls. If you could also enjoy yourself while you did good work, living the good life, so much the better. Wright recalled the elder minister's claim that the ACLU was God's special gift to conservative fundraising. He was funny, at least sometimes. But certainly not if he was named *The Light*.

Then there was Reverend John Broux, the president of America's leading Christian school, Florian Elder University. As always, the man was elegant, today in a beige Armani double-breasted suit with a green pocket square, even if everyone else was casual. Broux glanced up the Ark, shook his head and handed a porcelain teacup and saucer to an aide, saying, "I'll check out the serpent." Somehow, the sun was backlighting his red pompadour as if he were on a stage. He seemed to have his own ever-present spotlight. The man had simply laughed at the briefing saying, "My heart tells me this is false so it must be." Then he pointed at the president, saying in sudden controlled fury, "Implement your promise! God is waiting." He too was convinced he was the logical choice to lead.

Wright turned back to a group of fifteen teenage boys and led them up the steps. The air smelled of newly sawed wood with a hint of animal waste. "Just what we'd expect from the description in the Old Testament."

He moved slowly, pausing to rest and pull up the front of his pants to keep them from slipping under his stomach, conscious as always that he was America's premier conservative radio preacher, beloved and listened to every week by millions, known for his humor, or attempts at it, often at his own expense, to break down barriers. He was at the top of his career, yet if he were honest, he was miserable, and not just because of *Misago*. Some said he would be a perfect Prophet or The Light as some called the position. He himself wasn't sure, he had his doubts.

"Who cares what I look like when I work in radio?" He'd quipped on more than a few occasions when he addressed a live audience wearing his usual attire. Multi-colored aloha-style shirts with biblical themes were his favorites. He had them made for his own use and to sell on his website along with prayer cloths and pillows embroidered with favorite Gospel quotations. He knew many mocked him for this, some thought it tacky, some joined him and hawked their own lines but everyone was unanimously transfixed by his gross receipts.

Adam was his middle name but in his line of work he thought it more effective as a first name. Certainly better than Jerome.

He thought again about his new role as chair of the Congress, better known by its initials, CCC. It was a great honor. It increased his radio ministry even as his presence softened the group's hard-edged image. As part of that deal, his recent sermons focused more on sin than love and quality of life. That troubled him. Maybe they could split the difference someday on the tricky business of interpreting the Bible. He pulled out a roll of antacids and popped two in his mouth.

The CCC had been relentless in its efforts to bring Jesus back into public schoolrooms and replace Darwinism with the truth of creation. Many didn't seem to understand that the separation of church and state did not apply to Christianity, the founder's faith. Some called the CCC an American Taliban. Which was nuts. The Bible made it clear what was the true faith. It was a painful indictment. Yet even Christian leaders sometimes got it wrong. Years back, Pope Francis had said the term *jihad* did not mean a holy war but rather a kind of spiritual struggle, not unlike what Christians did in their own proselytizing. With religion and politics, facts were often twisted for advantage.

"I want to dramatize the Bible and recapture the cinematic thrill of *Jurassic Park*," he'd explained to the two board members. "We can't leave a beast as exciting as the dinosaur to the other side." The two were also key contributors to his misery index.

Standing at the top rail, Wright scanned the young faces from his hometown of Chillicothe, Ohio. "Boys, tell me the chapter and verse where it gives the measurements of the Ark." Several hands shot up.

"Samuel."

The gap-toothed boy grinned. "*Genesis* 6:15, sir."

"Excellent. And what was the size of the Arc? Mark."

A blond teen in a blue sports coat cleared his throat. "It was 300 cubits long, fifty cubits wide and thirty high."

"Well done. And how big is it in feet? Rolph?"

"What?"

"Son, how long is a cubit using our measurements today?"

"Ahh, I'm not real sure. Wait…a cubit is eighteen inches," the minister's son finally responded with the obvious help of a friend.

"That's correct," his father confirmed, hoping he masked his disappointment with an upbeat voice and smile. "So, the ship was about 450 feet long and about seventy-five wide. Not a lot of room to have two of every animal on Earth." He pointed into the hold. "But look how packed they are in here and the clever use of technology to bring in water and food and take away waste. That technology was obviously lost after the Flood but recreated here by those who have researched history."

The sky was partly cloudy and the temperature warm, a beautiful day for a tour of creation. Some rain would be nice, Wright thought, looking at the two ministers seated on a bench. A deluge would be ideal.

"How come you grew a beard, Reverend Wright?" a boy with a purple Mohawk asked politely.

"It makes me look more distinguished on radio."

"I think it makes ya' look like Moses," said a gangly boy with a large Adam's apple.

"Uh, thanks." He hoped it masked his double chin.

The minister had brought the teenagers from their high school to this inspiring amusement park for people of faith. Designed by an online gaming designer and providing a fully engaging sensory experience and featuring dinosaur animatronics, a place where ancient monsters roamed and the Bible could speak for itself.

"Wow, look at the baby T-Rex in the stall," yelled a boy wearing a green and white letterman's jacket. The creature did look realistic.

"Hey, there's two of 'em," said another jock in a blue sleeveless-shirt. "I thought dinosaurs were gigantic."

Perfect. A teaching moment. "Gather around me," Wright said. The boys drew close, looking at him and then away at the two playful dinosaurs. "They were big, but not as babies," he said. "Evolutionary scientists falsely claim that the Earth is millions of years old and that dinosaurs lived long before man arrived on Earth. But the Bible shows this isn't true. Genesis tells us that all land creatures were made on Day Six of the Creation, and that is the same day he made Adam and Eve. Thus, it is a fact that dinosaurs were made with man and existed with him in the Garden of Eden four thousand years before the birth of Christ."

"I thought they were vicious hunters," said a dark-skinned boy wearing a white puka-shell necklace.

"How'd Adam and Eve survive?" asked a teen with braces.

"Actually, they were friendly creatures in the beginning," the minister explained, "plant eaters. They got along well with Adam and Eve. But with Adam's sin, God changed many aspects of life—including dinosaurs. The Tyrannosaurus Rex was turned into a killer, a carnivore," he said. "All part of the price the Earth and its inhabitants paid for man breaking God's commandment. That's a lesson you need to take into your daily life. Live according to God's law."

Wright watched his son in the group of boys, worried that Rolph seemed detached from his family. His grades were slipping. Something was wrong. A black and blue mark on his cheek last week Rolph had laughed off with the claim he ran into a locker door. Wright needed to find a way to break through. One complication was Wright's fear that his son saw him as an embarrassment, an irrelevant old joke to today's generation.

The shy curly-haired teenager—always complaining about being overweight and favoring thick, black-framed glasses and strategic dabs of acne cream—stayed at the back of the group as if trying to distance himself from his dad and all the talk about sin.

Wright felt that boys needed a solid understanding of the Bible to ensure they had the skills to prosper and guarantee their lives beyond this one. He believed it taught humility, and every responsible Christian adult had a personal duty to help offspring find the path to happiness and salvation.

Later that day, after dinner and prayers, the portly minister invited the group to join him in taping his weekly radio show. The two board members declined. Perhaps it was best. He recalled a comment the elder minister whispered about his redheaded colleague: "He'd be a good man if he wasn't such a horse's butt." Tomorrow the horse's butt plus the American Eagle of Christianity and the board Executive Director, Sister Esther, known for her disabling assaults with tongue and cleavage, would meet with a Catholic cardinal to plan their attack. Was he being punished?

As he finished the sound check, the teens seemed excited. He enjoyed a live audience and was disappointed that two of the boys, including his son, didn't attend. The technician started the countdown: "Five, four, three, two, one…"

"This is Pastor Adam Wright of the Wright Radio Ministry welcoming you to another evening of Scripture and lessons for living in God's grace. I have in my audience a group of fine young men from Chillicothe Christian High School in Ohio."

The boys glanced at each other, grinning at the surprise introduction. He hoped his message was something they could tell their parents and brag about to siblings and schoolmates. "My topic for this hour: *Chastity Before Marriage—A Gift from God.*"

9.

Main Library, San Francisco

Daniel held the metallic canister in his palm, a cargo of stardust, sensing the fragility and power, before carefully repackaging it into the valise. He zipped up the sides, pressing his lips together, focusing on the task to keep his hands from shaking. Saito set down his phone and turned to him. Daniel hadn't noticed when the man had returned or how long he'd been gone, remaining silent for several minutes in Saito's presence, staring out the window at a large Victorian monument commemorating the founding of California, set midway between the library and the Asian Art Museum.

"Amazing," Daniel mumbled to himself. "I've never…" His heart raced; his mouth was parched. Did he want this to be true or not? Waving away Saito's attempt at a response, he logged onto the library's wifi connection. Several English language editions of Japanese news sites confirmed Wada's disappearance.

"All right." He leaned forward on his elbows, voice a little rough. "Yoshito has gone undercover or been kidnapped or killed. The implications scare the hell out of me. Do you really believe someone is trying to snuff this report?"

"Yes." Saito's hands formed fists that lightly touched the table-top. "He told me the prime minister cut a deal with the American government to suppress the findings in exchange for continued U.S. naval intervention in the latest standoff between Japan and China. Apparently, your president involved religious leaders in his decision-making process, risking a major war to ensure silence on *Misago*."

As part of his work, Daniel closely followed and wrote about the well-known leaders surrounding the president. "This is a scary time in America. The CCC is a priggish group, full of bile, superiority, and dismissive of science. They advocate ending American democracy because it's superfluous now that—quote—*true Christians* control Congress, the Supreme Court, the presidency and a majority of state governments. This is thanks to massive voter suppression, thuggish social media, and use of police and even the military to quell protests. Gun ownership, semi-automatic and even automatic weapons, with good old boy patriot groups, is widespread. I'd have hoped for more from Walton. He's an intellectual of the right, a man of sophistication who addresses criticism with a forthright honesty and wit that's disarming, unlike one of his predecessors, basically a con man, who called any criticism fake, denied all his extramarital sexual trysts, his crooked business practices and spoke in monosyllables. Yet Walton's also a political pragmatist. To his credit, he has so far not publicly declared support for the Kingdom movement although he likely has done so privately. Another option supported by some, is Walton naming himself president for life. A Supreme Court decision, quite a shock to many, makes the president immune from the law for any official act. It's a tragedy."

"Wow. But how do you really feel?"

He smiled at his friend. This whole situation seemed crazy but he instinctively trusted Wada and knew he could believe Saito. "Apologies if I'm rambling and a bit incoherent. The contents are beyond another *Alien* sequel. What this suggests, the idea of a conspiracy…"

"Certainly, it wouldn't be the first time unpopular findings were suppressed to meet some short-term political benefit," Saito observed. "You once had an EPA director who didn't believe in global warming, likely because of the siren call of big oil money and his ingesting too much lead paint as a child. Not so long ago you had a president who didn't understand evolution or much of anything scientific and degraded science and truth. There are many examples."

"All true. Yet few appreciate what it takes for government to work, the trade-offs not envisioned by the Founders. Still, I'm an optimist. America will correct itself and be stronger than the buffoonery of some officials."

How could he explain this in journalistic terms that people would accept? "It's like an intervention by ET or maybe *Close Encounters of the Third Kind*. For people of faith, a very upsetting supernatural divinity. This delegitimizes the Christian and Jewish concept of creation unless they want to admit *Genesis* got it wrong."

Daniel rested his clasped hands against his chin. "Fascinating." These findings were almost incomprehensible, a kind of religious infinity mirror. "You know, for centuries Catholics believed the soul of a child who died before being baptized went into a special holding place called *Limbo*. Until Pope Benedict announced this religious tenet was suddenly inoperative." He pressed on his eyes, dealing with his own strain. "Such management simplicity is impossible with *Misago*." Birthing a new god was not for the squeamish. Nor was killing an old one.

"Why?"

"The Christian Bible bonds Adam and Jesus, they're inseparable, a beginning and an end. You cannot have one without the other."

"That makes no sense."

"Adam committed Original Sin; Jesus is the Savior. If there was no Adam, as *Misago* seems to prove, there was no Original Sin, no need for a savior, no need for Christ. The Apostle Paul makes that point. Religious leaders will have two choices: Ignore this physical evidence and continue the status quo, knowing their core beliefs are bankrupt, fighting to discredit *Misago*. Or accept this truth and faith re-sets to square one."

"Amazing. I'd never made that connection. Hopefully people will be curious."

"Perhaps, but I'm not optimistic because it gets worse. If the key tenant of Christianity is false—commit to Christ, support the church, go to heaven, and enjoy life ever after—then hope in the hereafter is trashed. Heaven itself is at risk." His temples pounded with his mulling of the fallout, the fear and anger that seemed inevitable. "If parishioners believe the results, then their rage turns on the church itself for deception. No church would accept that, self-preservation is in all our genes. They'll attack the discovery as the work of Satan, perhaps in the guise of science. Ugly for sure, perhaps deadly."

A heavyset woman with a massive red beehive and wearing a generous chartreuse muumuu appeared at the end of the book stack a few feet away and slowly scanned the titles. His heart jumped. She looked like Edna Turnblad from *Hairspray*, his favorite cult movie. Its star was a man in drag called Divine. How he loved this city. They were both silent until she moved on.

"I need time to think." Did he really want to be involved in something this fantastical given everything else in his life? But it was by far the biggest story of his reporting life if true—a huge unknown—he had an obligation to take it public. That's what good journalists did, wasn't it? Or was it best to look away from a story with such calamitous potential? First, he had to verify; proof must be absolute. It had to be done with exactitude. He had no idea how, and somewhere in his brain, his Jesuit teachings were shouting *yes* and *no*. He would do nothing that might endanger Wada. If Daniel became the lightning rod, would fanatics target his family? How high the price? He pictured his young son, Garrett.

"Do you know that there are over 10,000 distinct religions in the world," he said, recalling his research, "and 150 of them have a million or more followers? This discovery has the potential to offend the teachings and traditions of many of them."

The scientist seemed to know that Daniel didn't expect an answer.

Daniel looked out again at the giant 1880s Pioneer Monument, a mix of life-size bronze statues dramatically depicting the worldview of California's founders. Yet it was an edited piece of history, its backside empty, sanitized for modern tastes. There had once been a Spanish vaquero and Catholic priest standing in triumph over a prostrate Native American. But critics proclaimed that section was offensive, glorifying the harsh subjugation of the indigenous people, and it was hauled away, an ugly part of the past locked up in a storage shed. Yet, it was also about the destruction of one religion and culture and the triumph of another. Ancient native gods and civilizations had perished thanks to Spanish steel and European diseases.

He mused, "Religion is held to a different standard here. American media and politicians tolerate actions they condemn elsewhere. America is a land of *must-believe*." Leaning forward, he cradled his chin on clasped hands and felt his indignation rising.

"Martin Luther King, Jr. said something like this: '*Nothing in the world is more dangerous than sincere ignorance and conscientious stupidity.*' He was explaining the rationalization for slavery and the vilification of African Americans. In the late 1970s, one church still justified its discrimination against African Americans because the Bible said, '*the Lord had cursed Cain's seed with blackness.*' The NAACP sued and just before trial commenced the head of the church had a vision that God had changed his mind. Amazing how shifting public opinion and lawsuits can motivate God to alter his views. The line between nonsense and church doctrine is sometimes hard to discern. What might happen if *Misago* left the righteous naked in the public square?"

Saito smiled wryly. "You're on a roll."

Daniel started to laugh and kept going. "Even now, the Supreme Court supports the view that faith trumps equal rights and respect. You don't want to serve gays in your business? Just announce such people offend your sincere religious beliefs and you can give them the middle finger. Our so-called impartial justices often represent the political party that appointed them, or faith, or personal prejudices. Not the law. The last session reversed gay marriage, leaving it up to states. How smug was their reasoning. There were demonstrations, hundreds of thousands of LGBTQs and their allies, in the streets in nearly every major city. In some cases, police and National Guard units were used to control crowds and intimidate people. Media coverage was limited. A huge protest march was set in Washington, D.C. but military units were stationed on all major roads into the capital and buses were turned back. Hotels, pressured by the religious right, or even owned by Christian nationalists, were closed. It was a stunning rebuke to free speech. A dozen states immediately outlawed gay marriage. How long before racial minorities are no longer protected?" Daniel rubbed his eyes. "I never thought I would see this kind of thuggish behavior in government."

"I saw some coverage of what happened. Stunning. I cried. America was the leader in free speech and human rights. Now it has turned against its own Declaration of Independence. Humans are political and imperfect, I guess. They create churches for lots of reasons."

"Indeed. They also make shifts in liturgy as a survival mechanism, mid-course corrections on a long journey." He reached over and patted Saito's forearm.

How would people react to this? Truth was no protection. This truth, if validated, changed everything. Social upheaval was possible. Inescapable. He gazed outside again, into the light, and Saito was quiet, giving him space.

"Old gods do not die easily."

Daniel coughed, recalling the quote from Neil Gaiman's *American Gods,* wondering if that had been in his head or he'd said it aloud. "Apologies again. My mind is a bit of a free-association thinker and wanders. Every god is the true one until they're no longer in vogue. Apollo was the hot Roman god and when Rome conquered Egypt, Osiris and his crew got dumped. Centuries later Apollo and his pals were tossed for a political deal with the rising Christians. Is Amun-Ra still hiding in the Sun and wind? Where will Jesus fit in this pantheon? I do ponder such crazy things from time to time."

"This seems like a good time for such analysis. People are entrepreneurial. I suspect a new god quickly gets folded into old traditions."

"Perhaps, but the obstacles this time will be overwhelming. Many Americans don't even believe in evolution."

"I read that."

"A big percentage mostly or wholly believe that angels and devils are at work in the world."

"In Japan, many, perhaps most, believe in the spirits of their ancestors, or *kamis,* floating around and sometimes interfering in someone's life." Saito leaned back in his seat. "But for these people, these Americans, I suspect Darwin means life has no purpose, there's no higher destination. People feel comfort believing the world was designed for a reason, with humans on top," Saito said. "They want reassurance that life is not just an accident of genetic mutations over time."

They looked at each other, processing the implications.

"One hope was that millions of Americans were angry over voter suppression, delegitimizing black families, women moving closer to chattel than at any time in a century, queers angry at their losses, discrimination championed by an effete and out of touch Supreme Court. The kettle has been boiling for years, could it be ready to whistle? Could *Misago* prove the final energy spike for an eruption?"

Daniel felt sympathy for this smart, talented man, undertaking an almost impossible intervention to help his friend, now in danger. That was admirable, the discovery delicious. Saito inspired him for another reason—an out gay man, comfortable, confident, sexy, and brilliant in a hostile culture. Daniel's own experience with Jesuits was often bleak; some sanctimonious clerics preaching hate for LGBTQs even as more than a few bitterly suppressed their own urges, clouding their objectivity, and others openly sought sexual release in and outside the church. Most Jesuits were good men, but certainly not all, some of them in powerful positions. His own feelings were impacted by such suppression, and his modest experience in consensual activity in church made him question the sanity and sanctity of such teachings; gays were not lepers, and were, in his opinion, children of God. His views on pedophiles, often protected when they should be defrocked, exiled or worse, were negative in the extreme.

He put his laptop in his pack. Standing, Daniel carefully squeezed the valise into the nylon bag. He could do this. It was his role as a journalist and this was the biggest story of his life. He would bury his doubts, take it public once satisfied of its veracity.

"We should hide this in case people connect us to this project," he said. "Then plan what needs to happen."

"Where?"

Watching Saito's face reflected in the window, he swung the backpack over his shoulder and held it tight. His voice was melodramatic to bolster his own confidence as he turned toward him. "Sir, I think we shall visit Wyatt Earp."

Looking confused, Saito followed him quickstep out of the library, across the street and down a steep escalator to the subway tunnel for the Bay Area Rapid Transit system. It was a twenty-minute ride to the City of the Dead.

10.

City of Souls, Colma

"Where we're headed, the dead outnumber the living." They were in a seat facing the aisle on the BART train, surrounded by scores of riders holding onto ceiling rods, swaying butts in their faces as the train rocked.

"Great," Saito responded, squeezing tight against him as man in a suit forced his way onto the bench.

"In Colma, here are about 1.2 million dead people and about 1,200 live ones," he added a few miles further on, knowing he was being disrespectful but enjoying it. The crowd had thinned as their train exited the city.

Saito checked his news feed as MUNI sped through the tunnels and eventually came above ground. When the man to his right finally stood and walked to the door, he slid to the side to give Daniel more space then turned to him.

"Why here? What does Wyatt Earp have to do with us? Wasn't he a cowboy?" He sounded annoyed. "I also want to kiss you."

"Ohhh. Taking your last comment first, I like the idea." He leaned into him and kissed his cheek. "Maybe more back at my place. I'll want more than one. As to the first question, Wyatt was a famous western marshal and outlaw. He died in California in the early 1900s. His remains are in the Hills of Eternity Cemetery in Colma. It's a Jewish cemetery, although he wasn't." The last passengers left at another stop. "We need to find a place to leave this satchel and we need to do it now. It's not safe with us or in any normal place I can think of. Forget public lockers—they're gone because of terrorists. We need time to plan. We have a family tomb in Colma where my mother's buried with my great grandparents. Not far from Wyatt Earp's grave. I always carry the key because it's ornate and reminds me of her. I still occasionally stop by for a visit and was there many times as a boy."

"Not exactly a place you'd expect to store space dust," Saito said, looking relieved.

At the cemetery, they walked toward a structure larger than most. It looked like a small stone church with arched door and windows. There was a cross on the roof. Daniel noticed a man in the distance disappear behind a tomb and chided himself for feeling spooked.

The bronze and glass door unlocked and opened with effort. Inside, he stepped to the marble altar, moved a pewter vase with dried white roses, and lifted the thin marble top.

"When I was a boy, my family used to come here not just to bury relatives but to clean up the place and pray." He looked inside. "I used to keep things in this hiding space. The first time I opened it, I found an old Bible and a rosary."

He took Wada's black valise from his pack and put it into the secret space, slid the marble top back into place and topped it with the pewter vase.

Daniel looked at his mother's crypt, ran his fingers slowly across the carved marble inscription, feeling the shape of her name.

"An appropriate home," he pronounced, "for a piece of heaven."

Buena Vista Terrace, San Francisco

It was early evening when they entered his second-floor apartment in the century-old yellow and blue Victorian duplex perched on the side of a steep hill below Buena Vista Park. The lights on the Bay Bridge and downtown Oakland were becoming visible in the distance.

Daniel fixed ham and cheese sandwiches and carried two plates to the kitchen table. They ate in silence.

"You said you were on sabbatical," Saito said. "What's your new focus, if I may inquire?"

"I'm writing a fourth book on religion, this one dealing with the conflict between science and faith and the trashing of science in the name of dogma. Also, the refusal of some faith leaders, many evangelical, to consider anything other than the exact statements in scripture even if the accuracy of those words are easily refuted and run counter to law. It's all part of the rise of Christian nationalism and some extremists who go even further."

"Never heard that term before."

"It's a bit like a backdoor effort to establish a state religion which is prohibited by the Constitution. One example: religious organizations often seek to provide social services under government contracts, meaning they're reimbursed with taxpayer dollars. Most are Christian. Not bad in itself. But under the Orwellian banner of religious freedom, many want exemption from the kinds of anti-discrimination laws by which nonreligious businesses must abide. If it's against your sincere religious beliefs, whatever that means, you don't have to do it. If your church is anti-gay, discriminate based on your beliefs while getting government funding. Congress last year outlawed all abortions in America, following a Supreme Court decision overturning established law on the subject. I mentioned overturning gay marriage. The tide is turning against liberty and people are cautious in states where governors are predatory. People who hate are now comfortable being in public, wearing their disdain for others proudly. It used to be bigots avoided the limelight. Now many who support equality are cowed, often by armed militias. Many politicians are anxious to support this kind of religious takeover for their personal short-term gain and to hell with any long-term impact on freedom and fairness. It's insidious. A dire threat to freedom."

"Scary. How far along are you?"

"Finished with research and through several drafts. My publisher likes the early chapters. Now I need a few months for final polishing." He smiled. "Never ask an author about his books unless you want a lecture."

"That cuts amazingly close to our current project. Perhaps your book could be incorporated into the *Misago* story. I'm curious, does your family no longer live here?"

"My grandparents are in Florida but kept this unit as an investment and to give me a free place to stay when in the city. Let's go into the living room to talk."

"Before then, may we turn on some music?" As they carried their glasses of Sauvignon blanc, Saito stepped close and whispered. "Just as a precaution if anyone is listening."

"How loud?"

"Very."

"I didn't seek this out," Daniel said looking at the cityscape as Arthur Rubinstein began to play *adagio*. He could feel the adrenalin ebbing even as the ramifications and his limited resources jabbed his brain. He needed a plan.

"No," Saito answered, "but here it is."

"This doesn't happen to everyday people." He picked up his glass.

"Perhaps, but because it's happened to you, you're no longer that same person. Have you heard of Francis Crick?"

"What? Yes. The scientist who won the Nobel for discovering DNA."

"Right. Tio and Yoshito once got in a lively argument over one of Crick's essays that suggested because some exceedingly rare elements were necessary to start life, perhaps some were deliberately transmitted to earth. Directed Panspermia."

Daniel shrugged.

"Wada thought Crick's paper was more satire than science, an insider's joke, and talking about the supernatural makes us mentally lazy. Tio—who I think thought the same thing but enjoyed sparring with Yoshito, kind of a game—said she was surprised her colleague was so rigid. Wada replied, 'It comes with age. Certainty is restricted to youth.' "

Daniel laughed. "A great relationship and two extraordinary minds."

"Tio performed follow up tests on both *Hayabusa* cargos and the more robust *Misago* regolith," he said just above a whisper, "and developed plans with Dr...."

"Nathan," Daniel suggested, thinking they should be less open on names. It was Yoshito's unusual middle name, selected by his mother, he was told, who was a student of the American revolution and admired a man hung by the British as a spy, a patriot.

"Yes, Nathan, who brought in other scientists and divided research into two levels, one open, the other closed except to a trusted few."

Daniel watched and listened closely as he gave details. Bravado was giving way to reality. How do you confirm the incomprehensible? The implications for society deeply troubled him. In the back of his journalist's brain, a voice kept repeating, "Don't play the fool."

Rubinstein pounded a series of dissonant cords. Daniel's mouth was dehydrated. He took a sip of wine. "Asteroids fall into the atmosphere all the time. Many reach the surface. Why hasn't this been discovered before?"

"Perhaps it has."

He hadn't thought of that. An intriguing possibility.

"It's been a long day and I suspect you're wearing down," he said. Saito looked exhausted. Daniel reached over and put his hand on the man's shoulder, appreciating the excitement of colluding over a secret that could shatter human perception of God. "I guess we're officially co-conspirators."

Rubinstein struck the final notes *pianissimo* and the audience at Carnegie Hall erupted in applause.

"Yes, I guess we are."

"You're welcome to spend the night, if you like, or I can take you back to wherever your bags are. Or have them delivered."

Saito turned, wrapping his arms around Daniel, and pulled him into a kiss. It started gentle and soon deepened. He unbuttoned Daniel's shirt and put his hand inside, rubbing his chest.

"Perhaps I can show you your accommodations?" Daniel managed to get out as he stood, coughed, and pulled his guest to the master bedroom.

11.

Apostolic Palace, Vatican City

The cardinal examined Vega's image on the computer screen. Father Alito paced behind him.

"If Dr. Wada was killed, the body has yet to be discovered," Vega said in his always-precise Italian. "If he left the country, it was not under his own name. If in hiding, his location remains secret. His JAXA office looked like it was vandalized as well as his Takayama home. Traces of his blood were found at his home, even a bloody hand print and a neighbor told police he believed he saw him being abducted."

"I can read your expression. You have suspicions." The earlier briefing by Vega had shaken him to his core. He glanced at Father Alioto now sitting beside him.

Vega smiled, perfect white teeth reflecting on the screen. The cardinal was amazed yet again that someone like him was capable of murder.

"I believe the Japanese were prepared to put Wada under house arrest or even stage his death to protect their position. But my contacts are perplexed at his disappearance. I do not think they are being coy to hide incompetence. Either unknown parties abducted him or he acted first and simply disappeared on his own, making it look like he was kidnapped to cover his escape. Either is plausible."

The cardinal leaned back in his chair and continued to listen and observe the image on his screen.

"My understanding," Vega continued, "is that Wada argued vigorously with top space agency officials and the prime minister over sinking the discovery in exchange for continued action by the U.S. Navy. Later, when a deal was cut with the Americans, Wada accepted it without argument. Such a man would not show passivity without an alternative plan in place."

"You sound like you admire him."

"Your Eminence, I admire intelligence and courage. There are few with such virtues in today's world. He is also said to be a man of good will. That is his reputation. If I may continue?"

The cardinal nodded. "The prime minister is largely ineffective, an aging prima donna. My instincts suggest the scientist faked his kidnapping, a tactical distraction, and has a scheme in place allowing him to work in secret."

"But you have no sense of what that might be?"

"No. Because he is a major scientific figure, Wada could prove embarrassing if he resurfaces and goes public. There is motivation for the prime minister to silence the man, even kill him. His agents are likely on the hunt. We also don't know yet if actual space granules are missing."

"Romaldo, we must find him and the package, quietly, if we can. While I'm intrigued, my first loyalty must be to the church. We've been seriously weakened by our scandals."

The Vatican's moral authority was continuing to evaporate. Monsters he'd protected, even rewarded. His shame was at times overwhelming. He knew or should have known what was happening. The blindness of friendship and ambition must never again cloud his moral duty. But would he have the clarity and backbone when they were needed?

"It would be better not to argue about *Misago* publicly even if we would likely prevail in the short term," the cardinal continued.

"My concern is not just for the Catholic Church to survive this decade but to live forever."

"I understand, Your Eminence. We are working with police. I'm focused on what my intuition suggests are high value targets, people further removed from his inner circle. May I inquire how the Holy Father is reacting? I fear for his health."

"Your concerns are shared. He did not respond well and his condition is delicate."

The cardinal had to help the pontiff into his bed after he first briefed him on the discovery. The man seemed at first befuddled, then angry. It was dispiriting to see his friend in such a state.

After a moment, he sensed Vega staring at him, waiting. "I suspect you have an opinion on all this, Romaldo. You know I value your views."

"Thank you for your courtesy. This is not just another theory. As much as we may not want this information public, we need to make sure that God is not seeking to communicate with us. This church has changed and weathered much over two millennia."

Vega paused and sipped water from a carved crystal tumbler. "Some of the American Protestant churches are comparatively new," he continued, "some less than a century old, almost independent operations tied to the popularity of a particular pastor, television program and the services offered. Many are more about politics than a consistent faith. They have different needs."

Vega set down the glass, intertwined his fingers and touched his chin, looking directly at the cardinal. "Suppression as a temporary tool so one can study and learn absent public scrutiny, is appropriate." His tone was respectful but almost stern, uncompromising. "Suppression without curiosity, suppression for its own sake, in perpetuity, simply to preserve the status quo may be an offense to God."

Father Alito whipped his head toward the screen. The cardinal showed no reaction but felt a jolt, a punch in the gut. He rested his chin on folded hands as he considered the statement.

"There is much complexity and wisdom in your words, Romaldo. I must think about them. I have obligations to my church. I like to think they are consistent with my obligations to God. You suggest perhaps they are not."

The two men assessed each other as the cardinal considered the implications. He owed the man his life. He was an ally and benefactor, a man of staggering wealth.

"Your words are strong, my friend, but also insightful and provocative," he said slowly. "Thank you for your honesty and for challenging mine. That is a virtue lacking in vast organizations, particularly ones as sanctimonious as churches." The cardinal felt a mix of admiration and apprehension. "Please give me some time on this and let us talk again soon."

Vega nodded respectfully and the screen went dark.

Martinez sat in silence, pondering the challenge. "Vega is a man of great insight and confidence," he said softly, as much to himself as Alito. "Few men, none that I know, would have the courage to make such a statement to a cardinal, much less a cardinal charged with defending the faith. What is disturbing—he may be right." Was he himself strong enough to face truth with such courage? And what about his church?

Alito replied, "You're the real power in a church with over a billion members. You make tough decisions every day. He's not just an advisor, more like a sage, and from the rumors, a warrior."

The cardinal smiled, accustomed to the perpetual admiration of his aide which was reassuring if meaningless. "I believe you're correct about him," he said, confident the priest knew only some of what Vega had done for him over the years. Such a man had his uses. But should he always be so complacent about someone just because he supported his cause?

"Do you ever wonder about him, Guido, and how he often shows up wherever major events unfold?" How was it possible? How was it that he had found a desperate monsignor in Bethlehem and saved his life? Now, one of the first outsiders to know of this catastrophe.

"Your Eminence," Father Alito said, ignoring the question, "is there anything I can do to help when you meet with the next group of cardinals this afternoon?"

"Find me bullet-proof vestments," Martinez answered with a wan smile. His peers, not known for their curiosity, rationality, humility, or ability to accept challenge, were not taking the news well, some in denial, some angry. They looked to him to solve this crisis. Unlikely. He feared the Holy Father would not long survive. That chaos would compound the catastrophe.

"There is value in reaching out to American clergy," Alito suggested tentatively, "as we are doing, to test their willingness to work together. Thank you for your work in setting up a meeting. A single voice, a coalition of believers, is strongest."

"Yes, we do need allies, Guido. Reverend Adam Wright is always helpful and will be at the conference at Lake Tahoe, but some of the others…" He left the thought unfinished.

Vega. The man's words had touched something hidden deep and he felt shaken. Obligation to church and God. Could they be different?

12.

"I miss you, Jesus." Did he just say this aloud or in his head? "Are my words your words?" This time he heard his own wistful voice. There was no response.

Reverend Wright ran his fingertips over the curve of his roll top desk. Tambour— he recalled the term for the half round strips of wood glued to canvas. He hooked a thumb in the indent at the base and lifted it open with a whoosh. This desk, crafted in the early 19th century, had first belonged to his grandfather; it was designed as a perfect place for writing letters, supporting the daily long-distance correspondence of the time. Inside were small drawers, pigeonholes, and shelves. All the clutter neatly hidden behind the element that gave the desk its name. In a tangled stack within were press clippings of his work and the rough draft of a sermon. He liked to write by hand, something more permanent than floating words on a shimmering screen. The desk was a bit like his life, all somber and composed on the outside, often a muddle inside, and from a side view, much like his physique. The analogy made him laugh.

He pulled out the wooden mid-back banker's chair with brass

castors, adjusted the blue and white flowered cushion, a surprise sewing club project by his wife, and, making sure his ample body was properly aimed into the swivel seat, he sat. From one unfortunate crash he'd learned the value of heedfulness instead of replacing a beloved piece of furniture. He looked out the multi-pane window covering one wall, framed in red trumpet vine on this sunny day in Chillicothe.

He picked up a yellow note pad, wrinkled from the ink and the press of his hand as he wrote, and reconsidered. The words returned. *Jesus, I do miss what we once had.*

His eyes and memories roamed the contents of the dark oak shelves that filled two walls, crammed with books, photos, awards, and the flotsam of his life. He remembered his heart bypass operation a year ago when he flatlined on the operating table and was brought back to life. He'd glimpsed burning lakes, fire, devil figures—the pits of Hell. Had it been a warning? Or just a dream under anesthesia? Another bit of detritus best kept hidden by his mental tambour. That experience had done something to him, shaken his confidence, his certainty.

Wright set the script aside, in no mood for writing, and picked up a handful of recent newspaper clips.

"Wright Praises Supreme Court for Reversing Gay Marriage Decision," one headline stated. The story continued, "It should be left to each state as the court has now done." Another story: "Only married heterosexual couples should be able to adopt, Congress of Conservative Christians Chair warns national conference." He sighed and pressed forefingers to his eyes.

"I miss the Gospels," muttered. He thought again about his decision to quiet skeptics on his Board by preaching less about Jesus and more about sin. He was also being pressured to support creation of God's Kingdom. He liked the concept of government by divine guidance or by officials who are regarded as divinely guided. But he got heartburn thinking about some of his board members setting policy. Iran was a great example of how this kind of government could lead to a religious dictatorship with vast human suffering. Three members of his board believed God wanted them in the role. Ludicrous. He picked up and tossed the clips in the trash. Putting his feet on an open drawer he leaned back again in his chair and entwined his fingers behind his head until a knock at the door brought him out of his reverie.

"May I come in?" his son asked.

"You're asking?" That seemed unusual for the often sullen teenager. Rolph entered, tense, clearly troubled.

"What's wrong?" Wright stood, closed the door and gestured toward the sofa. The teenager was trembling. His lips were white and tightly pinched as he sat in a far corner. The boy avoided looking at his father, instead staring at his lap, his hands pressed between his thighs. A trickle of sweat ran down his forehead. Rolph opened his mouth to speak and then coughed. He closed his eyes and tilted his head back, swallowing and biting his lower lip.

Wright, alarmed by his son's behavior and suddenly nervous himself, sat next to him and put one hand on the boy's shoulder. "Please tell me what's wrong. It can't be so bad."

The boy jerked as if recoiling from an electrical shock. He took a series of deep breaths, exhaling loudly as he sat up straight and rocked back unsteadily to gain control. His voice was taut, the words tumbling out. "You're going to get a call—from Michael's dad. I…we…I…have brought shame to you and the church. He found us…together. I am sorry, father."

The teenager bolted to his feet and turned his back, stepping to the window, too ashamed to face him. "I don't know what's happening to me, I feel like, sometimes, I don't know who I am." He steadied himself by holding onto the wall with one hand, the other clenched into a fist held tightly to his mouth. He blurted out, almost a cry, "It's worse. I need to be honest. I…I sometimes think I should've been a girl." He snorted, blowing out a snotty mess onto his hand. "Shit!" He rubbed his fist onto his jeans. "Could this get any worse? This isn't how I was gonna tell you."

Wright stared at the empty seat, praying this was some kind of teenage prank. He held his breath trying to calm himself. His heart pounded; he felt light-headed, confused. Was this a relapse;

was he back in Hell? His legs were wobbly as he stood and went to his son. God ordered Abraham to sacrifice his son Isaac. Was this such a test? He pulled several tissues from his desk and handed them to Rolph. His son was transsexual? He'd read about it, not sure what to think. Was that better or worse than being gay in Scripture?

This was ridiculous. He was retreating immediately into his judgmental preacher world and not his role as a dad. *"Found us together."* What did that mean?

He wrapped his arms about the boy's chest and pressed his cheek against the back of his head. Rolph stiffened but didn't move. The minister wanted to show support while he figured out just how to handle this calamity. A minute passed in silence save for Rolph's ragged breathing. Perhaps he was being too dramatic, too ready to judge.

"Could you explain what you mean by *'together?'* I can be a little dense sometimes."

Rolph blew his nose again and coughed. "Please don't make me say it. We were naked."

"I see. And you said… *'sometime.'*"

"Yeah. I've known for a long time." The boy's voice cracked and he inhaled loudly, seemingly anxious to end the humiliation and to get at what was hurting most.

"I know what you say…about people…people like me…in your radio shows. I'm an *abomination*." His voice quivered, tears streaming down his cheek. "Kids at school beat up a boy and spit on him. They said he was…was…queer. I didn't mean for this to happen. It just did. Mom knows. I just told her."

His son pushed his head back, his nostrils flaring and his lower lip pushed out as he steeled himself for the logical consequences of his action. "I…I understand if you want me to go away."

"Oh, my God, NO!" Wright squeezed him tight, holding his boy before turning him around. They faced each other, looked away, then back again, both unable to control the tears and finally unwilling to try. Wright grabbed another handful of tissues. Must he choose between the love of his son and the love of his church?

As he held the child he adored, the son he bragged about to friends for his accomplishments in school, the minister thought about his harsh denunciations of homosexuality and the LGBTQ+ alphabet nightmare, never knowing he was condemning his only son. Should honoring his beliefs mean casting out his son?

He recalled one of his predecessors trying to expand the political agenda of the CCC beyond opposition to abortion and homosexuality to include poverty and global warming. But the board had forced that minister to resign to maintain a tight focus on sin. Now his son had committed what his faith said was one of the vilest of sins. Why was that, he wondered? The why of it had never mattered until now.

Wright took a tissue and wiped his son's nose. The boy didn't resist. The minister tried to smile but settled for just stabilizing the quiver in his lips. "I love you, Rolph. You are my son. Let us pray together and seek understanding."

"But will God listen to someone like me?"

The minister's voice was strained but warm as he said firmly something he had never said aloud before: *"God created you."*

13.

Haight-Ashbury, San Francisco

"Did you know that a majority of American Protestants and a third of Catholics believe Jesus will return by 2050?" Daniel sipped apple juice, his emotions seeming to flutter between anger and astonishment. "You can appreciate the distress if Misago makes a substitution in the cast of this play." He and Saito were in the People's Café on Haight Street, sitting by an open window looking out on homeless teenagers mixing easily with aging hippies in the urban neighborhood.

"Are you a religious man, Daniel?" Saito was determined to learn his secrets for the sake of the mission. At least that's what he told himself, not his own curiosity.

"I've been disillusioned about religion for a long time," Daniel responded. "But this discovery strips away certainty for both believers and atheists." He clasped his hands under his chin. "People have gone to war over less."

"I'm trying to understand your thinking prior to the special delivery package," Saito said, between bites of chicken dumplings and Napa cabbage. "I think you're avoiding the question."

"You're pushy."

"You're sensitive." Saito's voice was more friendly detective than scientific researcher. He reached over and took one of Daniel's hands. "Sorry. Please? Either you have faith or not, isn't that right?"

"For most people that may be true," he said, looking amused, squeezing Saito's hand and entwining the fingers. "But sometimes you're just not sure what you believe and faith can be a matter of doing things because others expect it. I think for most people they adopt their parents' faith and their circle of friends, neighbors and churches reinforce it. I'm something of a deist, I guess, like many of the founding fathers, sons of the Enlightenment. God came, created, and left, giving man the ability to think and reason. That was his gift."

Daniel turned sideways in his chair, stretching his legs. He looked at Saito, considering his words. "In college, I read a book called *The Sparrow*. An odd novel by Mary Doria Russell, with some words I adopted as my own and they cling to me still. A young priest named Sandoz said:

> *'He was aware of his agnosticism, and patient with it and rather than deny the existence of something he couldn't perceive himself, he acknowledged the authenticity of his uncertainty and carried on, praying in face of his doubt.'*

"I am that priest. I'm Father Sandoz."
"You're a complicated man."
Daniel shrugged. "Some people practice religion and never question its authenticity. I think that's where it starts. *Misago* will change that. People may come to view their beliefs in pre-and-post *Misago* terms." He dipped a garlic fry in ketchup.

"I have Jewish friends who say Judaism is less of a religion than a culture with traditions they enjoy," he said. "They practice religious holidays yet are agnostic. I'm not sure if you call them people of faith or not. But they have no doubt whatsoever that they're Jewish." He rubbed the napkin over his lips, took a drink of juice and smiled. "Of course, there is what I'd consider a controversial view that being a Jew is genetic and DNA tests have been used to provide proof. I guess using technology to confirm heritage and thus faith is to me a dangerous proposition. I've a Mormon friend who says the church with its inward focus is great for business, a ready-made market. I'm not sure where faith and making money intersect for him. A single parent I know attends a Pentecostal mega-church. She goes for the day care. How do you classify her on the faith scale?"

"But you studied theology."

Daniel knew he looked surprised. "Yes. I was in a Jesuit seminary for a couple of years. My mother was very Catholic and she died in my teens. I thought pursuing the priesthood would honor her memory and somehow, help change the institution. My father…" He left the rest unsaid, his expression tightening, perhaps remembering some past horror.

"Is everything all right, Daniel?"

"Yes, sorry. I was a ridiculously pious kid. Insufferable. Rigid. As an altar boy, I'd had the temerity to be upset with the way a few priests and even nuns were so casual about their religion and ignored teachings of the church, some even criminal." He stopped as if old demons demanded attention.

"You were hurt once," Saito said with sympathy. "It shows on your face. Would telling it help?" He was pushing, perhaps too hard, venturing into private areas still raw. Daniel was outwardly confident and articulate but there was more there, something dark had shaken him.

Daniel looked at him, considering the question. "I'd rather not go there."

"I want to know who you are, Daniel. I care about you. Wada has great confidence in you. I was intrigued on many levels when we met as you know. I'd like to understand you more."

He touched Daniel's hand on the table, squeezed and pulled back. "We need to know each other to manage whatever lies ahead. You were once a devout Catholic. That may be important in our planning."

Daniel's voice caught, dropping to a murmur. "When I was

about eleven, I was approached by a priest, a close friend of my mother." He turned the butter dish around. "In the confession booth, he said he'd seen me looking at another boy and wanted to know if I had unholy thoughts. I wasn't sure what he meant. I had feelings of attraction to other boys and girls in my age group, but I wasn't even in puberty so it didn't make sense to me. A day later he called me in for consultation. He made me stand and walked up to me. When he touched me, I didn't know what to do. I didn't resist; didn't know I could. I felt powerless. I couldn't hit a priest. He was someone I admired. He said God wanted me to do this. *'It is our secret,'* he told me. Who could I tell? My drunk of a father? My sick mother? My abuser was a *priest!*"

Daniel looked out the window, humiliated. Saito grieved for him. Now he understood some of his pain related to his father.

"Sorry, I should not have gone there."

"Please. I want to understand." He picked up Daniel's hand and brought it to his lips, kissing it gently.

He continued, his words halting: "I tried to avoid him, refusing to give up my faith, my mother's faith. I put it aside and tried not to think about it when I entered the seminary years later. He was an aberration, I was convinced. Also the archbishop was a self-centered jerk. I still wanted to serve God as a tribute to my mom. I wanted to help change the system so people like him couldn't prey on children or any other parishioner. It's amazing how humans can compartmentalize their brains and lives."

"What happened to the priest?"

"A nun, Sister Joan, found me crying after a particularly ugly encounter. I begged her not to tell my mom. Sister took me to the archbishop and told him. He just looked at me like maybe I was lying, wasting his time, just a stupid kid. The priest was his friend. He said he'd check on my story and dismissed me. Sister was furious. I felt foolish, then angry. Maybe this was a secret part of the church I was too ignorant to understand. I heard later she accused the priest in front of the archbishop and others." He paused, taking a breath.

"Father Thomas was transferred to Rome to serve at the

beautiful San Luigi dei Francesi, an art-filled cathedral. Sister Joan was sent to Guatemala. We exchange letters every year or so. She was wounded long ago in a firefight between crooked police and a criminal gang. But she survived and lives in a convent. Every time I smell Aqua Velva, I see the priest's smug face and relive the injustice."

"I wish someone had been there for you."

"For her, too. The old boy's network within the church was powerful. I assume it still is judging by the lawsuits and stonewalling."

"There is hypocrisy in many religions, perhaps most. Yet believers point to all the good faith brings, often, I suspect, willfully blind to the evil."

"Yes, although there is something humbling and beautiful listening to a choir soloist sing *Ave Maria*." He paused again, a far off look in his eyes. "In seminary I met numerous gay students and priests. Some were active sexually even as the church officially condemned such acts. I once saw a bishop verbally humiliate a Franciscan Brother for having sex, even as the bishop was a regular in our living quarters prowling for hookups. Yet most of those I worked with, studied with, served with, were truly fine men and women of conscience seeking to do good."

"Were you always attracted to men?"

He exhaled, folded his hands, and looked directly into Saito's eyes. "I once kissed an altar boy. Or rather he kissed me. A similar experience in seminary, more than once and, to be honest, more than a kiss." He shook his head. "But that was the hothouse of our dorm. Outside the church, I was equally attracted to women. One, an attraction and devotion that compelled me to leave seminary."

"Thank you for your candor. I feel privileged. It deepens my confidence in your understanding and capacity to deal with this discovery and the fallout likely to come if it goes public."

Daniel smiled. "I appreciate your comments but time to change topics." His voice became upbeat. "This is not the conversation I expected with a smart, charming, and sexy astrophysicist and baseball coach. How about your life, Dr. Saito? Given how I've just humiliated myself, I hope you'll be just as entertaining."

"Fair enough. I've been a chemist at Mitsubishi's Space Division since I graduated from grad school at Berkeley—as I think you know. I did my thesis on a project at JAXA. I have a great job, travel a lot in the States and Europe where we have some sophisticated clients and jobs involving robotics and solar energy."

"Really?" He shook his head in mock surprise. "This isn't entertaining. Can we move beyond the LinkedIn profile?" He smiled, one eyebrow a question mark.

Saito laughed, enjoying the repartee. "Well…religion-wise—I love the beauty of Shinto with its emphasis on nature. But I don't connect my essence as a human being with religion. I've never married. The kind of marriage I would want isn't legally settled yet."

Daniel nodded, a tight grin on his lips. "One issue at a time, I think. Put down your guard, Saito. Either you believe in God or you don't, quoting an insightful Japanese scientist." He lifted both his palms. "Well?"

Saito smirked, enjoying Daniel's ability to shift emotions and direction. "Did I mention my BS degree is in biology? I believe Darwin is right and I see no hand of the divine in the creation of life."

"So, you're an atheist and not a fence-straddling agnostic?"

"That's not an either-or question. It's far more complex as I suspect you know but are, as you say in this country, *giving me shit*."

"Lay it on me. I'm ready to be enlightened." Daniel looked expectant.

"I've never been afraid to take a firm position. But such intellectual honesty may be easier in Japan than America." Saito reached over again to Daniels hand and kept it there. "Tell me what is the greater hubris: Certainty that God exists even with no proof? Or, certainty that God doesn't exist, also without real proof?"

"You just said the issue is more complex."

"Let me add two more: Isn't the agnostic taking the honest

position, given lack of proof? Or try this one—What is the greater hubris, continuing to believe in God the Creator, ignoring and seeking to suppress physical proof the position is bankrupt? Or, believing no god exists when our evidence says maybe he does?"

Daniel put his other hand on top of Saito's. "Excellent analysis. Your wisdom and insights are stimulating. Now we are in *Misago* reality. Does that make you a believer?"

"A believer in what? There is more we don't know then what we do."

He leaned back and pushed his plate aside, grinning. "Except for this new proof of a god's existence, everything's the same."

"Assuming it is a god. That's the easy part," Saito said. "Your friends, the Jew and the Mormon, what will they do if their comfortable world is suddenly hollowed out? The single mother looking for childcare may not worry about it unless her church collapses."

"People will be upset, confused, conflicted. Okay, moving beyond this," he said, "have you ever had any life altering experiences, unexpected ones, hopefully embarrassing ones, that made you wonder about your role in life?"

"I rode bare chested on a float during an LGBTQ+ Pride Parade in Tokyo when in my early twenties and was voted, 'Hottest Man.' I hadn't realized there was even a contest. I had to go up on the stage wearing just a leather thong and boots."

Daniel was bent over with laughter. "I want a photo!"

"It gets worse. I didn't know my younger brother brought my parents to see all the weird people. I hadn't come out to them."

"*Oh, fuck! No!*"

"*Fuck, Yes!*" He wiped his eyes. "I can laugh about it now. But it took a couple of years."

"Did you get a tiara?"

"Please. Do I look like a guy who would wear a tiara?"

"You're stereotyping. Butch men can wear feminine objects."

"So, you think I'm butch?" Saito started to giggle and couldn't stop. "Oh, it was horrible, even with a crown. But then my parents and I had a good excuse to talk, at least when they were willing to let me in their house again. They were fine with it. Eventually."

"Do you still have the butch crown?"

"Honestly, not so butch. My mother keeps it."

"Did it attract a handsome prince?"

"I did the parade to help a group that provided outreach to homeless queer youth. They were desperate to have half-naked men to draw attention to their organization. I don't date a lot. My career keeps me traveling, studying, and analyzing. My parents are disappointed I've not given them grandchildren."

"You're brave and dedicated. I admire that. I certainly wouldn't go on a stage mostly naked. Of course, I don't have the physique either."

"I assumed you liked my physique, given the glorious attention you pay to it when we are intimate. I truly do admire yours as you have likely noticed. Thank you. My turn, again. May I inquire a little more about your family life? Wada said you divorced a year or two ago and it might impact your views on your church and what to do with *Misago*."

"Gads. You're relentless. My marriage was annulled." Daniel's face twisted into a grimace of bitterness. "The church said it didn't happen." He struggled to regain some control. "I married very young. We had a son, Garrett. I published my first book, great reviews, little money. I ended up in journalism after a brief stint in public relations and was lucky enough to get on the staff of the *New York Times*. I published two more books. My third was a best seller. We had a little more money but evidently not enough for her." He stopped.

"Go on. What happened? Please?"

"Ten years in, she came home one day and said she'd met someone else."

Saito saw the pain in his face, the honesty, a rarity in his experience. Hopefully this was cathartic for him.

"I don't usually talk about this stuff. Maybe you're my new therapist. It turns out he was a wealthy older man with connections." The muscles flexed in his cheeks. "The rich new man in her life made a seven-figure donation to the church. The local archbishop claimed there was no connection between the annulment and the money. That did it for my identity as a Catholic. Now I see my son every other month, sometimes on special occasions, and Garrett seems disturbed. I know he's angry and I don't blame him. He didn't deserve any of this."

"When was this?"

"The breakup and taking of my son happened a few months before I made my visit to JAXA."

"I'm sorry," Saito said, saddened by how such a good man had been hurt. "Dr. Wada made a good choice. You're a complex man, Daniel Duboce. Your son is lucky to have you in his life."

As they walked up Haight Street, a young man without shoes held up a sign as they walked by—*Will Work for Drugs*—and offered a toothless smile. Two San Francisco policemen rode by on horses. Both officers tipped their hats.

"We need to understand our enemies," Saito said as they strolled around the edge of the park. "Who wants the data?"

"The FBI. I suspect Japanese police."

"Perhaps."

They jumped to the edge of the sidewalk as two shirtless tweens raced by on skateboards cutting between them and a dozen boisterous preschoolers holding onto round rings tied to a rope and guided by elderly nuns in white habits.

"You were saying?"

"If President Walton went to his religious allies, they're likely involved. Japanese news media is covering the disappearance but doesn't know what it's about. The media is key, at least what is left that is free."

"In what way?"

"It's the only hope to rip off the government gag and outmaneuver repression."

14.

Buena Vista Terrace, San Francisco

Daniel was surprised to find a tall swarthy stranger at his front door, smiling, impeccably dressed in a dark gray suit, white shirt and a pink and blue swirl patterned tie. Saito walked up beside Daniel.

"My name is Romaldo Vega." The man nodded, offering his hand to each and bowed slightly at the waist, like European nobility in an old movie. "I am hoping to be of service as someone who knows a little about what may be happening in your lives at the moment."

"About?" Daniel asked. This wasn't a door-to-door salesman and this wasn't the season for politicians. He was alone so not a Jehovah's Witness. Too old for a Mormon on a mission. His accent was intriguing and hard to place.

"Asteroids. May I come in?"

Daniel paused, processing the disclosure. So, he was already a target. Intrigued, he stepped aside and invited the man to enter. Saito looked alarmed but followed Daniel's lead.

Daniel pointed to a chair and Vega sat, legs crossed, leaning back, a picture of confidence. They sat on a black leather sofa across from him.

"Why are you here?"

"At this moment, on this issue, I'm helping the Catholic Church. Among other things, I support the fine work of His Eminence, Cardinal Diego Martinez, Prefect of the Congregation for the Doctrine of the Faith at the Vatican in Rome. It's in that capacity that I am here. He has taken considerable interest in you."

"Doesn't he lead what used to be called the Inquisition?"

"It's not been called that for a long time. Today it is the office responsible for maintaining and defending the integrity of the Catholic faith and to examine and proscribe errors and false doctrines."

"What's this to do with us?"

"Your involvement with Dr. Yoshito Wada and the *Misago* space probe." Vega's voice was calm, matter of fact.

"Why should you be interested in us because we know Dr. Wada?" Daniel asked. "Any Google search can show my connection. I'm a reporter and did a major story on JAXA."

"Let us not be modest, Mr. Duboce. A package of material related to the space probe is now officially missing, likely taken by Dr. Wada who is also unaccounted for. I would like to find that package."

Daniel picked up a notepad from a side table and started writing to remember details and see if it made Vega nervous. But the man didn't seem bothered and spoke in surprisingly full sentences, no contractions that he noticed. Most unusual, maybe pretense or, more likely, multi-lingual and being careful.

"Where did you hide it?" Vega asked, each syllable stated with precision.

"Where did I hide what?" Daniel asked, still trying to place the accent and stilted language. *How could he know? He doesn't. He's just fishing, like a good reporter might do.*

"The package of materials Dr. Saito received from Dr. Wada that he apparently delivered to you, Mr. Duboce, for reasons not yet clear to me."

"How do you think you know this?" Saito sounded more curious than upset. "What makes you believe Yoshito gave me something to hide?"

"To get proof out of the country for safe-keeping. I certainly would if our positions were reversed. I believe you took it when you left Tokyo."

Saito raised an eyebrow. "Quite an assumption."

"Dr. Saito, your call and voicemail to Mr. Duboce from Japan as you prepared to travel here, mentioning Dr. Wada and JAXA—"

"So, in addition to your religious talents, you also wiretap? What else don't we know about you?"

Daniel looked at them both in surprise. He didn't remember a voicemail from Saito. But he'd just traded in his old phone and got a new number, tired of all the crank calls. He leaned back in his chair trying to assess the man. Vega seemed to be reciprocating.

"You are now players in one of the great issues of our time," Vega said, "as you surely know. You are both bright, socially committed individuals of great moral standing. History could be changed by what you decide."

When they didn't respond, he took out a blank business card and a Mont Blanc fountain pen and wrote his last name and phone number in elegant script. "Please consider my comments. I would like to talk again early tomorrow. For breakfast," he said, handing Daniel the card. "Be forewarned. I am persistent."

As the door closed behind Vega, Saito pushed a finger across Daniel's lips.

"Rubinstein," he whispered.

Daniel nodded, turning on the stereo before gesturing for him to follow. He opened a door at the central enclosed airshaft in the building and headed quietly down the stairs to the lower unit. He rapped lightly on the unlocked door as he opened it.

"Woesha," he whispered. He repeated her name again as they stepped into the kitchen.

"What, Daniel?" She emerged from the den wearing an emerald-green flowing dress, a red and yellow headscarf. She wrapped her arms around him and kissed his cheek, leaned back examining him, wet her thumb and wiped off lipstick before turning to Saito. "Hi handsome. I'm glad you found him."

Daniel put a finger to his lips. "I need to use your landline," he whispered. "Could you turn up Ray Charles? My apartment might be bugged."

"Georgia...G-e-o-r-g-i-a..."

Nodding, she jacked-up the volume. It sounded like they were at competing concerts until Saito closed the door.

"Bruiser, it's me, Daniel."

"You sound like you're in a bordello. I can hardly hear you."

"I need your help. I'm onto the biggest story of my life. Remember the piece I did on the Japanese space program a year ago? Turns out, hidden behind the scenes, is a story of a spectacular scientific discovery and a coverup. If this pans out, it could be the greatest story of all time."

"No shit?"

He sounded dubious, a man who'd seen, heard and exposed almost everything in his four-decade career. This was a useful counterbalance, a way to test reality. Daniel continued, "I'll be sending you material via encrypted email. Use the same setup when we partnered on that mafia story. You know the code. I'll include details on where to find everything you need for proof."

"Got it. What'd they find that's so exciting?"

Daniel gave a summary while Bruiser listened in silence.

"OK. Interesting. Great for *Nova.*"

Perfectly suspicious, just what was needed. So Daniel came at it from a different angle, appreciating the challenge in getting a hard-nosed newspaperman to accept such an unexpected and consequential set of facts. His godfather listened patiently.

"What're the politics?" Bruiser's voice was curious but still noncommittal.

"The Japanese government has cut a deal with President Walton to quash the discovery. Dr. Wada has disappeared, perhaps of his own volition, kidnapped or killed. A space scientist and close associate of Wada is with me. He was told by Wada that religious advisors to Walton were involved in the decision-making,

I'm guessing members of the Triple C. We've just been contacted by a representative of the Vatican. He wants to talk tomorrow. He assumes we have the proof. There is also a Japanese police investigation that one man at JAXA is dead, maybe suicide, perhaps murder."

"Murder!"

Daniel thought that might clinch it. "I'll text my new number. It's likely bugged but you can leave messages in code."

"I'll bite." Bruiser did the growl laugh he'd often heard. "Start sending copy. Even just snippets. I can compile it if need be."

"If you don't hear from me in several days, pick up the package in person from the location I'll send you, and run with it. Meanwhile, I'll start transmitting material. To be honest, Bruiser, my role has shifted. I'm a participant in the story, a source, one of many you'll use. Take the role as lead writer. I'll talk to my boss at the *Times*."

"This should be your story, Daniel."

"It can't be if I'm to be faithful to what I leaned in J-School. I know I'm a little old-fashioned."

"You work for the *Times*. It should be its story."

"Save me from your honor, Bruiser. You want this. I'll talk to my editor but I'm on sabbatical to complete another book."

"Ironic indeed. Yes I want the story. I was just being polite. Good book subject, maybe it can fit in with this, a long historical perspective."

"Perhaps. One step for man, one momentous crumbling of old assumptions."

"Not very quotable." Bruiser was silent for a moment before concluding. "Be careful. No story's worth dying for."

"Thanks. A great quote for your second Pulitzer."

15.

Embarcadero, San Francisco

Daniel and Saito stepped off a silver MUNI train across from the Java House, a one-story white clapboard building with bright blue trim, perched on the Embarcadero overlooking San Francisco Bay, midway between the massive Bay Bridge and the baseball park of the San Francisco Giants.

Leaning against a corner of the building was Vega, dressed in a stylish blue/gray suit, white shirt, and bright purple tie, next to a large window covered with a painted monster baseball and a banner reading *Giantropolis!* The man took a sip of coffee from a cardboard cup and raised it in salute. A shimmering gray and tan Bentley Mulsanne, clearly his, and a driver were surrounded by motorcycles and bicycles.

"An inspired choice, Mr. Duboce," Vega said as they approached.

"Let's get our food and eat in the patio," Saito said, "for privacy and ambiance."

A few minutes later at an outside table, Daniel began, "I assume you already have reports from the FBI and the NSA."

"Actually, I operate outside any government but cooperate

when there is need. You're being facetious about the agencies but you may not fully appreciate the precariousness of your situation." Vega became silent as a couple rose from a nearby table and walked past.

"Just who are you?" Saito demanded. "Where are you from?" The man seemed like an anachronism, a handsome man from a 1940s movie about Spanish royalty in the early 19th century. But he was very sexual despite the way he talked and moved, or, maybe because of it.

"I have a home in Rome." Vega touched a paper napkin to his lips before taking a sip of coffee.

"I have one in New York," Daniel said with a hint of exasperation. "Perhaps go back a bit further."

"Of course. My family originally came from what is now Syria and fled to what was then known as Andalusia, now called Spain. If we can return now to our business at hand, Mr. Duboce. I am no fool; neither are you. You are both here and I was explicit last night. You would not be with me now if there was no merit to my suggestions."

"Humor me, Mr. Vega. I still have no sense of you or your motivations. Fill in some of the blanks between 900 A.D. and last year."

He smiled, perfect white teeth. "Such a persistent journalist, Mr. Duboce. You know some history. Apologies for my inadequate description."

"I know you won't mind if I take notes," Daniel said, taking out his notebook and pen.

"As you wish. I read your last book and gave a copy to the cardinal." He pushed back from the table and crossed his legs, looking relaxed. "I was born into great wealth and great expectations. As a young man, I was taught to value practicality over dogma. I run our family philanthropic foundation. We funnel large sums of money, billions of euros, and personal involvement—that's the key——into problem areas of the world. We venture into quagmires others avoid. It may be the largest foundation you've never heard of."

"What's the name?" Daniel asked, looking surprised at the revelation. "Does it have a focus?"

"Anonymous," Vega answered with a shrug. "When you give away money by the truckload, no one really cares about your name. The traditional trappings of foundations offer no value for our work and just get in the way. They often seek a halo to raise money, burnish the reputation of the CEO and can have outlandish administrative costs. They're often staffed with young idealistic college grads with degrees in philanthropy guaranteeing beautiful words, noble ideas, great web sites and limited spontaneous outside personal engagement of consequence. I prefer work that is not searchable. I admire those willing to put their lives on the line for their cause. I—"

"Your focus?" Saito interrupted.

"Social cohesion if that makes sense. We work to minimize problems that split societies apart. We help institutions and individuals that promote civil society. The cardinal is such a man and I'm honored to help."

"Is that real?" the scientist asked skeptically, about an impossibly vague concept.

"I like to think so." Vega laughed before taking a forkful of pancake dipped in syrup.

"Do you ever lie, Mr. Vega?" Daniel was curious about a response.

"I never lie but…I am precise."

"I'll remember that."

Vega leaned forward on his elbows; his face grim. "A government leader's actions are not always thoughtful nor, unfortunately, are they always helpful for their stated cause. The *Misago* discovery and its ramifications can be seen as vital to American security interests. Anything that creates social instability aids those they consider terrorists, the term *de jure* for political opponents. Information that might cause people to second-guess their faith could be seen as destabilizing."

"You're exaggerating," Daniel stated.

Saito wondered if it was truth or theatrics.

"I am closer to being your friend, Mr. Duboce, Dr. Saito, than the governments in either Japan or the United States. They have made parallel decisions and now their credibility is at stake if your information goes public and the deceit exposed. Truth is the threat. Trumpian, I believe the popular term is: truth as an impediment to self-absorption and power. Scientific facts are particularly odious if they don't support ideological and ego needs of politicians. *Misago* is science threatening belief. Dishonesty is irrelevant to a sizable part of the American population open to manipulation. Self-interest is a powerful force. You're both a danger to the state. See me as an ally."

They finished breakfast in silence, eggs over easy, not quite crisp bacon and white toast. The situation couldn't be put in starker terms, Saito thought. Vega might be right. In America, in his opinion, one party put its own interests above that of the country; the other, from a distance, appeared easily intimidated and an out-maneuvered group of spoiled children. In Japan, politicians seem encased in amber.

"I'd like you both to consider going with me to a private home a few hours' drive from here." Vega now sounded like an old friend. "I am trying to persuade a group of religious leaders to talk with you. I will pick you up mid-morning tomorrow. Pack enough clothes for a few days."

"I'm not running home to pack," Daniel said, pushing back. "Are these the same religious leaders who convinced the president to quash *Misago*?" He looked straight at Vega. "The guys who like to play the God-card in elections, the ones advocating creating a theocracy in America, dumping democracy and individual freedom? The ones angling to be appointed our own Ayatollah?"

"Yes, some of them." He appeared to be trying to hide a smile. "It is an unusual group. Talking with you in person is high risk when they could just use other resources. At this point I would prefer not giving their names. I suspect you can guess. They will be confident you will agree with them because they normally only talk to people who agree with them."

"Where's the meeting?" Saito asked.

"In the Sierra Nevada mountains. Bring sweaters."

"Can you be more specific?" Daniel inquired.

"Lake Tahoe, east shore. A luxurious private estate in Nevada not far from Glenbrook."

"Why should we trust you?" Saito was skeptical but pleased the lure was working. "We don't know you. You're making major assumptions about what we may or may not have done."

"Do it for that underlying concern I suspect you both have about human frailty and how society might easily move backward. Do it for the sake of humanity. Do it out of your duty as a journalist, seeking truth, Mr. Duboce."

The envoy leaned back, relaxed, hands folded in his lap. "You are both thoughtful people and I suspect you're also at least broadly spiritual, open to understanding the complexities of nature. You are players in a major drama. The stakes are high. The meeting at Lake Tahoe will help illuminate the gravity. You will be safe. I guarantee it."

"Will your cardinal be there?" Daniel asked.

"Cardinal Martinez will be present. Is that a problem?"

"I'm not sure just what you may know of my history," Daniel said bluntly.

"May I inquire…"

"Perhaps another time." Daniel stood and gestured to Saito. "I'll call you this afternoon, Mr. Vega, with our answer. Thank you." The three men shook hands.

As they wandered down the sidewalk toward the Bay Bridge, leaving Vega amid the bikers and joggers, Saito knew Daniel was still troubled about what had happened to him in the church and it might twist his judgment. Vega was more then he seemed. What was the best way to assist Yoshito Wada, assuming he was free and alive? This invitation was too convenient. Opportunity or trap?

"The dynamics shift if we meet with the ministers," Daniel said as they walked down the Embarcadero and watched banks of fog perched atop the hills to the east, pushed by the warming sun, waiting for a chance to roll back down. It was a typical day in the City of Saint Francis.

"Assuming they are capable of an honest discussion."

"Is there an alternative?" Daniel asked. "How else do we meet them? I don't expect we'll convince them to change positions, but the more we know about how they'll react to the actual proof, the better we can plan and anticipate. I'll let Bruiser and my *Times* editor know where we are if we go missing, my phone has a GPS tracker. Assuming it stays with me."

"What about the cardinal, Daniel? Will you be able to separate your anger from clear judgment?"

He glanced down, considering the question. How would he react? Had Diego Martinez known about the rape of children? Had the man done anything to stop it? He had to have known. Hopefully he could make this ancient history. But he winced, his mind replaying the scene when his son Garrett was taken away, sobbing, to live with his mother and stepfather, two police officers making sure it happened. The bishop's smarmy expression telling him piously that the donation had had nothing to do with the dissolution of his family. The anger was fresh. But he had to suppress his doubts.

"*Misago* is bigger than one person. It's certainly bigger than me." He tried offering a reassuring smile. "Let's make a stop before we get home. I want to get something for Vega."

16.

NASA Complex, La Canada Flintridge, California

Dr. Tio Ito sat in a green cracked leather chair with worn wooden armrests, academic chic, in front of a desk piled high with folders and books. The room was part of the NASA complex about twenty-five miles from downtown Los Angeles. She had a view, through windows crusted with years of dirt, of a small garden in need of serious attention, but her focus was on an old friend.

Behind the desk sat Dr. Horace Newton, a balding man of generous girth and ruddy complexion, a career space scientist involved in a series of NASA projects, many coordinated with JAXA. Newton had helped on the *Misago* launch and tracking.

Tio had called him last night. "I have much to tell you," she'd promised, "prepare to be shocked." And asked to meet in private. The scientist, having seen stories in Japanese newspaper websites after friends alerted him to Wada's disappearance, readily agreed.

"You promised me news or a scientific discovery of epic proportions being suppressed by my own government. How could I resist? My first question: Is Yoshito alive and free? I've seen speculation in Japanese papers that he—"

"The last time I saw him he was alive, free and doing outreach. But we have not been in contact in recent days so I cannot give you a definitive answer."

He nodded, lips tight. "All right, I understand. How did you conjure passports and whatever else you needed to escape on such short notice?"

"We started weeks ago." Tio suppressed a smile, sharing the contortions of their plan for the first time with an old colleague. "We divided responsibilities. I copied reports, photographs and pulled samples of the granules in such a way that it would be very complicated for anyone to determine if anything was missing. The passport—I have several—was easy to arrange because of my position even in an age of terrorists. Getting new credit cards under different names presented no difficulty, nor getting multiple cell phones under various aliases. Ironic the role deception can play in protecting truth or spreading fear. It's surprising how easy it is to hide in plain sight."

Newton leaned toward her with intense curiosity. "What are you hiding?"

"What do you know?"

"Only speculation that some *Misago* cargo is missing."

Tio provided background on the deal cut with the American president.

"Reckless," was Newton's response. "What's so dangerous that the president would risk war with China?"

Tio moved to the computer on the credenza. "If I may use my memory wand to transfer data it will begin to make sense." For the next hour, she explained the discovery.

Afterward, Newton's face was drained of color, his arms crossing his chest alternating with pressing his hands together. "It takes my breath away. I understand the president's fear even if I don't accept his reasons. Hell, it frightens me. But it's a major boost in scientific knowledge, a new trajectory. Scientists need to take another look at their own craft." He whispered, sounding incredulous, "We've all been wrong. Hubris squared."

She took out a small silver canister from her briefcase. "Here are samples. Take these and draw your own conclusions. The information I downloaded will give extensive data on our experiments. Test everything. I also invite you to examine our methodology on regolith from your own mining operations. *OSIRIS REx* in 2023 may confirm *Misago*."

Newton took the cylinder and cradled it as if holding a newborn. Or nitroglycerine.

"My advice is to keep this closely held since the American government is certain to cooperate with Japanese officials in finding me and recovering this so it can be hidden forever. Horace, beginning now you'll be in great danger."

Newton rubbed a thumb over the stainless-steel surface. "I'll personally evaluate the material and bring in only people I trust," he promised. "We'll run your tests on our own past asteroid payloads. This is perhaps the biggest scientific discovery in history, certainly in space science, certainly in human biology. I'll be ruthless in my evaluation as you want me to be. But we need to let the world know. I'm proud to be involved, Dr. Ito, proud to stand with you and Yoshito. May he be safe. I'm ashamed of my government, but not surprised."

She picked up her valise. "Watch for an appropriate time to go public. Hopefully, it will be obvious."

"I'll be waiting for your cue. Be careful, my old friend, you'll soon be the most wanted person since Bin Laden."

17.

As the group relaxed in the main room of the lodge, Cardinal Martinez savored his last sip of chilled Napa Valley chardonnay, then stood to address them. He knew it would be difficult, given their prickly personalities, competitive instincts, and divergent angels-on-the-head-of-a-pin views on faith, but they had to hold together. Everyone who mattered from the absolutists was here and all drivers and staff were staying at a nearby Stateline hotel. The clergy would do their work in complete isolation except for Reverend Wright's decision to bring his teenage son. He'd insisted; they were working through some important family issues.

"Our special greetings to young Rolph Wright, our honored guest." The teenager barely looked up from his phone to smile and wave one hand while the four ministers applauded politely. They were the spearhead of America's evangelical leaders who championed creation of God's rule in America—a controversial idea he thought might be a bomb and for now, less important than stopping Misago. He knew at some point other faiths should be brought in, Protestants, Jewish, even Muslim, depending on the success of this venture but that would be trickier since this group were Christian absolutists, obsessed with the Kingdom Movement. Religious pluralism was not on their agenda.

He'd suggested casual dress. Father Alito, here as his aide, wore an odd knit sweater of pine trees and blue night sky he'd found in a cabinet in his room. Reverend Wright had on one of his trademark short sleeve shirts with Jesus on a sandy beach with hula dancers. Reverend Robinson's blue sweater featured a large eagle that looked remarkably like him. Sister Esther wore a trim-fit blouse and knit vest. Then there was Reverend Broux, in sports coat and tie, ever ready for his TV interview should a news crew happen by.

Stonehouse was rustic yet elegant, almost spiritual, one of the first structures built at the mile-high lake, remodeled, and expand-ed over the years and owned by a wealthy friend of the cardinal. A perfect place to forge consensus if that was possible. Martinez ad-mired the square-cut rafters, hand-hewn with an adz decades ago, that held the high vaulted ceiling of tongue-and-groove knotty-pine cross-planks. Something older than himself that still worked.

The south walls were formed from logs from the original cab-in while the other walls were river rock with large windows and a floor to ceiling fireplace, all constructed in the last decade. Natural wood posts supported the roof and an inside balcony at one end of the room with a master suite beyond. Everyone sat on over-stuffed chairs covered in dark green nubby chenille or on worn brown leather sofas with geometric Native American patterned pillows that matched the large rugs on the dark stained barn wood floor. A dozen crystal vases around the room held long-stemmed yellow and white tulips, sweet-smelling blue hyacinths and large branches of fragrant purple lilac and pink camellias.

"I believe you've had an opportunity to see your rooms and some of the facility and grounds," Martinez said, enjoying his role as host. "A few notes about the blue waters just fifty yards behind me. Tahoe is the largest alpine lake in North America, naturally formed, and a constant thirty-nine degrees a few feet below the surface. Brace yourself if you take a swim. I urge you visit the pier tomorrow and look to the southwest." He indicated behind him.

"You'll notice a familiar shape on a mountain peak. I look and see the cross. Others claim…" He laughed. "It's officially called Mr. Tallac. We all see what we want to see." He gestured to Reverend Wright.

"Mr. Michaels, our public relations and political expert," Wright interjected from his chair, "will be getting in tonight. He's been doing research and will propose a plan for the next phase of our efforts."

Conversation slowed as a short middle-aged woman, wearing a white apron and lace cap, entered and went to the fireplace at the center of the lakeside wall and, with a groan, dragged the heavy bronze screen to one side. Soon the logs were crackling.

The cardinal continued his welcome when the housekeeper left. "This is our official planning session now that the president has taken our advice and won Japanese consent."

He set his glass down. "Mr. Vega believes he has a lead on the missing scientist and the granules. It will be very helpful if we can get our hands on the asteroid debris and corroborating data, assuming it's in this country. That will make our planning easier and more focused. Mr. Vega has been meeting with an associate of Dr. Wada who left Japan about the time he disappeared. Also a young journalist from the *New York Times* who seems to be involved with the scientist. He hopes to bring them here."

"Bad idea," Broux drawled in his southern accent. "Keep at least one layer of staff, preferably more, between us and those who may need to be dealt with. Especially the press. We must have flexibility in denyin' involvement should things not go as we anticipate." He seemed uneasy and self-absorbed, a thumb mindlessly rubbing his cleft chin.

"John makes a good point," Sister Esther said. "We're here to plan, not negotiate. Leave that to others."

Sister was a name awarded by her admirers, a kind of honorific title, based on their love and admiration. She had never graduated from divinity school so she was not technically a minister but the media didn't know the difference and called her one anyway. She had a massive following on radio and was a big draw in churches wanting to spike attendance. Martinez thought she was more the female charismatic counterpart of the huckster Andy Griffith played in the 1957 movie, *A Face in the Crowd*, about a drifter and con artist who rises to great influence through television. The face of a former American president popped into his head. Her given name, from her real preacher father, was the same as an historic figure from the Bible: Esther, an instrument in the hands of God, averting the destruction of her people. In her early forties, she was beautiful in a severe way and had ample cleavage which she liked to display with thin, low scooped blouses. Whatever his assessment, he had to deal with her nonetheless, knowing she could play her popularity like a whip.

"What others?" Robinson asked. "We're generals. Do we send some Christian corporal to do the job? I think not. There's risk in leadership. *Bring 'em on!*"

"That's not what you said on the Skype call with Vega when he laid out the issue," Broux countered.

"A general can change his mind," Robinson responded with a dismissive "*humph.*"

"Generals need to understand the enemy," Martinez replied, smiling at Robinson. "I'd like to meet those who wish to harm the holy word. I want to understand them. Win them to our side, letting the light of faith erase any darkness. Having read so much about your individual powers to persuade, it would be a privilege seeing you all in action. This is indeed a God-blessed team of generals." Father Alito looked pleased with his cardinal. Martinez knew it was bullshit, a favorite American term, but hopefully well received.

"Well put, Diego," Adam Wright said. He stood and adjusted his trousers. He looked toward his son who was lost in his cell phone screen. "We're involved in a delicate venture. We took a risk when we made our recommendation on the conference call. We must show the same leadership and courage here. If we can turn people from a negative path and gather the evidence, we'll have done our churches a service greater than our parishioners may ever know. But God will know. Personally, I'm comfortable with Mr. Vega bringing his contacts here."

"If the president would hurry up and appoint the Prophet," Broux barked, "none of this will matter. We'd have control!"

"Perhaps we can discuss this more over dinner," Martinez said. "The dining area is directly behind us. If we can, let us take a moment to enjoy this magnificent sunset."

As the sun dipped behind the mountains, the clouds and lake turned purple and red, melding at the shoreline. Trees drifted from green to black; boulders along the shallow waters went from gray to charcoal.

"As I understand *Misago*," Sister Esther said, observing the fire through her wine glass, "it's an implication that God is not actively involved in our lives, that He created a mechanism to start life but did it almost casually, not Earth-focused. I must reject that."

"I understand," the cardinal responded, sitting next to her on the sofa. Reverend Wright was on his left, Rolph having retreated to his room after dinner. "It strains what we have always believed."

"And yet, and yet while we reject it," she said, "we also must be prepared to deal with the possibility that this discovery could go public and people will be confused." Her voice trailed off as she watched sparks from the hot pitch. "While it may prove some form of divine intervention, it may not be obvious that it came from a Christian god."

"That's the topic for tomorrow."

"I don't mean preparation just in the traditional way political campaigns are done. This is a more insidious threat."

Wright and the cardinal turned to her.

"It seems to me," she said, "that to fully inoculate our churches against a public battle over biblical accuracy, we need to be even more relevant and inspirational in people's lives. Many good Christians could be deceived. Charlatans will argue Scripture is wrong."

Wright watched her with growing admiration. "That's most interesting and useful, Sister," Wright said, intrigued but cautious. "Cardinal, as you may know, there's a debate in Protestant churches, particularly the evangelicals, that maybe a focus on sin and sex is too narrow. Some argue that we should be looking at broader issues to alleviate human suffering such as poverty, genocide, AIDS and human trafficking."

Were her words the hidden thoughtfulness of a contentious public figure? Or a set up? She was not someone to be trusted. Wright remembered her harsh words against him during the campaign for chairman. She had insisted, as a condition of his election, on a doctrinal emphasis on sin over love. Had the discovery frightened her into re-thinking her rigidity? He considered bringing up the issue that was troubling him personally.

The cardinal seemed guarded. "I concur about the importance of lifting up the lives of the less fortunate and my church has looked at a broader vista than sexual issues."

When Esther remained quiet, Wright decided to take a risk. "Jesus focused on the needs of the poor; sin was lower on his to do list. Can we build on that wisdom?"

He noticed Broux and Robinson begin to frown. They were sitting a few feet away, obviously listening.

"The Old Testament and *Leviticus* take the lion's share of admonitions about fornication, adultery and homosexuality," Wright said. "This has credibility because we believe it's God-blessed…"

"It is blessed and inerrant," Sister interrupted, pointing out the obvious.

"Indeed." How would they respond if he brought it up? This was an opening. Pursue it. "But this discovery infers otherwise. I think sometimes we focus on sin because it plays to the media and a section of our base, yet if we look back in time, propagation of the species was a survival issue for our ancient forebears, a tribe's strength depending on numbers and strict rules of behavior needed to avoid conflicts, and the purpose of sexual union was strictly to create more babies. That's not true today." He seemed to have everyone's attention. "In our sex dominated culture, people see joy as perhaps more important, celebrating God's gift. So, I wonder if a focus on *shall nots* is as relevant to a society with so many quality of life and survival problems? I'm no longer sure. It's also losing its appeal with younger people and that has long term implications."

The cardinal chose his words carefully. "You surprise me, Adam. It's useful to periodically question basic tenants. Yet, people need guidance. As you suggest, Jesus did preach about a range of social issues. I've not thought about a strategic shift as Sister suggests. But it has merit."

He wants to avoid conflict, Wright decided.

They watched the fire. No one seemed ready to go further.

Sister broke the silence. "So, less vitriol on sexual behavior and more emphasis on solving the challenges of human survival? That assumes they're not linked."

"If I may be bold," Wright said, trying to keep his nerve, "is worrying about gay marriage more important than fighting an attack on Scripture by *Misago*? What are the core beliefs that unite us as Christians? As humans? What will help minimize damage in a public fight?"

Esther stared at the fire. "You ask a great deal," she said, a muscle flexing in her jaw. "Combating sin is part of my DNA. Yet if the church is destroyed or damaged by this new scientific assault, issues such as this become irrelevant because society would no longer have a moral core. Still, I cannot set aside my beliefs about the truth of the Bible."

"I'm not certain Rome is ready to go that far either," Martinez said evenly.

Wright sipped his wine, wondering if God or Satan had set up this opportunity. Take the plunge for his family. "Let me add more complications. I brought up homosexuality and our opposition to it being driven by *Leviticus*. I've preached fiery sermons on this. Now *Misago* challenges the sanctity of those words. And here is a twist; someone close to me shared scientific studies that do more than suggest sexual orientation is determined by genes, by inheritance, sort of like eye color. It's not a choice. If this proves true, it would make it God-given."

Sister Esther jerked her head and snapped: "I'd not put any more credence in that kind of science than I do in evolution." Her tone was sarcastic. "Science needs to support truth—*our truth*. The homosexual issue is mostly behind us."

"Are you turning liberal on us, Adam?" The cardinal sounded surprised.

"God forbid!" Wright forced a laugh. One could never be liberal. Liberal was the go-to epithet in American conservative politics and he was surprised the cardinal had used it. He thought *enlightened* or *non-judgmental* or *human* might work too and its constant appropriation in this way destroyed its real meaning. But, baby steps with powerful people. He knew that his own journey had been a quick one propelled by family love and they were reacting without such personal insights. Agendas could change.

Martinez stood and turned to them. "A most interesting discussion," he said. "The real challenge of *Misugo* may be to our hubris. We are sometimes so convinced we know truth that we dismiss other ideas. Then suddenly something strips us bare and we look at the world anew."

Indeed, thought Adam Wright.

18.

Stonehouse Lodge, Lake Tahoe

Should he open with a prayer?

No, Mike Michaels decided. The board members were too jaded; save prayers for public meetings. He was hungry for the sale, the biggest in his career and it would lock in their business forever. If he protected the secret, how could they go to anyone else? He'd already been briefed after signing a non-disclosure agreement but the ministers were temperamental and sometimes quarreled. They were also competitive, hungry to be named the Prophet. He must avoid being caught in a crossfire yet he also had to take risks to impress them, even shock them. Convince them that he was the right guy, a man of faith but with an Old Testament sensibility. If one of them were named supreme leader, it could be profitable.

He glanced into an antique mirror in a redwood-bark frame and considered his image. The yellow polo knit shirt went well with his blond hair. The beige khaki pants and maroon penny-loafers were a good fit for the audience.

He was in a small meeting room, dreary and full of splinters, at the back of the main building, adjacent to where the group met last night. Davy Crockett would feel right at home here. He preferred clean, smooth surfaces, lots of marble and stainless steel, not the ambiance of a moldy cabin. The room was part of the original structure, he'd been told, with ten-foot sagging walls covered in knotty pine and a ceiling made with rough-cut timber and lumpy white plaster. The windows were wide and arched, swinging open to bring the garden and lake into the room. And bugs. He closed one drape near the screen.

Michaels took out a handful of folders bearing the elegant red and gold flame logo of his company: *Transcendent Communications*. He slipped in background information on previous campaigns and a recent article by a prominent Christian newspaper columnist.

"Mike Michaels is the perfect image of a talented, clean-cut, God-fearing young executive and I admire the contradiction between his innocent looks and the acidic effectiveness of his campaigns."

Innocence had its uses.

"Cardinal—black jeans!" Robinson teased as Martinez stood to open the session. "That seems casual for the second most powerful man in the Catholic Church."

The group sat in large, upholstered chairs amid scattered small tables. Apple iPads and electronic pencils as well as old fashioned lead ones and paper, iced water pitchers, glasses and bowls of assorted candy were within easy reach.

"Better black jeans than black robes." The cardinal clasped his hands together, looking relaxed. "Sister, gentlemen, thank you for joining us again today. Reverend Wright will introduce this session." Martinez sat and gestured to the board chair.

The minister finished a square of dark chocolate before stepping in front of the group. "Mr. Michaels has done research and developed a proposed strategy. He's our main agenda, our own

'Brand Manager for Jesus,' as *Time* called him."

Wright looked disappointed, Michaels thought, watching Esther adjusting her bra with one hand while checking her cell with the other, her charms elusive, at least for him. Robinson was doodling an eagle. "Later this afternoon, Mr. Vega will be joining us," Wright said. "He's left San Francisco with the two people we discussed last night. The FBI has classified the Japanese male scientist as a person of interest but doesn't know about our involvement. For now, I think it's best if it remains secret. We'll have a chance to meet with them tomorrow. Right now, please join me in welcoming our guest." Wright applauded as he sat.

Michaels smiled warmly as he stood. "Thank you, Reverend Wright—"

"Before you begin, I think we should settle this issue," Robinson interrupted in a harsh tone, startling the group. "What do we do with these two strangers if they don't agree to join us? What do we do if they say they don't know anything but we think they do? We'll have exposed ourselves directly to the enemy. Over time, there could be others."

The cardinal and Wright looked at each other warily. Clearly not a subject they wanted to address.

"When I raised the issue of expanding our circle on the conference call with Vega," Robinson continued, "Reverend Broux said we didn't need to deal with this till we reached the Jordan. I believe it starts flowin' through this lodge when Vega arrives. How far will we go to protect our faith? If we're not willing to go all the way, then perhaps Mr. Vega should take his human cargo elsewhere."

"I'm not ready to say how far I'd go. But we shouldn't be meek," Sister Esther added as she leaned back in her leather chair, pausing before using what she called her "godly amplification that startled and compelled attention," her preacher voice at full wattage. "Too much at risk. Even if we ourselves did nothing, we have our own shock troops that may act on their own. We need to remember they blockaded abortion clinics and even assassinated abortionists. One question: do we equate the murder of unborn babies as an evil comparable to ripping the guts out of our faith? We could be at the beginning of a holy war if we're not careful."

Wright had a sour expression, Michaels thought, perhaps wishing he had a cudgel to play whack-a-mole. But he just sighed and waited.

"Let me add," Sister said, head high, voice taunting, "in the big picture, when heaven itself's at risk, is murder a sin? If we're protecting Jesus, is anything we say untrue?"

"Yes, it is!" Wright responded.

"Sister, honesty and non-violence are capstones of our faith," the cardinal stated. "It is imperative—"

"Thanks for tellin' it like it is, Sister," Robinson snapped, sounding pleased. "I get tired of polite chatter. The souls of millions could be at risk, including those yet unborn." He growled, "Until there's biblical authority there has to be some controlling power in our society and today there's none." His voice climbed, matching Sister's righteousness and power. "America is weak. Just look at what we're even discussing. How is this tolerated? The whole idea of reward and punishment, an ultimate judge of all our actions, we've let that be taken away. When there is no vision of God and biblical justice, the people run amok."

"Hmmm. Yes. I always liked that speech. Let me ask it a different way," Broux stated. "Do we love our God less than the devout of other religions?" He raised his arms and turned to each of his colleagues. "Well?"

"No!" Sister said.

"Absolutely not," Robinson agreed.

"Excellent. Here's a test. A poll of Muslims worldwide asked if suicide bombings were justifiable in defending Islam. Sixteen percent of French Muslims agreed; forty-six percent of Nigerians. While the act is despicable, the fervor is not. I suspect there's no such passion among American Christians to support their faith."

"I don't like what's being suggested—Christian suicide bombers?" Wright was appalled. They were all conservative Christians here, in private, and no need to pander for media attention. "This is dangerous talk. I don't understand."

"Perhaps you don't understand because you don't have a real congregation!" Robinson sounded venomous. "You have a pretend church, you sell holy water and silly shirts showing Jesus surfing in Hawaii. I see my parishioners every week in my television studio audience. Who do you see as a radio preacher?"

Stunned at the vitriol from one of his own board members, Wright shouted, *"That's outrageous!"*

"Outrageous, yes, but so is *Misago* and its impact on Christianity. I'm willin' to fight for my church. Are you?"

Wright sputtered, clenching his fists, clearly debating how to respond to such nonsense short of punching him.

The cardinal rose. He stared at Broux who slowly descended back into his chair after nodding in deference. Wright continued to stand, his jaw clenched. Michaels had expected arguments on strategy but not personal rudeness and venom.

"We're not suicide bombing terrorists!" the cardinal said with an edge. "We are not jihadists! We are followers of a man of peace." He moderated his tone. "Perhaps we are a little uptight, given the topic. I can understand that it challenges our life's work. Reverend, those statistics have me worried. I hope and pray they're not accurate."

"Your church," Robinson said with acidity, his lifelong disdain of Catholicism leaking from every pore, "is the church of the Inquisition. Indeed, the office you hold condemned tens of thousands to painful deaths in defense of the faith during the Inquisition. Are you less willing to protect your church than your predecessors?"

The room was quiet as the two men stared at each other. Robinson looked smug; the cardinal's expression was hard.

One upmanship, Michaels thought, not really useful.

"That was long ago, Reverend," Martinez said. "The world has moved on and so has my church. We are men of peace and love. I would ask you to think about what Jesus would say if he were here today." He looked out a window for a moment, into the forest, and his voice softened. "In this peaceful setting, I ask us to return to our main focus and not engage in medieval chatter." The cardinal sat and the room was quiet. "Mr. Michaels, I'm anxious to hear your proposal."

Michaels stood and glanced cautiously at the group. The exchange should be interpreted as a measure of their fear, lashing out at each other, a bit of religious cannibalism, because it was easier to snap at each other than dismantle the discovery on its merits. They were also showing off, he suspected, displaying their righteousness, a kind of clerical competition. Maybe he needed to up his game and focus on his main audience. Martinez was Catholic and foreign, Wright a figurehead. The conservatives would control the vote and the service contracts. Play to them. "I'm humbled to be with you and hope you find my advice useful. We've done polling and focus group work since I was briefed on the general topic to be discussed here."

"Are you related to Pat Boone?" Robinson interrupted then shook his head. "Never mind."

Michaels started to respond and reconsidered. Faith scorpions could attack without logic and paralyze his sales pitch. "Polling indicates that practically no one has heard of the *Misago* space probe. Its recognition in the general public is less than two percent. With our audience, conservative Christians, it's statistically zero. People will find it hard to believe such a major discovery could come from a country they didn't even know was in space." He scanned the audience. Two were ready to take notes, one was staring out the window.

He slipped one hand into a pocket and gestured with the other, trying to look relaxed and confident. Never appear nervous in front of a client. "Paranoia about terrorism, both domestic and foreign, continues to hold sway in this country. If our issue surfaces, this can prove useful because it makes the public open to certain arguments and fears. There are also issues about science and complexity. This is a difficult story. How much detail will the American public absorb and understand before getting bored, confused or disgusted and tuning out?"

Michaels sauntered in front of the group. "How you define an issue can dramatically shift public debate or slow down decision-making if you don't like where it's headed." He leaned back against a table and crossed his arms.

"The Ten Commandments are now on the walls of thousands of classrooms across America. As we all know too well, efforts to teach creationism in public schools was not successful initially but we didn't give up. Strategically, the movement shifted to school board elections, sliding under the public radar, electing our people into decision-making roles. We also worked to redefine the issue and challenge textbooks to reflect more neutral views on man's creation. Evolution is a scientific term and in general the public likes science even if it doesn't understand it. Polling showed that by switching to the term *Darwinism,* support was substantially reduced. Evolution is a scientific idea. Darwinism is one man's idea." He smiled, pleased they were still more interested in chewing on each other rather than him. "Even the term *theory* is helpful. People don't know what it means. They think it's just speculation and not the prevailing view of most mainstream scientific organizations in the world. Confusion is easy to sow using their own words."

He turned and touched a screen to bring up his talking points. "We also funded important academic research."

"Do you have to use that computer?" Robinson said. "Just talk. It gives me a headache."

"No problem, sir." Michaels knew a few things about the causes of headaches. He turned his screen to black then faced the group again. He forced himself to smile. He had good dimples. "Creationism can be a loaded term. Although the Wilkins Institute didn't originate the name Intelligent Design, it was one of the lead evangelists on the concept as a scientific alternative, and it's one of our closest allies. It's had mixed legal results but the lesson is instructive. Now we emphasize, *Teach the Controversy.* Teach Darwinism if you insist, but also teach the criticisms. It's a fairness issue. This makes it easier to get into the classroom." The ministers looked more attentive. At least he hoped they were.

"Studies indicate that serious science has been largely eliminated in the classroom, particularly in poorer school districts.

Public education has been starved for funding as money shifted to private academies and mixed-bag curricula with few metrics. This is useful to understand as we craft our messages.

"Science is confusing to those most comfortable in a black and white environment. Something is or isn't true. The constant disagreements over scientific studies on diets, heart attacks and other health issues make science seem as unpredictable as the weather. The Bible offers firm answers that never change."

"Amen to that," Robinson stated.

"Let me be blunt on my next point because honesty between us is mandatory in crafting our campaign. The Trump presidency politicized science in the Covid 19 pandemic, likely costing thousands of lives, and wounded public confidence in science and academia for millions of voters. Denying the pandemic and rejecting masks became a political statement even if it spread the disease. If you don't believe in science and the opinions of experts then you see no correlation between death of friends and the disease. While the deaths were unfortunate, this plays to our advantage politically today. *Misago* is science and a readymade segment of the public is primed to dismiss it. As is our political media."

"Many of those were our congregants," Sister added with a shrug and a look that suggested she had mixed emotions. "We lost many fine evangelicals."

"But most survived. While at a horrible cost, it helps us in this horror we face now. Science and experts and all that. The state of public education is also useful. It has less time for critical thinking about complex issues and devotes more time to rote memorization or studying topics of marginal importance. All of this means poor training for learning to think and question authority. As an American citizen concerned about our competitiveness in the world, I think this trend is unfortunate. But as a campaign manager, it's useful, helping debunk new scientific discoveries because people don't understand the scientific method. People are also easily confused and distracted, thanks to social media. Increasingly they lack the capacity to think critically about complex issues. As an American and a professional communicator, I'm simultaneously appalled and grateful."

"*Hrumph,*" Wright mumbled.

"I'd like to give important learnings and then conclude with a strategy," Michaels said, ignoring the minister. "In several campaigns, strategists deployed similar tactics. Relentlessly attack opponents on their strong points, not just their weak ones. Use third parties to keep blame at a distance, segment the population into tiny slices, keep them angry, feeling aggrieved, and flood the Internet and social media with counter scientific truths. Look at the QAnon success. And AI has proven useful in deep fakes. Trump was a master at making up facts to meet his needs. Repeated often enough, with a big enough media megaphone, people become convinced. Never give any ground, always attack, don't obsess about accuracy, and the media will cover it and distract the public from more serious issues. How many thousands of hours of television and radio news were spent obsessing over Trump tweets and reducing coverage of complex issues of real importance? We've also benefited from attacking any mainstream media that doesn't accept our position, starting from the days of President Reagan. Media on bended knee is good, media that reports anything critical, even if true, is the enemy. Our own media is well trained to stick to talking points. The icing on the cake is now having competition between our growing media platforms on who can be the most righteous."

"I agree," Broux said. Others nodded. They'd all played roles in various campaigns.

"Belief, not fact, is what's important in a campaign," Michaels said. "Making up facts is a long American political tradition. The George W. Bush campaign shifted attention from his own questionable military record and diminished Senator Kerry's stature as a war hero. The Trump-Clinton campaign ratcheted this up. We all know the effectiveness of '*Clinton's emails*' and '*Benghazi.*' Effective distractions on essentially manufactured issues. Attack your opponent to cover up your own transgressions and do it in a never-ending loop. Make certain every public ally has talking points so they repeat the same words over and over."

"You're putting it in a negative light. We won that race." Broux sounded irritated.

"I'm stating it like it was because we are all friends here and it is useful to understand what works in a campaign. Understanding fact from political fiction is important to those making up the storyline. We will be in a nasty campaign if this discovery goes public."

Reverend Wright twisted in his chair. "If we are being honest about facts," he said in a disgusted tone, "I took part in the first Trump campaign. But frankly, after we got our justices on hundreds of courts including three anti-abortion openly pious jurists on the Supreme Court, his value was done for me. The disastrous response to the pandemic cost me numerous friends and I did not take part in his re-election campaign. Better a liberal who can at least attempt to manage the pandemic than a man who clearly was uninterested in trying and likely in hock to the Russians."

"I wouldn't go public with those views," Broux admonished.

"Just trying to be honest as Mr. Michaels has suggested."

Best to keep moving, Michaels decided. "Recently there was the Walton/Pilligrew race." The PR man made no effort to hide his snicker, knowing it would bring them closer, insiders in changing history. It had been delicious, full of opportunity. Every American in the room had played a role.

"The termed out incumbent president set such a high threshold for style and eloquence that Democratic Senator Pilligrew of Michigan seemed wooden and dull in comparison. Governor Walton looked like a movie star, another Reagan." Michaels enjoyed the satisfied expressions, knowing he was connecting. "But polls suggested the race was razor thin.

"The Democrat fumbled badly in the first debate on strategy for American troops fighting drug cartels inside Mexico; Walton was presidential even if vague on specifics. He also made a private commitment to the Board and Kingdom Movement leaders that he would implement their plan." Michaels was silent for a moment, a grin slowly growing. "Then there was the terrorist attack that wasn't a terrorist attack in Pennsylvania."

Michaels remembered the 9/11-style moment—a real October surprise. Fourteen people, mostly elderly, died in Pennsylvania and hundreds were hospitalized when cholera bacterium poisoned the local water supply near Harrisburg. The FBI began its investigation, offering little information and a vague statement that it did not appear to be a terrorist attack. The national media went crazy, demanding details.

The local police chief and District Attorney held a press conference announcing the arrest of an illegal immigrant from Iran who had come down through Canada but they declined to give details because charges were pending. All will be resolved in a few days, they pledged. The FBI claimed improper interference in a case of federal jurisdiction and denied any arrests. But conservative media pounced, accusing the FBI of fronting for the Democrats, railed about deep state interference, and fired up the GOP base on the immigration issue. The Democrats were pounded on their anti-torture stand: "Too weak to keep America safe" was the charge.

Reverend Robinson, Sister Esther and others claimed it was God's revenge, punishing America for its sins as He had the ancient Egyptians. They blamed homosexuals, abortionists and, in a surprising stretch, the judge in Harrisburg who outlawed Intelligent Design in the classroom. The CCC mobilized ten thousand volunteers in Pennsylvania for the onrushing election and flipped the state red. Three days after the election, the FBI announced the arrest of a hospital employee with a history of mental problems. There was no illegal immigrant from Iran. The Caucasian male, born in America, had access to research pathogens and had been recently fired and charged with embezzlement. The Republican DA was accused of collusion with Jake Machin, Walton's campaign manager, all of which was denied. No proof. The election was over.

Michaels' smirk melted into a broad smile. "The people in this room took the lead in mobilizing millions of Christians across America, people who were hungry to have a real man of God in the White House. You closed the sale that made Jeremiah Walton president of the United States." He applauded, as did Robinson, Andrews and Broux. The others just watched.

"I'm obviously pleased Jeremiah won," Wright said, "but what's the lesson from this?"

"Take advantage of opportunities," Michaels said. "End results matter. Winning is everything."

"So does the path we follow to achieve our goals," Wright said.

Broux whispered something to Sister. She smirked.

Michaels stepped to an easel, anxious to maintain momentum, afraid Wright could distract the others. He picked up a black felt-tipped pen, scribbled "Wada" on the top, drew a vertical line down the middle of the white paper then turned back to the group.

"I believe we can avoid dealing with the actual scientific discovery if we're clever and bold, as Sister urged earlier." Michaels felt his energy rising. "Whether the discovery is true or not doesn't really matter. We need to focus attention on the man who made the discoveries and destroy him."

He let his words sink in and turned back to the easel. "What are his strengths?" Michaels wrote in *hero* on the left and spun back to the audience. "He saved a man's life on the International Space Station, putting his own at risk, even after that man had carelessly crushed Wada's leg. He's a model selfless national hero. A movie was made about him in Japan."

"This doesn't sound encouraging," Wright suggested dourly.

"Let me sketch it out." He wrote in a series of attributes on the chart in tight print:

Devoted husband; Brilliant scientist; Effective manager; Risk taker; Not afraid to stand up to authority.

Impress them with Wada's strengths before offering a strategy to destroy him. "And finally," he said as he wrote in the final item on the left:

The discovery is legit.

"Are you saying he's some super-moral man and can't be defeated?" Broux demanded. "I won't accept that and I don't agree with your last point."

"We must know our enemy to vanquish him," Michaels stated, "should it become necessary. Here's what's important for us." He wrote in *Unknown in America* on the right-hand side. "Yes, Wada appears to be everything in the left column. But no one knows who he is outside Japan except a few space scientists. We will define him. Jake Machin, the president's political guru, and I are developing a dossier that can be used with key influentials in the media and government to strip him of credibility and make it nearly impossible to mount a defense." He waited, wanting them to ask for it.

"Please, tell us how," Robinson insisted.

"Yes, go on," Broux added.

"First the hero issue," Michaels said with satisfied authority. "There were three men on the International Space Station that witnessed what happened when he saved a man's life at the risk of his own. One is dead. The other two are Wada and the man who was negligent, now a U.S. Congressman from Texas and who, frankly, isn't pleased by the movie that mocks his incompetence. Fortunately, the film is in Japanese. We attack the heroism story as concocted by Wada, a man obsessed with personal glory, and the other man, the dead one, perhaps lied for money. The video that caught it all on tape was doctored. I can have experts attest to that and come up with technical examples. And AI is useful."

"Even if it's not true?" Wright asked.

"Yes, even if it's untrue," he answered. "We must focus on the big issue and remember this is not done in isolation. Wada openly challenged his bosses and the prime minister in resisting the plan to suppress. They have more than adequate motivation to attack his credibility. They need to cover up the cover-up. They can question his emotional stability, suggest problems they cannot disclose because of confidentiality.

"He's also well known in academic circles in Japan," Michaels said. "Jealous colleagues might be willing to challenge some of his scholarship on a variety of topics. A desire for attention and cash can get remarkable results. It certainly works in this country." He took another drink of water before he continued.

"The fact that Wada has proof of the discovery may not be all that important. We can charge it was tampered with. We can throw scientific arguments against it, showing how. There are some likely experts who would say so.

"The point is," Michaels said, gesturing widely, "if we're fully prepared, and our allies in media and politics and the clergy are ready, we can define the issue first. It then becomes a story that only lasts a few days and is gone."

"And the loving husband issue?" Wright asked and exchanged glances with the cardinal.

"That's the linchpin! His wife recently died after a lengthy illness. He loved her dearly, was totally devoted. He was so distraught it pushed him over the edge. We don't say anything that is impossible but when all the parts are added together, the message is devastating and, what's key, distracting."

Wright looked at him, forehead furrowed and mouth tight to one side. Michaels turned toward him, defensive.

"All we would be doing is making sure that contrary views are heard. Who's to say whether those views are correct? How are we to know? The democratic process seeks to hear all voices. Let the people decide."

"Don't apologize or let Reverend Wright's famous scowl throw you off track," Broux said dismissively. "Please continue."

"Thank you, Reverend." Michaels sensed he had allies, pleased he'd taken Broux's cue. "This is the story we want. A once great scientist, who did many good things in his career, falls into despondency over his wife's death and also because he fears discovery that he was no hero, that his past scholarship was flawed. Because he dominates his department, he's able to sabotage scientific findings from *Misago* to bolster his standing. Given the startling nature of the discovery, this is all very plausible and sad.

"The focus is on a fallen hero, not what he actually discovered. Because the findings on the asteroid are so unbelievable, we'll give people and the media a more acceptable alternative. People won't want to believe *Misago* is real so we will give them reasons why it's not. But to succeed we must be ready to define the issues, to plant the doubts first and keep repeating. Most reporters will accept this and go on their way reporting on celebrities and scandals that are easier to cover."

"That's quite a strategy." Sister looked and sounded impressed. "Cold-blooded. You live up to your reputation. I like that considering what's at stake."

"If you care about the outcome, leave nothing to chance."

"Where does truth fit?" Wright asked.

"Truth is determined by who wins. The greater the risk—the more lethal the requisite strategy. Losing is not an option."

"I'm not sure that works," the minister said, still frowning. "Abortionists initially won in the Supreme Court and we battled back for decades. We were finally able to take back the court but only through some blessed chicanery in the U.S. Senate. We finally overturned Roe. Angry women then stormed the ballot box, many livid about how we'd won. No, I'm concerned about the ethics of what we do here as well as just winning." Wright stood. "Looking back, I voted for Bush II but was frankly troubled by the Swift Boat shenanigans, mocking a war hero. It was shameless and I wouldn't be comfortable doing something similar with the reputation of the missing scientist. I'll not even comment on some of what happened under a later president, a philanderer we pretended was blessed by God. I sense a pattern. I like to think doing God's work means I don't have to be underhanded."

"Oh, come on, Adam! We don't even know the guy." Broux waved a hand. "I'm more interested in maintaining confidence in the Bible then I am over the reputation of some Buddhist-loving Japanese scientist I've never met. There are sacrifices in any war."

"You're really set to sacrifice him?" Wright said, incredulous. "Frankly, I don't want to be involved in character assassination. I don't know the man we're talking about, but we should deal with him honestly and fight the *discovery* if it goes public, not the man."

"I do believe our mission's strong enough," Robinson said from his seat, "our truth righteous enough, that we don't have to smear."

Sister stood. "Good points. This is more complicated than doing what at first seemed like the honorable thing. As a minister, I worry that the discovery is the devil's work. We talked about this on the Skype call with Mr. Vega. Do others still share this feeling?"

Broux reached over and patted her hand. "Yes, Sister. I'm concerned about the devil seeking to deceive us. Satan is real to me. I believe he walks the Earth. Satan's messengers may be on their way to this building today."

"Help me understand. If I've doubts about the proposed campaign," Wright said, arms crossed, "I'm a tool of the devil?"

"Certainly not," Broux said. "Since most of us are Protestant evangelicals, we're protected by our faith. All of us who believe in Jesus, all of us who are born-again, wear the *Armor of God*. We just need to work through how we want to manage this campaign."

"We may be protected from the wiles of the devil," Wright said with a shrug, "but we seem to be drawing different conclusions."

Cardinal Martinez cleared his throat.

Michaels turned and asked respectfully, "A question, sir?"

"Perhaps we should leave Satan for another time," the cardinal suggested. "Cold-blooded is an appropriate term, Sister. I feel a bit conflicted; I suspect we all do. Let's take a break. I know Mr. Michaels has more to tell us and I need to have the clarity of thought to assess it."

Michaels sensed success.

19.

Echo Summit, California

Into the fire, Daniel sensed, as they crossed over a seven-thousand-foot mountain pass and spotted a finger of Lake Tahoe, more like blue glass than water, at least twenty miles in the distance, jutting out from what appeared to be endless forest, dark green spotted with an alarming amount of brown, likely dead and dying trees. The road was a narrow shelf carved into the granite, the surface still icy from a recent storm, snow on both sides of the road. Inches from the right side of the car was a thousand-foot cliff. Miles later, dropping steadily in altitude, they finally reached the valley floor, passing scattered cabins, before entering the main city, South Lake Tahoe, clearly a town unencumbered with central planning.

Eventually the limo passed through Stateline, a nest of fifteen-story garish, brightly lit casinos, faded dandies in the daytime, announcing they'd left California and entered Nevada. A mile later, heading up U.S. 50, was a meadow with grazing cattle and an old relic of a stone cabin. The lake was now hidden by forest in the distance.

Tahoe had always fascinated him as a boy, camping out and

hearing tales around a campfire. The most popular stories were about bodies lost to the depths and occasionally rising to the surface perfectly preserved, decades, even centuries after death because the water was so cold bodies didn't decompose. The sheer size of the lake was startling, twenty-two miles long and over half that across. A good place to dump an uncooperative reporter and scientist, he thought and smiled at his own theatrics and sense of importance. He wondered if this adventure would be more Dante than Scout Jamboree.

"You can open your present now," Daniel suggested to Vega, breaking the silence, taking a paper bag from his day pack. Saito knew the contents but thought it bizarre when he bought it and rude when he'd teased and declined to explain. Daniel was curious how Vega might react to this obscure piece of history.

Vega took the brown grocery sack, one eyebrow raised, unfolded the top, reached inside, and lifted out a pineapple. He gaped at it and his placid, sophisticated facade seemed to evaporate. He giggled, covering his mouth. After an intense few seconds, he wiped some wet from his eyes. "Oh, you surprise me Mr. Duboce."

"Would someone please explain." Saito, clearly not amused, wanted in on the joke.

Vega, taking a moment to admire his gift, lifting it up, turning it, pointed to Daniel.

Pleased with Vega's response, Daniel explained: "Christopher Columbus completed his second voyage in 1496 and brought back a radical new fruit, what eventually was named a pineapple. It was completely unknown in the Old World and, most important, *not* mentioned in the Bible. The sweetness and shape made it a sensation. Even funnier, the top was seen as a crown. It became a favorite of royalty, often called *God's Fruit*."

"So much better and less encumbered with sin than the apple." Vega was still smiling. "Is *Misago* a pineapple?" The man grinned again, shaking his head. "Does this obscure voyage also bring unexpected delights?"

Twenty minutes later the limousine slowed and turned left

into a hidden driveway, no more than a break in the white guard rails, almost impossible to see. The car dropped at a steep angle, passed through a grove of redwoods and parked by one of the stone and cedar buildings in the compound, just a few hundred feet from Lake Tahoe. Two armed guards walked up and waved at the driver, cheerfully calling Urs Frisk by name as he stepped out of the car and sharing high fives.

Vega exited from the opposite side, bag held tight, walking around just as Urs opened the side door for Saito and announced, "Welcome to Stonehouse Lodge." The scientist stepped out, stretching his legs, and Daniel followed.

"These are our special guests," Vega said, making introductions. He pointed to one of the guards, "Donatello, please show them to their suite."

"This way," the man said, his voice gruff.

Stonehouse Lodge, Lake Tahoe

Inside the guesthouse, the two men found modern amenities despite the rough plaster walls accented with tongue-and-groove cedar planks.

Daniel placed pieces of equipment including his laptop on the wet bar and, working with Saito, set up his satellite uplink. The green LED gave him some sense of connection and power in a setting where their hand was weak.

There were three small bedrooms with baths, a cozy central living room with fireplace, sofa, and bar. "A preference?" Daniel stood in front of the doorways.

"Pick your favorite. Three bedrooms and two baths. Of course, we can always share."

After a shower, Daniel went to the well-stocked bar and heard running water in Saito's room. There was no need to dress up so he wore jogging pants and a sleeveless tee with a faded Area 51 logo, including a green Martian, pleased that he finally found a perfect use for the birthday gift from his son.

He found a pair of crystal wine glasses and opened a bottle of California zinfandel. Enjoying the complex sweetness of the wine, he stood at the large floor-to-ceiling window, looking at the lake through the forest. A guard was standing near the front door. The two men looked at each other. Daniel nodded, the guard didn't react, so he closed the drape enough to block the man's view inside.

Minutes later, Saito emerged wearing a pair of white boxers and a towel around his shoulders. He finished drying his hair standing before Daniel, shaking his hips to music that wasn't playing.

"Nice song," Daniel said with a smile. "Can you turn it up a bit?"

Saito started singing what Daniel assumed was one of the man's favorites from his rock band. His voice was a surprise, strong, smooth, riffs higher and higher, in Japanese lyrics Daniel didn't understand. But the way Saito moved his hips, hugged his towel in a loving embrace, bringing the terrycloth to his lips in a passionate kiss, it had to be about a steamy romance. It was surprisingly good considering there was no music.

Given the scientist's fast rise at his company, his travel schedule and research, how did he find the time necessary to develop and keep this kind of body?

Daniel thought about his own efforts to stay in shape, jogging, diet, free weights in a spare bedroom in New York. Infrequent medieval swordplay. He wasn't sure he was succeeding sufficiently for the effort. Saito was a few years younger, so maybe that could be his excuse or just credit the man's genes, always a reassuring analysis.

"Feeling better?" Daniel asked when the song ended. "One of my favorites."

"I thought it might be. Can I have wine too?"

Daniel turned around and stepped up to the bar. "It has a hint of raspberries and a touch of chocolate, almost jammy," he said, pouring a glass and trying to sound like a snooty sommelier. "California wine has remarkable texture."

Saito stepped up behind him, reached around and picked up his glass, taking a sip. "A rich bouquet," he said with laugh, sniffing the wine and pressing against Daniel's back, his free hand squeezing his bicep.

"What are you doing, my semi-naked friend?"

"Admiring a special man, so handsome and smart, in this romantic alpine setting."

Daniel felt his face flush. He turned around, set his glass on the bar, and wrapped his arms around the handsome scientist.

Saito sat his drink down as well and pushed down Daniel's jogging pants, pleased he wore no underwear. "What have we here?" Saito dropped down on his knees. "Let's get rid of all this restrictive clothing."

Daniel cleared his throat and tried not to groan as his friend got serious. "Tomorrow," he said in a melodramatic tone, "we meet a group of hard-headed, self-absorbed Christian fundamentalists who have a president at their beck and call. Unlike us they're protected by armed guards. One is right outside our door."

"Worried about all these godly men?" Saito pulled back and laughed.

"Maybe I'm concerned about your safety."

"Certainly, what I'm holding in my hand could be dangerous, given its size, although it certainly seems appreciative of my efforts, standing at attention and all. Maybe it's the excitement of sinning near all these religious types." He continued what he'd been doing before pulling back again. "You're worried about my safety beyond your dick? You certainly didn't mean this poor weak gay man on his knees before you? We're a team of equals, Mr. Sexy *Times* Reporter and I intend to give you the same options you are giving me."

"Good to hear that."

"We need to understand this saintly crew, get into their heads, make them realize there is serious opposition." He grinned as he focused on Daniel's erection. "They've just as much at risk as we do. Their arrogance may make them an easy target, just as you suggested on the way up here. We should look for opportunities to puncture their confidence if that helps our cause or be charming and ingratiating if it does not."

"Good answer." Daniel grinned and struggled to maintain a not so straight face. "For a *gay* man."

Saito stood, still holding on to Daniel. "Sir, I would like to invite you into my room to discuss more intimately what's important." He ran a hand over hand Daniel's ass.

"I think I understand your point. I accept your suggestion."

Daniel wrapped his arm around him and they moved into the bedroom, giggling as they leapt onto a bed.

As he pulled off his shirt, Daniel asked, "How do we describe the maker of the cubes? It could be an intelligent being who had the technological capacity and the curiosity to do it and did. He, she or it might not be a god at all, at least as we currently define the term."

"For this meeting, we should try to keep it in religious terms." Saito pushed Daniel onto his back and climbed on top.

"We need to stress God or a god-like being. Uhmmm. That's in their comfort zone even…even, that feels good…even if we have no idea if it's true or not."

"Somehow, I think I'm in your comfort zone. The risk, of course," Saito said, "is that if we don't reach agreement, we become a liability." He began kissing Daniel's neck between comments.

"They have power, ego, and a limited worldview. A dangerous combination."

"So, do we tell them about the satchel?" Saito asked, his voice distracted as he massaged a fine set of pectorals. "Maybe they're listening now or watching us. Do we give it to them or use it as a bargaining chip?"

Daniel flipped him over on his back, grinning. "I don't really care if they're watching! Maybe the show starts early." Discussing the nature of God was not his normal pickup line. He reached down. "Such a muscular butt."

"Don't talk."

Daniel flashed on an image of an old, grizzled minister watching on camera. He suspected the preachers would be shocked and angry if they knew he had sex under their roof with a woman, given their nature and the reason for meeting. With a man, it would be a beautiful sight to behold, fist pounding, shouts about fornication and quoting *Leviticus*. Maybe something they could hold in reserve for just the right moment if a distraction proved useful. He remembered spotting a box of prophylactics in a bathroom drawer. He imagined Vega ordering supplies.

"Spread your legs," Saito whispered.

Daniel laughed.

20.

Stonehouse Lodge, Lake Tahoe

"Here's another issue," Michaels said, remembering a point that would strike a nerve and build enthusiasm. "Some of you have written about the shockingly low levels of religious literacy in America, even among people who go to church weekly."

A low growl from multiple throats. "It's a sad situation," Broux said, sighing, "when conservative Christians can't recite the Ten Commandments or even state differences between Catholics and evangelicals. Many don't know why they believe what they say they do." He pointed to Sister Esther, remembering a column she recently published.

"It's the triumph of feel-good Christianity," she added. "Many recite 'Jesus Is Love' as a mantra but can't tell you much about the basic tenets of their religion. It's pathetic."

"If I may suggest that while it's tragic," Michaels said solemnly, "it means your congregations depend on your interpretations of scripture and core doctrine for guidance. Few can contradict. This opens strategic possibilities if we see a media hurricane approaching.

"If important religious leaders hold together, we could have key messages ready that suggest parts of the discovery are nothing new, they fit with some established but little-known doctrine, yet to be determined. This is why unity around this one issue—preserving the holiness of scripture—requires we speak with a single voice. The media will simply be confused since you are the experts. Most Americans get their news from sources that support their opinions. Those who might read contradictory views are not likely our allies anyway."

Martinez had started to laugh before catching himself. "Most interesting and prophetic, Mr. Michaels. Some may find this surprising but I see it as good planning." He glanced at Father Alito. "I have a small team of scholars, sworn to secrecy," the cardinal said, "looking at how we might co-opt the finding, at least what we know so far, should we want to go that route as Mr. Michaels is suggesting as a backup option. I don't propose any particular course of action, only that you may want to be creative in finding ways to blunt the impact. We can share ideas for a common platform."

The ministers looked astonished. Michaels understood that the cardinal would be in some measure useful and supportive of his plan. It was nice to hear a lack of diplomatic obfuscation.

"Although it took a few centuries, the Catholic Church eventually agreed that the Earth was round, that it rotated around the Sun and, painful as it was, we even accepted, in an obtuse theological missive, that evolution and Darwin were compatible with our doctrine."

Martinez rubbed his chin, a wry smile on his lips. "When the evidence is against you, there is no reason to reject what the rest of the world knows is true. The media is interested in controversy. Diminish dissent and you reduce coverage. We're seeing how we might do this with *Misago*, or at least have it ready. I like options and frankly I detest character assassination no matter the cause. We're bigger than that."

Broux squirmed as Esther and Robinson scowled.

The cardinal glanced again at Father Alito. "Are there ways we can say, no big deal, it fits in with existing beliefs? As several of us noted, religious illiteracy is widespread. An all-powerful God can do anything. People want to believe so we just need to make sure they receive our assurances of hope packaged in comfortable terms. The media, despite its interest in presenting facts and acting tough, is afraid of offending a religious public. That plays to our benefit."

"Very strategic, sir." Michaels smiled. Right on point.

"*CAR—DIN—AL!*" Broux stood, letting each syllable hang on his tongue. "My church, my university will not accept Darwin. We'll never twist our doctrine to accept *Misago*! We cannot and will not! If you negate Adam there is no need for Jesus!" He was shaking, lips curling into a snarl. "Our commitment to God is absolute! What you propose is apostasy."

The cardinal shrugged, weary of evangelical bombast and showmanship. "In the long run, survival of the fittest applies to religion as well as biology. As an institution in its third millennium, the Catholic Church knows a few things about survival."

Broux flipped a hand in disgust. "I'll not bend truth for political expedience."

Esther and Robinson looked indignant. Wright seemed surprised. Michaels cringed, obviously wanting to avoid damaging his own brand.

Martinez rose in all his stately magnificence and walked slowly to the red-haired minister. "A mighty oak was uprooted in a gale and fell across a stream into some reeds. Asked the oak: 'How could you reeds, so frail, survive while I, the mighty oak, fell?' Replied the reeds: 'You were stubborn and wouldn't bend.'"

Broux looked incredulous.

"Aesop, a Greek slave who lived six centuries before Christ, had much wisdom." The cardinal allowed just a touch of satisfaction to show in his eyes as he swept from the room, Father Alito racing close behind.

This session was over.

Daniel slipped on a robe and answered a knock at the door. A stout middle-aged woman, wearing a bonnet and doily-like apron stood behind a cart.

"My name is Ealga. Here is your supper, sir," she said with a light Irish brogue as she pushed it inside.

"Thank you," he said, surprised and appreciative. "Just what we needed."

She glanced at him, up and down, curtsied, giggled, closed the door, and then hurried to the main building.

He checked to make sure his bathrobe was closed then lifted the glass lid over one of the plates. Saito came up behind him, slipped a hand inside his robe, across his chest, down low and squeezed. With his other hand, he undid the sash. "You're so not Japanese," he whispered, blowing in his ear.

Daniel blushed, setting down the lid, Saito's meaning unclear but not the intent. As he turned, his bathrobe slipped off his shoulders and fell to the floor. Saito's hand cupped his butt. Daniel ran fingertips down the scientist's well-defined chest.

Outside, a guard moved in the shadows of the forest. Daniel took Saito's hand. They hurried back into the bedroom. Dinner could wait. Work on the presentation tomorrow.

21.

Stonehouse Lodge, Lake Tahoe

Daniel's editor and boss at the Times, Stan Pruitt, was thrilled with the potential story but pissed it would not be a Times exclusive. "You know you work for the Times," he argued, irritated. "You got the tip for work you did last year as a Times reporter."

"Yes, but my sabbatical began last week, a sabbatical you approved."

"You have one final story, as I recall, on the feisty new mayor of San Francisco."

"Given the gravity of this story and the government attempts to suppress it, I need someone local who'll have my back, someone willing to do what's necessary to help me survive. The *Times* still gets the co-credit and reporters you assign can be integral parts of the investigation and take their share of credit. It's a partnership. You know Bloomingdale's reputation. Depending on how this comes down, you'll be seen as a selfless professional working to advance human knowledge."

"Man, you really had to work that." With the statement, his boss acquiesced and the call ended.

Daniel pulled on his tan corduroy sport coat and stepped

onto the deck, the morning cool and sunny. His strategy session with Saito had been minimal, merely tossing ideas as they showered and dressed.

The same Irish woman with the lace apron and cap delivered breakfast on a food cart and took away the one from last night. "Thanks for the great dinner, Ealga."

She curtsied. "You are most welcome." She giggled as she hurried back to the main house, turning once to look at him.

He checked his zipper. What's so funny? Had she watched? He lifted the lid on the first plate.

"Grilled rainbow trout, rice and miso soup," Saito said as he walked up beside him. "Very nice. And this other plate has—raw bacon, undercooked eggs and cold, dry white toast. Obviously, payback for Java House." Vega had a sense of humor. Saito chose the trout and moved to a nearby bench.

"I think I'll just have toast," Daniel said, picking up one triangle, spooning on some orange marmalade and biting off a corner. He thought Saito was perfectly dressed—a lime green crew neck and a theatrical dark brown light-weight jacket with a standing collar and detailed silver buttons. Somehow Daniel's teal t-shirt, an old sport coat and khakis seemed less elegant, although Saito had squeezed his pecks, cooing, "Nice," which was encouraging.

A guard walked past twenty yards distant. The man stopped and inspected them before disappearing into the trees. Another guard seemed permanently placed a few yards from their door. They didn't look like the Swiss Guards at the Vatican; they were paramilitary. But blue and gold striped pantaloons with metal conquistador hats topped by red plumes might be a bit out of place. It was not clear if they reported to Vega or the cardinal.

He poured a cup of tea and sat next to Saito. "Not matcha."

"No, some kind of English tea."

"Last night was very special." Daniel lifted the scientist's hand and kissed it. Sex was good anytime but having it while preparing to duel with fundamentalist clerics over the end of faith gave it a surreal edge, particularly when he thought about a hidden camera.

Saito lifted his fingertips from his own lips to Daniel's. "And special for me."

The man was not shy in or out of bed and determined to display his experience and the joy. Daniel was feeling a bit like a teenager again, filled with excitement and possibility, the old demons pushed away by his affection for this amazing man. So what if the ministers knew? He picked up his steno pad with notes from their discussion early this morning. Time to focus on the day's work—and dangers.

"I believe our strategy is a good one," Daniel said. "So far they've paid no price for their decision. It's been easy. We need to puncture their confidence and let them glimpse the downside." He looked again at his notes wishing there were more. "They'll try to intimidate since from their perspective we're gnats and they're dragonflies."

Saito smiled. "Gnats are good; dragonflies overrated. I suspect an outspoken and exotic foreigner will make them uncomfortable."

"They've no idea."

"Imagine if I said I was gay."

Daniel laughed and then grew more serious, pointing toward the main cabin. "Speak of the devil."

Vega approached at a fast pace and hopped onto the porch. "I trust you found everything to your satisfaction?" His voice and demeanor were upbeat. Were his clothes ever wrinkled or a hair out of place? He wore slacks, a shirt with an open neck and no jacket, emphasizing his narrow waist and broad shoulders.

"Breakfast was—*exceptional*," Daniel replied with a smile. "Have some tea with us and watch the guards in the woods. They seem to like us."

Two quail burst from a nearby bush. "It's beautiful here," Saito said, watching the birds take flight. "It reminds me of the serenity of a Japanese mountain garden."

"Everything reminds you of a Japanese garden," Daniel teased.

Vega poured tea and sat on a bench across from them. "Wrong kind," he said. "My apologies. I shall make sure this does not happen again."

"I'm surprised you would notice such a detail," Saito remarked. "Thank you. Matcha would be nice or even an Americanized green tea."

"Are you ready to meet the crew?" Vega put down his cup and carefully rolled up the sleeves of his crisp blue dress shirt two turns.

"Who are they?" Daniel asked. "It would be nice to know."

"Some of the faces you'll recognize from television. There is Cardinal Martinez from Rome as I mentioned before, and his aide, Father Alito."

"Isn't Martinez known as a hard-ass fundamentalist?"

"Mr. Duboce, I suspect your source is misinformed. He's a man of great charm, intellect, humor, and compassion. He is not what you might expect of a man in such a role. He has a broad worldview. Give him a chance before you judge."

Daniel didn't trust Martinez or any church official. But he should be open minded. "Fair enough."

"Reverend Jim Robinson is another member."

"Ah, yes, Mr. Televangelist." Daniel knew the man's reputation and had recently watched him on television as background for a story. How close was Vega to the American Protestants? "He sees Satan everywhere and once called the AIDS epidemic God's retribution on homosexuals. He's also made similar comments after each major hurricane and earthquake. Amazing how that works. And he sees himself as America's new dictator."

"He is obsessed with Satan as are many in his circle," Vega said with a nod. "I'll not defend his statements on AIDS or anything else. Sometimes religion narrows our view of life, other times it expands it. Hate and ignorance are not limited to those of faith. Those in power are not saints, only men and women."

"Agreed," Daniel responded.

"Other representatives include Sister Esther Andrews, a television commentator and Pentecostalist from Texas, daughter of a famous Baptist preacher. Reverend John Broux heads Florian Elder University. The American group is chaired by Reverend Adam

Wright, a radio pastor. Also, there is a political consultant named Michael Michaels."

"Important people." Daniel rubbed his chin. Michaels? He once worked with a man with that odd double name during a brief stint in public relations. Interesting. He was impressed with the lineup and noticed Vega's tone was flat, unenthusiastic, when describing the Protestants. "I'm familiar with Florian Elder University. Biology is taught through the Bible. That certainly takes creativity and fact-straddling. And they want to take America back to the eighteenth century." He smiled. "Mr. Vega, your group has muscle. What do they want? What do you want?" Daniel leaned back against the wall of the bunkhouse wondering if he had the same agenda. "What are the expectations?" He finished his slice of toast, licking his fingers.

Vega stood and slipped his hands into the pockets of his brown tweed slacks and glanced at the lake. "I would like you both to join with us in our efforts to preserve public confidence in the major religious institutions in the western world." He turned to Daniel. "Religion plays a pivotal role in social cohesion, as we discussed. I believe you share that view and don't want to harm the Church you used to love. The bitterness in your heart, I believe, is fleeting."

The envoy sat. "Dr. Saito, I hope your views of peace and harmony as expressed in the dual religions of Japan would lead you to the same conclusion."

"Mr. Vega," Saito responded, his tone no-nonsense, "I believe in the power of the scientific process. We test every theory; if it passes those tests then others will respect it until it's overturned. How do you test religious doctrines when they are all hiding behind amorphous terminology? Ministers say we are just not smart enough to understand God's plan as a technique to deflect honest inquiry. Really? Ask for a definition of faith and people struggle. Hope? Trust? So many words can be used, all just empty terms in the scientific process. A low bar."

Daniel enjoyed both the man's steadfastness and the complex color highlights of his hair in the sunlight. He blushed, realizing he was distracted, and brought his brain back to the topic at hand.

"If religious beliefs cannot withstand the same kind of scrutiny," Saito argued, "I'm not sure I'm ready to abandon my principles for yours. Truth is important to me. As a scientist, I believe in biology, not superstition."

"Well stated, Dr. Saito," Vega said. "Before I forget, please notice in the meeting the centerpiece on the table is now graced with the pineapple. We'll see if anyone notices." He smiled at each in turn and it seemed genuine. "I knew you'd be well prepared and well versed. I suspect you will not be timid. This first meeting could be unpleasant. They're not known for good behavior in private settings. They may seek to seduce or intimidate. I wanted to forewarn before you enter the lion's den."

"Speaking as a man named Daniel, sir, that's an outrageous pun."

22.

Stonehouse Lodge, Lake Tahoe

Odd place for a holy war, Daniel thought, feeling the atmosphere a bit apocalyptic as the three entered the area behind the main meeting hall, wondering if a Knights Templar sword might be useful.

Crystal glasses. Native American rugs. Bowls of dark chocolate peanut clusters. Logs stacked to the ceiling on one side of the fireplace with touches of moss. Scowling old men, Satan likely hiding behind the bookcase. The morning sun pushing through the chintz drapes, splashing yellow chrysanthemums on a white plaster wall. Birds chirping in the pines, freesia in a dozen vases offering a blast of perfume. An oversized computer screen. Journalism had made him cynical about human motivation but he wanted to remain open and optimistic. The room was a perfect stage set, every part tasteful, as if designed by a gay man.

A heavyset man with a full grey beard walked up to them, extending his hand. "Welcome! I'm Adam Wright, chairman of the board of the Triple C," he said warmly. "We're delighted to have you here."

Wright was trying hard. Daniel had heard several of his radio programs and he seemed more likable in person. As the minister introduced members, he noticed the man seemed flummoxed that no one stood or offered a hand, perhaps too self-important, rude or angry to be polite. He extended a hand to the cardinal and felt an emotional jolt when their palms met, focusing on the man's eyes until Martinez looked down. Then it was a cold, crushing grip from Sister Esther and a smug expression, willing to look at him, confident and haughty. He considered what he'd read about her in news clips. Broux's hand was soft and lifeless. Robinson grabbed his fingertips, squeezed and pulled his hand back.

Then there he was, sitting amidst the saints. Michael Michaels, the man he had worked alongside in a brief stint in public relations. A prick and even more unsavory than the corporate bosses they'd worked for. Useful to know he was on the team.

"This is Mr. Michael Michaels, famous PR and political consultant to corporations and protector of the Christian brand," Daniel said with a full-tooth grin as if addressing an old friend. "Why am I not surprised to find you here?"

Michaels stood, looking irritated as they shook hands. "Yes," he said to no one in particular. "Mr. Duboce and I met when I was doing political strategy at a major telecom firm."

The cardinal frowned. Daniel suspected he was caught by surprise; so was Vega. Michaels was clearly pissed, Daniel's words jabbing his sense of entitlement. A good thing. These men, religious royalty, expected to know everything important beforehand. Perhaps Michaels never mentioned his previous employment.

"I'm pleased you're here, Michael," Daniel said, patting his shoulder as an irritating old college roommate might do at a class reunion. "This means I know what to expect in any political campaign." The man was known for scorched earth tactics, often light on accuracy. Michaels had contempt in his eyes but said nothing. Daniel continued to grin and squeezing the back of the man's neck, feeling muscles tense. "Isn't your claim to corporate fame bribing the president's lawyer to get a favorable merger ruling? How did that go?" Daniel sat, crossing his legs, his expression as flat as he could muster, not ready to mention Michael's indictment as an unregistered foreign agent and saved by a controversial presidential pardon.

Vega whispered to Wright before taking the floor. He began, "I thank the chairman for the opportunity to launch our discussions. I've had the privilege of spending part of two days with Dr. Saito and Mr. Duboce. I found them to be independent thinkers, people of conscience and wit. I suspect we have much in common as we search for common ground. Mr. Duboce, if you would like to start."

Saito took a seat up front, taking out a notepad and a black and silver pen with 142 hours of high-quality digital recording capacity. He clicked it open and squiggled, demonstrating, in case anyone was looking, that it was just a pen, then set it down, casually turning the top outward and squeezing the clip. Recording was illegal in California without permission unless to gather evidence of a serious crime but Daniel wanted accurate notes. Was suppressing the existence of a new God a crime? It might make a great Harvard case study someday. The topic demanded precision and no one had said this was off the record. The ministers settled back in their chairs.

"Sister Esther, gentlemen," Daniel began, "I've reported for the *Times* on the *Misago* project and know Dr. Wada well enough to consider him a friend." An overstatement but he wanted them to think he knew more than he did.

Michaels picked up his e-pad and stylus, planning his hatchet job, no doubt. The squawking jays outside seemed to be having their own territorial dispute.

"Dr. Wada is one of the most formidable men I've ever met. I refer to his intellect and passion for science and advancing human knowledge. Let me start with a broader statement about *Misago* to give context. I know you've been briefed on the discovery itself."

He studied their faces and demeanor, seeking clues. He and Saito had agreed to slice straight to the heart of the matter. Given the larger than life egos here, the approach seemed necessary.

"I suspect this is what you want to know: Is there proof, physical evidence, about what was found by *Misago* on the asteroid

Geographicos?" All heads lifted. "Is that proof safely under lock and key in Japan, held by government officials? Or is it more widely dispersed, more vulnerable?" He looked toward Vega. "Is it here in America?"

"Well?" Robinson demanded, slapping his palm on the table. "Answer your own questions!"

"The Japanese government has much of what was found," Daniel stated forcefully. "Dr. Saito and I have more. We control materials and research data that are unequivocal, plentiful, and easily understood, ready for distribution. They provide absolute scientific evidence of the discovery and its truth. The cache is safely hidden. Its whereabouts are known to those with the capability to take it public. It will be released in a few days unless we instruct them to do otherwise."

Silence. Scowls. A few clenched fists. Vega and the cardinal just watched, their expressions inscrutable.

"You're bluffing!" Sister Esther blasted.

"Prove it!" Broux demanded.

On cue, Saito stood and stepped forward, looking straight at Broux, his irritation trumping Broux's with a long stare with just a touch of curled lip. "I carried Dr. Wada's proof myself and gave it to Daniel."

"I don't believe you," Esther sneered.

"Enough!" Wright said, standing and pulling up the front of his slacks. "We're not here to argue. They have simply confirmed what we suspected."

"I don't bargain with thieves," Broux huffed.

"Given the stakes here, does that make you wise, afraid, or a fool?" Saito stepped back, his tone less harsh, almost playful despite his words. This group was not used to pushback, only the reverence given to those who chatted with God. But fear kept them in their seats.

Such a lion, Daniel thought, stepping forward and tapping his shoulder. "My turn. A story broke yesterday in Japanese papers that the government admits material is missing. Check it out. We have that material. Deny or accept it but it's your faith at peril.

We wouldn't have come here unprepared. Why take such a risk? Dr. Saito and I wanted the opportunity to meet with you face to face. You persuaded President Walton to cut a deal for secrecy. We want to learn more about your motivations beyond self-preservation. We understand the implications if *Misago* goes public. Mr. Vega has eloquently expressed his views to us. But we want to engage with you and we want to do it respectfully. Given the stakes, no one should act precipitously."

"Thank you," the cardinal stated with raised hands and voice. "That is our goal. You startled us with your declaration. But it's refreshing to begin with openness. Respect is imperative if we want to reach consensus, if that's possible." His expression suggested he was ready to pounce if anyone disagreed. It seemed to work, at least for the moment.

"Mr. Duboce," Wright said, slowly settling back into his seat. "You're clearly a thoughtful man. I've read one of your books and many of your news articles. I've seen you on PBS. I'm impressed with your thorough and impartial analyses. Could you offer us that same kind of analysis on *Misago*? What do you see that might lead you to even suggest going public?"

"Good question," Sister Esther declared.

Daniel glanced at Saito. He felt as if the curtain were going up on a Broadway stage and he was standing in the footlights without rehearsal or even a script.

He began, "We each see reality through our own prisms. I'm a journalist. Facts and context are paramount. How humans came to exist on Earth is a profound question many have wrestled with and come to very different conclusions. For most, the answer is God, although there are thousands of definitions of what that means in different cultures and points in history. Probably all of you reject the concept of life developing through chance and natural selection. That is your right. This discovery, if confirmed, has profound implications for all of us, since it proves the biochemical origins of life."

"It gives me no discomfort," Broux said, his tone smug, "because I don't believe it. My faith tells me it's untrue."

"A-men, brother," Sister added with a dramatic preacher shout.

"Please let him continue," Wright urged.

Saito stepped forward. "I'm a chemist. Science is real and this discovery is tangible. Is your faith? I hope you have enough curiosity to at least understand what you're so anxious to reject." His tone was matter of fact and respectful. "Let me share why I think *Misago* is explosive." He was a commanding presence, handsome, foreign, confident, and his words had the desired effect. The room awaited his explanation.

"*Misago* brought back stardust, crushed rock, regolith dating to the birth of the universe and a cache of valuable minerals and gold. This we expected. Yet scattered amongst the particles were perfect cubes made of some unknown but plastic-like material." He explained what was found with a splash of technical jargon in a no-nonsense voice. "One thing you likely have not heard is that Dr. Wada went back and pulled granules from previous space missions, *Hayabusa* I and II. The first returned in 2006, the second in 2020. Three sets of materials, each adding confirmation. Do all asteroids contain the cubes or just a few? My guess is only some but there is no way of yet knowing."

Esther and Broux exchanged glances. Daniel suspected fear and curiosity were compelling them to listen, not unlike drivers passing an accident on a freeway. But they were all part of this pile-up.

"The big issue has always been: how did the raw chemical elements on Earth assemble themselves into precursors of life? How did they survive the draconian conditions in the early solar system? The catalyst in these remarkable cubes seems to offer an explanation." Saito turned to the cardinal, a hand in a pants pocket, the other gesturing. "I admit that this is startling. It challenges both faith and science. What we don't know is if it was someone or something so advanced its technology seems godlike. Or—perhaps a real god. I yearn to find the truth." He stepped back and pointed at Daniel.

Esther grunted, lifting her head. Broux coughed.

"So, what does that mean for a journalist?" Daniel asked. "The *Misago* discovery essentially answers all three questions—chemicals and catalysts, delivery system and preservation. But for a journalist, that's not enough."

"Good," said Wright.

Daniel gave him a nod-smile mix. "I want confirmation from others. Let me tell you something else you likely don't know. You only heard part of the story in your briefing because Dr. Wada didn't reveal everything to the president."

The audience stiffened. "What don't we know?" Sister Esther demanded. "Why were we not told all the details? Why should I believe you?"

"Please," the cardinal said. "Let us hear what they have to say."

"Science is a process," Saito injected, "we suspect some things early, calling them hypotheses, and disprove them or confirm them later. We learn as we go. That is its power, a methodology to try and ascertain truth as it relates to our physical world."

"You didn't answer the question," Broux demanded, a muscle twitching in his cheek.

"Dr. Wada didn't share it with our prime minister or your president," Saito said, his voice showing surprising patience, "because his tests were not far enough along to draw a reasonable conclusion. Wada is a cautious man of science. He doesn't hold a press conference every time he learns something. I think you can appreciate his caution."

"What—don't—we—know?" Esther repeated giving equal loud pronunciation to each word.

"Answer her, don't talk nonsense," Broux said, his hands fisting.

"We're here at your invitation," Daniel said, suppressing an urge to slap them both. He believed they were sincere, much like he had been in seminary—Jesus comes to you, at least you believe he does, and is real, at least at that moment in your life. "I respect who you are, I will not insult your intelligence by being less than candid. We can stop the discussions and go our separate ways, if you prefer." He looked at the cardinal. "Or, you can hold us prisoners and someone else will release the data."

"You're guests, not prisoners," Martinez replied softly, looking startled. Vega seemed amused by the exchange.

"Go ahead," Broux said. "I need to control my impatience."

"The stakes are huge for all of us, sir," Daniel said, hoping for earnestness.

"Dr. Wada's team believes an intelligent entity created the nano cubes as you were told. But Wada also believes the cubes' interiors are not identical. A diverse mix was tossed to the universe to start the process of life in various physical environments, some quite unlike Earth's. That suggests possible life forms different from humans. As a journalist, I want to know how he reached that conclusion. I need other experts to test it. I also want to know what theologians have to say from a wide range of faith groups. Everyone should have a voice because everyone has a stake."

Realistically, how could honesty be achieved? Religious figures would likely adhere to their faith, except those few capable of self-reflection and able to step back and contemplate a different reality, ignoring their financial self-interests, social pressures and ingrained beliefs. Even great scientists, from certain countries, could find themselves and their families threatened if they didn't support certain findings. Religion was also a tool for social control. Without serious planning, the discovery could be highjacked into a PR campaign not unlike cigarette makers obfuscating the results of the first findings linking tobacco and lung cancer.

He leaned against a table, hands at his side, Saito perched on the top with legs dangling. The serenity of forest song mixed awkwardly with the distant roar of speed boats on the lake and seemed fitting background for the hostility facing him. The cardinal's placid bearing returned. Vega watched him closely, an inspection, rarely looking away.

Daniel continued: "*Misago* proves Darwin. But the words of most of the holy books about life created in the image of God—they are likely wrong." Subtlety seemed pointless.

The group squirmed. Sister and Broux rose, ready to walk

out. "The words of the holy Bible are absolute and irrefutable!" Broux shouted, pointing at Daniel. He moved to the side of the room and leaned against a wall. Esther went over to him. Broux's face remained as red as his hair. "Why should we believe the words of a snot-nosed ex-Catholic journalist and the buddy of some criminal Japanese scientist? The answer is we DON'T! And I'll not let you blaspheme the words of God as He directed them into the Bible. Wada's a fraud! This whole discovery's a fraud! It'll be exposed as such!"

Daniel looked toward the cardinal and took two steps in his direction. He didn't want to create a scene with Broux.

"People in America and around the world worry about their future," Daniel said. "They yearn for absolutes. Your churches provide certainty about scripture, sin, death and heaven. I understand why Dr. Wada's discovery would be frightening. On some level, it worries me too."

"Do you believe in God?" Robinson asked straightforwardly, no sneer, an honest inquiry.

"I once pursued the priesthood," Daniel replied respectfully. "But now the evidence shows a superior intelligence launched a process that created life. Perhaps different life forms elsewhere. The issue is, who or what is this entity?"

Broux shook his head. "You did not answer my question."

"The Christian god has a history of offering absolutes only to have to abandon them when human knowledge forced change. The earth is round," Daniel said quietly, extending his arms. "Murdering those who disagree is evil by any definition. So is using the Bible as a fig leaf to condone slavery or Jim Crow. I say no to a god that uses religion to enforce men's control of women's bodies. That attacks gays by quoting a line in the Old Testament that research suggests is a bad translation—all for the sake of having an enemy to hate and stir your base. But I look at the creator of the cubes as a second chance for humanity. A god not yet defined and therefore unencumbered with the evil of ambitious prelates over the millennia. Do we hang our prejudices on this new entity to guarantee someone political leverage or do we let discovery take an honest course?"

Vega lifted a finger. "An excellent proposition. Mr. Duboce—you speak in theatrical terms of your disenchantment with Christianity. But losing belief in God is often, I suspect, much more personal. With that in mind, may I ask…how?"

Daniel was surprised. Had he guessed and wants it on the table? Was it to shock the Protestants or his own cardinal? He looked down, taking a deep breath. This reached beyond what had happened to one boy long ago. He glanced at Saito; the man nodded in support.

"My mother was a loyal Catholic and my own fervor for the church endured despite what a priest did to me when I was a boy, not yet a teenager, claiming it was God's will. Who was I to disagree with a priest on God's expectations?" He struggled to overcome the quiver in his voice. This had been so difficult to admit to Saito, much less now to a group of hostile strangers. "I didn't understand that the term was rape. My parents never knew. As I grew up I convinced myself the abuse was an aberration. Years later, the dissolution of my marriage was engineered by an archbishop who took hundreds of thousands of dollars in exchange for an annulment. A church that would not police the rape of children by its priests, that destroyed families for cash… that ended my relationship and faith."

He paused, watching the cardinal. No readable expression. Anger pushed him forward. "I don't buy the argument that we simply cannot comprehend God's plan. If he has the power to save lives during a hurricane, then he has the power to stop the hurricane. A hundred and twenty-seven people were shot to death by a madman last week in Texas. People who survived thanked the all-powerful God. Really?" His voice was calm. "God is never at fault. Yet, if he exists, he is. Most likely, there is no god, I decided, because if there was and he allows the horrors that befall mankind, then he himself is a horror. Organized religion," Daniel went on in the face of their stony expressions, "priests and pastors can be as corrupt and cynical as any government, or as generous and noble. Just because they profess to be faithful and claim to speak with God is no excuse. The Oracle of Delphi made similar claims in its time."

The audience remained silent, some looking away to avoid his eyes. Robinson was open-mouthed. The cardinal's lips to had tightened to whiteness, his face a mask, a man with years of practice at maintaining the granite facade. Daniel stared at him through the lengthy silence.

"What may have happened to you as a boy was inexcusable," the cardinal said without a hint of remorse. "The Church took steps to make sure it never happened again."

May have happened? Daniel glared, flabbergasted. Was anyone in charge? "When I was eleven," he said, anger leaking through his pores, disgust crushing restraint, "I stood before the powerful archbishop of San Francisco. A nun brought me there. She'd found me with my pants around my knees, blood dripping to the floor. The archbishop said it was horrible if true. *If!* He dismissed me, I was not worthy of his time. The rapist priest was rewarded, the nun was punished. The church has stepped forward only because of lawsuits, public disgust and, who knows, maybe God was in there somewhere."

Fuck. Why was he debasing himself? He noticed Michaels smirking.

The cardinal's face was unchanged, only his eyes widened. Daniel glanced around the room. Even the forest was silent. Vega was looking at him with compassion, if Daniel read the man right. Saito had a tear on his cheek which only added to his embarrassment.

"What happened to you as a boy," Broux said, his tone compassionate, is inexcusable and disgusting. I'm deeply sorry. There've been no such scandals in Protestant churches."

"I wish your statement on sex abuse in evangelical churches were true," Daniel replied. "There are many cases and much denial. I urge you to investigate."

"If you go public with *Misago*," Robinson said in a soft, pained voice with just a touch of quiver, ignoring his comment, "you could destroy all that is holy. That is arrogance. Indeed, it's reckless!" He sounded sensible, the voice of reason.

"Please, let's not argue," Wright implored.

Saito responded, looking at Robinson, "We should not assume that hiding this discovery is in your best interests. Truth has a way of surfacing eventually. Perhaps you should consider being open on this, as profound and discomfiting as it is. I may not be Christian, Reverend Broux," he said. "I may not see Jesus as a savior, divine or otherwise, nor do I need or want a savior, but I hope you will see this discovery as an opportunity, not a threat. Remember, even if you suppress it, others may find granules on future space trips. It may also be found on this planet in geologic formations."

"Perhaps it would be helpful if you could talk about what you know about Dr. Wada and where he is," Vega suggested.

"Let me be precise," Saito said, "I do not know his whereabouts."

"Likewise," Daniel added. "I fear for his safety. He's the best man to lead the world in understanding and it's easier to dislike someone you don't know." No one, he noted in disgust, had challenged his statements about culpability for rape. They'd just changed the subject.

"Perhaps we should break here," Wright suggested. "It may do us all some good to slow our heartbeats, have some lemonade and walk in this beautiful forest Eden. Maybe we can fill our lungs with clean mountain air and open our minds and hearts."

"It was hard to endure," Alito told the cardinal and two others in the garden and added with a hint of anger: "He attacked you!"

"No." Martinez was firm yet gentle. "He spoke with brutal honesty. His pain is genuine and I pray he lanced it by baring his soul. It was a brave act. The church erred, grievously, multiple times. Still does." He himself had erred. "Let it go."

The cardinal's sin, and the pain he felt because of it, was excruciating. For years, he'd heard of Catholic clergy sexually abusing boys and girls, reading reports, news stories and settling lawsuits. Celibacy was not for the weak and someday the church might need to re-think that rule particularly if the qualified no longer wanted to serve.

Why had he protected wolves and abandoned children? Blindness? Cowardice? A misguided loyalty to comrades? He was as guilty as they because he had failed to force accountability using the power of his position. Money could indeed corrupt clergy. Pay-to-play in politics and churches should never be reality, but it was. A question flashed in his mind. Was Daniel God's agent? He pressed a finger and thumb against the bridge of his nose.

"How often are clergy compelled to sit and listen to their beliefs being skewered?" the priest asked, holding his hands tight together to mask the shaking. "Worse, our strategy called for us to sit and listen."

"Obviously not everyone followed the plan," Vega responded with a hint of irritation. He turned to Wright. "Let me be straightforward. They have tangible proof of creation and we want it. You're the most likable of the American ministers and might be able to connect with our guests privately if you're willing to stretch, show empathy and humility. Daniel is an intellectual and as you've seen, enjoys debate. Saito is clearly infatuated with him. So, Daniel is key. You could be vital to our success if you would engage with him away from the group, maybe on a different topic, something deeply personal, surprise him, shock him even, seek his advice, pull him in and drop any defensiveness. Remember too that his wounds from the church are still raw. I'm not sure what to do with that but it might be useful. Remember he has a son just a few years younger than Rolph."

The cardinal nodded, surprised at Vega's machine gun approach but agreeing with it. Saito was infatuated with Daniel? What did that mean? He was pleased someone was showing leadership. He no longer felt he could. "Yes, catch him by surprise, engage him intellectually and morally, if you can."

Wright, far from nonplussed by Vega's confrontation, looked flattered. "I don't feel very charming now, either with my board of directors or this young duo. I'll do my best."

"Excellent," Vega said. "Americans prefer a spoonful of sugar."

Wright looked at him balefully and started to speak, then just nodded, and left. He wandered up the path, deep in thought.

Martinez turned to his loyal assistant. "Father, please start human resources researching the San Francisco archdiocese about the time Daniel was a boy, perhaps fifteen years ago, maybe longer. Look for transfers, a priest and nun about the same time, and get names and history. I also want to know who the archbishop was and where he is now."

23.

Stonehouse Lodge, Lake Tahoe

"This relaxing technique is highly efficient," Daniel whispered as they sat on the pier with their feet dangling over the side. It was a chance to stretch out after working all morning on the final edits of his notes before forwarding them to Bruiser. He'd also sent a follow-up text to Garrett, asking again about plans for his birthday and repeating his new cell number. He moved his fingers over Saito's on the dock, keeping low key.

"You were amazing yesterday," Saito said. "I was proud of you. You shocked the piss out of them."

"Is that a good thing?" Daniel laughed. "Thank you. It means a lot. We made a strong team. You are the fierce Osprey, you are Misago."

Saito blushed. A charming reaction. Daniel decided to change the topic. "Despite all the arguing yesterday, I slept great last night."

"Really? You didn't seem to be doing much sleeping," Saito said in a Lauren Bacall growl, lowering his head in a pretense of shyness before slapping Daniel's thigh. "We'll see what today brings after the hostilities yesterday."

He grinned, wondering if Saito was a fan of 1940s movies. "Do you play Garbo in drag?"

"You will be punished tonight, in a specific way, for your disrespect."

"I think we held our own. It was good Wright called for a break and gave us the rest of the day and last night alone. Time to think and…"

Saito pulled him closer, kissed his cheek, rubbing his tongue in a circle. He felt aroused and excited that they could easily jump from sweaty lovers to celestial plotters in an instant. "Being alone with you can be distracting. But a good distraction, a perfect way to burn calories." He turned his gaze to the lake. "Essentially, they feel allegiance to their faith and way of life and are frightened at being unmoored. I expect nothing else at this point. You and Michaels don't seem too friendly."

"HELLO!" Reverend Wright called to them as he walked in their direction carrying a wicker basket. He wore brown slacks and a multi-colored aloha shirt featuring a smiling Jesus feeding the hungry under palm trees. Rolph was beside him, staring at his phone, apparently less than excited based on his hanging back ten feet from his father and scraping his flip flops as he walked, a bit pigeon-toed.

"So much for getting away from them," Saito whispered, waving. "Don't trust anything he says."

"At least he's the most pleasant of the bunch."

"I hope you don't mind if Rolph and I join you," Wright said. "This is a picnic lunch that staff prepared. May we?"

Daniel swiveled around to face the two, sitting cross-legged. "Please do. I've been looking forward to learning more about Rolph. My son's just a few years younger." The teenager didn't appear to hear him as he sat.

Saito, in faded jeans and a thin blue sweater, swiveled around, arms around his knees, and watched the minister, smiling but silent. Rolph was in mid-calf green pants and a blue t-shirt, his thick black framed glasses low on his nose, phone tight in his right palm.

Wright put down the basket then dropped to the deck harder than he'd planned—rolling onto his back with his legs up in the air. He groaned as Daniel and Saito grabbed his arms and pulled him up. The minister looked grateful and red-faced. Rolph looked horrified, finally setting down his phone.

Wright growled, "Ya need to make sure you've got other talents when you have the grace of a stranded walrus." He took out a red-and-white checked cloth from the basket and with Rolph's help spread it on the deck.

"Thanks Reverend," Daniel said. "We forgot it was lunch time." He patted Rolph on the knee who sat cross-legged a foot away. "Good to see you again, young man. I hope we can learn more about you."

"Cool."

"No need for formalities," Wright said. "Just call me Adam. As I told you last night, not many people know that I went to Catholic school as a boy. Much like you. But my first visit to an evangelical church captured my heart."

"We all find our own way," Daniel said, enjoying his efforts to be friendly. Even if he distrusted his motives, he liked him.

"I was moved by your story. I know it was difficult for you, difficult for you both. Some of my fellow ministers were not always graceful. Myself included."

"Neither were we," Saito said. "But an important opening discussion."

The minister spread out an array of sandwiches and chips, grabbing a chicken salad for himself. "You presented new issues and showed a mastery of detail we lacked. You startled us. We worry what else we don't know."

"I'd say our knowledge at this point is limited. More research is needed." Saito was letting his scientist persona take charge. "We may never decipher the intent of those who launched these catalysts into space although we have a long shot chance at eventually finding clues to trace them back to their origin. This is an opportunity for theologians and scientists to work together to unravel the mystery." He knew neither of them believed such a collaboration would be productive but it was important to state.

Wright asked, "Do you think we can work together?"

Daniel answered. "I have my doubts—Adam." It felt awkward using his first name.

Seeming to ignore Daniel's comment, the minister went on: "I was amazed at how your uncertainty reflects some of my own. You've the courage to express your misgivings before those who claim they have none. May I ask a personal question?" The man's face seemed guileless. "I'm seeking to understand different points of view. You seem worldlier than I."

"I'm not sure about that. Ask away."

"Your confession today…" He looked at his son. "Not an easy topic. When you had your encounter with a homosexual priest, did it darken your heart? How did you handle it?"

An odd question, especially in front of his son, Daniel thought. The boy had turned crimson and was holding the cell phone a thumb's width from his nose as if trying to hide. Could he be gay? Or maybe just confused? A good kid growing up in an uptight world. Maybe it wasn't about him at all and this was just a tactic to engage. Did they know about his relationship with Saito?

"That's a heavy question, Adam. First, a gay priest didn't molest me. It was a pedophile. They're quite separate. I'm convinced that gay is a normal part of the human condition. We're all created in God's image, according to the Bible. Frankly, in my teenage years I had a crush on a guy and we experimented, lots of men do according to research. That means we kissed. Then I met Trudy and realized I was also drawn to women. We are each unique, part of who we are as a species."

He reached over and touched Saito's knee, exchanging glances. If this was about Rolph, he would help. "If my son told me he was gay, would I love him any less? Of course not! If my son felt he was born the wrong sex or anything else that was different, would he not still be my son, or maybe my daughter? The Bible offers wisdom but also folly. Humans have learned a lot in the nearly two millennia since it was written. *Leviticus* forbids men from wasting their seed by having sex with other men, getting a tattoo, working on Sunday, eating seafood with scales or a fin or failing to include salt in any offering to God. A list perhaps important in the fourth century but ludicrous and destructive today. If you give credence to the list, then follow all items or reject them all. Consider whether such ancient prescriptions are relevant, fair, hurtful or just baggage. A wise man can see the difference. If you value your friend, be a friend. Try and understand his view. Have an open heart. That's the message of Jesus."

Wright sat frozen, looking baffled. "Ahhh, yes, thank you," he mumbled. "That's...very useful and wise."

Rolph was staring, open-mouthed. "You...you had feelings... for a guy? You kissed a man?"

"He was the same as me. Confused. Sure. Experimentation is part of life. Churches shouldn't seek to ostracize whole segments of the population over variances created by God himself. To be fully honest here, I still enjoy male company as well as female."

The minister leaned back, shifting his focus as he pointed to a hawk flying high overhead trying desperately to escape a group of small angry birds chirping madly, defending their nests. He waited until they disappeared behind some trees.

"Do you both personally think the asteroid discovery, if it went public, would make people lose faith in the god of the Bible?" He looked toward his son. "I've told Rolph some of the details. A dad should be open with his son." He grinned at the boy who bit his lip, looking thrilled for a change of topic.

"Actually, I don't. Not for a long time," Daniel said. "I think people will be shocked. Those predisposed to believe it, will; those who aren't, won't. But a new discussion will start among those who genuinely want to know the truth, not mythology. Major surprises may yet emerge from *Misago*. I would hope theologians with an open mind could be part of any dialogue. Truth and faith don't have to be enemies." As long as both sides are open and honest, a big stumble.

"Have you ever considered," Saito injected, "that the discovery marks the beginning of the end of faith and the first concrete steps toward certainty?"

Wright stared at him open-mouthed. "Yes, yes, ahh, maybe a topic for later. Daniel, you said yesterday you once believed in God. I found that encouraging."

It had been a long time since Daniel had a serious give and take with a clergyman. He realized Wright was trying to recruit him, an odd charm offensive. Daniel sensed the minister himself might be vulnerable.

"I put the rape aside and focused on God," Daniel said. "I wore piety on my sleeve after my mother died. I graduated from high school and college early and enrolled in a seminary, the youngest member. I met this remarkable woman at St. Ignatius Church. We fell in love and I left the seminary. She was the first woman I ever had sex with. But only after we were married. Now that's being a good Catholic boy." That should please him; a little purity never hurts. So why did it feel so embarrassing? And he was talking in front of a teenager. And Saito.

Wright looked surprised. "A role model."

"I felt abandoned by the annulment," he said, and focused on finishing his egg salad sandwich. When he looked up, they were all watching him. Rolph's phone seemed to have lost its allure. The confessional was working. "It confirmed my distrust of *revealed religions*," he continued. "Someone announces God has secretly talked to them and if they can convince enough people they have some special insight, a religion is born. Millions insisting something is true doesn't make it so. Somebody famous said that."

"Mark Twain." Saito grinned as everyone stared. "What? *The Adventures of Tom Sawyer* helped me learn English."

Daniel punched Saito's shoulder and grinned. "I have faith," he said, "in the potential of the human mind if it can operate freely, not mired in faith from ancient texts. Learn from history, don't let it control you." He stretched out his legs and leaned back on the dock.

Inspiration struck. "Have you ever read any of the works of the American mythologist Joseph Campbell?"

"Yes, I have," the minister said, wiping his mouth with a checkered cloth. "Fascinating man. He did a lot of work on comparative religions."

"I've seen him on PBS," Rolph added. "Really cool ideas."

"There was a kind of *what if* moment in one of his essays. In a political deal, the Catholic Church demanded that the Roman Emperor Justinian eliminate all its competitors so he closed the Greek schools because they taught the scientific method and emphasized reason as a way of thinking about the world. Campbell asked *what if* Justinian had kept them open and allowed them to spread? Instead of the Dark Ages, might we have had another thousand years of scientific achievement? Campbell felt it was one of the great turning points of history."

"You are quite a philosopher," Wright said.

"I need to find that episode," Rolph added, picking up his phone.

Daniel looked at the boy and smiled, then back to the minister. "*What if* President Walton doesn't bow to the pressure of the CCC leaders—people like you, Adam—and the *Misago* discovery goes public? What if he backs away from promises he secretly made to this board and the Kingdom Movement? Is this one of those moments?"

Wright didn't respond. But he seemed to be thinking, not ricocheting standard religious talking points.

"I'm babbling," Daniel said, patting Wright on his ankle. "This is way too serious for this kind of spring day at Tahoe."

As they exited the pier, Wright walked in front of the group. Rolph carried the picnic basket. Daniel reached over and rubbed Saito's back. The scientist reached down and pinched his butt. A promising new day, he thought, progress on two fronts.

Cardinal Martinez came into view ahead, walking down the path toward them. "Daniel, please come inside."

24.

Family Quarters, White House

Jake Machin always imagined himself as James Madison, the shortest American president, when strolling through the modern-day White House. In the afternoon, the halls seemed filled with the ghosts of Americans who had lived and worked here, the guards snapping to attention as he walked, all handsome in their dress uniforms. The Marines were his favorite, immaculately groomed men and women, dark blue jackets and pants with red piping, white belts and gloves. The Washington Post called Machin the nation's premiere political guru, "ruthless, admired and despised." Homely and bald with a stature of five feet two, his reputation was everything. Madison had been a towering five feet four. Close enough.

He came up the stairs near the Lincoln Bedroom where he'd stayed several times. He moved past the Yellow Room with the Truman Balcony, a favorite spot where he often stood with the president, and headed to the private sitting room. Machin preferred talking about *Misago* in private, just the two of them. He heard laughter and paused to listen, not wanting to interrupt, and admired a portrait of a dour Abraham Lincoln, six feet four, wondering how odd his conversation with him would have been. The president was with the twins, Sarah and Noah, for homework day, something he scheduled twice a week. Walton was six feet one, and was always seated when they talked, so height was rarely an issue between them. Even when standing together and feeling dwarfed, he knew proximity to power was more important, an equalizer.

He also knew Walton prided himself on being knowledgeable about the world beyond politics. He read widely, particularly biographies and history. "A conservative intellectual," *The Atlantic* once called him. Machin hated the quote. Not a quality popular with the base. Intellectuals think too much. Fortunately, while the president had strong opinions and asked lots of questions, he was rarely insistent on his point of view when it came to politics. Machin disliked the deal cut to cinch the election, promising to declare God's Kingdom, but it had worked even if he felt the advocates were more grifters than saints.

"Come on in, Jake," the president called and waved toward an open seat. The thirteen-year-olds, Noah and Sarah, sat on each side of their father, offering Jake smiles and hand waves. They had the red curly hair of their mom and each was a picture of innocence. The boy had on black gym pants and a hooded blue sweatshirt with a Harvard logo. She wore a pink plaid hoodie and tan Bermuda shorts. Neither wore shoes. The president was in gray cords and an untucked dress shirt. They are too casual, he thought, but, this was their living room.

"We're talking about Mark Twain. Their lit class is studying American novelists. Everyone has to team up and pick one of his books. They chose *Mysterious Stranger*. Feel free to toss in your ideas. We're almost done. Have you read it?"

"Ah, no sir. I stick with political science and marketing."

The president pointed to his son who said, "This was Twain's last book, set in the Middle Ages. It's known for its dark side, not humor."

"Tell me about the stranger?" the father asked.

"The man says he's an angel," Sarah answered. "The other

kids are in awe when he lights a pipe without a match. Not much of a miracle for an angel, it seems to me."

Noah raised his hand. "Then he says he's Satan." His voice cracked on the last word. He looked embarrassed.

Sarah finished his point. "But he later says it's just a name, and he's not the Satan of hell."

The boy burst in, "But I found a paper online that said the mysterious stranger was God. Do you think that's true, Dad?"

The father tightened his lips. Machin could tell he was searching for the right answer because the man always wanted to lift their thinking, challenge them, not dismiss or talk down to them, a lion training his cubs. It was an admirable attribute. Maybe he'd bring in a reporter to do a piece for Father's Day. "That's a good question. We know Twain liked to make fun of pompous religious leaders. He also had some difficult periods in his life, particularly after the death of his wife, and occasionally he lashed out. This could be one of those times."

The president touched his chin, a finger rubbing against his lips. "I remember *Pudd'nhead Wilson*. The schoolboy said: *'Faith is believing what you know ain't so.'* Many found that quite funny. He was a humorist, remember, and Americans loved the book."

Where did that come from? Dreadful. Machin was appalled but tried to keep a studied composure. The man would drop twenty points in Iowa with that kind of comment.

Walton sipped his coffee. "I remember Twain also said: 'One of the proofs of immortality of the soul is that myriads have believed in it. They have also believed the world was flat."

Machin held his breath to calm his reaction. Thirty points.

Sarah's grin seemed frozen. "Is it okay to say something like that?"

"I think it's funny," Noah said, pulling his knees up to his chest.

Walton watched his children. "Me, too. I like both quotes. Let's not be so rigid that we can't see humor. Faith is personal. Not everyone shares our views and we should respect those differences. Don't be afraid to take a contrary position, on any issue, particularly at this stage in your lives. You may face some blow-back but it will help hone your beliefs." He glanced at Sarah. "Talk to me about other parts of the book."

"Well, at one point the stranger kills people with a flood," she said, "and then says he can easily make more people to replace them. That would be a godlike power."

Noah added, "And there's the old woman about to be burned at the stake for being a witch. It was horrible. She confessed even though the charge wasn't true."

"What do we learn from that?"

"That sometimes," Sarah said, "just accusing someone can destroy them and we need to be careful when we make accusations. When she was tied to the stake, someone threw an egg and hit her in the eye. People laughed. But she was innocent. It was unfair. I don't think God would do that." Her brown eyes were wide and looking for affirmation.

"I agree, Sarah. Great discussion and much to think about. Go and talk about it, take some notes and we'll discuss it again after supper." He grinned. "Now I need to chat with Mr. Machin." He gave them each a forehead kiss.

"They're great kids, Mr. President," Jake said as the twins scurried from the room. "Let me also say I'm glad there were no reporters. Voters in Kansas would not be amused."

"No such voters here. What've you got, my friend?"

"My contacts have leads on a Japanese scientist who's a close friend of Wada. He's in California and hooked up with a reporter for the *New York Times* named Daniel Duboce."

"Duboce? Yes, an interesting man. I read his last book. Very well done."

"Duboce and a scientist, Dr. Hideo Saito, are at Lake Tahoe right now having some kind of meeting with Cardinal Martinez and four members of the CCC Executive Committee: Sister Esther Andrews, James Robinson, John Broux, and Adam Wright."

Walton looked at him, not responding for some moments. "Very thorough intel," he said cautiously. "I wish we were as successful in tracking terrorists."

"These two *are* terrorists, sir, if they're linked to Wada." Machin tried to correct him gently, knowing the man liked to wander and sometimes needed to be guided back. "If Wada goes public and damages his government or ours, that plays into the hands of our enemies."

"My friend, let's keep this in perspective. We sanctioned the move to silence the discovery and avoid some destabilizing reactions."

"Your action was prudent, Mr. President. It cost us nothing."

"Yes, I know. Putting aside the potential for war, it cost nothing except suppressing an astonishing discovery, exchanging truth for social cohesion. While I've doubts on the analysis, it would still make a hell of a public discussion."

"But we need to make sure America isn't distracted in this age of terrorism."

"Yes, the discovery would be a firebomb."

"I'm working on a solution. A sometimes-colleague, Mike Michaels, is also at the meeting. He and I discussed several options if this should break into the wider media in Japan and in the U.S. We've pulled together some research that will discredit Wada."

Walton ran fingers through his silver hair. "Mark Twain said laughter was the best way to defeat the devil. Now we destroy our critics as a first line of defense rather than engage with them."

"Mr. President, we're considering one strategy perhaps worthy of Twain's quote: make the discovery a source of ridicule, and the scientist a public joke to leave him with zero credibility."

"I know who Michaels is. To be honest, I'm not a fan. Is any of this true?"

"I'm not reviewing his research at this point, just focusing on my own. My goal is to have credible sources behind anything offered up as possible fact. But I've forbidden him to use anything without our approval."

"Possible fact? Yes, please stay on top of it." His face had acquired a wistful look, rarely a good thing. "Don't you ever wish political discourse could be honest? You sat through the discussion with my kids. They're troubled about the woman accused of being a witch by her frightened and ignorant neighbors. There's no way out for her but death. Once the attack machinery does its damage, truth gets lost. Her life is over." He passed his hands over his face. "I'd like to think I can at least meet the moral standards I teach my children."

"Scruples are wonderful, sir, particularly when you're in church. We're in politics." Thank goodness, the taping of presidential conversations was long ago confined to the Oval Office.

25.

Stonehouse Lodge, Lake Tahoe

The dual French doors were grand for a lakeside cabin, each one at least nine feet tall, flanked by generous ten-pane wall panels. As Daniel came up from the side, the doors were open and, given the position of the sun, the glass seemed to have a distinct patina, the wavy look of 19th century windows, offering visual distortion, almost an Impressionist blur. He loved this kind of antique detail. Yet the dark wood looked recent but made to look antique, same with the brass hardware, new but burnished to make it old, a serious attempt at symmetry in this five-star home, a marriage of styles, something old, something new, nothing borrowed, water blue, and forced to look harmonious. It seemed to match the task at hand. Probably not a useful detail for his report.

He noticed people inside, one small enough to be a child. Crossing the threshold, Daniel stopped, disbelieving what he saw, surely just the impact of a bad sandwich, then gut punched. How was this possible?

Garrett jumped from a chair; ex-wife Trudy sat stiffly with one hand gripping the armrest, the other holding the boy's wrist. Vega stood to one side, the butterfly emerging as a wasp. The boy watched, standing rigid, his black curly hair heavily styled and gelled, a new look. Daniel told himself to control his temper over what Vega had perpetrated.

"Garrett." Daniel stepped to him, hugging the boy, pulling him tight and away from Trudy, kissing the top of his head, and received a strong embrace that quickly loosened. His son seemed hesitant.

"Hi, Dad."

"Hey, big guy." Daniel held his shoulders, grateful yet alarmed and furious that he was here. "What a surprise." He stopped himself from confronting Vega. Sort out the dangers and options first. "I've missed you."

He watched his ex-wife exchange glances with Vega. Her long black hair was pulled into a French twist under a wide-brimmed black hat, and she wore a classic pink tweed Chanel suit and pumps plus diamond earrings and bracelet. Clearly, she was doing well with her new husband and displaying it. He looked down to Garrett. Vega had just upped the ante.

"I think you've grown since I saw you two months ago," Daniel said, running his fingers affectionately through the boy's hair. "No part in your hair now. Looks good."

Garrett twisted his head, clearly annoyed. He'd always protested when his father touched his hair, part of a ritual since he was a toddler. "Oh, Dad, I hate that," he'd say and generally they would both laugh. But now he was silent, looking at him, then away.

They had always been close, almost inseparable, but the divorce had been brutal. Garret continued to be deeply unhappy, sometimes angry, willfully indifferent, clearly strained at holding so much inside. Did he feel abandoned? Daniel had no idea how to break the shell surrounding the boy's heart. His mother was key: discover a way to dissolve the shield she hid behind, part hostility toward him, perhaps embarrassment over what she'd done and arrogance about the expensive lifestyle she now flaunted that he could never provide. His presence in their son's life was a contest to her, not what was best for their son. Limiting his time with Garret was a power she held over him. Likely she had a different view. Right now, in this room, the imperative was the meaning of Garrett's presence. Clearly a threat. Vega playing tough. Or was it the cardinal?

He said, "Trudy, you're beautiful and stylish as always." She rose and moved to him like a model in *Vogue*. He shook her hand, a minimal greeting as she turned her head, expecting a kiss on the cheek which he did not provide.

He glanced at Saito, unable to speak, knowing he must be in shock as well. The scientist looked wary, watching his new lover with his ex-wife and son.

Daniel gestured toward him, finding his voice. "May I introduce Dr. Hideo Saito, a space scientist working with me on a discovery of staggering dimensions. This is Trudy, my former wife and my fabulous smart and handsome son, Garrett."

"Madam, Garrett," Saito said with a nod, winking at the boy.

Garrett grinned. Trudy seemed irritated.

He spoke his mind: "Mr. Vega? Trudy? What's going on?"

"I asked them to come," Vega said, "and made arrangements for transportation. Your son is the most important person in your life. What might happen here will impact his life and the society in which he grows to manhood."

The guy was a rapier inside a jeweled box. Now his boy would be a hostage, leverage to protect a god that likely didn't exist and posh lifestyles and egos that did. With the guards on site, they could do anything and no one would know. Blowing up a religion could be suicidal and journalists were rarely understood or admired. He had to remain cool, mask his emotions and let this play out.

"And you Trudy, I haven't seen you in over a year." Daniel struggled to sound conversational, knowing she could become easily annoyed and defensive.

"I know you're surprised. Me too." Her voice sounded more like an upper crust Eleanor Roosevelt than a California working class woman, something new, and unfortunate. "How often do you get a letter from the Vatican asking you to meet with a cardinal's personal emissary?"

26.

Dr. Steven Combs was at his desk, twisting a paper clip, waiting for his friend, Yoshito Wada.

The Search for Extra Terrestrial Intelligence Institute, founded in 1984 as a private non-profit scientific research group, scanned the universe using sophisticated signal processing technology searching for transmissions from advanced civilizations. Combs was one of a hundred SETI scientists, all convinced that given a suitable environment and enough time, life had developed elsewhere in the galaxy.

Combs was one of the most recognizable celebrities in America due to his popular PBS science series, his distinctive New England accent and his looks: tall, thin, a salt and pepper crew cut and his mustache—white, flowing and waxed, set off by large-framed black glasses with thick lenses. He was every inch the nerdy, eccentric scholar, a man obviously comfortable with himself.

He'd been surprised when he got the call from his old colleague. Internet gossip among space scientists suggested Wada had disappeared along with some of the *Misago* cargo. Some news reports hinted abduction, perhaps murder. Then he'd heard Wada's distinctive voice on the phone.

Now Combs leaped from his chair. "Yoshito! I'm so pleased the dreadful rumors are untrue." They embraced at the office door. "Come in. I'm anxious to hear details. I can't believe what you pulled off on such a miniscule budget. NASA's *OSIRIS REx* mission to Bennu cost ten times as much and didn't strike the rare earth bonanza you did. Congratulations." He walked to his old-fashioned percolator. "I know you prefer a special kind of Japanese tea. Is coffee okay?"

"Of course. Remember I spent three years at MIT."

Combs handed him a ceramic mug filled to the brim and imprinted with a faded *E.T. Call Home.*

"I have something of great interest to show you." Wada pointed to a sleek palmtop on the desk. "May I use this for demonstration purposes?"

"Please."

Wada picked it up as they both settled into leather chairs. He pulled a memory wand from his briefcase, downloaded the data, and shared the screen. Combs listened and watched intently as his friend patiently unfolded the story of *Misago* and what they had discovered in the dust.

"I'm staggered," Combs uttered afterward, standing up and then sitting back down. "This is a twofer: a brilliant scientific discovery *and* it verifies SETI credibility, a new direction for research. How the money will flow!" He smiled, then his face crumpled. "All these years we've waited for this!" He grabbed a Kleenex to wipe his eyes and leaned back in his chair. "But this is a monster."

"Perhaps monsters from the id. If I may ruminate a bit, I've been thinking about the new field of neurotheology, my friend, the idea that humans, through evolution, have found belief in a god or supernatural entities as useful in building cohesion among separate hunter gatherers, and comforting to the realities of death."

"By any chance did you see my segment on the God-gene? I think it may be relevant."

"I've been a bit preoccupied lately. Sorry. Can I have a

summary?"

Combs laughed. "Yes, I do like to talk. I'm convinced belief in god is part of our neural circuitry as part of evolution. That contention neither supports nor diminishes the view of believers or atheists. This belief in something greater than ourselves helped define early homo sapiens, communal activities for the common good, and those most wired for such a life survived in greater numbers than those who didn't. That's the basic thesis."

"I think you're correct. What's interesting is this belief circuitry helped tamp down sometimes violent tendencies, and religion for millennia has been accepted as part of life, strengthening social cohesion. *Misago* could rip that belief system and release a terror of the unknown."

"I wish I'd interviewed you for my show. Settled religious beliefs potentially exposed as fraud? Not a popular move and likely to provoke a backlash of immense proportions."

"Or create a sense of wonder."

"You're such an optimist. Monsters from the id you said. Wait, I know you love old sci-fi movies. Which one is it from?"

Wada grinned. "*Forbidden Planet* from the 1950s. Members of a human expedition on Mars being slowly murdered think it's a creature from the planet but eventually realize that a machine they discovered can dissolve our social veneer of law and religion and release the mindless beasts of the subconscious."

"Yes." Combs laughed. "A very Wada-esque analogy. It works."

Wada handed him a tiny sealed container, samples of the asteroid and an additional data wand. "Do what scientists do, my friend. If you confirm my findings, I ask that you be prepared to support me in public when the time is right."

"You know I will. I know you need allies. That's why you're here."

"Yes, allies with unimpeachable credibility who won't be intimidated by impossible odds." He'd already made a half dozen contacts and Tio had an equally long list.

"Scientists aren't very good at fighting off the politicians, especially when there's motivation to disbelieve and distort our results. Are you reaching out to diverse groups?"

"I'm starting to talk to a few colleagues but I'm not sure how many I'll get to before being discovered. Two governments are looking for me."

"You need to cast a wide net," Combs advised, leaning forward. "Include the unexpected, people or groups you anticipate opposing you. It adds credibility and media interest. There is one that might be helpful."

"You're always rich with ideas. That's one reason I came to you. I sense from American policy debates that science is not always respected here."

"Let's be honest," Combs said ruefully, "scientific evidence is often misused for political and marketing or even religious advantage. Americans can be illogical, defensive and easily conned. It has nothing to do with education or income. *Motivated reasoning* it's called and it's ingrained. We don't listen to anyone with a conflicting view. To break through, the message must come from an ally, someone trusted. But Walter Cronkite died a long time ago."

Wada shrugged, curious as always about the American mind.

"*Misago* faces more than churches." Combs spread his hands. "A virtual machine of political sycophants, conservative media, think tanks, PR firms, pollsters, booking agents, even philanthropists. Liberal church denominations may get involved since it threatens them as well. Together they can instantly mount a national campaign, overwhelming anyone without substantial resources and experience. We'll need to crack open that apparatus while reaching your allies in science."

Wada shook his head but did not look surprised. "Suggestions?"

"One think tank with possibilities—a long shot—is the Wilkins Institute in Portland. It's a major champion of teaching school children that evolution is just an unproven theory on a par with the Christian view in Genesis, ignoring, of course, contradictions in the account and all other religious perspectives. The organization was involved with championing Intelligent Design as a counter to Darwin."

Wada shrugged. "Why would a group funded by the Christian conservatives support my findings?"

"Hear me out," Combs said, pursing his lips in excitement, eyes glistening. "The top administrator and I were college friends. She's a serious academic who strategized that conservative money could help feed her family while she explored issues of interest.

She's sincere about her belief in an intelligent being creating life but less sure she believes all the official theory and how it's being applied."

Wada sipped coffee and leaned back in the chair. "A serious academic who is not thrilled at what she's doing but is practical about the world—yet yearns for respect. I understand that."

Combs pointed to Wada's chest. "Your discovery might be the answer to a prayer if I pitch it right and engage the open young woman I knew in school. The I.D. theory these days—most of the excitement has evaporated. I need to find her own self-interest in this. I can't make promises but I'll try."

Wada stood and they shook hands. "You have my cell phone number. Please be cautious. I assume NSA is scanning for key words."

"I will," Combs said, "and I'll work in secret with some of my colleagues here and then contact possible allies elsewhere."

"I knew I could count on you."

"Be careful, my friend. This could get ugly." He twisted one end of his long, waxed mustache, relishing the fight ahead.

27.

Stonehouse Lodge, Lake Tahoe

Saito, looking grim and embarrassed, his irritation mixed with worry, headed out to the beach. They'd had no time to talk.

Daniel, struggling to be upbeat, draped an arm over his son's shoulder, gave him a nudge, walking out of the room and down the boardwalk to a fern grotto midway to the dock. They sat together on a bench while Trudy stood, looking unsure what to do before he gestured toward an Adirondack chair next to them.

"How did you get here, son?" He tried to sound calm, stretching his legs taut to stop the quiver in his knees.

Garrett was cautious but Daniel sensed a repressed exuberance. "Mr. Vega has this awesome private jet. We flew at nearly the speed of sound. A limo met us in Reno and we drove up here." A year ago, he would have been jumping up and laughing. Now he acted as if he shouldn't enjoy himself or couldn't. What'd happened to him?

"Start at the beginning. How were you contacted? What did they tell you?" He glanced at his ex-wife hoping she would understand their predicament and drop the emotional baggage. There was no time for that. Their son was at risk.

"Honey, um, Daniel, it happened really fast," she said, the annoying fake accent still there. "I received a letter from Cardinal Martinez, hand delivered by a priest from the LA diocese who waited for a response. It asked if I'd meet with his representative to discuss an issue important to Catholics everywhere but not yet public."

She twisted her diamond encrusted wedding ring, flashing a rainbow in the sunlight before folding her hands in her lap. "He said it concerned someone I was once close to. It had to be you. The letter offered to treat everything in confidence and asked me to do the same. I was surprised but intrigued. The priest suggested a time that afternoon. Mr. Vega showed up at my door."

"Then what?"

"It was just the three of us. Mr. Vega said he believed you were in possession of material that could significantly impact public confidence in the Bible." She stopped, appraising him, pinching her lips.

"Please, Trudy, go on."

She gave a convoluted description of the discovery. Vega had been clever. Precise, but skirting key facts, giving a false impression that focused on fear.

"He said you were undecided about what to do with material the Japanese scientist gave you," she continued. "He hoped we would meet with you and help you reach the right decision."

Daniel waited for her to continue but she was quiet. "And that would be?"

"That would be turning the material over to him," she said dismissively, as if it were the only option, "and agreeing to say nothing about this to anyone. He believes you want to be helpful but are torn because of your friendship with the scientist."

"And you, Garrett? What do you think?"

His son's expression seemed conflicted. The question was unfair. He was just a boy. How would he make any sense of this?

"Dad, I think the church is a friend to most people. I know you've been angry about what it did to our family." His voice caught and he glanced away. "I've some issues too, but I don't think we should do anything to hurt it. Mom likes it."

As he spoke, Daniel realized how much Garrett had matured. He was beginning to sound like a young man. Anger at the church and the breakup of their family was still close to the surface for both. Who knew what Trudy had done to sour the relationship?

"Mr. Vega said my feelings were important to you, Dad. Is that true?" He sounded vulnerable.

"Nothing matters more." He squeezed Garrett's shoulder and looked at him just as the boy glanced down.

"Let me tell you both what this is about," he said emphatically. "You're both adults for this conversation. Draw your own conclusions. Dr. Saito and I had an animated discussion with the ministers yesterday. It wasn't friendly. They're afraid and, honestly, I am too. They see truth as the wrong choice for a complex mix of reasons and I see it as the only path but recognize the...volatility."

Garrett offered a fleeting, enigmatic grin before returning his gaze to the forest.

"Here are the bare bones." As Daniel talked, his son seemed transfixed, listening intently, though trying not to show it, only his eyebrows shifting. Daniel hoped he was reading him right. Trudy just watched.

"So, it's like making life where there wasn't any life, from scratch!" Garrett interrupted. "Asteroids from beyond the solar system. Wow!"

"Exactly." Daniel beamed at this burst of enthusiasm.

"Stellar." The boy looked genuinely excited. "So, why's the church so concerned?"

"It's a big problem for Catholics, fundamentalist Christians and other religions because it doesn't jibe with their view of creation or the divinity of a God who made humans in his own image." He continued giving details.

Garrett nodded, mulling it over. Trudy was quiet, staring at the massive diamond in the center of her ring.

"So, what Dr. Wada found may profoundly change the way we think about life—and about God. Sound crazy?"

"Yes," Garrett said. "I have to think."

Trudy tightened her lips as they looked at each other, not as the antagonists they had become, nor the lovers they used to be, but like two people trying to reconnect. He needed to be honest if they were to understand the risk.

"I was brought here because I have something they desperately want. After the president reached an agreement with Japan to hide the discovery, Dr. Wada disappeared. But he gave materials to Saito and he brought them to me. I have them in hiding while I put together a newspaper series that I hope to publish."

"You really have the stuff?" Garrett looked surprised—and impressed.

"Yes."

"Cool." The grin returned and stayed longer.

"Many will attack *Misago* from all sides. This kind of religious conflict can lead to war, terrorism, the most awful and senseless kinds of violence. As you know, the Kingdom Christians control many of the power levers in this country. The federal government is conspiring to keep it secret and will of course use its power to protect the president. The FBI is involved. Stories I've seen on the web say the agency is looking for Wada, dead or alive, prisoner or free agent."

Both Garrett and Trudy looked truly shocked. The boy's eyes widened: "Do you know where he is?"

"No. I believe the government is wrong and the men in the great stone lodge in this forest are wrong. But I know there could be bloodshed if this goes public. So, what do I do? Tell me."

Garrett rubbed his face, his voice strained. "Dad, will you be okay?" He put a hand on his father's arm.

"Daniel, I had no idea," Trudy said, her voice quiet, a slight quiver noticeable. "I can hardly believe this is real. So, it actually happened?" She now seemed to understand the danger and sounded less theatrical.

"Yes, Trudy, it did." He wrapped Garrett in a hug. His comment to Saito about the threat to his family two days ago was no longer abstract.

They sat in silence before Garrett pulled away, looking back and forth between them as if making a judgment. He leaned forward on the bench, his elbows on his knees as he rubbed his face. Daniel put a hand behind his son's neck, massaging it gently, hoping it was reassuring. It was for him. The boy didn't push him away.

"I don't want to bring you shame," Daniel continued, softly. "Truth doesn't always prevail over a determined and well-financed opponent with an army at its disposal. We're talking about disproving a central tenant in three major religions. As a journalist, I believe in telling the public the truth about important events. I suspect it will get out even if I do nothing, but perhaps not in the way I could shape it, an honest telling, at least honest to me, as I perceive the truth of it. This isn't just about a lone reporter." He didn't want to overwhelm them but needed to make it clear.

"Even if the *Times* and the *Beacon* publish the story, they may not be strong enough to withstand the onslaught, the political hurricane. It could be wildly emotional, even violent, with religious leaders seeking to frighten their congregations. Major churches are massive business operations and will mobilize their full resources to survive. Boycotts would be the least of their worries. The government could threaten advertisers with loss of government contracts if they support either newspaper. It could even be worse. The FBI and other government agencies and Christian militias could shut it all down, take people into custody in the name of national security."

He wanted to raise the threats in a way that would challenge their understanding. Garrett could understand, he was confident, and hopefully also his ex, a good person if afflicted with a money tooth. "What do I do?" he asked. "How high a price can anyone pay for this kind of honesty in today's twisted version of democracy and a free press?"

Trudy looked paralyzed before offering a tiny nod, a swallow and slight opening of her mouth, silence conveying understanding, the façade defrosting. For her, this was now far more than a beach trip or a chance to diminish him.

"Dad, you should tell the truth." His voice had a righteous

tone, the confidence of boyhood, that the good guy wins, before reality teaches otherwise. "That's what you always told me and I'll love you no matter what." His voice broke. "You're my dad."

Garrett reached out, pressing his forehead to his dad's shoulder.

Daniel embraced him, swallowed, eyes welling, looking into the woods. Was this the breakthrough to rekindle the love of a son? All riding on the back of granules from an asteroid, questions about the legitimacy of faith, and men with righteous certainty. And guns.

28.

Stonehouse Lodge, Lake Tahoe

"UPS package for Dr. Saito."

The group was standing in the dining room finishing an early dinner, saying goodnights, when Ealga stepped forward, adjusted her lace cap and made the announcement.

"What?" Broux snapped. "A package, here, for him? Here? *Here?*"

"Yes Mr. Minister," she said, walking over to the startled scientist. "Just delivered."

"Thank you, Ealga," Saito said with a nod and smile. He'd been talking with her privately, trying to kindle a relationship. They might need secret allies.

"How did someone else know?" Wright asked to no one in particular.

Saito examined the label. "From Sacramento," he whispered, almost breathless, forcing people to tighten the circle around him, looking over shoulders, adding to the mystery and the obvious discomfiture of the ministers. He removed the brown wrapping, handing it to Broux who seemed flummoxed as he took it, glancing at the address before passing it over to Wright who promptly dropped it to the floor. Inside the box was a small package covered in gold foil, tied with a red cord. He lifted it out, handing the shipping carton to Robinson who ran his fingers through the Styrofoam bits.

"Open the damn thing!" Broux barked in frustration.

Saito removed the lid and a piece of cotton. He lifted out an ivory carving and held it in his open palm. It was about two inches long, an inch wide and just under an inch in height. It was part turtle, part dragon. It had fierce eyes and a double set of horns on each side, an extraordinary piece of ancient Japanese art.

"Cool monster," Garrett said.

"Yeah, really amazing," Rolph added, standing next to him.

Saito clutched the carving in his fist and grinned. "Thank you for another lovely dinner," he said heading to the double doors, exiting into the garden, trailed by Garrett, Rolph, Trudy and Daniel.

"Saito, what is it?" Daniel whispered, hearing ministers baying in the distance.

"Didn't you see it? It's a little carved beast with the face of a devil. Who knew he was here?"

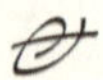

"What's it mean?" Daniel turned the ivory carving around in his hand. They were alone in their suite. Trudy had proclaimed exhaustion as they had left the dinner hall and took an upset Garrett with her to their cabin next door. Rolph looked dejected at being abandoned by his new friend, and said he should get back to his father.

"No one knows we're here," Daniel said. "What does it mean to you?" He handed it back and Saito held it in his open palm.

"It's a mythical eighteenth-century beast. I believe the dragon represents courage and the power of heaven. The turtle traditionally is the messenger. A message from heaven."

"Why delivered here?"

"Daniel, it's from Yoshito! From his family netsuke collection, one of his favorites. *He is safe!* At least he was when he sent this. He knows where we are."

He set the carving on the table.

"How does he know that?"

Saito hesitated. "He's monitoring me on an enhanced satellite GPS tracker in my suitcase that gives him exact coordinates over a wide area."

"What?" Daniel scooted forward on the couch. "I thought you didn't know what happened to him."

"I did not, do not," he declared. "I knew he planned to come to California. I called him twice on a designated phone but got no response and was afraid to try again. He told me if he suspected a device was compromised he'd destroy it. He had several phones."

"You had plans with Wada beyond what you told me? He's tracking you—us?"

"Daniel, there is something you need to know."

"Yes, I suspect so," he said acidly.

"Please sit next to me."

He did as asked, feeling pissed.

"Okay," the scientist said, "I hope we can trust Vega's promise on not eavesdropping." He looked around before continuing as if he could somehow see listening devices.

"Yoshito and Dr. Ito need to make personal contact with their network of space scientists. Many are old friends, several in California. If he stayed in Japan he would likely be arrested and have no leverage to change the decision. The plan was that while he got in touch with his old network, and Tio made her contacts, I would bring materials to you so the story could hopefully, when the time was right, appear in the *Times*. We assumed family and a wide circle of friends might be monitored if it was a high enough priority. If they were looking hard enough, we wanted them to discover me. That's why I was so insistent on hiding the materials until we could be certain."

"So that's how Vega found us. Your calls to me were like a flare."

"Yes. That seems an accurate characterization. Yoshito admires you as does Dr. Ito. They're depending on you. Wada needed help he couldn't ask for in advance."

Daniel stared at the floor. "You used me as a decoy. The sex, the seduction…was it part of the strategy?"

"No, Daniel. I really care for you. It felt right. We've shared much the last few days. I have deep feelings for you, admire you and want to be with you."

"Then why do I feel like a fool?"

"Please. Enough!" His tone was sharp.

Daniel could see irritation in Saito's eyes. But he was the one being played.

"Get over it!" Saito commanded. "Don't start feeling sorry for yourself. We have no time for bruised egos. The sex was hot. We weren't faking it. I sure wasn't. Wanting seconds and thirds did provide scientific evidence that you enjoyed it. Of course your groans, a couple of screams, gripping the sheets, grabbing my…."

"Stop it!" He was quiet, looking at Saito, the netsuke, back again. Think. With his brain, not his ego. His co-conspirator was right, the issues were too big to let personal feelings intrude. Saito should have told him at the beginning but if he had admitted it was a ruse would he have gotten involved? Probably not. That would have been an added layer of improbability. The sex was brawny, maybe even incandescent, the best he'd ever had or hoped for.

Saito kissed his cheek before nibbling his earlobe. Daniel laughed, ready to turn the page, and wrapped his arms around him. Saito was special, this new and stimulating conversation could wait. Their lips pressed together, tongues exploring.

There was an exuberant knock at the door. They looked at each other and shrugged; Saito answered.

"Hi, Dad, Dr. Saito," Garrett said, rolling a small travel case as he entered. "Mom said I should stay here tonight. Is that okay?"

29.

Wilkins Institute, Portland, Oregon

Sitting at her computer in the Spanto Telecom Tower, Elizabeth Cleaver watched a spider build a web outside her window before checking her email. As head of the Wilkins Institute, she felt like a fading celebrity. She had succeeded in being one of the key leaders on Intelligent Design and other Christian messages designed to undercut any science that opposed Scripture, but the glory days seemed past. No media calls in weeks and, the ultimate pain and humiliation, she'd been skewered in her last public talk to a supposedly safe audience by an old woman wearing a Ma Clampett flowered hat.

As she opened her computer, she noticed a message from Steven Combs of the SETI Institute. Their paths had diverged after she became active in the Christian movement. Combs had once teased, "I remain a man of science, committed to Enlightenment principles of reason over faith." In response, she had playfully poured a glass of milk over his head. Afterward they went out and got drunk.

He looked back at the computer screen. The subject line read: *"I hear music."*

Elizabeth jumped back in her chair and with a trembling hand, opened the document.

"Le Sacre du Printemps (The Rite of Spring)."

That was the entire message. She stretched her arms, reaching behind her neck as she felt a quiver. Steven liked riddles. Something big had happened. It would impact her world and would not be a pretty melody.

She googled *"Le Sacre du Printemps,"* remembering to breathe. She clicked on a music history site:

"The Rite of Spring was a controversial piece of music by the Russian composer Igor Stravinsky. When it debuted in Paris in 1913, it set off a riot in the concert hall. It was music that rejected the lush romantic melodies of the past in favor of loud, angular, dissonant, atonal noise, as some heard it. Audience members hissed. There were fistfights and police were needed to restore order. It startled audiences and deeply offended the musical tastes of the time even as it also launched a new form of music that future audiences would eventually come to appreciate."

Grinning, anticipation conjuring wild images, Elizabeth dialed her friend in California. "I got your email," she blurted as Steven answered on the first ring. "What does it mean? What have you found? Is it what I think it is?"

"It may be all that you imagine, all that I imagine, and more," Steven answered, pleased and cocky. "But we're on the early end of this. It's wrapped in complications and requires complete secrecy."

"What, what? *Tell me!*"

"I can't tell you on the phone. Can you come here today?"

"You're a pain in the butt! I'll leave tonight and text with details. What about Stravinsky?"

"This is music never heard before, never dreamed of, never imagined, music from the static of space. I believe truth to be something we both strive to achieve, my freaky friend, beyond the needs of our daily employment. I ask you to leave all that in

Portland and come here in the spirit of exploration."

'How can you tease me like this? Remember, I know your secrets."

"I'm sorry I have to be so nebulous. I admit to sounding like a jerk. You'll understand when we talk. Stay at my place and please, say nothing to anyone. I look forward to your visit."

30.

Stonehouse Lodge, Lake Tahoe

Dinner was grilled lake trout, vegetables, and endless talk about the ride several had in the cardinal's fully restored twenty-foot Chris Craft. Built in 1930 and powered by a 135 horsepower Chrysler engine it was very fast. "It was named Resurrection," the cardinal bragged, "literally raised from the dead many years ago when I was living in Los Angeles." He said he worked with mechanics and carpenters. Obviously, the man took great pride in the boat and his role in restoring it. Daniel had seen it, admired the beauty and watched the ministers get in it. He helped push them off, pleased he and Saito might have some private time.

As coffee was served, two figures in gardener's hats entered from the kitchen. One stepped forward a few feet from the table and removed his hat, setting it on an empty chair. He waited, lifting a cane against his chest.

Daniel glanced in his direction. *"My GOD!"* he yelled, jumping to his feet.

"YOSHITO!" Saito hollered as he leaped up pushing over his

rustic wooden chair.

"What's going on?" Robinson jumped to his feet, knocking his glass, plate, silverware, and a vase to the floor. Others bellowed, a cacophony as seats scraped the floor.

Daniel raced around the table to Wada and embraced him with a whoop, stepping back as Saito pushed in for his turn.

Tio stepped forward, removing her floppy hat with a theatrical flourish and bowed.

"You're here too!" Saito shouted and hugged his friend.

A guard stepped into the room, pulling his baton from his belt carrier.

"Behind you," Wada warned.

Daniel spun around and instinctively crouched.

The guard took two steps forward, trying to make sense of what he saw.

"Eci!" Vega's voice was loud and harsh. The soldier looked at him, nodded and backed out of the room.

Daniel reached over to his son, who was standing nearby, and pulled him toward their new arrival. "Garrett, this is Dr. Wada. The scientist you've heard about. This is another remarkable space scientist and a friend, Dr. Tio Ito."

"I am honored to meet you," she said in perfect English, slipping off a burlap over-shirt to reveal a stylish blue blouse, black vest, a silver and red bead choker, gray jeans and high boots.

Not exactly lakeside attire, and Daniel grinned, loving her sassy spirit, extending his hand. Tio surprised him, stepping past it, embracing him in a bear hug, a kiss to each cheek.

"Always stylish, Madam Scientist," Daniel whispered affectionately.

Everyone was standing, silent, jaws agape. Vega, the only one sitting, looked amused.

These are the holy men, Wada thought, looking at those staring at him. Probably no more than thirty seconds had passed. The surprise seemed to have worked.

"How did you find us?" The voices overlapped. *"Why are you here?"*

Wada leaned on his cane. "All your questions will be answered in time." He maintained a collegial, friendly tone. "Let us wind back the clock a few moments. The beginning is usually a good place to start. I am Dr. Yoshito Wada, Director of the *Misago* space program at the Japanese Space Agency. This is Dr. Tio Ito, one of the world's great astrophysicists and a JAXA colleague." He addressed the open-mouthed audience. "To whom am I speaking?"

There was silence until Wright rose. "Let me start as the chairman of the board. Welcome to Stonehouse Lodge, Dr. Wada, Dr. Ito. I'm Reverend Adam Wright, a radio minister and teacher of the Gospel. This is my son, Rolph."

Wada stepped forward, leaning over the table and shook the teenager's hand. "Lovely meeting you." The boy looked embarrassed.

Wright continued: "Let me ask each of us here to identify themselves and the groups we represent. Surely, we owe you that."

The clergy, words coming slow, defiance masking unease, gave their names and affiliations.

"An eminent group," Wada responded, crossing his arms, holding the silver handled cane horizontal in one hand. "First, how did I find you? Dr. Saito and I share a global positioning system satellite device. Finding you was simply a matter of following his GPS data."

Several exchanged rueful glances.

"You ask, why am I here?" Stepping closer to the table, he spoke in his slightly accented but perfect English. "This is my second trip to America in just a few weeks. On the first one, I met your president and gave him our early findings. This time I wanted to meet those who had the power to get an American president to threaten and bribe my prime minister and quash a major scientific discovery."

He focused on the cardinal. "Men so powerful and confident in the rightness of their cause are leaders I wanted to meet and understand. Human motivation is complex. Is it self-interest that propels you or some truth that I as a scientist do not yet comprehend? The pursuit of nature and its secrets are what my life has been about. This is a new mystery I want to investigate."

"I'm curious," Broux said with a derisive snarl, "about the sudden convergence of all of us here, as if it's some kind of grand scheme. You obviously planned this surprise visit in advance to gain some advantage. Dr. Saito and Mr. Duboce are some kind of decoys in your strategy?"

"I'm surprised at your imagination, sir. When I left Japan, I had no idea this kind of meeting would happen. I suspect you had little notice yourself. I'm in hiding because exposing my whereabouts does not seem strategic," Wada said. "Daniel is an honest man, and I believe one of the few who can understand the dimensions of the discovery—the science, the theology, the politics. Dr. Saito has been working privately with me, an ally. As for my exit from my homeland, Reverend, I'm a prudent man and acted as you yourself might if the situations were reversed. Our gathering here is unexpected but an opportunity to explore our mutual issues."

Wada stepped to the head of the table, looking at the ministers, resting his hands on the back of a chair. Some stared back, others looked away. He noticed Daniel smiling, leaning back in a chair next to his son, Tio and Saito on either side in complete understanding that this was a useful stage.

"The scientific discovery you seek to hide is mine. I led the *Misago* project. The Japanese people will someday take great pride in what their countrymen have done." He smiled, standing in the light from the wrought iron chandelier overhead. A blond dandy was feverishly taking notes. Must be the PR guy.

"Daniel, I assume the group has been told about the material Dr. Saito brought you?" Wada watched the woman preacher go rigid, clench her teeth, sticking out her lower lip. She would take some work; but never assume hopelessness.

"So, it's true?" Martinez asked. "You confirm what Mr. Duboce and Dr. Saito told us earlier?"

"I'm not sure what they said since I've not had a chance to talk to them. But some days ago, I asked Dr. Saito to be prepared to bring materials to this country believing it would be easier for him to get them out of Japan. He gave them to Mr. Duboce. Back to my question, Daniel, did you brief this committee?"

"Yes, I did, yesterday. Mr. Vega gave an overview to the group some time back on a Skype conference call. I added what new information I had. But Saito told me privately that there is more."

The group stirred again but remained quiet.

Wada picked up an elegant green crystal glass and filled it with water from a matching pitcher. He drank slowly.

"Yes," he said, pleased that the audience looked appropriately anxious. "There is much you don't yet understand and, indeed, this process is in its infancy. I invite you to think about this tonight: What if you are successful in blocking this? What of other discoveries to come? Will you always win? Will the Japanese government always be compliant? Indeed, it is my belief that there will be many other findings, some in space but others here on Earth. They'll not be limited to Japan. These granules have likely been coming to Earth for billions of years. But, we never knew we should be looking for them or dreamed of their existence. Now we do."

Wada watched the expressions of concern. "This will be an excellent topic for discussion tomorrow, if that's acceptable."

"Some of us would be interested in hearing more now if you're agreeable," Wright said, clearly not wanting to wait.

"I agree," said Robinson.

"Don't try to intimidate us!" Broux snapped with a hiss. "Just tell us what ya know. You're the one who had to sneak into this country and hide from police. You're hardly in a power position."

Wada looked at the man, smiled and spoke in an intimate and friendly cadence, at least that was his goal. The corners of his eyes crinkled. "I seek to intimidate no one, Reverend. I'm an old man, tired from the trip and would simply prefer to catch up on my sleep, gather my thoughts and talk tomorrow. You should be rested as well. Our topic and the consequences are enormous to us all. I assume I have access to a computer and, hopefully, a large display screen?"

"Yes, we have that and it'll be waiting," Wright said, sounding dejected.

"Excellent," Wada said. "I would like to retire now as a guest and not someone hiding as a gardener. Dr. Ito as well."

"Of course," the cardinal said, graciously. "We have empty cabins and would be delighted to have you both here as honored visitors."

Wada bowed slightly. "We perhaps see the world quite differently in some respects. I'm a scientist but I am also a participant in the culture and pageantry of two great non-western religions: Buddhism and Shintoism. While these have no association with Jesus they do marvel at the wonder and magic of the world. I respect your beliefs and hope you'll give me the same courtesy."

He rested his cane on the tabletop, waiting to see if anyone wanted to respond before continuing. "I believe we need to understand each other given the dimensions of what is at hand. Forces have been unleashed on both sides. I suspect what you will hear from me will discomfit you. Assimilating new facts can be unpleasant, shocking, maddening, if we don't like the message. But what is the alternative? Of course, I hope to learn from you."

Michaels used his stylus with surprising speed and noise. Wada was quiet. The PR man looked up, perhaps sensing trouble, and found Wada staring at him. The scientist shook his head. A chastened schoolboy, Michaels put down his pen. Vega watched the silent exchange and his smile widened when his eyes connected with Wada.

The scientist looked back to the group. "To stimulate our thinking for tomorrow, I offer something outside our mutual comfort zones, yours and mine, a brainteaser:

'Not only does God play dice, but... he sometimes throws them where they cannot be seen.' Stephen Hawking, the late great physicist, and an atheist, gets credit for that insight. He was responding to a reporter's question and making fun of Albert Einstein. Not many can do that."

Wada donned his most grandfatherly expression and assumed a non-judgmental tone. "Having faith means you don't require proof, and, frankly, that is fragile to someone like me, a scientist, who deals with the physical world and not speculation on the unprovable. But what if ultimately all things are provable? Might religion and science, working together, move us into a post-faith world? Do you want to be part of that kind of exploration about the nature of God and the universe? Gentlemen, I look forward to our conversation tomorrow."

He walked around the side of the table and shook hands with each person, making small talk like a good politician, wishing them good night, Tio right behind him, doing the same.

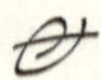

Georgetown, Washington, D.C.

Later that evening, Sister Esther kept her cell phone conversation short. "General, the missing Japanese space scientist is no longer missing. Wada is at the cardinal's retreat on the east shore of Tahoe. He has another scientist with him."

"I'll have agents sent immediately and arrest him."

"Not a good idea, Beau. It'll piss off the cardinal who's made him a guest. But more than that, there's a squad of armed guards here, rifles and pistols, all dressed in black like commandos, apparently working for him. The last thing we want is a shoot-out. The scientist promised to divulge more secrets tomorrow. It'd be premature to act. I'll keep you informed but be alert."

He'd do what he damned well pleased, but he said, "I'll fly to the coast and be waiting." Beauregard remembered the man when he briefed the president. All nonsense, of course, another arrogant atheist scientist telling him his faith was wrong. But as the Director of National Intelligence, the general knew this was a security risk. He rubbed a thumb up the large bumpy scar that ran from his right ear to his chin, a souvenir from a secret operation that won him the Congressional Medal of Honor.

His gaze drifted elsewhere, as it often did when he was reliving the glory, pain and justice, the highlight of his life, stitched to his sleeve. The story had been told in one Hollywood movie and the general's war exploits were made into a cable series. A little over the top but useful for his greater purpose.

Now he would defeat this new enemy his way. The devil take Sister Esther.

31.

Stonehouse Lodge, Lake Tahoe

The three scientists and Daniel sat cross legged on the floor around a small coffee table finishing their morning meal; Garrett was asleep in his father's room. "Perhaps we can have the conversation we didn't really have last night," Daniel suggested.

"Let me apologize again," Wada said, "for not letting you know in advance of my plans and seeking your support. It was impossible because events in Japan moved quickly. My situation was precarious. I'd prepared materials and, with Tio and Saito's help, was able to make my escape. My tracking app suggested my line dedicated to Saito was compromised so I disposed of it on the back of a passing garbage truck. Dr. Ito joined me yesterday."

"Understood," Daniel said, ready to move on. "So where have you been?" He wanted what Saito told him confirmed.

"I've been networking, as you Americans say. So has Tio. There is an international community of space scientists, informal, but still there. I briefed several who in turn will reach out further. She has done the same. Initially I assumed the FBI would be looking for me and was hoping Saito might prove a distraction, and this man Vega was a gifted sleuth."

"So?" Daniel asked with a sense of adventure. "Are there multiple sets of materials you brought?"

"Yes. In case I was caught or she was. I wanted to have additional material exported. Tio carried six sets. I carried ten."

A guard paused in front of the window. He looked straight at them before disappearing.

"I assume they're loyal to the cardinal," Daniel said, "although Vega gave the order for that guard to leave last night and the man instantly obeyed. It's odd. For now, they're not sure of our intentions. Best to keep it that way."

"The cardinal is shrewd," Wada responded. "I want to understand him better but we must be bold to succeed and there are risks. Tio and Saito volunteered to help." He pointed with his fork as he finished the last bite of apple fritter. "But Daniel, you were hijacked. You certainly have the right to withdraw."

"No. I'm a journalist. The *Times* and *Beacon* want this story and I'm now part of it. I'll play my role. But tell me, how did you persuade the Japanese press that you'd been kidnapped?"

Tio covered her mouth as she laughed. Wada turned to her, gesturing her to speak. "I disabled video monitors and rifled through Dr. Wada's office at JAXA," she said, "making it obvious there was an intrusion, and he had a trusted neighbor trash his homework area in Takayama. The man notified police and later disclosed he witnessed from a distance what might have been Yoshito's abduction."

"And your role at JAXA after Yoshito left?" Daniel asked.

"I left two days later. Certain members of our *Misago* crew continued doing key research in private and I wanted to make certain they could succeed at least for a few days or weeks. They made progress until guards were brought in to keep them out even at night. I used a fake passport and credit card provided by Yoshito, making various contacts with old friends and colleagues and met with him near the Tahoe Airport."

"Like synchronized swimming." Daniel looked at his watch. "We meet with the ministers in less than two hours. They were clearly shaken by the meeting last night. Vega is a big question mark. I'm not sure where he stands. I know it's crazy, but I'm pulled to him. He's a man of secrets but I sense integrity at his core world view."

Wada shrugged and walked to the cart. "They're most accommodating. Coffee and matcha. Not quite up to the Emperor's standard, based on the intensity of the color and bouquet, but close enough. There is even something here…" He held up a steel whisk and looked puzzled. "I assume this is supposed to replace bamboo." He shook his head. "It'll make it froth. Any orders?"

Tio and Saito spoke as one: *"Matcha!"*

"Okay," Daniel said with a laugh, "I'll take the full nasty tasting octane. I may need it."

32.

Stonehouse Lodge, Lake Tahoe

The clergy, along with Michaels and Vega, waited. An unaccustomed and discomfiting experience for the powerful, like schoolboys waiting for the headmaster.

The meeting was set to begin at eleven a.m. Fifteen minutes later, Daniel walked in with Garrett who was not invited. All part of the plan.

The ministers seemed surprised but welcomed the boy. He responded politely, "Thank you, sir, good morning to you too." Trudy, also not invited, entered a minute later, followed by Tio, Saito and Wada, who carried a leather file case under his arm. It was decided that Tio would work with Wada on the presentation, in the belief a female foreigner might further add to their discomfort. Adding to that, she was beautiful, stylish, brilliant, and outspoken. So, perfect. Daniel put his notebook on the table and took out a pen while Saito set a note pad at the top edge with an elegant black pen clipped to the handle.

Wada stood before the group wearing a black turtleneck sweater and pants, his long silver hair pulled back behind his head and tied with his trademark black cord and jade orca. "Madams and gentlemen," he said, sounding energetic and upbeat, "should I begin or are there other considerations that need to precede my presentation?"

"Dr. Wada," Wright stated, "please go ahead. We're anxious to hear what you have to say."

Wada handed a memory wand to Michaels as if he were a staff assistant rather than an arrogant PR powerhouse. "Please download," the scientist asked politely.

Michaels looked irritated, then confused, just staring at the blue tube, obviously unsure what to do.

"Here," Tio said, nudging Michaels aside "Let me." She entered instructions on the keyboard and brought up an artist's drawing of the solar system on the large screen, including the asteroid belt, circles marking the locations of all three asteroids, *Itokawa*, *Ryugu* and *Geographos*.

"Let us make certain we're all at the same starting point," Wada said, suppressing a smile. "The three JAXA missions targeting three asteroids had different goals. The first dealt mostly with testing new systems, autonomous navigation, robotic landing, and retrieval. The second was a more ambitious journey, blasting away part of the surface and certainly testing the upgrades in our technology. The third was about finding and laying claim to wealth and beginning serious extraction of rare earth elements. A mining operation. I was interested in pure science and my prime minister was interested in return on investment. It worked for both of us."

Wada highlighted a series of photos of the asteroids taken by the three spacecraft. He pointed to the screen as he talked, much like a teacher before his class. "Notice on the first asteroid, Itokawa has two main sections—a body and a head, according to one of my imaginative staff members. Another colleague thought it looked like a crystalline sea otter. See, this is the head."

Wright twisted his head as he looked. "Yes, I see it."

"Me too," Garrett added in high-pitched counterpoint.

Wada smiled warmly. Daniel tilted his head and scratched his chin, a prearranged signal in case the scientist got too technical.

"But enough about asteroid topography. What did we find?"

He let his words hang in the air. The ministers leaned forward. Damn he's good, Daniel thought and squeezed Garrett's shoulder. His son covered one hand with an open palm and gave him a secret thumbs up as Wada continued.

"A key scientist in the early *Hayabusa* probes, a genius contrarian in my opinion, died two years ago and left me a personal diary that hinted at something mysterious—if I used some counterrational steps, doing things that scientists in their wisdom and hubris contend will not work. It took me several months to decipher his code that hid the real message. He knew I loved detective novels, as did he."

The Jules Verne-worthy research scheme made this irresistible, at least to Daniel.

"We experimented in private at first," Tio said, picking up the story. "We were shocked when his hypotheses proved accurate. After *Misago* returned from *Georgraphos,* I compared samples from all three." She stood and made eye contact, hoping to spread more discomfort. "Yoshito only shared a small portion of the findings with President Walton. Most of the granules we retrieved were made of what we expected to find, the raw stuff of planet formation. But of the millions of microscopic granules retrieved from this asteroid, many were not what any mainstream scientist would expect."

With an amused schoolboy look, Wada pushed another key and a graph appeared showing four spacecraft: the American Eagle capsule on the Moon; Stardust, an early NASA project; China's *Chang'e 5* and the *Misago* module. "Let me also state that only a few times in human history has our species sent humans or spacecraft into the solar system and successfully brought back samples of what's out there. The Moon being the first target with multiple trips starting in the late 1960s."

He gestured to the screen and turned back to his audience. "NASA's *Stardust* flew through the tail of a comet and brought back its samples in 2004, a monumental early achievement. Two years later the first reports suggested major changes in how we think the solar system was formed. For brevity, I am only highlighting a few points. The next images are JAXA projects."

Daniel was pleased. Wada had everyone staring intently at the screen, not an easy feat with this group.

Tio put up a photo taken by the probes as they neared each asteroid for landing. "Do we fear or rejoice at new discoveries? *'Men occasionally stumble over the truth,'* a man once said. *'but most of them pick themselves up and hurry off as if nothing had happened.'* So which path will you take? The man, by the way, was Winston Churchill. As we go forward," she said, "as more countries and private companies get involved in space science, other samples will be brought back. The Astronomical Society of the Pacific has suggested that a modified vehicle and crew could take off from the International Space Station and rendezvous with a NEA— this stands for Near Earth Asteroid—in just a few months. Think what they might bring back. Prospectors in space suits with cargo storage far greater then *Misago.* Several billionaires are organizing such flights now."

The scientist paused, giving them time to consider the implications. She gestured to Wada.

"Thank you, Dr. Ito." He clicked to another photo. "I suspect you've all seen pictures like this. A scanning electron microscope image of an ant, magnified hundreds of thousands of times. I thought I might start here as a way to ease into a discussion of what we found."

Wada next brought up a photo of crystalline granules. "Here are photos also taken with the aid of an electron microscope. These are what we expected to find, various minerals in different crystalline shapes. This is nature. Our astronomical observations using light and x-rays told us what to expect and we were not surprised. But then we came across something most unexpected."

The crystal morphed into a photo of a cube. "This is a shape rarely if ever found in nature. Indeed, it is not natural. It's the size of a virus, invisible to the naked eye and here viewable only with the aid of a specialized microscope. This is many thousands of times smaller than the ant we just viewed."

Next came a group of cubes. "Here are others, all exactly the same precision cubes. Again, impossible in nature. Yet here it is, as Tio likes to say."

He glanced at her as he slowly turned away from the screen and looked at the audience. "One standard research methodology is to slice samples into exquisitely thin pieces and study them individually. But at first, we couldn't cut them using standard techniques. The surface was impervious. Again, impossible. Yet—there it was. With trial and error, we were eventually able to breach the hard outer-shell of the microscopic cubes. I'll be pleased to offer greater details to anyone who wants this."

Tio touched a key. Up came a view of a single cube, hovering and tumbling slowly on the screen. "We call this a nano cube, for want of a better term. As Yoshito said, it's the size of a virus. There are actually two shells. An inner one, made of protein, is not unlike what you might find in a virus. This is the catalyst. Around it is a second protective material, what you are looking at here. We're not sure what it's made from, only that it's impervious to everything except one set of chemicals."

She enlarged the image on the screen as the cube continued to slowly tumble. "Here we are with the outer shell and then we remove it electronically." She rotated the inside view. "Inside this first cube is what we would expect to find in nature—RNA and protein. There were also at least two elements as yet unidentified. I will get back to this in a minute."

Wada took a drink of water and let them look at the picture. He'd told Daniel earlier that his challenge was helping this non-scientifically trained and maybe science-phobic audience understand a complex discovery. Daniel thought he was doing very well.

"In nature," Wada said, "a virus is protected by this protein coat and it keeps it safe, up to a point, until it can find its intended host. If it's a flu virus and someone with the flu brushed their nose and leaves some mucus on a park bench, it will remain there for some time, viable for the right use, and waiting for the right host."

He turned back to the screen. "In looking at what we have inside the nano cube—if we ignore for the time being the unidentified elements—the rest in many ways seems like a naturally occurring set of chemical elements wrapped in some special quite unnatural shell that can protect them from space, apparently for billions of years, until it finds the right host. In space, extreme heat, cold and radiation can be deadly. This artificial shell seems to work well against these elements. Indeed, if we can someday determine the composition, it may have applications for space travel by humans."

Dr. Wada leaned back on the table. "When we got the mixture just so, a close resemblance to chemicals and temperatures likely found on an early Earth, the outer shell dissolved and the material inside started various chemical reactions. What we found was a transition from abiotic or nonliving to biotic, living matter, in its most basic form, certainly not life as we know it."

Some squirmed in their seats, bad students compelled to sit in detention.

"Like the flu virus can make you sick when transmitted to the right host, the cubes, when transmitted to a planet with the right set of chemical ingredients and temperature, can jump start chemical life forms."

The audience again stirred, looking uncomfortable but not bored.

"The early Earth was a very unfriendly place, say four to five billion years ago," Wada said. "I know some of you don't believe that timeline but I am hoping you'll bear with me. The atmosphere, science believes, was likely a mix of toxic gases, cut by lightning and bombarded by radiation. It was also pounded by asteroids crashing through the atmosphere and onto the surface of the planet. These were asteroids like the three we just discussed and perhaps carrying nano cubes. It's also possible these asteroids are fragments left when space visitors from beyond our solar system crashed into them." Up came a *Scientific American* cover with a cigar shaped visitor and headline, "Here's a tourist from beyond Pluto." He gave them a moment to peruse some highlighted copy. "How did it travel between galaxies? What might it have been carrying? Perhaps the cubes? Was it sent? Another followed two years later and others since then."

Broux coughed. Wada pointed. "A question, sir?" The minister shook his head. Wada continued, gesturing to the microscopic photo on the screen.

"There is a term called *panspermia* that applies here. In essence, the Panspermia Hypothesis states that micro-organisms or biochemical compounds from outer space are responsible for originating life on Earth and likely other places in the universe as well where conditions are right. This discovery would support that theory. The basic chemical ingredients for life were here, either from the beginning or brought by crashing asteroids or comets, and then other asteroids brought the catalysts necessary to stir the primordial soup to life."

Wada stood and walked back to the center of the room.

"Here is something else I found astounding. The cubes, we believe, were dispersed to more than Earth-like planets. I believe Daniel mentioned this yesterday so I will only briefly offer more speculation." He stopped, exhaled, and looked down, the image of a thoughtful man contemplating momentous issues. As he raised his head, his voice was just above a whisper.

"Our views of what constitutes life are limited, assuming, perhaps out of hubris, that any other life forms must be like us, carbon based. *Star Trek* was perhaps prescient in the varieties of life it conjured. As we continue to explore space, we may be in for some surprises. The implications for the biblical Genesis are significant, particularly as they relate to man created in God's image. More on that in a minute."

Daniel smiled, amazed at his staccato technique of giving information to stimulate their interest and then switching subjects to keep everyone alert. He noticed Broux's jaw muscle twitching and that Sister Esther had both fists clenched. The cardinal watched intently, slowly turning his gold ring. Vega's expression gave no hint of what he was thinking or feeling. Father Alito was visibly perspiring. Trudy, Garrett and Rolph remained transfixed. Saito, in the next seat, pushed his knee against Daniel's.

Wada watched the audience again for questions. The ministers stirred but seemed to be following.

"But there is something even more startling. I'm going to suggest to you that your vote to suppress the discovery was made with too little information. You accept established theology and seek to spread the word as gathered and interpreted by the founders of your religions—Moses, Jesus, Mohammad, John the Baptist, the Council of Nicaea and other individuals and groups you are more familiar with than I. Irritating scientists like me always seem to be challenging your sacred teachings."

Daniel thought his demeanor was natural and non-threatening. Wada leaned on his cane. "But what would happen if this discovery actually offered *communication* from the creator?"

Sister began to cough.

The cardinal flinched, his eyes wide. *"Cosa?"*

Broux was incredulous, "What'd you say?" Everyone seemed to be talking.

Wada held up his hands. "Reverend Broux asked a question," he said, helping everyone settle down. "This is my response. Whoever or whatever—man, god or creature not yet open to our comprehension—is communicating directly to us, his creations, through these cubes."

The ministers turned rigid, stunned at the audacity of this Japanese scientist making such a claim.

"Please continue," Wright implored, a tremor in his voice.

Vega smiled behind folded hands.

"As a scientist, let me answer by giving you a sense of how we know this. Under the most rigorous scientific methodology we examined the cubes in many ways. But we did not have to look far to make one startling find."

The cube on the screen continued to tumble forward, showing four sides. Wada then pushed a button and the cube rotated sideways. As it moved rapidly, a dark spot appeared on one panel, over and over.

"Let us stop it so you can see this one panel head on." The cube halted its trajectory on the screen; a circle came into view in the exact center. It was actually a smudgy maze of circles, lines and colors. "Let me show you the same exact object with a major alternation of the light spectrum."

The circle instantly appeared multi-dimensional, exquisitely detailed, infinitely deep and multicolored, like a great, complex work of art. "What do you see?"

"I see a circle, several circles," offered Wright.

"It looks a little like a cross section of a cell, as least my recollection of what they look like," Alito suggested.

Broux cleared his throat, seeming unsure if he should raise his hand or just speak. "It looks like a series of concentric circles. Then there is a square in the center and various smaller squares inside."

"Yes. Excellent!" Wada's upbeat voice was infectious. "I had the same initial reactions. Perhaps I'll make scientists of you yet."

He walked to the screen and pointed. "This too is not a form found in nature. Just like the cube itself, this clearly appears to be manufactured. Each cube we looked at had this identical mark imbedded on the outer hard cover with five exceptions. Each is precisely the same in all details except for the very central square in the middle of the circle. Each of the five variations seems to match the type of catalyst within the cube, at least the three we could get open. Sort of like a product name or maybe an ingredient panel in the center. The rest of the information in the circle appears identical in each of the thousands we looked at."

He stared at the cubes, giving his audience a chance to study the photo and think of the implications, before turning around to judge their faces.

"My early assumption here is that cubes for Earth-like worlds got one stamp, cubes for frozen worlds got another, and super-heated worlds got the third. The two types we could not open, we don't yet know the kinds of worlds they would seek."

"You said early assumption," Daniel said. "Has your view changed?"

"No. The more we studied it, the more it confirmed our initial hypothesis." He gestured widely, his voice rising, his diction precise. "The information—the art, the communication or maybe advertising or whatever it is that surrounds the central square—is a mystery. If I think like a science fiction writer, or a scientist seeking a hypothesis to explain it, or maybe a theologian who sees something divine—I might wonder if this is a message from whomever or whatever created them and distributed them through space. I think it actually is. Further, we suspect—but still have no proof beyond this discovery—that they were likely distributed throughout the galaxy, perhaps multiple galaxies, billions of years ago to create life—life that local elements, local conditions would dictate and shape." He studied the faces across the room, a smile on his face, eyebrows raised, clearly enjoying sharing secrets.

"How do we interpret it?" Wada then asked. He pointed to Wright, to each minister. "Should scientists alone do the work? Or scientists and theologians with a broad and open perspective and seeking truth, join with us in this effort?" He cleared his throat, almost a grunt, his expression serious. "I ask you to think about what I've said and then add this consideration. How does this work with the theory of evolution as proposed by Charles Darwin? I'd answer that it works perfectly and sets in place most of the key elements of his hypothesis."

Sister Esther stood and started to leave, then stopped, turning around as if conflicted—she wanted to move away from such apostasy but still needed to hear the full report—perhaps so she couldn't be accused of lacking the courage to hear the words. She remained in the back of the room, watching.

"Thank you for being willing to hear me," Wada said with respect. "I know this is difficult." He continued in a grandfatherly style. "I don't know what the other markings represent: words, art, mathematical equations, star maps or something else. If indeed these nano cubes, designed for different worlds, were distributed throughout the galaxy to jumpstart life when conditions were right, then life could be in existence on millions of planets with life forms unique to the conditions that created it. That has profound implications for Genesis and the thesis that humans were created in the image of God. It suggests that other life forms including carbon based ones may not be anything like us at all."

Wada tilted his cane handle toward the audience. Daniel wasn't sure how the ministers would respond to the next comments he knew were coming.

"If the maker of these cubes creates intelligent life forms on other planets, I suspect there're many views of God or none," he said with a shrug. "When I think of our history on Earth, mankind has prayed to many deities, some with radically different looks. Those in this room relate to the bearded God giving life to Adam as depicted on the ceiling of Michelangelo's Sistine Chapel. Looking back in time, I think of the dog-headed Anubis who reigned for two thousand years as the god of the dead in ancient Egypt; the elephant-headed Lord Ganesha of Hinduism; the lightning bolt throwing, carousing Zeus of ancient Greece; or Naga, the serpentine protector of Buddhism."

From his pocket, he pulled out the dragon-headed turtle *netsuke* and held it in his palm. "Or, this wise yet dangerous mythical beast you recently met that may represent a Shinto god."

"You're bein' insultin'. Do you really think we believe any of this?" Robinson snarled.

"Amen to that," Esther said dismissively. "This's baloney."

"I'm stunned by what you've presented, sir." Wright walked to the front of the room. "Like Sister Esther, I'm so agitated by this that sitting down is no longer an option. Essentially, your interpretation seeks to toss out two thousand years of Christian history." Wright laced his hands in front of his stomach. "Indeed, it eliminates thousands more of Jewish experience. It certainly runs counter to other religions as well. To accept this, we'd need to abandon our beliefs and the rich culture and tradition of centuries that surround them. It invalidates our holy books. That would profoundly impact life on this planet. We need to be open to science as a helpmate in life but not as something that dictates our beliefs."

"If I may dare to inject a layman's view," Vega stated as he stood. "I believe Dr. Wada suggests we have something never before seen, and certainly not proven, but a discovery that offers a new basis for religious interpretation as well as scientific speculation on the origins of life."

Daniel saw that all present turned to the man in silence and respect. Was it more than his money or was that sufficient motivation for this group? Vega went on without pausing for reaction.

"There are many controversies over Christian scripture and our understanding changes periodically as new evidence is discovered," Vega said. "Was Judas a traitor or simply following orders from Jesus? There are the Dead Sea Scrolls and the stone tablet called Gabriel's Revelation that suggests the blood of a messiah was necessary not for the sins of humanity but to bring redemption to Israel. Now there is *Misago,* perhaps making all the other questions irrelevant."

Daniel noticed Broux and Robinson beginning to look at Vega with suspicion. But Vega still had everyone's full attention.

"The proof of the Bible," Vega said in his distinct baritone, "is that its many authors and editors were inspired by God to write the truth. Yet new discoveries seem to occasionally suggest the writers may not have gotten it quite right in some areas. Indeed, in terms of science and ideas about the Earth being the center of the universe, it seems there were many miscommunications between God and the writers."

The cardinal watched warily as Vega continued with his discomfiting perspective.

"The late Holy Father, John Paul II, gave a tepid embrace of evolution in trying to bring the holy book into line with what we learned from science," Vega said. "Our faith evolves. This discovery offers an opportunity to perhaps, and I emphasize *perhaps,* read the words of the creator directly." The man paused as his eyes examined each person there. "Should we reject such an offer? Would God, whatever form he takes, want us to reject it?"

Vega sat, crossed his legs and picked up his glass, casually sipping while the ministers exchanged uneasy glances, obviously not sure what to make of his commentary. Daniel had to remind himself that Vega was working with the Catholic Church.

"That's quite a speech, Mr. Vega." Robinson slapped his palm on the table. "But let me tell you, son, I say *no way*! I'll not accept this discovery. I see no benefit for myself or my parishioners. My religion's just fine the way it is. We're on the verge of making this nation God's Kingdom. We don't need this bullshit!"

Tio rose to her feet. "I'm amazed that many Christians regularly believe they see communications from God or Jesus or Mary in light reflected from a skyscraper window or in the oil stain on the bottom of a skillet used in warming tortillas, or in dreams."

She moved beside Wada, protective of her friend and mentor. "In Shinto, sometimes its adherents believe they see gods in ancient waterfalls or twisted trees. So powerful is faith, and so fragile and insecure, that people seek signs everywhere to confirm their beliefs. Now we have what you could interpret with your faith as direct, tangible images of a creator and perhaps even text."

Cardinal Martinez coughed, ready to offer his view. "I'm intrigued with what I see," he said. "The Catholic Church will never abandon its faith in the holy Bible and our belief that we are created in the image of God. But Mr. Vega raises important considerations about seeking to understand this quandary."

Daniel thought the cardinal's tone and manner suggested he was conflicted or simply loath to contradict Vega.

"The Church has indeed been flexible in much of its early history in adopting even pagan beliefs that were popular, incorporating them into its dogma," Martinez continued. "That accounts for some of its early success. Mr. Vega makes me think about how this discovery might be integrated into our faith. I don't know. Certainly, I think we need to keep the secret at least until we are ready to know how to use it. My comments, of course, reflect my intellectual curiosity and private musings, certainly not Vatican policy. We should not act impulsively here. We need time to reflect."

The image on the screen remained—a series of concentric circles with squares inside. When there was quiet Wada continued. "Very good discussion. Perhaps now would be a good time to add yet another element."

A near silent gasp filled the room. Daniel covered a smile with his hands. Garrett looked at him and grinned.

"Please look again at the circle on the screen, the stamp that seems to be on every life-creating cube. We all see things through the eyes of our individual experience. What we are familiar with is where we venture first when there is something new. You are all Christians, except perhaps Tio, Saito and myself. We might have at least two different lenses at work here, but probably more."

He clicked on photos of numerous cubes with the circle facing forward. "I've studied Buddhism and Hinduism, religions of much of the world's population. I'm a scientist from a culture quite different from your own. An American scientist looking at this for the first time, Christian or Jew, would probably not recognize what someone from India or China or Japan would see unless he was Native American. There are amazing similarities between Asian and Native American images, created thousands of years and thousands of miles apart. Our imaginations have different starting points and experiences. What I see on screen is *not* likely what it is. But here's an attempt at explanation. I see a schematic visual representation of the universe. It bears some elements that remind me of a Sanskrit word, *mandala*. I use that term with caution and simply as a placeholder so we can have a single term as a reference point."

"What is that term again?" asked the cardinal.

"A mandala. Mun'-dah-la," he said trying to sound it out for the group. "In the Native American religious view, it means a circle reflecting that all life moves in a circle. Something a bit different in other cultures but related."

"Of course," the cardinal said. "I've seen them in my travels."

"Yes, Cardinal. But it's also much more than that and its symbolism in our world is what makes it seem so startling in coming from another." Wada turned to the computer and worked the keyboard. Up came the three different circle designs from the nano cubes and three traditional mandalas from different religions.

He paused when the loud squawking of birds filled the room from an open window. "The mandala," he said, ignoring the distraction, "is an ancient symbol found in some Eastern religions and, yes, in art, and is used in meditation, perhaps by a monk thinking of the world outside his body and the world inside. Here are examples of three on the left. On the right are three different designs from the cubes. I invite you to compare them." The room went quiet as Wada gave them time to study.

"Please continue," Wright urged.

The scientist looked at the screen before turning slowly to his audience. Daniel knew his interpretation would be as shocking as it was compelling.

"Essentially, a mandala represents wholeness," Wada said, "and can be seen as a model for the organizational structure of life itself—a cosmic diagram that reminds us of our relation to the infinite, the world that extends both beyond and within our bodies and minds. That is its earthly definition. I've no idea what the makers of these cubes intended and, as I indicated, there are big differences. But sticking with my anchor word, mandalas date to the earliest recording of history. The root of the word, through the lens of Chinese history, is 'manda' which means 'essence.' And the suffix 'la' means 'container.' By some definitions, a mandala is a container of essence. I would suggest that is exactly what each nano contains, the essence of life, the catalyst necessary to begin the process to create life."

"You venture far to come up with this interpretation," Wright suggested, a respectful challenge.

"Perhaps I do," Wada said, unthreatened and unthreatening. "I said we interpret what we see based on our experience and culture. Your interpretations likely are different and we should discuss them. Again, my term is simply a place holder. If I may, let me carry this further, then talk about possible implications. I offer no absolutes here, only ideas. The traditional center of a mandala has a dot, and it means seed or sperm. On each nano cube there seems to be the name of a catalyst, what some might call a seed or sperm."

Wada sipped his water, checking body language. "On the outer circle of a mandala we often find a ring of flames, so symbolically someone seeking to access the seed or truth or enlightenment within the mandala must pass through this outer layer and have his impurities ritually burned. When I think about this interpretation and think about the nano cubes passing through the burning heat of our atmosphere as the asteroid crashes to Earth, the symbolism again seems very appropriate. It makes this old scientist wonder about so many things. It seems spiritual in many ways."

The ministers just stared at the screen.

"This discovery is more than just science," Wada said. "What are these creators suggesting? Most of those in this room believe a Christian god created life in His image. If what I read in American newspapers is correct, one of the political goals of the CCC is to put more evangelical Protestantism into public schools. But selling direct Bible verse, particularly the words about creation in Genesis, has had mixed results."

He leaned toward Reverend Wright. "It's the ultimate conundrum, Reverend. How does something simultaneously prove your case while destroying it?" He stood straight again, glancing around at the group, his expression unreadable.

Daniel knew he wanted to be respectful yet create enough discomfort to help them open their imaginations.

"The theory, your theory, is Intelligent Design," Wada continued, "the idea that life was created by an intelligent source, a mystical obfuscation cloaked in reasonableness, a kind of non-Genesis theory to bring your God back into schools and other public places. I suggest that what you have before you is a Gordian knot, an intractable tangle of new science and old faith. It establishes absolutely one part of your belief system while demolishing others. And it does it with hard evidence."

Several started to speak then changed their minds. Wada waited in silence.

Finally, Broux began. "Normally I'm the most outspoken guy in any room. You haven't changed my mind, my faith is absolute and unshakable, but you do raise some fascinating philosophical issues. The cardinal suggests we need time to reflect. I'm not ready to scream at you—yet—so take advantage of the quiet to present your conclusions while my anger reflex is momentarily numb."

Wada walked to him. He smiled as they looked into each other's eyes. "Fair enough, sir," Wada said. "Thank you for this opportunity. Let me suggest that we have received direct communication from a creator or at least the Great Catalyst Maker. What we have received is billions of years old, not two thousand, and it's in a language we don't yet understand."

Wada was in his element, speaking as if before students interested in learning, not holy men hungry to destroy his work. "There are thousands of religions on this planet today and there have been untold thousands in the past," he said. "All of them might simply be wrong, created with inadequate information at a time when people were desperate for answers and had limited information."

Dr. Saito said in a loud voice, "As we consider the make of the makers, remember that any sufficiently advanced technology is indistinguishable from magic. Arthur C. Clarke offered that insight. And useful here." Daniel pushed his knee into Saito's while looking straight ahead.

"Indeed." Wada smiled at his friend. "Here we have the strongest evidence ever that some kind of creator exists, perhaps also a direct message from that entity. This creator could be a living biological entity from a place in the universe that is light years away and more advanced than any human being. Or it could be something else, divine and immortal, that we don't yet understand and is nothing like our traditional idea of God, except in its power and the role it plays in the universe." He paused for a moment, focusing on each person as they looked up. "Are these new choices the basis for a philosophical and scientific inquiry, to work together to try and unlock this message?"

Wada seemed to analyze their expressions. Daniel suspected most were somewhere between the anger of disbelief and the fear of truth.

"Do we have faith in the capacity of our fellow humans," he asked, "to present to them this new discovery even through it might lead to re-thinking some basic human mythology? Or does our need to maintain the status quo take precedence over science and truth? How far will you and others who hold your beliefs go to maintain the secret? One member of my staff, who leaked details of the information to the prime minister, appears to have been murdered, his body found with a fortune in yen, perhaps part of a payoff gone horribly wrong."

The group stirred. "That's horrible!" Wright said. Others nodded, looking stunned.

"Please think about what may have been done in your name and what violence may yet be unleashed. I ask you to consider: what is best for all of us and who should make that decision?"

Daniel gave a discreet nod of encouragement. Not that Wada needed one.

"Is humanity ready," Wada asked, "and indeed capable of bringing its faith forward to reflect new truths? If we seek to maintain our personal comfort with what we now have, what are the creators intending who launched these cubes into the universe? I suggest that over time we will be able to interpret the messages on these cubes and understand a little about those who created them. Perhaps someday we will discover the equivalent of the Rosetta Stone that unlocked the hieroglyphics within ancient Egyptian pyramids."

Wada remained animated and still had more to say.

"One question that will need to be answered is why would these new creators leave their name on a nano granule?" No one attempted to respond. "We might look to our own space ventures for an answer, assuming the creators of the cube are anything like humans on Earth. Why did Americans leave their names on the lunar lander?"

Wada pushed another key and a photo of the Apollo 11 landing capsule sitting on the Moon came into view. He zoomed into a close-up of the plaque.

HERE MEN FROM THE PLANET EARTH
FIRST SET FOOT UPON THE MOON
JULY 1969 A.D.

WE CAME IN PEACE FOR ALL MANKIND

"It was signed by President Richard Nixon and the crew of the moon mission. My answer, applying my human background, is that they wanted to brag, gain some measure of immortality, to lay claim to history, maybe even to lay claim to property rights."

Wada stood in silence. The question was impossible. "I wonder if it's perhaps suggesting there are or were competing civilizations or gods out there that made such nano cubes and tossed them to the stars. I don't claim to know the answer but just suggest that this is our future. This is the most compelling, the most complete and the most irrefutable information we have ever received on the creation of life."

Mike Michaels had had enough.

"No one will believe any of this, even if you're correct on all counts, which I doubt," he proclaimed. "It requires a rejection of everything we've known and been taught for thousands of years. The fact that your own government seeks to suppress it will just further discredit you and your message. Frankly, Dr. Wada, we'll win this fight and win easily."

"If you are correct, young man," he said, "does that mean human fear will triumph over truth and the creator of life?" He waited for a response. "Do you win by praying to a god that may not exist? If you're concerned about heaven and hell, where will this new god fit? Could your soul, as imagined in Christianity, be at risk if you make the wrong decision? Perhaps Heaven has no interest for you."

Michaels crossed his arms in silent disdain.

"This's bullshit, just like I said when we were first briefed!" Robinson said with contempt. "The Bible's very clear in *Genesis* how man was created and I don't believe any of this silly interpretation of yours. Hell, some of my followers still don't believe Americans landed on the Moon. They think it was a Hollywood stunt."

"Which view of *Genesis* is correct, Reverend?" Daniel asked, ready to play his part in undermining their certainty. "Genesis I or

Genesis II?" He knew this was dangerous turf.

"Both show God creating man," Robinson responded. "They're essentially the same."

Wada pretended to be puzzled. "I didn't know there were two."

Robinson looked at him, then out the window, shaking his head, apparently done with the discussion.

Wright, leaning against the wall, smiled, anxious to fill the void on his favorite book, as expected. Wada gestured for him to step forward.

"Let me try," Wright said. "For the benefit of Dr. Wada, Dr. Saito and Dr. Ito—*Genesis* does have two distinct sections that refer to creation and they're slightly different. *Genesis* 1:26-28 has man in the image of God with dominion over the earth. *Genesis* 2:7-8 describes Adam's creation in the Garden of Eden. In *Genesis* 2:23-24, God takes one of Adam's ribs and forms a woman and brings her to him." He went on for several minutes giving extensive detail.

"Wonderful," Daniel said. "You bring it down to its essence. Of course, according to some, in Genesis I, women are equal to men. But this isn't the time for that debate." He paused, considering his pitch. He glanced at Garrett sitting next to him who looked up, tilting his head, urging him to go on. Daniel suppressed a smile. "My point is that Genesis is flexible and our topic today is creation. I wonder if what we see in this room is a discussion between *Genesis* I and II. Dr. Wada is the son of Adam I seeking to understand the science of the universe. The members of the CCC are like Adam II, looking for the image of God not in mathematical formula or science but in the wonder of sunlight on a warm summer day, the sweetness of roses, the majesty of starlight in the mountains. All of it is within the context of the Bible. Can we stretch the confines of *Genesis* to accept new physical scientific evidence?"

"That's an unusual embellishment of the two versions of *Genesis*." Sister Esther offered a forced smile in making the comment, as if struggling to be accommodating.

Wada wondered how long she'd endure such talk.

"If I understand it," she stated, "you're suggesting that what the good scientist presents might fit in with Adam II's desire to establish an intimate relationship with God by understanding the message He has sent via *Misago*, expanding the confines of *Genesis* as you suggested. Correct?"

"I hadn't thought about it exactly like that."

"Good, because I don't think it fits if you did!" She waved a hand dismissively. "*Genesis* is not confined, let me correct you. What's been presented here is way beyond the words of the holy Bible. No clever reinterpretation will bridge the gap."

"You're right Sister. This is *bull crap!*" Robinson shouted, overturning a candy dish as he stood. "You sound like some silly drugged-out San Francisco fruitcake poet trying to pretend he's got some insight into God. *You-do-not!*"

"Please," Martinez snapped. "We need to remain respectful and on topic. That is what Dr. Wada has been doing in his presentation and, as men of God, we can do no less."

"Thank you for your admonition, *Car-din-al,*" Robinson said sarcastically as he sat. "Let me say that I see NO advantage in this for us. I like the direction America's headed. The views of our Savior are now taken more seriously in the public square than they've been in a century. We've got strong voices in Congress and in the White House. Good Christian judges sit on hundreds of benches across the country making sure the Constitution respects and reflects the Bible."

"Amen," Sister added. "We'll soon have a Christian Prophet above the president and Congress. If it's me, know I have the same view as my friend."

There was quiet in the room.

Mike Michaels was the first to break the silence. "As science fiction, the presentation gives me goosebumps," he offered. "But I don't believe it and neither will the public. Reverend Robinson is right. The polls are with our current mission. This is a distraction. Is it true? Who can know? Who cares? The public will reject it because they don't want to believe it. We should support them since it advances our position."

"Your lack of curiosity about life astounds me," Wada said as he stepped toward Michaels. "People accepting it? Not at first. But over time people will become excited. Many will at the outset when they understand it is serious science. After all, it is the truth."

"The truth often loses, Dr. Wada," Michaels said with a shrug, "particularly if the other side has a good P.R. man."

"For the record," Martinez reminded the group, "truth is always our goal. I too felt some goosebumps. A message from God—in his own words! *If*—*if*—that is what this is. I keep asking myself if God is seeking to contact me. Or is it the devil?"

"With all respect, Your Eminence, they have no real proof that any of this is true," Michaels said testily. "It's just photos on a screen and we all know you can easily manipulate photos. The whole thing is just pieces of something smaller than the human eye can see and needing microscopes manipulated by atheist scientists to verify what's there. This isn't proof people of faith will accept."

"An interesting point," Wada said with an impish grin. "A group of ministers who believe man should take on faith claims of a virgin birth, life after death, walking on water, stopping time, original sin, feeding the multitudes with a loaf of bread—this group wants proof."

Wada's smile widened. "I couldn't agree more, Mr. Michaels. You're right to ask." He looked at Tio and Saito, then back to the others. "If I offer the group a challenge, if I give you additional proof, hard evidence, will you use it to confirm what I've said? Or, are your statements about seeking God's truth simply hollow rhetoric?"

"Truth is always the goal," the cardinal said.

"Agreed," added Wright.

Michaels frowned.

Wada looked back at Saito, then Daniel and nodded once.

Saito rose quickly, squeezed Daniel's shoulder and whispered in his ear: "Key time, sweet lips."

Daniel reached into his coat pocket and handed him the key to his family's crypt. They'd discussed this as a possible tactic and the timing seemed perfect.

Saito's voice was confident and respectful. "We have presented our findings and you, all men and women of faith, have asked for proof. Here is what we propose. To show you our good faith, I'll give you the location of the granules, photographs, and other materials I brought to America just a few days ago and delivered to Daniel. You're free to go to it, study it, take it to faith-friendly scientists you trust and make your own interpretations. Or, leave it. I suggest that your sign of appreciation, proof of your quest for truth, would be to engage with us, science and faith working in partnership to understand creation."

Saito picked up a notepad from the desk and wrote down the location in Colma. "It's in a Catholic graveyard."

Martinez seemed startled, as did the others. "That is indeed a sign of good will," the cardinal said as he stood, breathless, walking to the front of the room. "Thank you. This is an important moment." He extended his hands to all three scientists.

Michaels seemed satisfied. Daniel assumed he was convinced Wada had just unilaterally disarmed. Robinson's expression suggested they were fools.

Saito handed the note and key to the cardinal.

"Perhaps we should take some time to ourselves or meet in small discussion groups," Martinez said, "and pray for God's guidance. I don't believe I've ever had a day like this before."

33.

Stonehouse Lodge, Lake Tahoe

"I did not expect this overture." Vega was standing with the cardinal and Father Alito in the garden just outside the French doors. "Nor the moral challenge—the ethical obligation they've given us."

"Agreed. But it was stimulating. We need to follow through." Martinez gestured to the priest. "Guido, please find their materials. Get them, guard them and call me to confirm." Taking the paper and key, Alito scampered toward the parking area.

At the end of the pier, Sister Esther spoke in quiet confidence. "Once we get the material, we've no need of them."

The red-haired minister nodded. "Have you made the call?"

"Yes."

City of Souls, Colma, California

Bruiser opened the door to Daniel's family crypt in Colma's

vast cluster of graveyards with only minor difficulty, his lock pick set matching the challenge. He wanted copies of everything and all of the actual granules. Fake ones were fine for the religious types since they likely wouldn't do research anyway.

Emotionally it was more difficult than he'd anticipated, all the memories. His knees wobbled as he looked at a faded photo taped just past the doorframe: Bruiser with Daniel and his mom.

He walked to the back of the crypt and stopped before the altar with a vase filled with dried white roses. "Laura," he said, "do you know my friends claim my first wife looked like you? But certainly not the next three." He pressed fingers to his eyes to slow the tears.

Daniel had told him to wait a week if he'd not heard before going to the crypt. He was early and it was best Daniel didn't know he was rushing. "Close enough," he muttered, his curiosity and fear for Daniel overcoming patience. This was just too tempting after he'd read Japanese news accounts on Wada. He placed the vase on the floor. From what he had been reading from Daniel, he could scarcely comprehend what must be hidden here. He took off the marble top, reached inside, wondering about spiders, and pulled out the black case.

"Heavy and well made," he said to himself, feeling a rush. If the Japanese news speculation was right, this adventure could be brutal in its outcome. "Hopefully," he grinned and hummed the name of the space program to the tune of the *Halleluiah Chorus* as he worked.

It had been many years since he'd won a Pulitzer, received death threats, and survived two attempts on his life for uncovering criminal activity in California gaming. A dozen elected officials and tribal leaders had gone to prison. He enjoyed wide respect among old school journalists but the younger reporters, those into vapid smiles and puffball reporting to match their hair, saw him as quaint, a fossil hungry for the glory days of long ago. Now he headed a newspaper with an old name that was struggling to survive.

"Mis-e-ag-o," he hummed louder as he squatted on the floor

and opened the case, his knees challenging his efforts to sit. He opened his own bag and compared the finely crafted *Misago* cylinder with what he had brought to replace it. "Shit!" Then he shrugged. "Who'll know?" He looked at his own version of glass tubes, done with the help of a friend and a Bunsen burner and filled with sand from the ashtray he kept on the roof of his building. He unhooked the *Misago* container and looked inside. He shrugged again. "Oh, well."

He opened his hand-held and reached for the first of three memory wands. It took two tries but finally the information downloaded. He replaced the wands back into the case.

There were a variety of loose photos and a letter to Daniel from Wada. He took out his favorite spy camera for high pixel digital images. Finished, he replaced the tubes with the asteroid dust with his special smoky cigar version. He returned the valise to the hiding spot and yanked his arm back faster than any creepy arthropods might react. He replaced the marble top, put the vase back in place and took a photo of the altar for possible use in the story. He turned and once more contemplated the grey marble wall with Laura's name.

Standing outside, under a canopy of trees and the rolling lawn before him, he felt peaceful. He flipped the pack over his shoulder and screamed, "I'm alive all you fucking pansy-ass journalists! This is real news. *I love you, Daniel!* Thank you!"

A squirrel stood on its hind legs assessing him, gave a bark-like grunt and dashed up a redwood.

Stonehouse Lodge, Lake Tahoe

"I'm going for a jog," Daniel announced. "I need to calm myself."

Wada, Tio and Saito looked up from the table where they were discussing expanding contacts with scientists. "I thought we had an agreed upon relaxing strategy," Saito teased in a throaty voice. "I'm so ready to do it again and again until we reach perfection." He grinned and turned toward the door.

"What strategy?" Garrett asked, looking up from a video game on his phone. "Can I come with you?"

Father and son dashed down to the beach. Garrett stomped both feet in a shallow pool of water, drenching his dad, before taking off, Daniel in close pursuit.

"You're so going to get it!" Daniel yelled and laughed as they raced beyond the Lodge grounds and into the forest.

As he rounded a stand of redwoods and manzanita, Daniel almost smacked into one of the guards holding Garrett by the shoulder. The boy was squirming.

"Let me go!"

"Don't touch him!" Daniel slapped the man's hand away, put an arm around his son and pulled him back. *"What's going on?"* No one touched his son.

Another guard stepped behind him, holding a semi-automatic rifle across his chest.

The older guard, the team leader based on his stripes, with black hair and a linebacker build, the man he'd seen looking into his room, touched the handle of his pistol, his lips in a snarl, ready for a fight, his words chilling: "You are not authorized to leave. Return to your cabin."

"Nor are we prisoners, Sergeant. You're out of line. I will discuss this with Mr. Vega." He put his arm around his son and they turned around. "Race you back!"

Family Quarters, White House

Jeremiah Walton checked his watch before using his phone from the family quarters at the White House. It was answered after a partial ring.

"Good evening, Mr. President."

"Good afternoon, Your Eminence. Time for our scheduled talk on our new favorite topic."

"We had a surprise last night at my Tahoe retreat. We had

several. First, Dr. Wada, the missing Japanese scientist, showed up along with his assistant, a woman named Dr. Tio Ito, and presented some startling material. Obviously, he's not dead, nor kidnapped. Second, he confirmed that he did ship over materials and offered to share them with us for our own evaluation. Prepare yourself for a summary of what he didn't tell you when you met!"

The president was silent with shock. Jake Machin had briefed him about the meeting and Duboce attending but Wada showing up was stunning new information. He'd never shared with anyone his relationship with the prelate, not even Machin.

The cardinal checked his notes as he spoke and informed him of the meeting rapid fire.

Walton gasped, covering his mouth, honest with his emotions before a friend. "Are you done?"

"Do you want more?"

"Not really. Do you believe any of it?

"Jeremiah, he is impressive. I guess what I don't believe is that he's lying to me. He believes it and so does Duboce plus the other two scientists. I'm not sure. But the public could respond in any number of ways."

"Why now?" Walton asked. "You know what we're planning on doing with the Kingdom Movement?"

"I do. A rigid theocracy. Are you expecting my blessing?"

"Would you give it?"

"No. Nice try. You will be forcing everyone to buy into one religion's point of view and discarding religious pluralism as well as democracy. Of course, what I understand of the state of democracy is that it is in tatters. You could end up in a civil war."

"We are where we are. We control the military and there's a small army of patriot groups ready to engage. What you suggest are reasons I've held up on announcing support. You should have heard the howls when the CCC was briefed on *Misago*."

"You may control the levers of earthly power but that does not mean you are noble in what is being proposed. I say that with deep respect for you as an honest man who loves his country."

"You think there may be something to it? As you know, I did

meet Wada. If I had to pick one word to describe my reaction it would be fear. I was afraid the discovery would be seen as an attack on Christianity and Islam and all our nutcases would retaliate. Truth seemed secondary to peace. It seems outlandish, unbelievable. I wondered if I was being conned."

"I don't believe it's a con, Jeremiah. His evidence and openness are persuasive."

"I need time to think, Diego. I also need to confer with my science advisor."

"Good idea. And your minister."

"That's you of course. Let's talk again at our scheduled time. I'd like to keep this between us at this point, at least our personal conversation. I understand your need to communicate with the pope—just don't tell him about our conversations."

"You want me to lie to the pope?" The cardinal laughed.

"Tell him you took my confession and it's privileged," the president snorted. "Maybe he'll think you converted me, Diego! You may get extra points." The president took a deep breath and his normal demeanor returned. "I trust your judgment. You've been a wise counsel on many occasions. This will test us all."

34.

Stonehouse Lodge, Lake Tahoe

"I'm concerned that the worst case is already beginning to happen," Michaels told the CCC members later that evening in the cardinal's room. "The story is starting to leak. Japanese papers are expanding their coverage beyond just Wada's disappearance. They're now speculating on why he disappeared and whether it's related to the missing space dust or the death of another JAXA scientist. The kidnapping of such a visible and respected man is a powerful news hook to capture readers along with speculation on what would compel such an act. If the story stays with Japanese newspapers, no one cares. Our constituents don't read them. But today's Tokyo version of the International Herald Tribune quotes an unnamed Japanese scientist that the kidnapping, murder and theft are related to a startling scientific discovery."

He held a printout. Robinson grabbed it, pulling it close to his nose.

"This could get picked up in the U.S., just as an oddity," Michaels warned. "We don't want to lose control of the media."

"So what do you propose?" Robinson asked.

"That we go public." He knew this would get them excited

and then he could turn it his way. And win.

"We cannot!" Robinson stated. *"We will not!"*

"Please let me finish," Michaels said. "What I'm suggesting to you is we make this a joke. I propose we destroy Dr. Wada's credibility by making him a laughingstock and force any scientist or reporter who wants to support him think twice about soiling their reputation."

"I like it," Sister Esther responded. "Yes, a joke. I like that."

"I suggest we tell the story much like it is," Michaels continued, "but leak it to a publication such as the *National Muckraker*. Let them cover it like the latest Elvis sighting or UFO landing and abduction. We can make *Misago* sound just like that. So, when Wada does make his pitch…"

"We don't know if he will," said the cardinal. "He did give us access to the stolen material. And we will examine it."

"I suggest we do it anyway," Michaels argued, "as protection. Who cares about Wada or the other two scientists? He'll have to figure out how to answer questions on his kidnapping. I can get some of our columnists and maybe a late-night talk show host to make it a joke. A Japanese scientist suddenly seeing space aliens. Dr. Wada, claiming we were made by oval-eyed monsters from Alpha Centauri. How sad it is that he fell apart after the death of his wife and whether he was really a hero that day on the Space Station. If we play this right, the discovery will become a joke."

"Unless other scientists go looking in those asteroid craters," Vega said. "Or, other space missions bring back additional nano cubes. Or, the government of Japan changes and new leaders learn the truth and want Japan to get credit, new leaders who don't care what late night American comics or grocery store tabloids have to say. You're proposing a sort-term tactic that will someday be uncovered and prove humiliating to Christianity; certainly an embarrassment to the people in this room."

The cardinal nodded, his expression grim. "Then there's the issue about truth and ruining the reputation of an honest man."

"I've been listening all afternoon," Sister Esther said harshly. Clearly, she'd heard enough. "Romaldo, you're a smart man and

I respect your views and what you do, your generosity, but I'm concerned about the larger needs of the Christian church. I'm not sure we should want to engage in a discussion in the media. If this is a message from God, He'll understand our caution. If it's not, I don't much care about the makers of these nano cubes nor do I believe it."

"I agree. Let's go with Michael's plan," Robinson said. "Short term's okay. Preserve the status quo. We can fight other battles if they develop."

"Yes, focus on Wada." Broux sounded less enthusiastic. Wright was silent, looking troubled.

"Remember there are risks in any strategy," Vega warned. "There are no guarantees it will go as Mr. Michaels suggests. You heard Wada's elegant presentation. It's not a joke and the questions are profound for each of us. Or should be." His voice slowed, becoming ominous in tone. "The revealed religions of the world are at risk. Bad short-term solutions may make our long-term goals more elusive. When this is exposed, and I assume it will be, confession will not add to the dignity or legitimacy of our churches."

Martinez glanced at Wright and turned to the others. "I suspect Romaldo is right, but there appears to be consensus among the Americans. It is your country. I'm a guest. This is your media; you know it better than I. Mr. Michaels is your consultant. Reverend Wright: proceed or not?"

Bingo, Michaels thought, Wright has the same set of problems. He needs unity among the ministers.

"Reluctantly, I suppose," the minister said, "but I share your discomfort."

Michaels lifted his head in triumph.

Vega looked at him, smiling in a way that was not reassuring.

City of Souls Cemetery, Colma

In early morning darkness, a black sedan wound through Holy Cross Cemetery. The car made repeated stops and a man got out with a flashlight. Eventually it pulled in front of the Duboce family tomb.

Two men went to the entrance, a stout man in a cap and a tall slender one in a clerical collar. Within minutes, they opened the door and entered. A lantern lit the room, a crypt glowing with red, yellow and blue visions of the holy family in the graveyard. Fog circled the crypt, disappeared, and returned.

The two stepped outside and secured the door. The priest, wearing a hero's grin, carried a black case. Both returned to the car which became enveloped in the mist as it sped away.

Across the park, an infrared camera with telephoto lens finished snapping a series of photos.

35.

Beacon Building, San Francisco

"You should see the photos, Daniel, they're great," Bruiser said with a chuckle. "Father Alito should be ashamed of what he told the locksmith."

"He had a locksmith?" Daniel asked, scrolling down the volume on his phone. "I gave them my key."

"I guess they wanted backup or maybe didn't trust you." He laughed. "Loony Tunes. I had the PI who did the stakeout find him. The holy guy paid with a credit card and said he was working with the Archdiocese in San Francisco and needed to retrieve some personal items left at the crypt by a man who was dying. Do priests often lie?"

"He may not get into heaven." Daniel enjoyed the new twist. "Have you received my last batch of copy?"

"Hot stuff, Daniel. The encryption works well. I have two other reporters doing background on everyone involved and the *Times* has half a dozen reporters on it, all coordinating back through me, I might add. We'll be ready. Be cautious. The FBI is hunting Wada and who knows what they'd do with you. And the ministers, at least one or two, might want him found."

Stonehouse Lodge, Lake Tahoe

"I have news."

The cardinal walked into the living room. "Father Alito just called. He has the case and everything seems to be there. He's taken it to the Archbishop's residence where it will be safe. I must say hiding it in Mr. Duboce's family crypt was clever. But now we have it. I'll take it to Rome for testing."

"Oh. Excellent, excellent," Wright said, looking jovial. "That should make our task easier. I'm so pleased they're willing to be helpful. Actually, I'm surprised given the nasty confrontations. Perhaps God spoke to them."

"I'm feelin' good myself," Robinson said, dimples flashing. "I guess my irascible personality didn't distract too much."

Michaels' smooth tone was counterpoint to his smirk. "As a follow-up, gentlemen, and as part of our insurance policy, my team is already making contacts in creating a new national source of amusement for those who read supermarket tabloids."

Vega poured a cup of tea. "Let me ask a question of the group. They offered the material as a sign of good faith. Is our response what Mr. Michaels is doing or will we offer something in similar spirit?"

"It's too early to know. We haven't discussed our own next steps beyond Mr. Michael's campaign," Wright offered. "I'm certainly supportive of the Vatican follow-up."

"This has been a good team effort," Sister Esther said, deflecting the issue while readjusting her blue silk scarf around her shoulders. "I didn't really have confidence that different denominations could work together."

"Me neither," Robinson added.

"I'm curious," she said, loudly enough to turn heads and lifting a finger toward Vega. "In this ecumenical moment, maybe I can learn something about the stories we hear about the secret society of *Opus Dei*. I know it's a lay group focused on promoting conservative Catholic values but it was started during Franco's rule of Spain back in the thirties. The stories of self-flagellation and other extreme practices mixed with super piety are intriguing. True or not?"

"Actually, madam, I am not a member and suspect rumors of bloody uber-rituals are greatly exaggerated." Vega offered a wry smile.

The cardinal looked down, fearing what might be coming and did a quick prayer under his breath. He knew the man's gracious formality masked a wicked sense of humor and justice. He could be lethal, verbally and otherwise if provoked.

"Oh. Sorry," she said. "I assumed, given your position, that you were a member. But I guess you can be a good Catholic and not be *Opus Dei.*"

Vega glanced at the cardinal with a raised eyebrow. Martinez rolled his eyes. *Please be gentle. We are recruiting allies.*

"Actually, madam, I never said I was Catholic."

"But—you work for the Catholic Church. Don't you?"

"The cardinal and I collaborate on issues of mutual interest. This is one. I am not nor ever have been an employee of any church."

All side conversations stopped.

"So—are you Protestant?" she asked. "Born again? Just what are you?"

"Neither."

"*Only* a *born-again* Christian can wear the *Armor of God*, sir," she responded, her voice brittle. "Do you accept Jesus Christ as your personal savior?"

Vega rubbed his chin and glanced into his cup of tea, clearly in no rush. "I guess I don't feel the need to don magical armor to see evil. I'm a man of good will, instincts and eyesight," he said slowly, his tone soothing as he looked at her. "My focus is joining with others on a quest to preserve the traditions of revealed religions—all of them—the Catholic Church and your own, to help hold humanity together."

Robinson brought his fist down on the table and shouted. *"Damn you!* You've been at the center of our talks. Are you a Christian? How do we trust ya' if you're not?"

Vega's expression was impossible to read. The cardinal assumed the man was enjoying himself. Vega took a sip of tea and set down the cup. "I am an ally," Vega said, with exaggerated elocution, meeting his stare, one eyebrow slightly raised.

With elbows on the table, Martinez rested his forehead on open palms and closed his eyes. *This too shall pass.*

"We've a right to know," she insisted, sounding stressed. "Those beliefs, all that we collectively hold dear, are central to our decision-making. Do you believe you're accountable to God? Just who and what are you, sir? Are you an atheist or a Unitarian?"

"Rest assured, I'm neither of those," he responded, hiding a smile with his hand. "Most religions teach that all men are ultimately accountable to God." Vega leaned against the edge of a table across from her chair, his tone friendly and professorial. "Earlier, Sister, you talked about this as an ecumenical moment. In that spirit let me offer a view from a holy book we have not discussed. The *Qur'an* holds that every human, Muslim, and non-Muslim alike, is responsible for their deeds and will be judged by Allah. I believe it is Surah—that means chapter—Surah 82.13 that deals with judgment day: *'Most surely the righteous are in bliss, And most surely the wicked are in burning fire, They shall enter it on the day of judgment.'*"

"Are you a *MUS-LIM?*" Robinson's voice was an octave higher than normal.

"I believe judgment, if there is one, will be based on character and actions, not adornments worn on our sleeves or around our necks, certainly not with empty piety," Vega said, looking satisfied.

"Cardinal!" Robinson was standing. "This's, this's unacceptable!" he said with spittle flying. "A…a…*MUSLIM!*"

"I do enjoy your sense of ecumenicism," Vega replied with a shrug. "Disparaging any religion or belief other than your own is common in the competition between faiths for membership and money but it's ultimately destructive to social cohesion. Loud dramatic inflection, my friend, is unnecessary." The warmth of his smile and tone softened his words. "Volume does not add to clarity or insight." He gestured respectfully, glancing at the white-faced cardinal and back to Robinson.

"You…you insult me? Sister Ester was on her feet. "You're as bad as those damned homosexuals destroying the meaning of family and love! I agree with Reverend Broux." She was almost hissing. "You're even worse than homosexuals, worse than liberals and atheists."

"I agree with Reverend Broux." Sister Esther was on her feet. "You're even worse than homosexuals, worse than liberals and atheists."

The cardinal noticed Vega's smile was gone and his face now blank. Even Vega has his limits, the cardinal knew. Perhaps he'd decided the cause would be better off without her. He knew Vega had donated major sums of money to each of their churches and had also intervened when they asked for help on sensitive issues. Although not with Sister. Vega was not someone you wanted to cross. This will be interesting.

"I will not comment on liberals, whatever that straw term means. Homosexuals? What does that have to do with our mission here? I appreciate that some American religions fixate on sex, but our problem is far beyond different views on piety. Some embrace gays, others loathe them. Focus on our purpose."

"Morality is everything to our church," Sister replied in a sharp rebuke.

"I'm certain of that, Sister." He paused, looking amused. "Your church's tight embrace of a president who was a serial perjurer, sexual predator, philanderer and thief who conned his followers for money and sought to destroy democracy and embrace enemies. Your role in promoting a fake terrorist attack in the last election certainly clarifies the accuracy of your point. Yet your moral code, such as it is, becomes irrelevant if your churches disintegrate because your flocks move away from Jesus if he is proven to be only an illusion. Let us keep our focus on what is important."

"You should not be here," she snapped. "You insult our faith, mocking sincere views on homosexuality and—"

"Millions don't share your fixation. Despite a seriously regressive U.S. Supreme Court. America, I believe, has moved on. You should too."

"Many Americans are fooled by the power and wealth of the homosexual lobby. But we're not. And our words are spreading around the world." She sneered, tossing her head back as if she had now won the debate.

Vega stood; his eyes focused on hers. "I was not going to do this but your thoughtless hostility..." His voice was hard, the menace unmistakable. "You have blood on your hands, Sister. Someday you shall face justice. If I did not see *Misago* as a greater threat to social cohesion, I would certainly not be willing to work with you or even be in the same room, such is the level of my disgust with you and people like you. History will not treat you well, I suspect, and Lucifer, if you believe in him, awaits."

"Don't you dare insult me or my allies in Christ!" Sister growled, inching up to his face. "You don't know anything about God if you're a Muslim!"

"And if *Misago* is true, then neither do you."

She swung her open palm toward him but he easily intercepted her wrist and held it firm, twisting it until she squirmed. "Let me go you pretty boy apostate!" She splattered his face with spittle.

"Let her go!" Broux demanded, standing but not interfering. Nor did anyone else.

Vega yanked her close, his voice a knife blade as he pulled the scarf from her neck and wiped his face. "I practice no religion that I will discuss here and I do my best to hold society together even as some seem anxious to tear it apart for absurd issues of feigned piety, mindless ambition, and a natural human function like sex." He let her go with a shove, driving her back a step, forcing her to grab the back of a chair to retain balance, and tossed the scarf at her. "Focus on reality instead of nonsense. Be forewarned, I am not always a gentle man." He winked at the cardinal.

"If you cannot work together on such an issue as *Misago*, perhaps you deserve to lose. Your faith is at a precipice and you play games. Think carefully about what you decide. Cross this new god at your peril. And, your public relations campaign is the work of a fool." Vega shook his head and exited the room.

Martinez took a deep breath and exhaled. He'd never seen the man so angry. Fortunately, his own pious voice came easy. "God is served by many people and many religions," he said. "In this challenge from *Misago,* all people who believe in God, any God, have common purpose. Mr. Vega has served the Catholic Church with great effect for many years. He is a good man and important ally to all of us." He gestured to Sister Esther who was purple with fury. "Trust me, we *need* him. Now, I think we have more important things to worry about. Let me add, he did not say he is Muslim, you inferred it." The cardinal stood, picking up his briefcase. "I have calls to make."

Vega was standing under an arched lattice covered in star jasmine, so fragrant the cardinal sensed it a dozen yards away. The man seemed to be examining the exquisite white flowers, nothing on his mind except the perfection of nature, certainly not his confrontation with some self-obsessed clerics.

"Romaldo, you did that on purpose. We need them, and mocking them is not a way to build alliances."

"We all need our boundaries expanded, Your Eminence." He took another inhale and turned to him. "Knowledge is constantly expanding except to those frozen in a world of rote memory and pettiness. The issue before us is so staggering in its consequences that fools may not add much value to the fight. We need people of courage and imagination to have an honest discussion, should it go public. When the emperor is naked, tell him. My patience is limited, given the stakes."

Palo Alto, California

On a quiet cul-de-sac, the San Francisco Symphony recording of Igor Stravinsky's *Le Sacre du Printemps* played softly on the stereo in the home of Dr. Steven Combs. For hours, he and Elizabeth Cleaver had reviewed Wada's data.

"You know I really hate this music. It's programmed every

few songs," Elizabeth said, sitting at the kitchen table.

"Of course. Why do you think I'm playing it?" Combs looked at his friend, smiled and gulped the rest of his coffee. "It reminds us of what *Misago* presents."

She put down a stale glazed donut, licking sugary fingers. "I keep thinking about yesterday when you took me to Stanford," she said. "My palms were sweating, my throat dry, my heart racing and all I did was look at the images on the screen. The implications are so big that I'm still struggling." Elizabeth looked at her longtime and unlikely friend. "You've asked me to join you in this to bring some fundamentalist think tank respectability to your new cause," she said. "That could ruin my group financially. What's wrong with a regular paycheck, a comfortable religion and a house in the suburbs?"

Combs leaned back in his chair, folding his hands behind his head. "Absolutely nothing. But here's another possibility. Your leadership could greatly expand your base as an organization that takes off its blinders when confronting a new scientific discovery. Surprise your supporters and confound your critics! You're on a quest. Your credibility will skyrocket. Your media coverage will be heavy and I suspect even your funders will be worried about dumping you in the middle of a very public debate. There's also the possibility of other non-Christian sources, funding from groups and individuals that want this new clarion voice of reason to continue being heard."

"But *Misago* undercuts the purpose of the Institute," Elizabeth said. Then she laughed at a new thought. "I might not get invited back to the White House for one of those fancy state dinners."

"Yes, but maybe the next president will be less politically pious and you could get asked to parties that are actually fun. One part of your equation—an intelligent designer created life—wins over part two—in the image of God."

"We never state that." She sounded defensive.

"No, but that's what ID is about. Think bigger," he said with a sense of urgency. "Think history. We're on the cusp of what could totally transform human spirituality and open new windows on science. Imagine if we eventually translate whatever is on these nano cubes. Even as a longtime atheist, I get shivers. You may never have this opportunity again."

"I get shivers too, but a window that offers a new view of reality is quite different from the one you jump out of and plunge to your death. Jake Machin and the CCC will destroy anyone who dares go public. More than just reputations. They're vengeful."

Combs rubbed his eyes, exhausted from hours of hard chew discussion. "I never claimed there weren't risks," he said. "With jeopardy comes opportunity. That's why I think your organization can be key in altering perceptions when this goes public. It will make conservatives look at it seriously, not just reject it as liberal science."

"You sound confident it will go public."

"I have no doubt. This is the genie of creation and the lamp has been rubbed." He giggled. "Apologies for that dreadful analogy. My brain needs rest. Talk to your key people, you miserable Christian, at least those committed to something beyond the status quo and might see the value in jointly seeking to understand this revelation. I capitalize the letter R."

His friend was silent.

"We're also doing some research with colleagues at Berkeley," Combs continued softly. "Sharing it only with those we trust. If I can set up a meeting with Wada, would you come?"

Elizabeth snapped her head back. "Yes, absolutely, you arrogant atheist. I'll fly back this morning and be ready to join you and Wada any time. I'm still undecided about what to do, but I hear the Siren's call. I just need to figure out if it's pulling me to the rocks or to glory."

"To glory," Combs responded, holding up a glass of orange juice.

36.

Travis Air Force Base, Sacramento

"Where are you now, general?"

"A military installation two hours south."

"Good," Sister stated with satisfaction, holding her cell phone before her face to view him. "We have Wada's space dust. Actually the cardinal does."

"Do I understand he has nothin' left of value?"

"Correct. Some talked about a good faith effort to study it. I see no need. The findings are lethal to faith. The cardinal's man is openly disrespectful and may not even be Christian."

"What?"

"Never mind."

"So what do we do with Wada and the others?" The general assumed their views meshed. Crushing the discovery was the right move. Rumors, tips from staff members loyal to God who had called him, suggested the president was vacillating. Best to hold that intel close.

"Shouldn't you be the one telling me?"

"He's a terrorist, perhaps an unwitting one," the general responded, ignoring her snide remark. "Wada's bombs are disguised as science."

"Agreed."

"Duboce is a journalist. He'll want to go public. We can't allow that. He'll be stopped."

"Our exposure of the biased liberal media for years is helpful. It's all fake when it does not support our worldview, such is the righteousness of our cause. Our truth supersedes all others."

"Yes, Sister. Strategic and prescient. Plus creating our own media with reporters who know our truth. I'll bring some FBI agents to Tahoe."

"Excellent. I have some special contacts who might be helpful as all this evolves."

Beauregard touched his keyboard and a map of Lake Tahoe's east shore popped onto his screen. "Looking at roads there, you appear to be fairly isolated. A highway on one side, up a steep embankment, the lake on the other. There's an active Episcopal religious camp and parking lot to the north and private homes and a meadow to the south. Control of the site seems easy. Given what's happened, any chance we can trust the Swiss Guards?"

"They obey Martinez and they're armed. You'd need to be cautious. We don't want an international incident with American soldiers shootin' Vatican security guards."

"Agreed." He picked up a recently printed photo. "I pulled details on Duboce. A pretty boy but he apparently can handle himself." The general smirked. "I'd like to see how tough he is. I'll be in Tahoe later today. Minimum force. I don't need more."

Spanto Telecome Tower, Portland, Oregon

Elizabeth Cleaver was back at headquarters by late afternoon, feeling anxious as her team members entered her office. It was foggy outside, obscuring her view of the high rise across the street. She had pulled four chairs from the table in her small space, setting up a large computer screen on a table in front. It was all mid-century shabby, considered poverty chic in some design circles as long as you ignored rips and stains on seat fabric. She'd asked to meet with them in private and cancel all other activities, promising news that was world-shaking. She needed to be in top form.

Titus Jones, known both for charm and bombast, was heavyset with pale skin offering dramatic contrast to black hair gelled and combed straight back. He was key, Elizabeth thought, popular with religious conservatives and a prodigious writer of tracts. At forty-five, he headed the Center for Science and Faith, the heart of the Institute, and focused on campaigns promoting Intelligent Design in public schools.

Dr. Stanley Jianguo, articulate and intense, was the Director of Finance. His round steel framed glasses, too big for his small face, made him seem much younger than his thirty-five years.

Chikae Swung claimed his given name meant "God's Power" and he was indeed an animated and popular speaker. At six-feet-five inches he had become a frequent basketball player among black teenagers in tough parts of the city. He managed Public Policy and Legal Affairs. He was forty-seven but looked older because of his graying hair.

"Are we clear for the rest of the afternoon and evening?" Elizabeth asked. "I think we will not want to be interrupted once we start."

Nods all around.

Elizabeth clasped her hands behind her back and looked at her team, all professionals as well as friends. "This is confidential. None of us will disclose the content of this conversation to anyone without my consent. If anyone has a problem with that, please speak now so you can be excused. I'm sorry to be so difficult, but it'll make sense once I start."

"Don't be a pain in the ass, Elizabeth. Talk," Chikae taunted. "We'll follow the rules—we're Christians, remember?"

The others nodded.

She walked to the door and twisted the lock closed with a theatrical click, then turned down the lights. Her computer was already prepped. She'd been rehearsing with the materials for the past half hour. She couldn't be facing a tougher audience.

"I've spent the last two days in Palo Alto at a friend's home. I think you're familiar with Dr. Steven Combs of SETI Institute. Yes, the one who has the PBS series and the handlebar mustache. We were college friends at Cal and he remains a trusted friend. He's privy to information that's the political and theological equivalent of a ten-point earthquake on the Richter Scale."

"Hmmmm. I read somewhere that a ten isn't possible," Chikae offered. "The earthquake in Revelations was an estimated 8.9. The same article said an eleven would split the earth in two."

"About the same," Elizabeth responded. "In terms of western civilization, this would rival it if it goes public and if the data holds true. It was shared with me in confidence and Dr. Combs has given me permission to show it to you and seek your advice. Darwinists and Christians can sometimes agree."

All three men leaned forward, curious.

"Have any of you followed stories about the missing space scientist from Japan, Dr. Yoshito Wada of the *Misago* space program?"

They all shook their heads.

"Here's what some of the newspapers have been publishing in Japan." Elizabeth flashed through several English language web pages with headlines about the kidnapping.

"Let me start with the discoveries on three distant asteroids and bring you up to date. As I talk, please think about how this impacts our work and our future."

For the next hour, she worked through two-dozen images, of *Misago* and the nano cubes, some prepared by Wada, some she'd worked up with Steven Combs. The three associates asked an occasional question, but otherwise sat quietly, rapt. She left up an image of the mandala. Then faced her audience.

"Reactions?"

Chikae shook his head. "It's science fiction. Your buddy is playing a bad joke on you."

"It does sound like that," Titus suggested, staring at the screen. "Yet, suppose it's not a joke. Then, stunner!"

"It proves our case for Intelligent Design!" Stanley shouted and then covered his mouth in embarrassment. "Sorry. It's astonishing, ridiculous, mesmerizing, fun, and wild. I could think of adjectives for a long time. My question—is this legit?"

"If it is, I think the big issue," Titus stated, "is whether it would trigger wars, terrorism, jihad and assorted other violence! People want their mythology true or not. Some are willing to kill if it's challenged. Remember Salman Rushdie? The Ayatollah of Iran issued a death sentence because of the way his novel interpreted a verse by Muhammad. Imagine how the Muslim world would react to this."

Chikae countered, "I don't think the fear factor should be part of our decision-making. If we do nothing the story may unfold anyway and we'll have less chance of influencing results. Suppose liberal Christians had a heads up and acted to involve themselves. Would we be able to play catch up later?"

Elizabeth extended her arms, pleased at the direction. "Each of you asks the right questions and shows the right skepticism. I spent many hours on this, including use of electron and other microscopes at SETI and Stanford. I've seen the nano cubes. Dr. Combs believes it's real and has met with Dr. Wada who's in the U.S. secretly and brought samples. He's seeking to build a case to overturn the ban put in place by the Japanese government."

Titus sat, his arms folded. "You said the CCC board was behind the president's decision to keep this secret. Are you sure? I know they were instrumental in Walton's election but this is beyond any payback I've ever heard about. Those guys are big supporters of I.D. They are also rumored to be pressing the president to declare America under the leadership of God. Whatever that means. They rule, I guess."

Chikae rose and started pacing. "If this is true, if this is true," he said, "it both destroys and supports our mission. It undercuts the foundation of Christianity as we know it. But it's also very exciting." He gave a bitter laugh.

"I can understand why the CCC wanted to keep this quiet," Stanley said. "I suspect most folks just won't believe it."

Elizabeth nodded. "I agree. But are we most folks? Where do we want to come down on this kind of cataclysmic discovery? Do we keep it secret or take it forward? Do we stay quiet and implicitly support its suppression? Do we go public at an opportune time and urge its study but remain neutral? Do we go further and stake a claim on this, essentially riding the back of the tiger?"

The three stared at her. She knew her questions were impossible and their minds were racing.

"I find myself torn, as you are, but here's the core issue. Do we seek to preserve the past or do we embark on the creation of a whole new religious foundation for mankind?"

"Stop! Not so fast." Standing again, Titus gripped the back of his chair. "These are huge questions and I'm not ready. We need to talk this through."

"My friend," Elizabeth said, "that's why I asked you to clear your calendars. That's why we're here, the four of us, to work together to discover and interpret and understand. That's what our Institute's all about and this is the biggest issue we've ever faced by far."

Titus cleared his throat and began to talk with a slight quaver. "Even if this goes public in a big way, it could take decades for this to play through."

Chikae: "We look at issues long term and our pledge is to find or develop policy options to strengthen America and its religious core."

Stanley raised his hand. "But we exist short term," he said. "We live by our annual fundraising. If we're tied to this bombshell it could piss off most of our donors."

"May I speak a little heresy?" Elizabeth didn't wait for a response. "I believe Intelligent Design is a brilliant concept born in a think tank as a PR tool. It worked effectively for years. In the face of legal failures and criticism from the scientific community, we've opened American public schools to alternative views of creation, our stated goal."

Titus looked skeptical. "You want to declare victory like Nixon in Vietnam? You want to abandon Intelligent Design to the atheists?" There was a nasty edge to his question.

"I agree with Titus," Stanley offered. "A new idea, no matter how stimulating, does not a new mission statement make." Then he laughed. "Of course, with this discovery there may not be any atheists." He paused, raising his head. "Or, maybe we all become agnostics in the sense of what we've believed."

Elizabeth nodded. So far, so good. "We may have early results back from Steven's own research team by tomorrow." She stood and pressed her palms together to calm her nerves for the big question. "Would you be interested in meeting privately with Wada? Remember he's being hunted by the FBI."

"Yes!" All three spoke in unison.

"Excellent. We proceed cautiously."

"Go ahead, Elizabeth, dream big," Titus said. "That's what we do. What are you yourself thinking?"

"Thank you, my friend," she answered. "I think this is a thunderbolt. Publicly we exist to examine natural and supernatural theories on the creation of life. This discovery shows the hand of an architect. We have it directly from the creator, and maybe in his own handwriting, if I may take some poetic license?"

"Too much license, actually," Stanley said, teasing.

"Given the heads-up, is it best to stay on our current path and ignore this discovery, indeed work to discredit it when it comes out as it surely will eventually? Or, do we take a major risk, shock the hell out of our own constituency and the national media, take a leadership role in the movement to study *Misago* and maybe, just maybe, be part of the elite group of humans who begin to shape a new religion based on the discoveries and our conservative values? Where lies our value? Where lies fame and glory?"

Stanley: "Where lies money? As CFO, we'll need money to keep this think tank solvent and do all these exciting things. Let's be honest. We're hired guns and our religious conservative bosses may simply go elsewhere. An honest hired academic-gun can turn into an unemployed and discredited academic-gun."

Chikae: "Wait guys! I can work anywhere. I didn't leave my integrity at the door when I signed on. I like the money but I also have pride. If we handle it right, we can keep donors engaged. We should consider Elizabeth's proposition. She's not suggesting abandoning Jesus. This thunderbolt needs creative thinkers who can turn its electricity into useful Christian current."

Titus: "Boo! Bad imagery. Let's focus on doing what's right. I love a good fight. I'd hate to see the liberals grab this thing and run with it. Or the agnostic scientists! But I believe the Christian right—if it's smart—will want to be a player on this, running with the discovery and not just trying to block it."

Chikae: "Time out, guys, too many metaphors." The group laughed.

Stanley: "I think we could argue that we're out front to keep options open for conservatives, to be part of the inside planning so we know what's going on. I think some donors would agree."

Elizabeth said, "We might find a path that brings glory, puts us back as key policy players, supports our conservative values and pays the bills! And, it might be fun."

Chikae stood and moved closer to the screen. "Can we look again at the three nano cubes with the circular markings?"

The others followed.

Stonehouse Lodge, Lake Tahoe

Michaels detested being kept on hold as if he were merely a low-level hired gun. He wandered near the boathouse, hoping to stay out of sight. The sun was low on the mountains across the lake.

"Yes," Jake Machin said finally, his voice cold.

"Mr. Machin, Mike Michaels here. You said to keep you informed. The group is supportive of moving ahead with the campaign to go public and discredit the discovery," he said, his words tumbling out. "Actually, I should say the American clergy. The cardinal was negative. He thinks this could backfire. The *National Muckraker* is interested and we're ready to contact various blogs and maybe even comedy writers at the major late-night shows as soon as it's out." He sounded breathless.

"An amusing strategy, Michaels. Maybe it'd work. Depends on luck."

"I want to be optimistic, sir."

"It's not enough. Fortunately, the stun dossier on Wada is nearly complete. If the president approves, I'll drop it with one or two key columnists when and if the time is right. Nothing until then. Your staff has been very helpful. The JAXA director, Wada's boss at the agency, is trying to find a psychiatrist who's willing to state that he treated Wada for depression. They have money. It shouldn't be a problem. That's the last piece."

"What about a JAXA scientist attacking Wada's credibility?"

"It's in the works. They're looking for someone, perhaps in financial trouble, who can be coerced. One credible scientist will condemn another. A pile on. The media and public will be confused and eventually lose interest. Nothing turns people off more than complexity."

"Great. And without the granules or photos there's no proof. Be forewarned. The cardinal and even Reverend Wright keep talking about truth. I'm not sure if they're serious."

"Are they fools, Michaels? Are you? Truth is not the issue, winning is. Winners write history."

As the phone clicked off, Michaels decided he couldn't disagree.

37.

Harrah's Casino, Stateline, Nevada

Martinez saw a familiar face on the screen. "Please thank the White House staff for setting up this secure video conference," he said, sitting inside a small studio in Harrah's Casino at Stateline on Lake Tahoe's south shore. "I assume it's just us." He had come to the hotel where his staff was staying so he could conduct other pressing business. Never had the normal demands of the Vatican seemed more tedious.

The president nodded. "I thought it might be nice to see each other, Diego, and despite the early hour it makes you look saintly. Perhaps it's the static. It's supposed to be secure. Of course, Richard Nixon probably thought the same sitting in the Oval Office."

"So, caution is prudent. There's also irony in a Catholic cardinal sitting in a Nevada casino."

Walton grinned at his old friend. "Just avoid the slot machines, not much return on investment."

"Have you reviewed the updated JAXA materials?" the cardinal asked, ready to get to the point. "I assume your delivery service is even better than the pope's."

"I don't get direct transmissions from heaven like you but the

State Department is relatively efficient. The Japanese prime minister was surprised. He knew nothing about any quasi-mandalas. I suspect Wada has been holding back. Now I'm anxious to know more."

"I need to absorb what I have which is unsettling enough."

"Is this a curse or an opportunity?"

The cardinal pinched his lower lip. "I sense you're in one of your moods, Jeremiah, and need to talk. So, I'm listening, my friend. An appropriate role for a priest."

The president leaned forward, put his elbows on the desk and folded his arms. "You know me well. Until now I've only looked at *Misago* as a threat. Invalidating Genesis is not a little thing. Intellectually, I dismissed what it's about. I can be slow sometimes." He looked lost, as if trying to determine which way to turn in a labyrinth.

"Just talk, my friend," the cardinal urged.

"I've used religion as a convenient political campaign tool," Walton confessed, "but this is different, more lethal. People will be afraid or angry. There are about three hundred million guns in America and rationality is not a requirement of ownership. One gun club sells bullets from a vending machine. Add in armed Christian militias and assorted fevered groups. How do I manage it?"

"Selling fear is not a good long-term strategy, Jeremiah, and certainly not healthful for democracy. That admonition of Franklin Roosevelt in the darkest days of World War II —'There is nothing to fear but fear itself'—still holds true today. Remember, America is more than a superpower. Your nation is a noble dream, in many ways almost mythological, a symbol addressing human longing for a life where individual talents and initiative determine success and happiness, where government is a helpmate, not some ossified social system. The hunger for freedom and justice is ingrained in our souls and despite its shortcomings America is still the hope."

"I suspect you're right, even if we've often fallen short." Walton shrugged. "So, now I'm the president of all the people, at least that was my oath, and I'm looking at the most provocative discovery in the last 2,000 years. We're keeping it hidden for the moment. Good or bad? I thought I knew, Diego. I'm glad you admire Roosevelt. Me too and I liked Reagan for the same reason." The president sounded more energized being back on politics. "They were optimists who sought to inspire with a grand vision, asking people to believe, to have hope and not just fear. Obama was that way too. Most presidents end their terms and wonder what they did that mattered. Generally, it's a war that defines a great presidency, like Lincoln and the Civil War or Roosevelt and Pearl Harbor. I have *Misago*. What do I do? Right now, I'm trying to hide it."

"Are you talking to me, Mr. President, or history?"

Jeremiah, tugged back into his private world, seemed to stare through him. His voice was a whisper when he came back. "You helped me find myself once long ago, Diego. When I lost confidence, lost my wife and son, lost direction, lost an election and was adrift. You found me and gave me heart and belief in myself."

"And you, Jeremiah, took a despondent cleric and convinced him that there really was a loving God, despite the evil and misery of the world that overwhelmed him. You taught him that he still had a role to play."

"Yes, two men burned out at an early age with too much grief."

The two stared at each other, reliving horrors impossible to forget.

Walton began again. "Let me try something on you, Diego, something you might find a little heretical, given your position and my record. It's something I was thinking about when we set up these meetings. If I can continue my soliloquy, I think about Jefferson." He lifted a document from his desk. "A famous quote of Jefferson's, etched on his memorial in Washington, takes on a different meaning when you see it in context. It's a letter to Dr. Benjamin Rush, a signatory of the Declaration of Independence. It's the raw Jefferson, what you might find in the first draft of a letter written in quill pen.

'I promised you a letter on Christianity…I have a view on the subject which ought to displease neither the rational Christian nor Deists, and would reconcile many on the clause of the constitution, which, while it secured the freedom of the press, covered also the freedom of religion, had given to the clergy a very favorite hope of obtaining an establishment of a particular form of Christianity thro' the U. S.; and as every sect believes its own form the true one, everyone perhaps hoped for his own, but especially the Episcopalians & Congregationalists. The returning good sense of our country threatens abortion to their hopes, & they believe that any portion of power confided to me, will be exerted in opposition to their schemes. And they believe rightly; FOR I HAVE SWORN UPON THE ALTAR OF GOD, ETERNAL HOSTILITY AGAINST EVERY FORM OF TYRANNY OVER THE MIND OF MAN. But this is all they have to fear from me'."

Martinez absorbed the words before offering comment. "So much wisdom, so many questions raised in such a few words. Not much has changed in two centuries other than the names of the religions. Every faith believes it's the chosen one and all others are wrong." He started to smile and then pulled back, dark issues surging in his head. *When does faith in a loving god surrender to hubris and human ambition? God sometimes seemed like an afterthought in the competition for followers, power and money. Abraham was at the heart of all three great western religions but that commonality was often abandoned in acts of violence not for God but always in His name. The examples were endless.*

"Is America on a dangerous track?" the president asked. "Should we pull back and return to the view of the Founding Fathers? Is that a discussion we can even have? Another question might be: Is *Misago* a vehicle for that dialogue? What direction would it take us? The final question might be—am I the man to do it?"

"Tough questions, Jeremiah. I suspect you're suggesting that you're in a unique position to change things if you decide it's the right thing to do. Only Nixon could go to China and talk with the

Communists, and only a born-again president can seek greater secularization or lead the nation in a discussion about *Misago*."

Martinez watched his friend's reaction. "Your mother named you Jeremiah after a prophet who warned of the oncoming destruction of Judah if the nation did not stop its idolatry and immorality. Be careful of what you reap when you deal with this whirlwind called *Misago*, dear friend, as well as religious intolerance. What *Misago* offers is dangerous and unpredictable."

"Caution is always well advised, Diego. I recognize and fear the danger. Now we seek to suppress it." The president scratched his cheek and looked back into the screen. "But if it's a message from the creator, why wouldn't we listen? Is there no upside? I guess that's my question. Is it possible for us and other men of good will to separate our prejudices from our ability to understand and reason? You're the keeper of the faith of Catholicism, but you're so much more than that. You're a man who can think and who values reason. You don't denigrate the capabilities of the mind to make it easier to accept the contradictions of dogma."

"You give me too much credit," the cardinal said. "When you offer your heart to a cultural phenomenon such as Catholicism, it's difficult to disengage. Let me say it's inspiring to know that the chief of state for the world's most powerful nation is capable of thinking big and bold. Some of your predecessors were fools pandering to the darkness. But I know you'll temper it all with the insights and wisdom gained in a remarkable life. That's what leadership is supposed to be but rarely is. I'm just not sure what I can advise other than caution. Dip your toe slowly into this witch's cauldron. I would like to reflect on it and talk again." He smiled, they both nodded, and closed the connection.

The cardinal rubbed his eyes and lowered his head. Trying to remain upbeat and helpful to his friend had left him exhausted.

"He greatly admires Your Eminence," Vega said as they exited the communications booth. "He is intellectually ambitious yet risks much if his pride and hubris overtake his political instincts. You advised caution and he would be wise to listen."

They were headed back to Stonehouse in Vega's town car, sitting together in the back seat for the half hour ride. Vega asked, "Would you be willing to offer some of your shared history? Please know that I understand if I probe too deeply."

Diego didn't respond at first; his relationship with Walton was long, painful and complex. When he eventually spoke, anxious to be honest to a man who had saved his life, he felt uplifted even by the dark tale, given the brotherhood it had birthed.

Vega said, "His official biographies deal with his narrow loss for Lieutenant Governor of Colorado many years ago. And that on the evening of that loss, he, his wife and young son left their headquarters and all three were shot by a man intoxicated by drugs. Walton managed to knock him to the ground and pound his head on the sidewalk until his skull cracked."

The cardinal's voice broke as he said, "Jeremiah lost all hope and purpose. Biographies don't mention the self-doubt that nearly destroyed him, just the heroism and attempted defense of his family that eventually re-launched his career."

Vega said, "Even serious biographies are vague about what happened afterward. Some have suggested the rejuvenation was because of God but your name in effecting this has never been connected to his. I know I venture perhaps too close to private truths and you should feel no obligation to share more."

The cardinal turned in the seat and looked at Vega, and said after a silence lasting minutes, "When I was a boy, a great earthquake hit Panama and much of Central America. Thousands were killed, including many in my village. I didn't understand how God could allow such a disaster but my priest and family prayed fervently to thank God for our survival. I assumed I just wasn't old enough to understand."

He looked out the window, admiring the beauty of a spring meadow along the shores of Lake Tahoe, taking strength from it before continuing. "Eventually I went into the priesthood, loving God, putting my doubts aside, and I rose quickly through the ranks of the church. You already know I became a monsignor in Argentina during the dirty wars, the *Guerra Sucia,* state-sponsored terrorism that killed thousands. Thousands more simply disappeared. The true evil of men drunk on their own self-importance. I was arrested several times, even tortured."

He pulled his sleeve back and revealed a jagged scar. "I'll never forget the words of one military leader about the death squads:

'As many people as necessary must die in Argentina so that the country will again be secure.'"

As the car passed through the Cave Rock tunnel, he began again. "Traveling with two nuns, I came across a school in a rural area. The children had been caught in a fight between rebels and a death squad. Those not killed by bullets died in a fire. We tried to help. It was hopeless. I cradled a boy in my lap." He held the invisible child in his arms, brushing back the blood-stained hair on the child's forehead. "I had no means to save him as he and I sat surrounded by two score of murdered children. He passed to God in my arms."

Tears welled in his eyes. "I left Argentina and through the church sought refuge in a Catholic sanctuary outside South America. My order sent me to the mountains in Colorado so I could be cut off from the world as long as I needed. I was shattered and could not comprehend how a God of love could abandon children and let them die at the hands of criminals. Nor how the Creator of the world could allow his progeny to perish in natural disasters. To be told that men simply cannot understand the needs of God left me cold and agnostic.

"On one of many long and solitary hikes I met a man not unlike myself, broken, abandoned and having lost his faith. In the beginning, we used only our first names and were slow to reveal our history as we met frequently and sat and talked and wept over weeks and months. His name was Jeremiah Walton."

The cardinal turned and put a hand over his eyes, seeking to shield long suppressed emotion. Vega pulled a handkerchief from his pocket and handed it to him.

"Together," he said quietly, wiping his eyes, "over a long summer, fall and winter we rediscovered ourselves, God and purpose. A few years later, gunmen in Palestine kidnapped me and you came into my life. God is indeed mysterious in the connections He makes."

38.

Stonehouse Lodge, Lake Tahoe

"It's time to make like Moses and flee Egypt," Wada said, grinning slyly as he looked up from his pre-lunch matcha in their regular meet-up space in Daniel's room.

"It's dangerous for non-Jews to talk like that," Daniel responded. "But I agree. It's time to part the waters."

"Does your confrontation with the guards mean we're prisoners?" Tio asked.

"The guards, at least those two, seem to think so. Don't know if Vega gave them orders or they're just bullies. Physically, we're vulnerable because we're dangerous. Vega warned us back in San Francisco. Michaels is ruthless," he said. "If he's working with President Walton's political hit man you can bet they'll try to destroy us politically via the media."

Wada stepped to the window. A Swiss guard stood a few yards out into the woods. "They watch us. Strategy suggests we not take chances. My rental car sits a mile north in Camp Galilee. An ironic name considering what we are about."

"What about Garrett and Trudy?" Saito asked.

"We need to get them out," Daniel replied.

"I believe we're the target," Yoshito said, "not them. I sense Martinez is a man of integrity and will protect them. Who owns the guards is the big question and if it's Vega, are we sanguine about his intentions?"

Daniel raised an eyebrow. "I guess my proximity to the Catholic Church makes me less bullish on the cardinal."

"Of course they'll go with us and we need to make sure they understand the risk both ways," Tio said as she stood.

"Wise counsel," Saito added, standing next to her.

Daniel set down his tea. "Thank you. I've been thinking of a diversion to add to our margin of success. It's a bit complicated but might work."

Saito touched his shoulder. Wada hurried to be next to him. "Tell us, Daniel."

The East Shore, Lake Tahoe

Thirty minutes later, Daniel went searching for his ex-wife. He spotted her on the beach. Wearing designer jeans and a light sweater, she was reading a romance novel. Garrett, in red swim trunks, was playing fetch with a black Labrador, likely from a nearby home. Trudy watched Daniel approach, her back stiffening as she closed her book.

Garrett skidded to a stop on his knees, sand flying, with the Lab in close pursuit. "Cool dog, huh, Dad?" He tossed a piece of driftwood and they covered their eyes against more flying sandas the dog pivoted back to the water which was slightly warmer at the shore.

"We need to get another dog," Daniel said, wiping sand off his shirt. "It was tough when Jackson died. We all loved him."

"I'd love it!" Then Garrett looked downcast. "But—my stepdad's got allergies and is obsessed about dirt."

Daniel smiled, pleased to help him in a way Trudy could not. His career as a journalist might soon end, given his personal involvement in a story of this magnitude, and he had a free place to stay in San Francisco, not an insignificant advantage. "We'll find a new friend on your next trip, a rescue. He can live with me. I may be spending a lot more time in the City."

"*Yes!*" Garrett yelled. The Lab, dripping wet, ran toward them and bumped the boy's leg, ready for another toss. They wrestled and ran down the beach. "Mom," he yelled, "Dad says I can have a dog and he's moving back to San Francisco!" He bounded into the lake with his new friend, apparently oblivious to the cold.

Daniel shook his head, grinning as he dropped down cross-legged beside her. He needed to get them away but wanted her to understand the risks. She also needed to be enthusiastic and buy into the plan. A cascade of past arguments with her flashed through his head. It had to be her idea.

"So," she said, "you want to get him another dog?"

"He can stay with me."

"Garrett or the dog?"

"Ugh, the dog with me full time and Garrett part time."

"Are you sleeping with Saito?" Her voice was sharp. "I've seen the way you two exchange glances and the way he touches you. Are you gay? I never thought you were. Why did you marry me if you were gay? Are all priests gay?"

"Please. Enough. Not all priests are gay, just a small percentage to my knowledge. I wasn't a priest, just a student studying for the priesthood when I met you and fell in love. I had feelings for men, even some teenage experimentation but when I met you, all that fell away. I loved you with all my heart and wanted no one else. But meeting Saito established that I am bisexual."

She gazed at him in dismay. "I…I don't know how to respond. My husband's gay. Sleeping with a man while I'm here with our son."

"Ex-husband. You divorced me, remember?" Don't attack. He told himself. Stay focused and find out if there's a real problem. "I've no idea what offense I've committed in finding someone in my life. Certainly Garrett's seen nothing that should upset him. I would say Saito and I are dating. Yes, we're having sex. Are you comfortable since we have both moved on?"

She watched Garrett running down the beach, and her demeanor eased. "Yes. I think I can accept it because you're an honorable man. We have gay friends. He'll be fine with it." Her expression changed, a bit shrewish. "Let me ask, did you sleep with any men while we were married?"

"I kept my vows." This really pissed him off. "Did you sleep with Gerard McIntyre before you divorced me?"

"This dog offer is just to get Garrett closer to you."

She drove him nuts. Never answer a question when the answer is difficult. "Let's not fight. I just think boys and dogs go together." They sat staring at the lake. Why were conversations with her always circular?

"Daniel, do you hate me for leaving you?"

"I'm sad about it but I've moved on. You weren't getting what you needed and I understand. Now I just want my son to stay in my life."

She watched Garrett jump into the water with the dog. "You know I was never like you, into ideas and politics and social purpose. I like comfort and I want my son to grow up with money and go to good schools. Is that so bad?"

His mind filled with many thoughts, not all of them friendly. "We all need different things, I guess. I'm sorry I wasn't enough for you but I understand and hold no grudges. I wish you happiness and hope you won't deprive me of my son."

Her eyebrows pinched together, either surprised or suspicious. "I'll never use your homosexuality against you with Garrett."

"I'd hope not. You're a good person and I like to think we were in love. I certainly would never do anything to create tension in your relationship with our son. He is far too precious for games."

"Garrett loves you desperately and misses you. I didn't realize it until this visit. He idolizes you, he's just as afraid of losing you as you are of losing him."

"I can't compete with vacations and fancy clothes. The *Times* pays okay, as long as the job lasts, but nothing like what you married into."

"Garrett isn't blinded by money." She looked down. "Just me, I guess."

Don't go there. "He'll soon be a teenager. Teens can become self-absorbed. Status, clothes, and cars." He realized her upper crust accent had faded.

"You treat him like an adult. That's really important to him. And…" She paused. "And you were really impressive with your passion and arguments. I'm proud of you. So's Garrett. We're both blown away."

Son and canine friend collapsed next to them. "We need to talk," Daniel said, his tone urgent. "I ask your confidence for this conversation."

Garrett moved closer. Trudy just watched, eyes narrowing.

"You were brought here to influence me to support the clergy," he said.

"Did it work?" Trudy said bluntly, almost dismissively, then seemed surprised at her own words.

"Don't worry. I still have a mind of my own. I'm a reporter and the *Times* is going to cover this, as is the *Beacon*. When it goes public, there'll be a ferocious political effort to discredit it, maybe even destroy the reputations of Dr. Wada, myself, and the papers. You know we turned over materials that Saito brought over," he said. "The cardinal will do what he will with them. Hopefully it'll distract them. But what you should know is that I intend to get out of here tomorrow morning along with Yoshito, Saito and Tio."

"*What?*" Garrett looked alarmed.

Daniel said, "No easy task with the guards. You came here as guests of Mr. Vega. He and the cardinal are honorable and will see that you're taken back." He wanted to be honest about the dangers but not frighten them. Trudy needed to be adequately motivated.

"For the scientists and myself—we aren't sure if they'll let us go and we don't intend to ask. They may not have finalized their plans and the time seems right. Keep quiet about what you know; act surprised when we disappear." He held his breath waiting for their response.

Trudy encircled Garrett with an arm, pulling him close, her unspoken message clear: Our son comes first.

"Can we go with you, Dad? You're trying to do what you think is right. I want to be part of it and not left again." He sounded panicked, his eyes pleading.

Daniel was taken aback by a single word, "again." He had to play this out with her. "You're safer here with your mom."

"Only if Mom stays!" Trudy had a determined look and her voice was no-nonsense. "Garrett told me about the asshole guards. We'll go with you. I think Mrs. Mom needs to show solidarity with son and father. I don't want to trust Vega's goodwill given how he lied to us."

Garrett grinned, embracing her.

"OK. We're a team," Daniel said, immediately relieved, pleased at her strength and solidarity but concerned about the dangers ahead as they wrapped their hands around his and squeezed. "It's a hike but here's the plan…"

39.

Stonehouse Lodge, Lake Tahoe

Sitting on a bench behind a bank of ferns, Daniel read an online edition of the *Times* while enjoying the morning sun. Saito was nearby, waiting for Wada to emerge from coffee with Reverend Wright. The plan was already running late. Eventually the two men came out.

"Yes," the scientist said in parting conclusion to their conversation, "I think Buddhism is more evolution-friendly than most religions because it doesn't believe in permanence."

The minister thanked him, nodded to Daniel, and headed to his cabin. Wada glanced in his direction and rolled his eyes, heading slowly down the boardwalk, moving blissfully as he had counseled earlier and Daniel had laughed at the term.

A guard blocked Wada's path in the pines. A burly man in his thirties, the guard gave him a contemptuous look before stepping aside.

"And good day to you, too," Wada said, tipping his fedora, continuing his stroll, admiring the garden. The walk, taking a circuitous route, should help flush out the guards, as it just did this one, so they would know their locations. And it was blissfully done.

Saito stood up from the stone bench, stretched and hummed a tune that Daniel thought sounded familiar, and casually sauntered to Tio's room.

Daniel stuffed his laptop in his backpack and ambled to his cabin as blissfully as he could. A few minutes later, he left with Garrett. They went to Trudy's cabin and knocked loudly before entering.

"Mom, I'm here with Dad, look decent." Garrett came out wearing his own large backpack and strolled with his father down the boardwalk to the boat dock, talking excitedly about science class in school.

Tio went to the main lodge to signal Ealga. The two had become friendly, not difficult since most of the men ignored her. The housekeeper seemed taken with Daniel, likely found him sexy, but money was key: the pay for part-time work at Stonehouse was seasonal. The woman had been receptive to a substantial cash offer. The ministers were in the small conference area as they'd announced earlier. Tio walked through the great room in the lodge, saw Ealga, smiled and nodded. The woman touched a finger to her eyebrow in reply.

Tio went to the dining table, picked an apple from the fruit bowl and headed into the garden, munching contentedly. She strolled blissfully to her room, stopping once to listen to a low flying plane.

There were only two guards visible on the main grounds. They followed behind Garrett and Daniel at a discreet distance.

Wada checked his watch and turned back toward the cabins. He had seen no other guards. He entered Trudy's room. A moment later, the two quietly exited with light packs and disappeared into the forest.

Tio reached her room in the next building and in a clear, carrying voice said, "Yoshito, I've been thinking about what you said earlier..." She then closed the door behind her. Saito was waiting.

Father and son were on the dock, talking about the ecology of the lake. Daniel pointed to a group of trees turning brown and explained the beetle infestation rampant in the Tahoe basin. Garrett asked about the exhaust from the Chris Craft in the boat dock and its impact on pollution. Speaking in his best broadcast interview voice, Daniel explained the workings of an internal combustion engine. "I'll demonstrate with the Chris Craft." He took Garrett into the covered boathouse at the end of the dock. They left the door ajar but blocking the interior view from the boardwalk.

Daniel retrieved the key from behind the driftwood on the wall where he'd seen the cardinal take it when he took the ministers for a ride. He grabbed cushions and life jackets to start making dummies for the seats. Garrett dropped his pack to the floor and pulled out several shirts and baseball hats. They fit the clothes loosely over the cushions as they had practiced in their room, using pillows from the couch.

As they finished, a fire alarm sounded in the lodge.

Vega shouted for the guards.

Daniel and Garrett ran onto the dock as if curious about what was happening. Thick black smoke billowed menacingly out open doors and windows. Paid for grease fires could be messy and useful, Daniel thought, and was pleased they had brought plenty of cash for the trip. The two guards tailing them dashed to the lodge followed by a third patrolling nearby.

Watching from her cabin, Tio nodded at Daniel though a window, then she and Saito grabbed their packs and left, headed north.

Father and son stepped back into the shed. Daniel turned on the motor, set the automatic navigation system and guided the boat out of the slip. He checked wind direction and they pushed the classic 1930s Chris Craft toward the center of the lake.

Seeing no one, they fast walked down the dock and disappeared into the woods. "We meet at a grove of sequoias a mile north and fifty yards from shore," Daniel reminded Garrett.

They spotted Tio and Saito a short time later. As the four neared the rendezvous site, Dr. Wada waved his brown fedora and whistled a birdcall. Trudy, dressed in white pedal pushers with bright pink accessories, fanned both arms overhead. She was hard to miss. The two turned and walked into the redwood grove as they raced toward them.

"Shit!" Daniel yelled. A mountain-sized soldier in Army camouflage fatigues stepped from behind a tight crop of trees and grabbed Yoshito and Trudy by their necks. The man had a gray buzz cut; his shirt stretched tight over muscular arms and chest. Both resisted, but it was a one-sided fight. The soldier took their punches with a grin, playing with them. Then he saw Daniel and immediately shoved them to the ground. He had an eager look.

Still two hundred yards away, Daniel sprinted, not quite sure how he'd handle a guy built like a Transformer from the movie.

"We'll both take him out!" Saito shouted, running next to Daniel.

The soldier stepped a few feet closer and stopped, focused on Daniel, waiting, pounding his Hagrid-sized fist into an open palm.

Trudy jumped up, indignant and screaming. She hit the soldier's bicep with both fists and kicked his calf. He laughed, not even turning his head, pushing her to the ground.

Wada used the distraction to stand, straightening his jacket. He took the bottom end of his cane and swung his arm back, rotated the cane twice as if making certain of his calculations. The Osprey flew, crash landing into a spot just in front of the distracted man's right ear. The soldier froze, then tottered. Wada stepped behind him, examining the man's expression. "Yes, that's the spot." With satisfaction he tapped the back of the man's neck and, like a falling tree, the soldier toppled stiffly forward, the side of his face smashing into a pinecone.

"Ouch!" Wada winced and stooped to check his pulse.

"Are you all right?" Daniel shouted as he reached them, bending over, hands on his knees, panting. Saito was next to him, an arm around Wada and helping him stand. Tio and Garrett were a few steps behind. The soldier's collar was askew, showing a series of stars.

"He's unconscious," Wada said, sounding unruffled as he turned to Trudy. "A fine strategic distraction, my dear. Thank you." Wada stood and rubbed his bird. "He will regain consciousness soon. Prudence suggests restraint."

"You just did a smackdown on some general!" Daniel felt caught between impossible options. "How do we handle that? You could've killed him!"

"I want to fly like an eagle, till I'm free…"

"Appropriate, Dr. Saito," Wada responded. "Although technically it's an Osprey."

"Are you both nuts?"

"Daniel! Daniel!" Saito said, "remember we're being *blissful.* It's a song by the Steve Miller band. I thought it appropriate. This giant attacked us, not the other way around."

"It was self-defense," Wada responded, "and given the issues before us this seems like a minor transgression. He will be unpleasant when he regains consciousness. May I introduce General Beauregard, your Director of National Intelligence."

"Shit!" Daniel shouted, throwing up his hands. "Garrett, grab the rope in your pack." Muttering obscenities inside his head, Daniel rolled the soldier on his back, lifted him into a sitting position and pulled his hands behind him. Garrett wound the white cord around each wrist.

"Beautiful square knot, son."

"I don't recall this in the Scout handbook," Trudy remarked.

It took all of them to drag him to a small tree, binding his arms and chest to the trunk. "Dad, we need a gag."

"How about this?" Trudy suggested, unwinding her pink scarf.

"Lovely," Saito said, stretching the fabric across his chest. "Beautiful but a waste on him."

"It's your look," Daniel said, taking the scarf, knotting it in the center and then tying it multiple times around the general's mouth and head. He turned to Wada.

"Yoshito…" Daniel started to lecture, upset that he'd taken the risk.

"You're most welcome," the scientist said with a nod. "It was my turn." His expression seemed cherubic and then his eyes hardened. "The wartime scars on his right side may go nicely with the new ones on his left."

The group jogged to the paved parking area forty yards ahead, nervous but cautious as they stayed out of sight, running between clumps of manzanita and ferns.

Garrett spotted two soldiers at the far end of the lot, distracted in conversation, and ambling in their direction. Tio pointed toward two other men in suits about twenty yards near the exit of Camp Galilee.

After the soldiers passed, they hurried to Wada's rental, a blue Toyota SUV.

Daniel opened the door and flipped the unlock switch. They crawled inside, Garrett taking up a spot by the rear window in the storage area. "Stay low or lean back, look anywhere but at the guards, and maintain as much mystery as we can. This could get bumpy."

Daniel peeked over the dashboard, knowing they had only a few minutes before the prisoner was found. No soldiers in sight and the men in suits seemed preoccupied with their phones. Texting had its uses. He assumed they were likely FBI given their suits at a beach and stiff posture.

A crowd was exiting the chapel and returning to their cars. A line soon formed at the gate with each doing a California stop before driving on.

Daniel started the engine. "Okay, kiss the mats and hold on. Tio, take my phone. Bloomingdale's number is written on a piece of tape on the back. Dial it on one of Yoshito's phones. We don't want it traced—which may or may not mean much at this point."

He clicked on his safety belt. He knew Bruiser was familiar with the area and the *Beacon* had a large northern California circulation. Maybe his godfather would have an idea. If not, he would come up with something. Maybe hike over the hills singing like Julie Andrews in *The Sound of Music*.

"May I borrow your fedora?" he asked Wada. Daniel pulled it low over his forehead. "Do I look like Frank Sinatra?" Somehow being silly encouraged calm.

The car inched across the lot, pulling in line behind other vehicles. As they reached the entrance gate, the agents were working their thumbs overtime. Daniel rolled down his window and slowly passed them. The agent looked up from his phone, stooped lower, catching part of Daniel's face before silently mouthing, "Shit!"

"Must zee bishop in Carson! May Jesus bless!" Daniel barked with a bad Swedish accent, gently nudging the accelerator, trying not to spin the tires in the gravel. He didn't want to appear reckless.

"Stop!"

"What bishop, Dad?"

"Hold on! We may have company."

40.

Highway 50, Stateline, Nevada

"Bruiser?" Daniel yelled at the speakerphone, heading toward South Lake Tahoe. "We're being chased by FBI agents. I have Wada, Garrett, Trudy, Tio Ito and Saito with me. We're passing through Stateline."

"Your kid and ex-wife?" Bruiser whistled in disbelief.

"No time to explain! There's only so many ways out of the Tahoe Basin. They can easily set up roadblocks. Suggestions?"

Stonehouse Lodge, Lake Tahoe

"The rescue craft should report back soon," the cardinal informed the assembled ministers, sitting in the overstuffed chairs by the fireplace.

"How'd they get away?" Robinson sputtered. *"Inexcusable!"*

"They were never prisoners," Wright answered after taking a sip of his latte. "We weren't ready to do what needed to be done if they were, at least I wasn't. I believe the exchanges were healthy, even if somewhat emotional, and we each learned a great deal. We have the granules. I'm not quite sure what will happen."

"Obviously they plan to go public," Sister said, looking at him with a touch of derision, extending her forefinger—the candy apple red nail embedded with a small diamond—to push a slice of lime down into her vodka tonic. "Otherwise they wouldn't have left like this."

"Perhaps," the cardinal said, tired of the theatrics, "but they were not sure of our intentions either and may simply have decided it was time to go and they had no responsibility to say goodbye."

"It doesn't really matter whether they're here or not." Michaels had his head back, trying to look powerful, his voice mocking. "The *National Muckraker* should move with the story tomorrow and we'll follow up with contacts in select media for commentary pegged on that story. It'll be a joke in a week. The dossier being prepared by the president's office with my help will discredit Wada if our initial sortie doesn't work. There's also the possibility of arresting them for theft. Or as terrorists."

The cardinal shook his head, finding Michaels easily as obnoxious as some of the others. "No charges on the Chris Craft." He pressed his hands together, considering his next statement. "I wish I had your absolute confidence, Mr. Michaels. Perhaps their story will be dismissed, should they choose to tell it, but many once doubted the virgin birth and Christ's ascent to heaven from the cross. Now it's the heart of our faith."

"Your hypotheticals are irrelevant," Sister sneered. "General Beauregard personally brought up his men last night. In the boat or on foot, it doesn't matter. They'll be found and locked up. And that'll be the end of it."

"You called him?" Wright asked, squinting in disbelief.

"Somebody here has to have balls."

South Shore, Lake Tahoe

Daniel darted through the heavy traffic at Stateline. Garrett was the first to notice a black sedan moving erratically behind them, steadily getting closer.

"I think it's the guys from Camp Galilee," the boy said as his father ran a red light. The sedan was gaining.

As they moved beyond Stateline on the four-lane road, traffic was heavy and sluggish in both directions. As he neared a signal, the red light was about to turn green.

Daniel swung hard left and punched the accelerator.

Looking behind, Garrett shouted his approval. "The black car's stuck way back. I don't think they saw us turn." Everyone cheered.

They headed up Pioneer Trail, slowing to the speed limit. "This takes us through the forest toward Echo Summit. Not much traffic here," Daniel said with relief. "It's okay for the rest of you to sit up and relax. For now. Call Bruiser back and let him know the description of our car and location."

They rode for several miles through pines and scattered cabins before reaching Highway 50. Taking a casual left, Daniel pulled into the center divider, working his way into heavy traffic. Within a mile, the road narrowed, one lane in each direction.

"Where's that turnout?" Daniel asked, trying to hide his anxiety with a tone of calm.

"Hey, blissful, remember?" Saito said.

"Just ahead," Trudy responded, equally calm.

On their left was the oncoming lane of traffic and a thousand-foot drop inches beyond. On the right was a sheer wall of rock and a few gnarled stunted conifers leading up to the peak of the mountain, over seven thousand feet high.

Garrett continued his backward commentary. "Not sure if it's the same black car but one just tried to pass. Kinda reckless."

"There's the truck," Tio said, pointing to the right as they neared a turnout.

A large blue *Beacon* delivery van pulled alongside. The driver, a bald middle-aged man with a puffy brown mustache and ruddy complexion, gave a casual salute with one hand and waved for them to move forward. The truck forcefully inserted itself into traffic behind Wada's SUV.

The two vehicles drove for a quarter mile as the road narrowed further between rock outcroppings. The van gradually slowed to a stop at the narrowest point, turning slightly to fully block the lane. No one could pass because of the heavy onslaught of traffic coming the other way unless they wanted to risk a head-on collision and hurtling over the cliff.

The driver turned off his engine, put on the flashers and got out, pretending to inspect the motor. Cars immediately backed up behind him. He shrugged and acted apologetic as cars began to honk, a few drivers screaming obscenities, as the traffic backed up down the mountain. The opposing traffic continued, each car just a few feet apart on the icy road.

"This's so cool," Garrett said as he kept up his play-by-play. A mile ahead, with no one behind to see where they were going, the SUV pulled into a turnout, drove behind a clump of trees and parked.

A woman in jeans, a plaid flannel shirt and gray flecked hair exited an old maroon Volkswagen bus. "Hi," she said with a friendly smile, holding out her hand as they got out of the SUV. "I'm Melissa. I think you met my husband, Indiana, the truck driver." She laughed, running fingers through her short-cropped hair. "Mr. Bloomingdale said I should call him that. Really, his name is George. I couldn't believe the call, but he's helped us out of jams many times and we live up here. We're honored to help."

Tio walked over, arms wide and gave her a hug. "We really appreciate your taking this risk."

"Thank you," Saito added with a salute.

"I'll drive you to San Francisco," Melissa said. "You may want to enjoy what comfort you can find, sorry there're no seats. Please use the newspaper bundles to sit on. There won't be much traffic for the next twenty miles, just locals, headed toward Sacramento. We don't want anyone to spot you in case they get questioned. Mr. Bloomingdale urged caution."

"Thanks," Trudy said, extending her hand as everyone stepped into the back, rearranging stacks of newspapers for seats, or squatting on the metal floor.

"Is abandoning my SUV going to hurt the prime minister's credit rating?" Wada asked impishly. "I rented it in his name."

Tio and Saito groaned.

41.

They were almost to Kyburz, thirty minutes down Highway 50 before Daniel could pick up a decent signal on his cell. Melissa pulled into a turnout and waited for him to transmit since wireless reception was tricky. Except for an occasional face peeking out a window in surrounding cabins, anyone watching would think she was alone.

"Sirens!" Mellissa warned. "Ahead! Coming towards us." A half dozen black SUVs and two sheriff's cars raced past them, lights flashing.

"Cool!" Garrett shouted, looking out the back window, "but TV is better."

Daniel finished a lengthy write-up on the gathering and escape, checking his pen recorder on several quotes. He hit send and the coded document beeped to Bruiser.

The van's passengers engaged in sporadic conversation passing through Sacramento headed to San Francisco. It was lightweight stuff about fast glimpses out the window, weird cars, Garrett's schoolwork or other topics, ignoring what was really happening.

A text pinged, a coded note from Bruiser. "Got it. Check this out."

Daniel clicked the link and smiled. "Ever heard of the American Institute of Aeronautics and Astronautics, the AIAA? Sounds pretty official to me. They open a three-day conference in Oakland tomorrow."

"Of course," Wada said, excited. "Yes, a good group. Let me see the site." Daniel lifted over his laptop. "Excellent," Wada announced. "It has a huge membership, over 30,000 nationally, so hundreds will likely attend a regional event. It deals with engineering and science in space and defense. They meet frequently to discuss space issues." He showed it to Saito and Ito who nodded in agreement.

With a wide grin, Wada looked up from the screen. "The Osprey will land here. No guarantees, but this has real potential. The agenda says Dr. Steven Combs is speaking to the group at their concluding session. I've already met with him about the discovery. He's an ally. He and a Harvard scholar are debating the morality of weapons in space. I'll call him now and try to insert a clandestine new entry in the agenda. Starting now, we have three days to rally our forces before the AIAA announcement. Are we agreed on going public?"

"Yes, absolutely," Tio said with conviction. "It'll help cut through the attack that's coming. This is a great forum."

Saito nodded, "Yes, perfect," he said with a somber voice. "I wish I could be there. I have a rare George Reeves Superman tee that would be perfect. But, I'll be more useful recruiting allies in London."

"Who's George Reeves?" Garrett asked.

"*Oh, man.* Homework assignment. He was the first Superman on television. Let me see if I can find a link." Saito took one of the burner phones.

Tio looked up from examining airline schedules. "Saito, you can catch a flight tonight. I'll make reservations." While she looked up the web address, she picked up a canvas bag and pulled out a stack of passports. "Here. I think you'll like this one."

"Oh, so perfect. Yes, definitely George Takei. Wow!"

"You're gonna be Lieutenant Sulu?"

"Sure am."

"Good choice," Garrett giggled.

"At least two people from my company will be at the conference. I'll give them a heads up to meet me at the airport."

"Wear George and take a selfie," Garrett suggested.

Saito rubbed the boy's hair.

"Daaad, my hair!" Everyone laughed, including Garrett.

Daniel picked up one of Wada's multiple phones and dialed San Francisco. He put it on speakerphone.

"Daniel, here. It's a go. Wada has a contact. Dr. Combs."

"Great," Bruiser said gleefully. "I saw your note at the end of the last transmit. Finding a way to break this story so people of faith don't feel abandoned or crushed will be tough. People may be confused, go into denial, get really pissed off, grab their guns. Sort of a damn the torpedoes moment. Fuck, I love this!"

"Remember, Garrett's in the car and we're on speakerphone."

"Sorry. I agree *fuck* is a bad word. Moving on, the Japanese press is full of speculation. So is SETI's web site. We can toss in some of what's happening with the FBI search. The White House is mute, probably paralyzed. Really bad form, but good for us. It gives us another angle—what're they hiding? We'll start the rolling buildup tomorrow and each day until Wada presents at the conference, both papers working in tandem. The full story will run in the morning, before he speaks, getting a detailed factual record out there. Then live coverage at the conference itself. We won't reveal the location publicly or in any stories but I'll have some private conversations with key reporters and anchors I want there, particularly network talent. I may leak a variety of sites just to keep the government spinning."

Daniel scooted next to Saito. "Sorry we're separating."

"Me also. But the London conference is perfect to pick up hundreds of contacts. I've presented to the group several times. We each need to maximize our individual talents. I'll miss you." He turned and kissed Daniel on the mouth.

"*Eeeewww,*" Garrett groaned. "Kissing." He started to giggle and everyone joined him, including his mother.

42.

Dr. Steven Combs sat in a small classroom at the Jesuit-run school talking with Yoshito and Tio. He'd briefly met Duboce, his son, ex-wife and Dr. Saito before they headed to the airport for Saito's trip to London and then Daniel's apartment.

They waited for the Wilkins Institute leaders to appear; a text indicated they were close. "Please remember these are religious conservatives but also research academics," the SETI scientist advised, apprehensive but hopeful. "They take pride in their work and want some validation from the larger scientific community."

Wada pulled up various graphics on his handheld in preparation and linked it to a larger screen. "Agreed," he said. "We must find the sweet spot of their self-interest and ours."

Combs shrugged. "Given the tradeoffs it's perhaps half a loaf but it's a cosmic-size loaf and puts them back in the heart of the international scientific, religious, and intellectual battles that will be forthcoming. Play to their ego and vanity as we discussed and we'll have our best chance of recruitment."

There was a knock at the door and a tall dark-haired woman stuck her head inside. "Steve? Great—this is it." She entered with her colleagues, walking up to Combs and giving him a warm embrace.

"Thanks for agreeing to meet us here. I'm Elizabeth Cleaver, Executive Director of the Wilkins Institute," she said, stepping over to the scientists and shaking hands. "These are my colleagues…"

Combs set the stage. "In my discussions with Elizabeth, we talked about the value of meeting face to face and being able to hear first-hand what Dr. Wada and Dr. Ito have discovered. Given the gravity of the topic, I'm going to risk sounding a little pompous and say when the history of this discovery is written this meeting may be seen as a turning point." He hoped it wasn't too over the top. The four academics stirred slightly in their seats.

Wada picked up his handheld. "If it seems useful, Dr. Ito and I thought we'd do a brief summary of key parts and then answer your questions."

"Sounds great!" Chikae said and sat back to watch and listen.

The two scientists went through the highlights.

An hour later, Titus ran his fingers through his black-gelled hair and folded them behind his head as he listened to Wada's conclusions. "This mandala is just an assumption," he said, starting the questions, "kind of seventies goo and I'm having a hard time with it. Way too mystical."

"Not even an assumption," Wada said disarmingly, "just an observation by someone who is familiar with the art form. In any event, it is hardly an exact match. It looks much like the design of a mandala; I certainly would never say it is one."

"But the similarities are startling," Elizabeth said. "It's also a useful shorthand on what to call the hieroglyphics, at least for the time being. Perhaps a more neutral term can be developed that doesn't have eastern religious overtones."

"Whew!" Stanley exhaled. "My brain's on overdrive when I think about this and look at the data. It's preposterous. It simply can't be true."

"You know, Dr. Chang, you sound just like Dr. Wada when we began to appreciate the dimensions of the discovery." Tio said.

"We were so startled that we kept the discovery secret from some of our colleagues and certainly the broader scientific world. He saw things that could not be. We needed to test and test again, fearing being seen as fools if we didn't have rigorous research behind every detail."

Chikae tried to keep his voice flat but was not entirely successful. "Clearly this validates at least part of the I.D. theory." He was sitting next to and towering over Tio. He leaned forward on his elbows. "It scares the hell out of me with all its implications for faith and social unity. Some of our own donors might strap on suicide belts to destroy its advocates."

Titus walked to the screen and turned to the group. "I'm not sure humanity has the collective maturity to handle this," he said. "Except for the Catholics who play 'rope-a-dope' much of the time when they're attacked while other religions go nuts. Can people of good will discuss this without creating chaos?" Titus leaned against a wall as if needing to do so.

"That will depend in part on how it is presented and by whom," Tio answered.

Wada continued. "I'm a scientist and don't expect anyone to take my word on the discovery. We seek to challenge the findings of others, to spot holes in theories. Dr. Combs has examined my reports and the granules themselves. I believe Silas spent time with him as well. I urge you to do the same. You're research academics and should take my word for nothing. You're welcome to my findings to determine if they're real. If you concur, then we talk about next steps. If you don't, then there are no next steps."

"Well said," Chang replied, impressed. "Your non-defensive tone will serve you well in public debate. Silas vouches for your findings. I trust him. I'm struggling with this but I'm also excited. My legs are rubber."

Elizabeth examined their faces. "Thank you, Stanley for that vote of confidence, I treasure it."

Chikae slapped his palm on the table. "Okay, count me in on this. It's too big not to be a player. Wilkins Institute must be part of this—a risk, but what a ride!"

"There're lots of books and articles and glory waiting for those with the steel to see this through," Elizabeth said, struggling to stay calm. "I say that not as an enticement but more a matter of fact. The issue could revolutionize the world. I'd like to see us a player."

Three Institute executives looked toward the one member who had not committed and who was closest to key donors.

"Okay, guys, my turn," Titus said as he rubbed one of his sideburns. "I think we can sell our supporters by saying we're doing this to be on the inside and help direct it. That's the truth. This is so big people with our world view need to be part of it. I suspect it will also open new doors and some donors may be afraid not to continue giving to cover their bets. It keeps us a player. I'm in."

Everyone applauded. "I think we should take a group photo," Elizabeth said. "This could be important history." She paused for a moment and added, "I want Julia Roberts to play me in the movie."

43.

"The story for the day of the conference is looking great," Daniel said, closing his computer. "I redlined a few suggestions. Will the headline really be as big as the bombing of Pearl Harbor?"

"Nothing less." Bruiser was peeking out the window, barely moving the drape at Daniel's apartment. "That red-haired guy in the blue Chevy is still out there."

"I know, we're under surveillance. The FBI's looking for Wada. If they wanted me dead, Red would have knocked."

"Don't assume civility and politeness." Bruiser sat and looked at his laptop screen. "A lot of people are really frightened. Red may just be a decoy. Hopefully the jammer should knock out anyone listening. That's why I brought two."

Daniel was worried about his friends making contacts with other scientists. Saito, someone who stirred feelings distinct from the issue at hand, was in England, perhaps already at the conference. Tio and Yoshito were in a hotel near the airport. "I'm hopeful the Wilkins Institute will do a press conference. Seems a stretch."

"Yes. I suspect they will. Fame and glory are aphrodisiacs.

Think about the opportunity for a religious type announcing the discovery of an actual god."

"You're going to hell." Daniel went to the back bedroom. Garrett was playing video games; Trudy was taking a nap. A car would pick them up in less than an hour for the airport and a return to Beverly Hills.

He draped an arm over his son's shoulder. "Are the zombies winning?"

"No way, Dad!"

UC Berkeley, California

Tio and Wada walked through Sather Gate and the Student Plaza in the heart of UC Berkeley. Hundreds of students were text-walking all directions, sixth senses providing avoidance control. The duo headed north toward the McCone Earth Sciences Building. Wada was meeting with Dr. Phil O'Connor, a prominent geologist and a friend since grad school.

"He's well connected and has always taken a strong interest in my work," Wada said as they worked their way through the crowd. "Phil can excite his peers about the possibility of finding the cubes in existing rock strata on Earth near ancient meteor craters, assuming they're there. Our conversation yesterday showed he was intrigued and anxious to help."

They spotted the building in the distance and stopped on a hillside in front of the building. "I'll call you when to join us."

Tio waited on a bench as he hurried down a slope past a group of students relaxing on the lawn and playing Frisbee. He entered a small plaza, also filled with students, before passing through the glass doors of the main building. O'Connor's office was a small room on the second floor, down a hallway connected to a reception area. Wada smiled at a young woman standing by a file case and went down to the open door.

The professor was sitting behind tall stacks of papers on his desk and surrounded by bookcases that long ago reached capacity.

"Phil," Wada said with a grin. "You and your office look unchanged since the last time."

O'Connor stood and extended his hand. He was a gangly man, awkward in his movements, his fingers bony. Long light-brown hair streaked with white looked as if it needed a good combing and shampoo; his mustache awaited its bi-annual trim. His face was filled with dismay.

"I'm sorry, Yoshito," he said, choking.

Two men dressed in gray, their faces covered, rushed into the tiny office from a room across the hall.

"Yoshito Wada?" one asked gruffly.

"Why, yes, I am he." Wada turned to look at them. One had a rifle to his shoulder aimed right at Wada's head, muzzle about six inches away. The other held his weapon across his chest. It was over in a moment. Wada was slammed against the wall, his arms forced up. He was frisked; then handcuffed. His cane dropped to the floor and was pushed aside.

Two other FBI agents entered and watched as Wada was shoved face down and his cell phone and computer bag seized. He was yanked upright by one of the men in gray.

"Yoshito, I'm sorry." O'Connor was tearful. "I wrote your name on my desk calendar and the FBI called when I was out and talked to the secretary and she checked."

"Shut up professor," an agent snapped, "or you'll implicate yourself."

O'Connor gaped, looking confused.

Wada listened but remained silent. Odd, all his preparation to avoid electronic surveillance and they'd found his name written on a paper calendar. He chuckled at the irony.

"What's so funny?" an agent screamed in his face.

Wada looked at the overweight, over-caffeinated, balding agent. "Life," he replied, calculating whether his contacts to date were enough to match the coming fury.

The man seemed angered by his response. "You're under arrest. Don't resist and you won't be harmed. Come with me."

"Is there a particular charge?" Wada asked, curious.

"Terrorism."

Wada was grabbed by the shoulder and marched out of the room. He heard O'Connor shriek in agony and betrayal.

"Can you be a little more specific?" Wada asked as he was pushed through the hall and down the stairs, a gunman in front and behind. He knew Tio was watching and didn't look as he was propelled from the building, head high, and was rushed through a group of gawking students. Several held up cell phone cameras and Wada glanced in their direction so they could get a good facial shot.

"Move outta the way," a guard yelled. Wada was shoved, falling face first into a white van.

"Bastards!" Tio seethed under her breath. She saw the men with rifles, their faces covered, and the two FBI agents. Students were standing open-mouthed. She watched until the van pulled away, noting the license number, and then took out one of Wada's cell phones and dialed.

"Emergency. Meet me where you and Saito talked after Angel Island."

She waited ten minutes, then cautiously went down to the building, and stood before the chattering students. "The man you just saw arrested is the scientist mentioned in today's *Beacon* and *New York Times*. His name is Dr. Yoshito Wada, a top scientist at the Japanese Space Agency. Find it, read it, spread the news, make it go viral. I saw you shooting videos. Can I get copies?" Several students stepped forward.

Inside, she found the professor sitting at his desk, face in his hands, cursing, stopping only when he saw her. She spotted the silver Osprey peeking out from under a table and picked up the cane.

"I believe this belongs to Yoshito," she said. "If I can, I will be in touch again. If not, do what you can on your own. Pull yourself together," she ordered. "We're depending on you. I know he gave you some details last night. Check this website and use the password indicated. It will go public in the next twelve to twenty-four hours. Prepare your posting, make sure it's your best work because you'll be speaking to history. You'll know when the time is right. Network aggressively with your colleagues."

She handed him a slip of paper and was gone.

44.

Private Quarters, White House

The pope had died in his sleep last night, not unexpected given his heart, and Misago. The College of Cardinals was gathering, waiting for second-in-command Martinez to arrive, the president knew, all protocol abandoned, the Vatican in chaos.

After expressing his condolences and concern, Walton went straight to the point of this call. "My Director of National Intelligence wants to charge Wada with terrorism and have him disappear. He was arrested earlier today."

"He's no terrorist."

"I know but my staff believes his freedom threatens my presidency. And the story is breaking, although still hazy."

"My challenge also seems unsolvable," the cardinal said in a sympathetic voice. "My church is in turmoil. My peers await me in Rome for an emergency conclave. Difficult decisions lie before us. They are afraid. When you and I wandered that mountaintop long ago, the world was a bleak place for us. Yet we found hope. I'm feeling morally confused again, my friend, my energy fading. I'm not sure I can give you the guidance you seek, at least not from my heart. Only from my head as dictated by my obligations to the Church. I cannot do both."

Jeremiah understood, worried about his friend and confidant. The man had stress lines and dark circles under his eyes that were not there a month ago. "Perhaps I should be counseling you today. The essence of faith is not requiring evidence but when contradictory proof comes at you in a form that is this difficult to dismiss..."

Both men were quiet. The president was the first to continue. "When you make a commitment to the entity you think is God, is that forever even if something more concrete comes along that suggests the initial message was wrong? What's the role of the clergy?"

"People do change religions."

"Yes, but do they change gods?"

The cardinal rubbed his gold ring. "This has never happened before, Jeremiah, at least since Emperor Constantine created the Council of Nicea to sort out the differences in the early church."

"Yes, where 300 old men declared Jesus divine on a 153 to 147 vote. At least no Russians."

"I'm pleased your sense of humor remains intact. It was vital on the mountain top." He shook his head and smiled in reminiscence. "Back to our topic, do I protect my church at all costs? Do I shield my flock from the cataclysm change can bring? Do I study this for a long time to try and understand it and go on rationalizing as if nothing has been altered? I have no answers."

The president's mind raced as he said, "Think ancient history, Diego. Think about the rapid growth of your own church, a tiny, repressed sect in a Roman Empire that was crumbling. Your predecessors saw opportunity and took it. Today there's no empire set to spread the new religion, but there is the media."

"You make my head hurt," Martinez said. "I'm just trying to deal with my fellow cardinals and the future of my church."

Walton understood the strain yet still needed to think aloud to someone he valued and most of all, trusted. Only one man fit that description. "I keep going back to our conversation about Thomas Jefferson. His letters show a man of the deist school. Is that what *Misago* confirms?"

The cardinal looked skeptical. "That is one possible interpretation," he said.

"Don't jump too quickly. As Wada said when I met with him, findings are preliminary. He does not see the divine, only a superior intelligence. But if it's true, as you suggest, the irony is that religion still mocks the Enlightenment for diminishing God and His warm embrace."

The president leaned back, feeling even more uncertain.

"Speak to me, Jeremiah. Speak to me."

"Is it a twist of fate that people such as you and I and Wada would be the ones suddenly faced with this question? Should I bring American resources to help people comprehend this? Can I win politically and morally by being on both sides of this? Do I move ahead declaring America God's Kingdom and set in motion what needs to happen to create a theocracy and dump democracy? Not that democracy isn't already on life support."

The cardinal returned the intense stare of his friend. "I have no idea about the timing unless this new god, if he exists, is watching and maybe smiling as he messes up people's minds. Political leaders lie to stay in office, to pump their egos, to keep their societies calm, to help their allies, to amass power, to smite enemies. Let me add, sometimes clerics do too. In this case, we don't know the truth."

"But what does your intellect say?"

"That's unfair. When I wear my red cap, I believe in my heart that God created man in His image and sent His son to redeem us."

"You don't literally have that hat on now. What if *Misago* is true, hat or no hat? How much new information do we need?"

The cardinal frowned as he pondered the issue and seemed unsure himself. "Faith insists I stay with my established beliefs. My intellect urges me to see what this is about," he said, looking uncomfortable. "You're asking me if my duty is to 'God the creator from the asteroid' or 'God the founder of my church.' I'm not sure it must be Church vs. Creator. I hope not."

Jeremiah held out his hands, palms up. "What else is it then?"

"I need time, my friend. And I'm already late. The next days will be difficult."

"I know. Find wisdom and peace. My staff thinks I'm nuts."

"Our demons have much in common and they show no mercy."

"My thoughts go with you for the conclave, my friend."

Main Library, San Francisco

"Hey," Daniel said cheerfully, nearly an hour after Tio's call, giving her a hug and sitting opposite her in the same library carrel he and Saito used before, overlooking the Asian Art Museum.

"Has it only been a month since I called you?" she snapped, irritated. "Where have you been?"

"Being tailed," he replied spreading his arms in innocence. "I dumped him somewhere between West Portal and the back alleys of Chinatown." He grinned, raising his eyebrows in silent apology. "What's the emergency?"

"They arrested Yoshito in Berkeley. The FBI was waiting for him, two men with face masks and rifles, two others in business suits. He was handcuffed and pushed into an unmarked van. Students were taking videos and I have copies of three and more coming. Students are posting and linking the *Beacon* story."

As she picked up Wada's cane and placed it on the table, for Daniel it became real. She played one of the most dramatic videos. He felt helpless and angry, not sure what to do or say. Her eyes were damp. He touched her hand and struggled to breathe. Anger wasn't useful, he needed to channel his energy into taking this public. Truth was the best revenge and Wada's best hope for freedom.

"He had a contingency plan for contacting other scientists, as I recall, beyond what Saito is doing."

"I've a list of about fifty email addresses for people he knows around the world," she said. "I also have a personal message from him and a web address and password for them to contact that gives details. I did send a coded text to Saito telling him to go public tonight." She looked at her wristwatch. "He's now likely meeting with a large gathering of well-connected biologists and astrophysicists. This will be in addition to his already vast list of contacts. He is a remarkable man," she said touching his arm.

"Yes he is," Daniel responded putting a hand over hers, wishing the man were here but pleased he still had the help and support of such a remarkable scientist.

She smiled then returned to the main subject. "Yoshito's planned email says he's sending this if authorities intercept him. He asks them to network but remain silent until the story breaks. Always the optimist even as he plans for the worst. These are people he's worked with over the years. Most are in the U.S., some in Europe, a few in Asia. Some he's contacted before. It's powerful."

"I can imagine," Daniel said, a shiver down his back. "Okay let's do it." He pulled out his laptop. She pulled two flash-drives from her purse. "Maybe attach some of those student videos. Drama is motivational."

After downloading the addresses and messages from Wada and one especially dramatic arrest sequence, he read through the material and was pleased to scan the multilingual web site. Saito had obviously added new data. Daniel patched into the library's wireless network. Tio moved her chair next to his as they read.

"Effective," Daniel said. "The subject line's a little unnerving." As he spoke, his voice betrayed the stress: "The Osprey Has Crashed."

He sent the messages individually to bypass spam filters, pushing send many times. "It'll take a while to bring the web site down once it's discovered and it's well protected. By then it won't matter. Others will download and forward the content."

"That's the hope." She rested a hand on his shoulder. The simple act was reassuring. "I'll start calling a few key contacts."

He nodded. "I need to figure out a legal strategy. The conference is in its first day. Wada needs to be there." He scrolled through his address list.

A half hour later he stood, stuffed the laptop into his backpack and announced, "I'm headed to the ACLU."

45.

SAN FRANCISCO, CALIFORNIA (NY Times and SF Beacon)—The cargo from the Japanese spacecraft Misago is "a scientific and religious bombshell," according to two American scientists who have seen the results. President Walton has been mute on whether he has joined with the Japanese government in suppressing the findings...

Sistine Chapel, Apostolic Palace, Vatican

Cardinal Diego Martinez was on his knees, praying. He looked up to the giant golden crucifix on the altar before him, then up, up to the light from the high windows, then up even higher to the glory of creation as magnificently rendered by Michelangelo Buonarroti.

He strained to see the detail from Genesis and the bearded, noble face of God. He wondered, given the *Misago* discovery, if it proved true, how closely the face of the maker of the cubes would match this glorious depiction by the Renaissance's greatest painter.

"Why now?" he said to himself. "Or, do I already know?"

The cardinal came to the basilica often for contemplation,

sometimes mingling with thousands of excited tourists who walked through each day and stood in awe, as did he. But the tourists were gone today, mandated by centuries of tradition; just Martinez and his peers were present, a time for denouement and inception, an end and a beginning witnessed by God.

The room was forty-one meters long and over thirteen wide, the exact dimensions of the Temple of Solomon. As he slowly rose on stiff knees, he looked at one of his favorite paintings by the early Renaissance painter Pietro Perugino, *Christ Giving the Keys to St. Peter.* The prophets surrounded Jesus. In the background was the triumphal arch of the great Constantine, the first Roman emperor to become Christian, linking the Catholic Church and its popes as heirs to the Roman Empire.

"I wish it were so clear today," Martinez whispered, trying to look composed now that he was standing. A heavy cape was added to his shoulders by an aide and he took a staff, running his fingers over the cross on top, feeling a strange sense of calm as he walked through the first set of doors in the Chapel with his fellow cardinals.

St. Francis Hotel, San Francisco

Peeking out a door and seeing the crowd in the Colonial Ballroom of the St. Francis Hotel on Union Square, Elizabeth Cleaver found the spectacle surreal. The press conference was set for the lobby but when nearly a hundred reporters showed up, security had moved it to a larger meeting room. A simple press release about *Misago* to a media starving and desperate was better than free champagne and gift bags. "All right," she whispered to her colleagues. They were all fighting grins and twitchy kneecaps.

A score of microphones with network and station logos were clamped and taped together in an impossible twisted stack. A dozen television cameras glowed with red lights in the back of the room. The four walked out quietly, faces morphing into serene and serious masks despite the cacophony.

Elizabeth stepped forward and waited for the room to quiet, made introductions and held her arms high for calm.

"The Wilkins Institute has carefully studied the findings from the spacecraft *Misago*. We have seen the reports and actually inspected the granules at Stanford University and its high-resolution microscopes and were able to meet with Dr. Yoshito Wada, the Director of the *Misago* program, who is in California. Or was. We also talked with another Japanese scientist traveling with him, Dr. Tio Ito."

There was loud rumbling in the audience. Several started to scream questions. She held up her hand. "Please, let me finish."

"*Where's Wada?*" one man shouted.

"Please. We believe the discovery is real, as reported today in the *Times* and the *Beacon*. We state that fact as an organization that has championed greater ties between science and faith. The discovery offers substantial evidence, hard evidence, on how life began on this planet. But for all that we now know, there is far more that we do not. At least not yet. It has profound implications on faith, and, indeed, on the nature of science."

There was a collective gasp in the crowd.

"What's the discovery?" a woman hollered.

"*What?*" a dozen voices demanded.

"We believe the evidence is worthy of consideration by all Christians and people seeking understanding and evidence of the source of life on Earth, whether that source be extraterrestrials or a divinity unlike the traditional view of a Biblical God."

She paused, taking in the awed, frozen faces before her. She had expected bedlam, not this utter, stunned silence.

"Details of the discovery will be revealed tomorrow, eight a.m., Pacific Time, at a location to be announced later as a safeguard to prevent the government from shutting it down. Please understand our caution given the forces at play. Our excitement at this discovery is so strong that I will personally be introducing the main speaker. I can today confirm reports in Japanese media: the discovery is being suppressed by the governments of the United States and Japan. It's our belief, it is the view of the leadership of the Wilkins Institute, that these findings should not be hidden despite the honest motives and good intentions of the president and his religious advisors. Indeed, we believe the findings must be brought into the sunshine. The implications are so colossal that humanity is at risk to do otherwise."

The reporters, recovering themselves, seemed to collectively surge closer, tighter, desperate, shouting questions. A half dozen guards locked arms keeping the reporters at a distance.

"What was found?"

"What evidence?"

"Where's Wada? Is he in detention?" Elizabeth glanced at her colleagues, then back to the crowd, holding up her arms and waiting for silence. "Dr. Wada has disappeared. We suspect he has been seized by the FBI to ensure his silence. If so, we ask the president and the Director of the FBI to release him, NOW! He is no criminal, he is no terrorist, he's a scientist. This is a grave injustice not only to Dr. Wada but to a world that will hunger to learn what he knows and to help us interpret the meaning of granules from space."

Elizabeth took out a piece of folded legal sized paper from her jacket pocket and held it up. "The Wilkins Institute has joined with an unusual alliance—the *Times*, the *Beacon*, journalist Daniel Duboce, three Nobel scientists, the ACLU and other truth seekers. On behalf of these groups, Mr. Duboce has filed a Writ of Habeas Corpus in federal district court demanding information on Dr. Wada's whereabouts." She looked above the faces, toward the bank of television cameras.

"To our friends in this Administration: This is not the right way. To our friends in the religious community: Wait for the evidence before ye judge." Her voice lifted higher, picking up a preacher's cadence. "And as we pause until tomorrow, I offer one line from *Revelations*:

Behold, I stand at this door, and knock: if any man hear my voice, and open the door, I will come in to him, and will sup with him and he with me.'"

Elizabeth stopped and watched the reporters, daring them to interrupt. Everyone just stared. *"And the voice,"* she said with a dramatic lifting of her arms, *"is God."*

A moment of silence. Then reporters screamed questions, spiked with colorful obscenities, apparently upset by the obfuscation. Elizabeth was delighted. Her board of directors had been stunned by the news on the emergency conference call an hour earlier. But they either understood or were too numb to disagree. Now, joyously, they were in the eye of the hurricane.

She and her three colleagues waved, pivoted, and scurried for the back door, flanked by security police as the crowd surged. She'd needed to hype interest in the announcement and position Wilkins Institute as a critical partner. And she had.

"A little thick," Chikae said as they dashed down a corridor.

"And melodramatic," added Stanley. "Of course, I like drama."

"But effective." Titus said, shaking his head. "What've we done?"

Elizabeth suppressed a chuckle as they squeezed into a waiting car, ready to disappear for the night at a secret location not known even to their spouses. It was imperative that they avoid the fundamentalist and political avalanche that was coming. They had to finalize their Qs & As and spend hours practicing brilliant spontaneous quips to startle and silence opponents, made ready for YouTube and talk shows, not unlike the way Churchill had for his impromptu rehearsed witticisms in Parliament during World War II.

Olympia Conference Center, London

Saito walked to the center stage waving to nearly a thousand members of the International Planetary Society, a major association promoting the exploration of space. When he had earlier outlined the findings, the president of the association, Thurgood Gommel, was stunned and agreed to put him into the agenda, as much time as he needed.

"Thank you, Thurgood for allowing me to intrude on your busy schedule. I think you will find it's a remarkable diversion.

One you all may remember for the rest of your lives. I will let you be the judge if you think I am being hyperbolic."

He picked up the handheld mic and brought up the first set of slides. "Let me tell you a story that will change your views on heaven, God and science." He grinned, enjoying the excitement, and pleased to be part of this elite group of scientists. "I am here to inform but also issue a call to action."

46.

Vatican Square, Rome

"This is Cynthia Bertolouci, PRI International, just outside the Vatican. Half an hour ago, white smoke rose from the chimney near the Sistine Chapel, signaling the College of Cardinals had reached a decision and selected a new pope.

"The crowd, estimated at over a million, many waiting here for over two days, screamed its approval and anxiously await an announcement.

"There was speculation that a split in the ranks of the cardinals occurred over the *Misago* discovery," the radio reporter said, "and would lead to a long and difficult selection process, that an ultra-conservative choice to protect the faith or perhaps an elderly caretaker might be selected while cardinals continued to argue what they should do to meet what early reports suggest may be the greatest challenge to the future of Catholicism in its two-thousand-year history. The cardinals have reportedly been briefed on the discovery while the rest of the world awaits details."

Oval Office, White House

The president leaned back in his chair. "Wilkins Institute said that? That's gutsy of Elizabeth Cleaver, maybe suicidal. They could become pariahs and lose all their funding."

Machin grimaced as he read the rest of the story that had just broken on CNN.

Walton stood and began to pace. "We can't control it!" He pounded a fist into an open palm. "First *Misago* and now the bullshit with Beauregard. Have you seen the report on him?" He walked around and leaned against the front of his desk. "He's meeting with some alt-right and Christian military types. It's all part of *Misago*. He sees it as an opportunity."

Machin pinched his lips. "Think he'll try and turn the military against you?"

"Treason? A coup?" The president frowned, his voice deep, his words precise. The general and others had been working for decades to build a Christian army. Previous presidents had looked the other way. Some units might follow him. "He's a legend, nuts, and righteous. I meet with him later today, supposedly a standard intelligence briefing, and I'll try and force his hand."

"Deal with one crisis at a time, Mr. President. The revelation going public is a potential blowout. Beauregard can wait."

Walton gave an anemic smile and put a hand on Machin's shoulder. "Good advice, my friend. I'm worried Beauregard may go after Wada."

Vatican Square, Rome

"For those just joining our broadcast, the College of Cardinals has announced its choice for the new pope—Cardinal Diego Martinez from Argentina, generally seen as the number two man in the Vatican, and most closely associated with upholding traditional Catholic doctrines. Ironically, the cardinal joined the conclave only after it officially began. Holding the conference so soon after the death of Pope Julian also broke protocol, and speculation is that it's all related to the *Misago* discovery, details of which are just starting to emerge. The cardinal has reportedly been closely involved with the revelation."

Her voice was barely audible above the screams and applause of the faithful in Vatican Square.

"His selection of a name may offer clues on how he will act. He has chosen to name himself after the beloved, legendary 262nd pontiff, John XXIII. In picking the name, he shows his confidence in aligning himself with a humble but determined pope who sought to modernize his church.

"Pope John XXIV, now wearing the official vestments of his new office, continues to wave at the crowd. He's the second Hispanic pope, born in Panama. He is standing at the rail of the balcony, acknowledging the adulation.

"His leadership will be sorely tested given the challenges that faced the church even before the *Misago* discovery. He's stepping to the microphone, about to deliver his first papal blessing. What goes through his mind, we wonder, as he assumes his new role in these times?"

West Wing, White House

Presidential Press Secretary Dennis Myers, often teased for his princess white complexion and unkempt black hair, chewed on an arm of his horn-rimmed glasses as he considered options. The pressroom had been stuffed to capacity for hours with angry reporters, in no small part because he'd declined hundreds of requests for comment since the story broke.

A former star journalist for the *Atlantic Monthly*, a liberal in a conservative White House, he was known for candor and a fanatic devotion to pumping iron. Even though he was losing the battle of his waistline, he wanted to win the fight for his reputation in this impossible job and not be seen as sycophant nor fool as had some of his predecessors. He was furious at being placed in this situation. Just two months ago he'd been writing tough investigative journalism and had taken this job only after his old Army buddy, Jeremiah Walton, begged him. He'd been a Green Beret captain, Walton a lieutenant in the never-ending Middle East wars.

This morning Myers had distributed a vague and meaningless statement indicating the Administration was sorting through the conflicting rumors and claims. He'd handed out a similar one an hour ago adding a line about having no information on any Japanese discovery.

He knew his former colleagues in the media expected more. It was humiliating personally and for the president. He'd never seen senior staff so skittish and secretive and, worse, Jeremiah had pointedly avoided him.

47.

"What happened to your face, General?" One side of the man's face was a canvas of lacerations and dried blood trauma; the other his famous ridged scar.

"Terrorists, Mr. President. Hand-to-hand combat."

"Please be careful, we need you. You're in full dress greens. An event later?" This was clearly not a normal briefing.

"Thank you. I like my uniform."

"I like it too but you're in a civilian job now. Suits are good. Please be seated."

"There's a rumor that you've made a decision to switch your position on *Misago*." The general's tone suggested it was more accusation than question, hostility just below the service.

"And your source?" So much for subtlety.

"Given my responsibilities, I seek out information that deals with threats to national security." He offered a self-satisfied smile. "Some communications are not so secret."

"*What?*" Walton was stunned. Only two others knew he was wavering. Martinez and Machin.

"Chats with a certain Catholic prelate shock those who love

Jesus. Some IT techs know that, ultimately, we all serve God. They came to me. True heroes."

"So, you eavesdrop on private, privileged conversations?" The president did all he could to keep from grabbing the man. He held his breath and let it out slow, struggling for calm.

"To keep America safe no communication is privileged." He lifted his head defiantly. "I was with you and Jake Machin when Wada gave his presentation and the discussion on closing it down—but silence since then. Why cut me out? Now you equivocate. America—indeed Jesus—deserves better." His hands gripped the arms of his chair. "I'm your friend. I want to help you do the right thing for God, country and even your own soul."

"If you listened carefully to my private conversation, then you know I've made no decision. Right now, *Misago* is leaking and we must find a way to control it. But enough theatrics, General," he snapped. "Don't overstep your boundaries." Walton glared.

Beauregard eventually looked away, acting more bored then intimidated.

Ignore the hubris, he told himself. Get it out now. This is being recorded. The president stood and casually put his hands in his pockets. "Remain seated. You said in your call you wanted to talk about Elizabeth Cleaver."

"Correct. As Director of National Intelligence, I intend to arrest and confine her. At least when we figure where she's at."

Walton walked to a window near his desk, looking at the garden, his hands now clasped behind his back. He selected his words with caution.

"We should be careful. Cleaver is a U.S. citizen and has many allies, allies that supported me in the last election and who supported your appointment. They're good people. Hold off. In any event, it's not part of your portfolio. You have no authority to do it." He faced Beauregard.

The man stood. "This is no time for bein' timid." The general ran a thumb down his scar, a frequent habit, then over to the patchwork of new wounds.

Perhaps he's reminding me of how he got them, the president

thought, and about his public support as a national hero.

"Tell me, General Beauregard, are you not personally identified with the movement to bring Jesus into army basic training, to turn our military into a Christian army?"

Beauregard again showed no emotion. "Yes, sir. I've been part of the effort to bring faith to our soldiers. I'm proud of it. They need Jesus to give 'em strength on the battlefield."

"But doesn't the faith that you bring, Christianity, prescribe that all soldiers need to accept Jesus as their savior, be born again? You reject all other religious views. Correct?"

"Yes, sir. There's only one Truth." Leaning forward, the general placed one hand on the desktop and pointed the other at Walton. "Do you really not understand?" he said incredulously. "There's no authority except from God and my mission and the mission of thousands of Christian patriots like me is to bring all the armed forces under Jesus. And we're winnin'. Those who oppose us, like Cleaver and her turncoat devils, do the work of Satan." He was silent as his eyes narrowed. He settled back into his seat and waited.

Feeling as if he had been punched, Walton returned to his seat, leaning forward on his elbows, needing to press against something firm to steady his nerves. Such words were better suited for a Protestant revival, not the Oval Office. What's this about? Was this insubordination, treason or just the ranting of a nutcase general? Legally it would be a crapshoot to take his stars, given the politicization of the courts. He knew what was happening in the military—the pressure, the proselytizing, often from senior officers to worship Jesus. It was supposedly a means to build unit cohesion even as it marginalized and sometimes radicalized non-Christians. No president had ever intervened, it was too costly politically. Now democracy itself might hang in the balance because no one had had the balls to stop it, including himself.

Beauregard folded his hands, touching them to his chin. "You need to hold fast to your original instincts and not vacillate for the good of America. Don't try to change God's standards—change yours. I'm tryin' to be your friend. Your authority comes from

God and your actions, if you allow *Misago* to go public, strip you of legitimacy. Don't twist about just to meet some findings from godless scientists. Show your spine. God's law must prevail, not mans'."

"And you know God's law?"

"Yes, sir. I do."

Buena Vista Terrace, San Francisco

"Please reconsider your rejection of my offer, Mr. Duboce… Daniel. You need protecting beyond the police." Vega's voice was strong on the speaker phone even if he was in his private jet flying back from Rome and approaching an East Bay private airfield.

"Stay the course," Bruiser said, standing next to his godson. "You don't know him. His guards could protect you or make you a prisoner. Trust the police."

"I assure you, Mr. Bloomingdale, he would be no prisoner. Police are not enough."

"Why are you helping now?" Daniel asked, confused by the man's call. "You work for the cardinal."

"And Daniel is Ex-Lax in his holy water," Bruiser snapped.

"I work for no one. The cardinal is a close ally on many issues. On *Misago*, he's loyal to his church yet conflicted by the implications, as am I. My advice: Let me help. Do not in any way expose yourself in public."

The three men were quiet for a moment before Daniel responded. He had few allies and he liked Vega but was suspicious of his fluidity on a topic that cut so deep.

"Thank you." Daniel said. "I sincerely appreciate your concern and your kind offer but we'll trust the police should we need help."

His phone chimed a text. Garret and his mom were back in Beverly Hills.

48.

Oval Office, White House

"I'm concerned by the ferocity of opposition to the Misago discovery and the story's only beginning to leak," Beauregard told the president. "You need to plug it. Intel indicates rabid hostility and fear among Arab leaders with just the first dribbles of detail. Even here there's hundreds of threats emergin' against you personally and Duboce and others associated with it."

"How serious?"

"The *Times* and *Beacon* stories, Japanese media and posts on the Internet are creatin' fear and hostility," the general continued. "This *Misago* bullshit is trying to cut off Jesus at the knees."

"Don't you think that's a little dramatic, General?"

"No, Mr. President, I don't. This Japanese crap is a direct assault against this country's most cherished beliefs and values. I suspect much of America will oppose you if you allow this to escalate and once they understand the implications. You must come out clearly against it and start ordering the perpetrators locked up. Denounce it as fraud, a coup by science. Show your fist! Ditherin' is unacceptable to real Christians. Worse, it is just gettin' in the way of our long delayed plans of re-making America as God's nation."

The president held his emotions tight. He folded his arms to remain steady, wanting to sound casual. "I'm curious—have you studied the *Misago* findings?"

"I've read enough and I've discussed it with key Christian leaders and other senior military commanders who love Jesus. Civil unrest and even violence are possible. I know what happened at Stonehouse Lodge. We have a Christian Army that depends on Jesus and His love to guide and protect them in battle. It's a bindin' agent for warriors. This discovery mocks the values and faith our soldiers hold dear. If there're demonstrations or even riots in opposition to the discovery, I don't believe the military will move against Christian Americans protectin' their faith."

The president's forehead tightened. "So the short answer is no. Yet you're ready to start a civil war over what you've not taken the effort or time to understand."

Beauregard snarled but remained silent.

"Are you suggesting there are circumstances under which the military will not be loyal to its Commander in Chief? I believe Americans are more thoughtful and curious than you suggest. Calling out the military is only done in emergencies. But if I needed them to maintain order, I would expect and demand loyalty."

Beauregard was quiet, looking past him.

"Did you not take an oath to support the Constitution?"

"Yes, sir. The Constitution is a blueprint for a Christian nation." His voice was unequivocal. "There is no such thing as separation of church and state! We'll not allow the treachery of *Misago* to prevail."

Remain calm, he told himself. Bad political appointments can come back and bite you on the ass. The man even has his Congressional Medal of Honor around his neck. Why?

"What would you do if I gave you a direct order, General?"

Beauregard was stone-faced as he responded. "I'll not work in opposition to my faith and Jesus Christ. Neither will many fine officers in the military and God fearin' soldiers."

Walton pushed a hidden button under the drawer on his desk. Three Selective Service agents and two soldiers burst into the private office from three doors, pistols in hand.

The general rose with dignity from his seat and faced the men. The president held up a palm to keep security from advancing further.

"Gentlemen, thank you for answering my summons. Please lower your weapons but remain with me. Let me continue this conversation with all of you as witnesses. General, please face me. I know you as a man who values honor and truth. Remember you speak now before your president, fellow soldiers, and, indeed, before God."

Beauregard turned in crisp military fashion as if he were on the parade ground and faced the president. His expression, seen only by Jeremiah Walton, was subtle but unmistakable—a barely perceptible smile.

He expected this, wanted this, the president realized, working to conceal his shock. He knows it'll go public and he wants to lead the revolt. It's part of his challenge. He wants a public crusade, to be seen as persecuted for his beliefs, a champion for Christ, facing down Satan. That's why he's in dress greens. It's for the media, a photo op. Walton exhaled slowly, knowing the next few minutes were the start of a new drama.

"Who is the Commander in Chief?"

"You are sir," the general said stoically. "But Jesus Christ is Lord."

"And what did you just tell me about the loyalty of our military?"

"I said your actions, if you fail to protect our faith, will be seen as treason by many in uniform, perhaps even some in this room. We cannot divorce Jesus from the military. We'll not be a secular fightin' force. If you allow *Misago* to go public, real Americans will be disgusted and turn from you. There could be mobs in the streets. The military will abandon you. Arrest me at your peril. It will not hold."

"And you just informed me that, as a commissioned officer, you would not obey my orders?"

"That's right. Not if they included using the military to suppress the dissent of honest Christians."

"Do you believe we have entered the End Times, General?"

"Many believe we have and those who know think *Misago* marks the beginning. I suspect it may be true."

The legal grounds on sedition and treason were quicksand and this man had a plan and allies. "A few moments ago, you said that you and others in the military were ready to advance if I did not retreat. What were you suggesting? A coup?"

Beauregard shook his head in disgust. "I gave you a way out. You're preparing to betray our faith and mock our Constitution and values. You don't deserve to be president."

"General, you are hereby relieved from your position as Director of National Intelligence and I shall take all steps necessary to remove you from any active role in the military. Your stars are forfeit. Gentlemen, please take Mr. Beauregard to a holding cell."

As the general turned to the soldiers to be led away, he glanced over his shoulder. "What's the charge, Mr. President?" His voice was taunting. *"Protectin' Jesus?"*

The president had been played, Beauregard wanted this, to be a martyr and this would be his recruiting song.

Walton pushed his intercom button as the door closed behind them. "Please summon the Attorney General, the Secretary of Defense, Mr. Myers and Mr. Machin. Code Red."

Sistine Chapel, Rome

Diego Martinez, still struggling to comprehend how his life had changed in an instant, continued to humbly wave to thousands of the devoted shouting in the plaza below.

As he moved to the large microphone at the railing, he noticed it was old-style, something out of *Evita*, antique but obviously still functioning, his favorite type of technology. It gave him hope.

49.

Nob Hill, San Francisco

Agent Jeffrey Lewis, all FBI prim in a gray ill-fitting suit, hair slicked back, examined the ornate gold leaf framed mirror in the hallway outside a small Nob Hill apartment. The area was part of an elegant baroque-inspired building in one of the City's wealthiest neighborhoods. He checked his pistol before slipping it back into a shoulder holster. Satisfied, he watched two men in black, their faces hidden by dark ski masks and carrying assault weapons. Another agent, Jerome Higgins, was on one knee nearby, going through a small canvas bag.

Lewis was impressed with the twisted columns and the *trompe l'oeil* paintings of elaborate gardens on many of the interior walls. Several of the smaller units, like this one, were *pied-à-terre* owned by rich couples who lived elsewhere in the Bay Area and used them when they came to the opera on weekends. The apartments were also popular for men who maintained mistresses. It must be nice, he thought.

Higgins pointed a heat-reading meter toward the apartment, confirming someone was inside. They assumed it was Tio Ito because an agent, returning a book at the Main Library on her day off, saw Ito leave the building and knew who she was from office bulletins and photos. She had followed her to the apartment and a stakeout was put in place. A title search found Carroll Bloomingdale owned the property.

With the team ready, Lewis gave the order. Rifles at their shoulders, the two SWAT team members kicked in the door and rushed inside. The agents followed with pistols drawn.

The first rifleman was greeted with a book slamming into his face with such force that it knocked him sideways; he screamed a profanity as his nose crunched and he fell over a chair.

Tio grabbed the rifle barrel of the second gunman who swung the butt around to hit her in the head. She easily ducked and snapped her foot up sharply under his chin, knocking him back into the two startled FBI agents.

Lewis dodged the falling rifleman, stepped into the room and raised his pistol as he screamed: *"Surrender!"*

She shoved his arm aside before he could finish the word and rammed a fist into his mouth, splitting his lip, knocking him backward into a table that flipped over, a ceramic vase shattering. The first rifleman jumped behind her and pounded the rifle butt into the back of her head just as she started to leap toward the agent. She fell unconscious.

"Fucking bitch!" Lewis wiped blood off his mouth as he stood. "We should've shot her."

"My nose is broken," the first rifleman mumbled.

"You know the orders," another agent said, getting off the floor. "Take her alive."

Transcendent Communications HQ, Chicago

"Did they accept the offer?" Mike Michaels asked, feeling lighthearted—everything vital was coming together. "Fantastic. I love the penthouse. Yes, business is about to double. When do we sign the papers? See you tomorrow at five." He thrust his arm in the air in triumph and snapped shut his retro style cell phone like a castanet.

He looked out the window of his fortieth-floor office with its glass walls and view of downtown. The furnishings were modern and sleek. He swiveled his desk chair and glanced up at the poster-sized framed enlargement of a *Time* magazine article calling him "Brand Manager for Jesus."

Humming his favorite song from *Cabaret,* he scanned news highlights on his computer screen. *"Money, money, money…"* The Wilkins Institute coverage was extensive. He knew Duboce had to be involved. "Fucking prick." He didn't need to read more.

His secretary, petite and brunette with a 1950s Donna Reed flip, knocked on his door. In a smoky drawl, she announced, "The staff's ready and waiting, sir." It was her shtick and he loved it, encouraging everyone to express themselves visually and give energy to the staff.

He walked purposefully down the hall to the glass room with another dazzling cityscape view. A dozen managers and assistants were waiting, an interracial mix of men and women—talented professionals he had worked hard to recruit. Each was perfect in looks, talent and ferocity.

"Have you seen the full video on the Wilkins Institute press conference, sir?" Tom Lowe, a thirty-year old manager in a red *God Rocks* t-shirt, sounded upset. "It's viral on the Internet, crazy, no questions, over in four minutes."

"Yeah, I've seen enough. Clearly they're traitors. Duboce is behind it. Somehow, I suspect he'll be the spokesman or at least at their event. The story is just starting to break and we need to get ahead of it, set the tone and narrative."

"We're already moving forward on several fronts, sir."

Michaels nodded. "Of course. That's what we do. We must not be distracted. The issues are bigger than one group or person. They're trying to discredit faith itself. We're HIS brand managers." Others nodded around the table; two of them clapped. It was good to be able to inspire.

"The Institute is tough to attack given their track record. There are no obvious weak spots in Duboce's history," Lowe said. "I've been trying to find out as much as I can about him. He seems like a solid citizen, good father, and all that."

"I've known the man for several years. We'll bring him down," Michaels responded, thinking of an angle, smiling when the idea emerged. Given the stakes, why not? "Hit the blogosphere with stories about Duboce being divorced by his wife for physically abusing her and her son." He felt a tingle in his shoulders. Sometimes you must stoop low when evil was at your door in order to lift up a greater cause. "Yes, I have sources that say it's true. After a couple of days, come back with a hint that he was sexually molesting the boy but make sure our name is not associated with the charge. Get some obscure web jock looking for attention to make the accusation. It doesn't matter if they're crazy, that may be useful." Fake news, real news, truth—what matters is winning. "See that it gets spread. We need to shift the debate from the discovery to the credibility of those who made it public."

Michaels watched his aide taking notes. "Say court records were sealed because of the shocking, graphic nature of the abuse, closed at the wife's request to protect the child," Michaels said. "Quote a source that insisted on anonymity out of fear of reprisal. We can keep building on this."

"O—kay," Lowe said slowly, sounding skeptical. "That will sink his clean guy image and be impossible to refute. I like it. I just hope your sources are solid."

"Of course, but sources don't make much difference on the Internet or those who love conspiracies, reality television, tabloid scandals and our favorite network." Many lived for this, willingly embracing a false narrative if it supported their predispositions, prejudices, or just for fun. The rumor of a pedophile ring in the pizza parlor in Hillary Clinton's campaign had been almost too easy. He smiled at his team, feeling back in control. He knew the ex-wife's denial would only help keep the story alive for weeks.

50.

Buena Vista Terrace, San Francisco

"What the fuck?" Daniel read an email from a researcher at the Times. He was sitting at the small oak pedestal table in his dining nook, staring at his cell phone and ignoring a cheese omelet and lightly burned wheat toast.

"What?" Bruiser asked taking off his chef's apron.

"My paper's been scanning for any reference on any site, including the dark ones. Here's their first shot, quoting unnamed sources that I physically abused my wife and son and that's why I got divorced." He set his phone down. "Fuck, fuck, fuck."

"We knew it was coming. Playing dirty is what they do. I got a note from my own people earlier this morning and was going to talk to you about it. After you eat. So eat and we'll talk."

Daniel looked at his plate.

"The eggs are my specialty," Bruiser said in upbeat bar banter. "Definitely Michelin three star and you don't want to insult the cook." He rubbed Daniel's shoulders. "Eat." His godson was depressed by what happened to Wada and Ito and worried about Saito. Now this.

Daniel picked up his fork and moved the eggs around, finally taking a bite.

"The website's notorious for extremist views," Bruiser said, "popular with even those to the right of the Alt Right, even some of the Alt Left. Also, Bigfoot sightings. The platforms don't really care as long as it gets eyes."

Daniel stared ahead. "The ugly black boot of oppression. I knew it'd come, but this is faster than I expected. Key scientists, friends, are under arrest and now these lies about my family."

"Political campaigns often have no soul. A troll likely planted the story. Since you're not well known yet on this issue, it's one of the insiders. Any ideas?"

"Oh, not much doubt. Michaels heads my list. Then the president's political guy. The worms who work for them in the dirt."

"My own guy on staff says this was likely planted to get picked up in any reporter's Internet sweep of names. It's designed to look official, as if quoting the actual divorce decree. Remind you of any recent president?"

"Let's not go there. Then there's the fact that I've got a male lover and a young son. I can imagine what'll happen. What rhymes with sodomite?" A disgusted laugh.

"This is moving fast. Our goal is to overwhelm. Drown 'em. Make these early hits look false and malicious. We're trying to unmask the writers. We will. The conference is designed to create an earthquake."

Daniel's phone rang. "It's Saito."

Brusier watched as they talked, picking up Daniel's fork, spearing some egg and bringing it to Daniel's lips. Daniel smiled indulgently and opened his mouth as he listened. "I miss you too," he said and hung up.

"Saito said the conference went well, nearly a thousand attendees. He was booked as an emergency thirty-minute add-on and spoke for three hours. He was mobbed, people desperate for more information. They passed a resolution for continued research and respect for Wada and JAXA but they're holding back till there's some kind of signal to go forward. Wada's website is apparently being well used and it's not yet public, just the secret password." Daniel grinned. "This's helpful. I knew Saito would rock."

"I don't believe they'll hurt Wada. Just hide him for a while. Tio's receiving treatment for the bump on her head. She'll be fine." He'd received a tip from a woman across the hall from his *pied-a-terre* and had been there within minutes of the break-in. "You should've seen the agent's lip. She apparently kicked the shit out of two gunmen and pounded the agent before they got her. *Such a woman!*"

Daniel's cell phone rang again. He looked at the name, let it ring twice and punched the speakerphone so Bruiser could hear. "Mr. Vega."

"We need to talk soon," the man said with urgency. "I've landed and am on the Bay Bridge. Are you at your apartment?"

"Yes. Why?"

"To help you prevail," he said, his tone calm yet insistent. "Trust me. You turned down my offer of help before. Please reconsider and stay there. The forces against you are strong and ruthless."

"I know. Wada's been taken by the FBI." There was silence. "Tio's been arrested too." He pressed a fist to his forehead, controlling his anger and fear. "I'm being accused of abusing my family."

"How is Dr. Ito?"

"Recovering. Some FBI agent knocked her unconscious. Classy guys."

The anger was giving him strength, Bruiser could sense it, vengeance bringing him out of the darkness. And thank whomever that a lover was back in his life.

"Let me make this pledge," Vega asserted. "This will not go unpunished. I will also find the author of the smear."

"Why should you care? You're one of them."

"No! I am not! Trust me. I'll be there in twenty minutes. My views have shifted. Controlling the message is key to managing the chaos. Proximity to Sister Esther pushed me to reconsider, as did observing you and the scientists. My goal is social cohesion, not any particular religious view."

"Having experienced Sister in person, I can understand."

"When the story breaks, it must be managed or forces will crush you. I can help. You have friends. Avoid exposing yourself in public without protection."

Daniel disconnected and turned to Bruiser. "You heard. Vega wants to help. Should I be nervous?"

Bruiser finished the last bite of his toast. "Hear him out when he arrives. You'll need allies, assuming he is one. Even if he's not, you might learn something useful. No danger in talking."

The publisher walked to the front window and pulled back a drape to peer at the street. "The media's going bonkers on this, boy. Your filing in federal court is blood in a piranha pool. Since all signatories refer inquiries to you, Daniel Duboce is the man. Camera crews are on stakeout in front. Plus lots of your neighbors."

Daniel moved beside him and Bruiser slung an arm around his shoulder. "Snap out of this, Daniel. Reach inside like you did when your mom died. Be depressed when you're old. *Not now!* We need to act. We need payback. You're the only one who can deliver. *Do it for the fuckers who wrote that article! Do it for Wada! Do it for Tio and Saito! Do it for truth! Do it for vengeance!*"

Bruiser pulled him tight. "These reporters may be an opportunity. Challenge the president. But don't give away too many details on the discovery. Save that for your presentation in Oakland. Reporters don't know science. But the conferees do."

Daniel stared. *"What?* You're kidding. Not me!"

"You're the only one left. Saito's in London and on this topic, he'd have zero credibility as a foreigner, too handsome, a young guy with an accent, no gravitas, a funny name, a non-Christian talking about Christianity. Get real son. It must be you."

"I saw the reporters," Daniel said in a quiet voice. "I'm not sure what to say or even if I've the mental clarity at the moment." He pulled away and stood, slipping his hands into his pockets.

"Reach inside and find it." He fought to keep from losing it himself, watching Daniel in such a state. "You're a respected journalist and a player. This is breaking internationally and no one can figure out what it is. Now, kidnapping and smear. So, make them hungry for more but don't give away everything. Give us tremors before the Big One." He pushed to sound genuinely excited as he talked. This was a crucial opening. "Earthquakes bring tsunamis. Make it so."

"You make it sound so simple."

"You're very articulate, Daniel, and you look like a fucking pretty boy stud on TV. You'll do well. These days pretty is more important than content on television. You have both. Drip sincerity: talk directly into the cameras, ignoring reporters, eye contact is crucial with viewers. Now go get cleaned up. Change into something appropriate. Wear a jacket."

Daniel ran his fingers through his hair and wiped his face. "Give me twenty minutes."

51.

Private Quarters, White House

Pope John rubbed his lips as he stared into the teleconference screen. He looks very tired, the president thought.

"I don't know whether to congratulate you or offer my condolences," Walton said to his old friend, smiling.

"You make my head hurt," Martinez said. "I'm just trying to deal with my fellow cardinals, an intransigent papal bureaucracy, media demands and all this about *Misago* threatening the foundations of the church. I was elevated to solve it. You should have heard the speeches. Such a special time to become head of my church." He laughed. "I'm so pleased you're president. It was a perfect reason to insert your call to the front of the mob of sycophants, well-wishers, and reporters at my door."

Walton saw the strain yet still needed to think out loud to someone he trusted. "My plane lands in a few minutes in Los Angeles," he said. "Then I do my usual fundraising and politicking. This issue is all that's on my mind. Politicians today wear religion as a suit, God-con is epidemic, and I certainly have put it on and will again tonight. Now it seems even more hollow."

"Speak to me, Jeremiah. Speak to me. We all do the holiness

"

thing from time to time."

"What if all this is true?"

The pope frowned. He'd done nothing but think about the issue and seemed unsure himself. "My indecision may make me a terrible pope. You're asking if my duty is to the stardust or the Bible."

The president held out his hands. "What else is it then?"

"I need time, my friend. I have the backpack from Mr. Duboce and we'll examine it after assembling the right team. I also have a not inconsequential number of official duties now that I wear the triple tiara." He grinned. "You should see it, Jeremiah. Maybe you should get one too. A unique fashion statement."

"You can pull it off, my friend. It's good your wit hasn't been crushed by your new wardrobe. I've ordered the FBI to bring Wada to LA so we can talk again in private, assuming he's safe. My staff thinks I'm nuts."

"Our demons have much in common."

Buena Vista Terrace, San Francisco

Woesha Jones, Daniel's best friend and neighbor, was sitting on the top front step of the building as he and Bruiser opened the front door to the two-story duplex. "You look hot!" he said.

She jumped up, giving him a hug and kissing his cheek. She wore a familiar ensemble—emerald green flowing dress, a red and yellow *Kente* headscarf and large gold hoop earrings.

"I was wondering when you were going to come out," she said, wiping lipstick from his face. She gestured to the waiting mob of media. "I didn't want them disturbing you so placing my rump here seemed to keep them at a distance." She laughed, squeezing his shoulder. "Nobody fools with Mama. I have that effect on people. They're talking weird shit."

"Wait till you hear the reality," Daniel said, taking her arm, whispering, "Let's do this."

The three walked down a dozen steps to the sidewalk. He

wore the blue sports jacket and the striped button-down shirt she'd given him for Christmas. The skies were fog-free as Daniel stepped before the bank of microphones in the driveway five feet in front of his garage door. The crowd merged into a half circle around him, maybe fifty people and the shouting started immediately. Five crews with shoulder-mounted cameras moved forward. Photographers started a steady snap, snap, snap.

Woesha stood next to Bruiser on Daniel's right, unsure what this was about but anxious to support her friend. Behind the news media were dozens of onlookers. She smiled at their octogenarian Russian neighbor, Mrs. Palenko, a few feet away and holding onto her walker, her hair in rollers covered by a faded floral scarf, blowing Daniel a kiss. They both loved the woman.

"Daniel, you have an admirer," Woesha said, pointing to the elderly woman. While reporters spat out questions, Daniel held up one hand and ran over to Mrs. Polenko, kissed her on the cheek, hugged her and then stepped back to the microphones. One television crew went live and the reporter started a quick introduction adding to the confusion.

Shouted questions became a cacophony. "Please, one at a time," Daniel shouted, looking confident as he held up both arms for quiet. "I'm happy to answer your questions as best I can but not all at once." He smiled broadly. A photographer stepped in front of him and was quickly grabbed by a reporter angry that his camera shot was blocked. The reporters were ravenous. Daniel pointed to one young woman.

"Thank you. Cindy Beacon from KRON TV 4. Your name is on a filing in federal court seeking the release of Dr. Wada. The filing claims there's some kind of cover-up dealing with a discovery in space. Can you clarify what it means?"

Daniel's smile evaporated. "Dr. Wada was taken into custody by FBI agents," he said, "and with the help of the ACLU, the *Beacon*, the *New York Times*, several prominent scientists and others, we went to court to determine where he is. The court has not yet acted. Let me also say that another Japanese scientist, Dr. Tio Ito, has also been kidnapped by the FBI after being physically assaulted."

Shouting started again but he ignored it, looking down and running his hands over his face. He looked up, raising his arms. "Please, let me talk." Suddenly the stretch of street in front of his house had never been more serene. Clearly no one wanted to miss a word.

"We hope to have a court ruling in the next few days. I can now confirm there's a cover-up by the Japanese government as well as our own and that the discovery is politically and theologically explosive. Dangerous enough for high government officials to kidnap and perhaps worse." He paused. Every reporter was shouting again.

"Yes, Mic," he said pointing to Mic Jones, a heavyset man with a gray ponytail and goatee, masticating slowly on his ever-present chewing gum. He was an old friend and publisher of the left-leaning *Bay Review.*

"Whadaya mean 'explosive?' What'd they find? Why would they kidnap to hide it?"

Daniel took a shallow breath. "The discovery made by Dr. Wada, Dr. Ito and their colleagues at the Japanese Space Agency involves a find on an asteroid far from Earth, actually three asteroids, over many years. It will dramatically shake human understanding of how life was created. Anyone who's seen it is afraid. I'm one of them." He paused again for emphasis, looking at the suddenly silent crowd and at the house across street where someone was leaning out her window to watch.

"I wasn't expecting this press attention and haven't prepared anything for discussion," he said, his tempo quickening. "Frankly, I wasn't planning on going public. That was up to Dr. Wada. But now he's in a holding cell and cannot speak. The same with Dr. Ito. I hope they're both alive but I have no information. So, here I am."

As a dozen questions were shouted at once, one high-pitched voice lifted over the others. *"Are you Satan's man?"*

Daniel searched the crowd for the questioner. He was a bearded, slender young man, a scowl on his face, dressed in drab green overcoat that seemed too big for him. The tone was hostile and accusatory.

The man looked angry. Deranged, Woesha thought. "Let's get our boy out of here," she said in Bruiser's ear.

"You want to destroy public faith in JESUS!" he shouted. Several people standing near him moved away. Bruiser and Woesha came up to Daniel on either side. "Let's move," she said, trying to pull her friend back to the front steps and inside the apartment. There were no police here.

Daniel resisted. "That's not true." He moved two steps back, looking confused. "Your question doesn't make sense. Up till now, I've made no public comments on the discovery nor has anyone else."

"*Liar!*"

The man, less than ten feet away, pulled a pistol from his jacket. A bullet hit Daniel in the chest, slamming him back into the garage door. Bruiser twisted around and grabbed his godson, shielding Daniel's body with his own. A second bullet missed Daniel's head but took out most of Bruiser's ear. The third pierced the publisher's forearm. The crowd screamed and fell back.

Both men collapsed in what seemed like slow motion into the garage door, Bruiser holding Daniel tightly to ease the fall.

Feeling more banshee than human, Woesha leaped toward the assassin.

"MUTHERFUCKENBASTARDSONOFABITCH!" she roared, wildly waving her arms as she stomped forward.

Mrs. Polenko turned her walker around, shouting obscenities in Russian. She moved with surprising speed toward the man with the beard. The gunman backed up as if unwilling to fire on women.

Mic Jones heaved his clipboard at the assassin, hitting him in his forehead, drawing blood. "*Bastard!*" Mic screamed, spitting out his Juicy Fruit.

The bearded man stood frozen then shifted his gun toward Mic, Woesha and Mrs. Polenko as they closed in. The lens of a television camera swung around to his face. Looking confused and frightened, the man turned and ran to the end of the block, heading left toward Buena Vista Park.

The immediate danger gone, Woesha turned her head back toward her friend. Bruiser had lowered Daniel to the ground, still shielding him, ignoring his own wounds. Blood was splattered across the garage door and the wood shattered. The bullet must have passed through his back. Bruiser crawled over him on his knees, blood streaming from his arm, his face wet with tears as he rolled to the pavement and lay beside Daniel, cradling him in his arms.

A *People Magazine* reporter hit 911 before she stooped down next to Daniel and put a white handkerchief over the massive wound in his chest. "Looks like it went through. Yes! We need an ambulance—and police!"

Several photographers moved in. She leaned over Daniel, looking up at the cameras, making sure she was in the photo, perfect for a magazine cover story.

Woesha grabbed the woman and yanked her back. "Outta the way, silly bitch!"

Daniel looked at his godfather and whispered—"Bruiser." He went limp. The handkerchief was saturated. Bruiser Bloomingdale's scream echoed down the street of two-story buildings.

At the corner, a cameraman dashed after the assassin and caught a glimpse of him running toward Buena Vista Park. He zoomed in just in time to catch his face as he turned. A well-dressed man shoved the photographer out of the way and sprinted up the hill, moving with the power and speed of an elite warrior.

52.

Beverly Hills, California

"Dad's okay. Dad's okay."

Garrett repeated the endless loop in his head. His mom and Uncle Bruiser had told him: "Your Dad's is doing well, considering. Ignore the news reports."

He was supposed to go back to San Francisco this weekend. News stories were horrible. Would they lie? He tried not to cry. Be tough, Uncle Bruiser and his mom repeated. Ignore the news. "Your uncle is in the hospital with your father," his mom said, "and he knows what's really happening."

He was just another student dressed in a regulation gray knit shirt with a school logo, blue cotton pants and black leather shoes with a military shine at St. Dominic Catholic School in Beverly Hills. His curly black hair was clipped short on the sides as the strict rules required. He hated the look. The girls all wore navy and white checked skirts with white knit shirts. He thought they looked ridiculous.

He gripped the edge of his desk, trying to concentrate, trying not to think about his father. There was no one to talk to. They didn't know he was Daniel Duboce's son. It was his stepdad who attended PTA events and met his teachers. His mom told him going to school would help him think about something else. Uncle Bruiser had been strongly against it but his mom said he had to do it because his stepfather insisted.

He was one of twenty students in civics class. His teacher, Joshua Dufty, a sweet-natured man in his first teaching assignment out of college, wore what he often did, blue slacks and a gray check sports coat and tie. He looked like the model on the school brochure promising scholarship, discipline and wholesome values, nothing like those free-wheeling public schools in San Francisco.

The interminable morning finally ended. In the forty-minute lunch break before math class Garrett and two students headed to the cafeteria. Andrew, an African American boy, was perhaps his best friend. Kristin, a slender redhead, always made him laugh. They all got soft drinks, protein bars and stepped into the adjacent passage, a popular place to hang out.

A tall middle-aged man dressed in a baggy charcoal pinstripe suit walked up to him. "Garrett Duboce?"

"Yes," he confirmed, wary of strangers.

"My name is Jonathan Brinks. I work for your stepfather. I have a car waiting at the corner." He pointed toward the nearby cross street where a black sedan sat idling. "He needs you to come to his office."

"Why?"

"He wants to make sure you're safe. Don't know more than that. He just told me to bring you." The man put a hand on Garrett's shoulder, pressuring him to move. The boy backed away.

He wrapped a hand behind the back of Garrett's neck. "We need to go *now!*"

"No!"

Every student in the alley watched. The man grabbed him by the arm. Garrett's drink dropped to the asphalt.

"No! Leave me alone! I don't know you!" Garrett kicked his leg, slugging him with a free hand; his backpack slipped off.

Kristin and Andrew began yelling and charged. The man pulled a small caliber revolver from his coat and pointed it at them. "Come with me or your friends get shot. Your choice." They stopped, gaping, while other students shrieked, ran or took photos.

Garrett's arm was twisted behind his back. Helpless, afraid for them, he stopped resisting, nodded in defeat and was marched to the car. One disaster after another. Why?

The man opened the back door and thrust him inside. The gunman elbowed in next to him and slammed the door shut. Garrett tried the handle on his side but it was locked. He caught a quick glance of his friends and others watching as the car accelerated, tires slipping on loose gravel. He tried not to shake. Act tough. Did God hate him?

Up the street, a second car pulled into traffic.

53.

CHICAGO, ILLINOIS (Chicago Sun Times)—A group of prominent Protestant ministers, a female Christian media star, a Catholic cardinal who is now pope and a political campaign consultant known for dirty tricks met secretly with reporter Daniel Duboce just days before he was shot. The topic dealt with release of a secret discovery by Japanese scientists…

California Pacific Medical Center, San Francisco

"You've looked better," Bruiser told his godson while adjusting his own sling and ignoring the ache in his phantom ear. "But you're alive and you'll be pretty again. But best you don't have a mirror." He was grateful Daniel was alive. He looked so helpless in the hospital bed.

Daniel's voice was strained. "I don't remember much after the shooting."

Bruiser had stayed all night as doctors performed emergency surgery and then he sat dozing in a chair beside the bed, ignoring the bullet hole in his arm, wondering if it would leave a dramatic scar, great for conversation and attention. Also a partial ear could be a big draw. The first shot had pierced Daniel's chest, above and to the right of his heart, but missed vital organs. His condition was delicate, as one doctor stated, but stable. Don't get him stressed, she'd insisted, let him rest.

"You were brilliant at the press conference, boy. I counted twelve satellite trucks at the hospital just now. O.J. Simpson didn't get that many."

Daniel looked pale, an intravenous needle in the back of his hand attached to whatever was in the plastic bag above; under his nose was something described by a nurse as a *nasal cannula* for oxygen; patches on his chest were attached to a machine tracking vital readings on his heart, two lines coming from somewhere under his gown going to boxes with orange lights but no winking green ones like on television. Bruiser felt nauseous as he watched a nurse change the dressings on Daniel's chest and back. The gashes were dreadful, the exit wound the worst, and he felt ashamed. He'd talked him into going out and failed to pull him away fast enough from the gunman. He closed his eyes. Crap. How to stay upbeat? The nurse stepped away.

"I called L.A. three times, Daniel. Trudy and Garrett are okay. I talked to Garrett from the ambulance. The shooting went live on TV, went everywhere. I had to claim I was your father. Your kid knows you're okay and police are guarding you."

"How's Garrett?"

"Doing his damnedest to be tough. I told him you asked me to call and send your love."

"But I was unconscious."

"Still a good story. He's at school today. Trudy and her knucklehead husband felt it best. Garrett'll be here this weekend. Officially you're unconscious. I worked it out with the doctors to confuse the creeps behind this." Bruiser placed his hand on Daniel's forehead checking his temperature the old-fashioned way and gently rubbed his hair. His godson was quiet now, eyes closed, likely asleep.

But Daniel said, "Thanks for protecting me. I know you tried to get between the gunman and me." He watched Bruiser before he spoke again. "Are you okay? How're Woesha and Mrs. Polenko?"

Bruiser swallowed hard. "I'm fine, just a couple of minor

holes. Woesha was here for hours till I sent her home. She is one loyal and feisty woman. Mrs. Polenko was here earlier. They love you and they scared the shit out of the assassin. Don't mess with them," he said with a strained grin.

"You've always been there for me." Daniel patted Bruiser's good arm.

The godfather turned his head aside. It was a struggle not to cry. Gotta be strong for him. Gotta be.

"Did they catch the guy?"

The publisher looked up at a ceiling-mounted television, avoiding eye contact. "Yes," he said, not wanting to lie and worried it would upset his boy further. "He's dead. Not many details yet. You have cops outside your door. The mayor ordered protection."

"What motivated the guy?"

He shrugged. "My reporters say he was in a Protestant fringe group. Doomsday nuts and maybe with a connection to a local church. Cops are checking it out. Maybe the same scum that planted that crap story."

"But why kill me?"

Bruiser heard someone clearing his throat. He looked up and saw a tall, well-dressed man standing inside the closed door.

"Mr. Bloomingdale, I presume?" The gentleman walked to the bed and reached over, patting the startled publisher on the shoulder.

"And you are?" Bruiser asked, looking at the stranger's elegant well-fitted suit. He reached around to the back of his hospital gown and pulled it tight to make sure his butt was covered.

"Romaldo Vega," Daniel said.

"Of course." Bloomingdale was cautious, raising an eyebrow. The description fit the voice he heard on the speakerphone. "How'd you get in? With cops and reporters everywhere?" This guy was way too pretty.

"I'm well connected with the police." He glanced at Bruiser before turning back to Daniel. "Police alone cannot keep him safe. I would like to supplement with my own security."

"Why are you helping now? You work for the cardinal. Wait. The guy is now pope. This discovery is rat poison in his holy cracker."

Vega looked amused. "Actually, that wafer is often called a *hostia* or sacramental bread, made with flour, pure water, yeast and salt." He turned back to Daniel. "As I told Daniel, I work for no one. Pope John is a close ally on many issues. On *Misago*, he is loyal to his church yet conflicted by the implications, as am I."

"Yet, as I understand it," Bruiser said, brushing aside the man's attempt at humor, his tone harsh, "you briefed the Christian leaders on the discovery and took part in the cover-up. You tried to get Daniel to defect and brought his kid to Tahoe to convince him your side was right. You messed with *his* family. And he is *my* family. Why should we trust you?"

"You are as I have heard you described and you should be skeptical," Vega said, sounding respectful. "After much reflection, I have changed my position in part because I have come to admire our mutual friend. I believe he has the wisdom and skill to survive and lead what is to come."

Bruiser crossed his good arm over his chest and rested it on the sling. "And what's that?"

"You have seen the media frenzy." Vega was confident, unblinking, somehow warm, reassuring and matter of fact. "It will become a whirlwind. My efforts to keep it secret have failed. Since you both did much to create the furor, perhaps congratulations are in order. I believe my talents will now be most helpful in containing the fallout. Mr. Bloomingdale, only a handful of people knew of Daniel's connection to *Misago* and the assassination plan had to be hatched before he filed in court. Powerful people want this discovery buried. In a few days or weeks when the actual details are out, thousands, perhaps millions will be filled with a sense of betrayal and disrespect. Most will not believe it at first but many will see it as science seeking to destroy faith."

Bruiser touched his ear stub bandage and winced.

"Are you all right, Mr. Bloomingdale?"

"Go on," Bruiser said with a wave of his hand. "Just a bullet hole in my ear, not my head."

Vega turned to Daniel. "The motivation to kill you was prevention. After this goes public the motive will be revenge and to further the goals of ambitious clerics and politicians. Some people will lash out; a few will seek martyrdom if we do nothing. Our strategy must be more than defense. There are too many soft targets to protect."

"The *Beacon* will support him," Bruiser declared.

"The power of your newspaper, while great, is not sufficient," Vega said. "It's one-dimensional. We must communicate on a visceral level to those who might contemplate violence. And viral." His voice picked up slightly in volume, more preacher-like, yet painfully sincere. "We must communicate in a way that makes leaders and pawns step back, communicate in a way that makes them think powers are at work they do not understand and put them at great risk. When the subject is religion, you need to understand the street as well as the cathedral."

Bruiser's head snapped upright. "You did it, didn't you? It was a way to communicate fear. You're Gabriel!"

"Who's Gabriel?" Daniel asked.

"Despite the obvious dangers," Vega said, ignoring the question, "this is also an opportunity. Are you strong enough to have this kind of conversation now? Your health is important to me."

"Please," Daniel said.

Bruiser felt a rising sense of alarm. Keep his yap shut. For now.

"The world prefers the status quo," Vega said quietly. "People fear change. But if God is communicating it might be that some of our assumptions have been seriously mistaken. Both the pope and I feel it. But we do not yet understand the message."

Bruiser watched Daniel, worried he might be too weak for this kind of discussion. But his godson was following the conversation closely; his eyes clear and focused. And the man was fascinating, handsome, charming, stylish, and likely a murderer. He recalled how Daniel had described him in his early copy.

"The fact that we have physical evidence is irrefutable," Vega said. "We need to study it and apply God's greatest gifts—man's sense of curiosity, our ability to think and reason. We must be bold and willing to go where the journey of discovery takes us and set aside calcified assumptions that may bring us comfort but deflect truth. We need to bring the scientific method into this quest for God. Both sides—science and faith—are going to be skeptical. And they should be."

"I agree," Daniel said in a whisper, his eyes wide. Bruiser sensed he was surprised by the comments.

Vega touched Daniel's shoulder and smiled. "Good. If I may continue? I wonder if God is saying our journey on this Earth has taken us to a point where the next adventure begins. The discovery was not possible before science reached its current state of development. Did God allow us to find it now to strengthen our faith but perhaps not the faith we have known in the past?"

"Some will disagree," Daniel said with effort, "and say it's Satan. That includes your friends in the Triple C."

Vega grunted, a smirk on his lips. "Everyone is entitled to their own superstitions."

"I think you're full of it," Bruiser said dismissively, convinced he was a con.

Vega laughed and shook his head. "You are a delight, sir, as are all those close to Daniel. It speaks to his character. So, you still doubt my motives? Obviously, I've lost my touch and perhaps come across as some doddering shaman."

"Doddering?" Daniel tried to laugh and coughed again.

Bruiser touched the side of his godson's face and watched closely to make sure he was steady. "Manipulative, unscrupulous and dangerous might work."

"Apt descriptions all, Mr. Bloomingdale, and deserved."

"Since we're having such a good time," Daniel said, trying to smile, "any insights on who wants to kill me?"

"I'm pleased you have the strength for humor." Vega put both hands on the bed railing. "The CCC and its allies are afraid. Some are networking. Enemies are not limited to that section of Christianity."

Bruiser felt a little overwhelmed but intrigued. "Mr. Vega," he said, "I think you're weird but I appreciate your support of Daniel. I also think you never answered my question about Gabriel."

"I would like your permission to bring my own security to your protection, your home and family."

"I think the police are fully capable. We should not have gone out there for the press conference without them," Bruiser said. "My mistake."

"You're assuming police would have responded without violence first," Vega replied. "Do I have your permission, Daniel?"

"Stick with the police, Daniel. I know the Chief and all the captains. They promise full protection. I don't trust this guy."

"Maybe we should follow the law for now," Daniel said.

"As you wish." Vega touched a palm to Daniel's forehead and held it there. "The doctors tell me you shall recover if careful," he said. "Clearly God was not with the assassin." He stepped back from the side of the bed.

"Gentlemen, I see Daniel as a leader, perhaps an apostle, of a new faith linked through science to the creator. I have work I need to do as part of my…communications plan. I must leave now and will return soon."

Vega bent slightly forward at the waist. He exited the room.

"What the fuck am I supposed to think of him?" Bruiser demanded.

Daniel smiled and closed his eyes.

54.

Downtown, Los Angeles

The sedan drove at the speed limit, making no unusual moves as it exited Beverly Hills headed east. Forty minutes later it pulled into the driveway of a small apartment building. In the back, the driver parked next to a stripped-down SUV up on blocks. Windows were broken on three units. Two men, Garrett held tightly between them, got out and entered a first floor studio apartment.

"Why don't you tell me who you are?" Garrett pleaded when the door closed.

Each man held one of his arms. He'd asked the question repeatedly in the car and the last time was slapped hard in the face. That convinced him to ride in hostile silence. He was frightened at first, but the slap really pissed him off.

"I know you don't work for my stepdad," he said a little more defiantly and waited for the reaction. They yanked off his school jacket and shoved him in a chair. His hands were pulled behind his back. He tried to stand and was slapped again. Once he was bound, they seemed to relax, taking off their coats. The fat one sat on the bed, the tall one in a chair facing him.

"You're a smart kid," the big one said. "No, we don't know

your stepdad. Your real father is involved in somethin' a lot of people want kept quiet. Or—Angel Gabriel may pay a visit." The men snorted.

Garrett was defiant. "It's no hoax! You don't seem like religious types to me."

"We're not," the tall man responded, sounding a little friendlier. "But we do work for people who care about such things. Since your old man didn't die, they hired us as backup to make sure he has the right incentives to keep quiet. Don't know who tried to kill him. Wasn't our group. He's not very popular."

Garrett tried to sort out all that had happened and found it impossible. Had his mom told him the truth about his dad's condition? Why did his father send him away after they got close again? Would his kidnapping make his dad worse? What were these creeps going to do? He was stressed beyond crying. What more could happen? Overwhelmed and helpless, he continued to pull at the ropes. It rubbed his wrists raw but it was a distraction.

The men watched television, occasionally exchanging comments in a language he didn't understand. They flipped the dials to see if there were any stories about the kidnapping. There were none.

After two dull shows, the tall one announced he was getting burgers. He exited cautiously, placing his gun in a shoulder holster under his jacket. The fat guy watched the TV while Garrett was lost in anger and hopelessness. Fifteen minutes later, someone knocked. The fat one, gun drawn, opened the door and the tall one stepped inside carrying two bags of food. The hamburgers were put on a table. Taking off his jacket, he pulled the holster over his head and slung it over the back of a chair.

"I'll take off the ropes so you can piss and eat but you have to promise to be good," he snarled. "Try anything and I'll break your fuckin' arm. Clear?"

"Yes, sir," he said, wanting to knock their heads together.

"Leave the door open."

Garrett glared. They were trying to humiliate him. He left the door ajar, open to view. He looked around. No windows. No way out.

The front door splintered; the lock ripped from its thin casing. Two men in ski masks rushed inside with automatic rifles at their shoulders, ready to fire.

"Freeze!"

The tall guy—Garrett saw him reflected in the mirror on the door—lurched for his gun. An intruder slammed a rifle butt into his head, sending him sprawling over a chair and onto the floor. The tip of the barrel jammed into Brink's ear, drawing blood.

"Yield!"

Meekly, the kidnappers complied. Their hands and legs were cuffed, black hoods pulled down over their heads. An intruder advanced to the bathroom door.

Garrett swallowed. Who else wanted to kidnap him? "My name is Garrett Duboce," he said, struggling to remain calm. "I'm ten years old. I'm in fifth grade. I don't have a gun."

A black boot pushed the bathroom door fully open. He could see the tip of a rifle.

"Please. Come out," said an accented male voice.

Garrett stepped cautiously out of the room, arms up, palms open, like he'd seen in TV crime shows. The men pulled off their masks. He shook his head as he stared at a muscular man with short blond hair. A guard from Tahoe, the friendly one.

"Jurg?"

CPMC Hospital, San Francisco

"Daniel, stay down!" Bloomingdale tried to hold his godson in the bed. "It's being investigated."

"I need to be there, he's my son!" Daniel pleaded.

"There's nothing you can do. Police are on it. I talked to one of the chiefs myself two minutes ago. The best thing you can do to help Garrett is stay in bed and get well."

"Good advice, Mr. Bloomingdale."

They both jumped and turned to the door as Vega entered

and quickly walked to the bed. "I have good news." He put a palm on Daniel's forehead. "Lie back, please." He gently forced him back to his pillow. "First, my apologies for not following your instructions. But I had my security team put the school under surveillance. I was surprised to learn he was at school, seems counterintuitive, but I'm glad my men were there. Your son boarded my private jet for San Francisco ten minutes ago. Trudy is with him. Both are safe. Two of my soldiers followed the kidnappers to a downtown site and rescued him."

Daniel gasped. Bloomingdale gripped the bed railing to steady himself.

"He is a little shaken but excited to be joining you. Thrilled. He should arrive here in about two hours."

Daniel pulled himself forward in the bed and touched Vega's arm. Pain caused him to freeze. Both men helped lower him back down. They waited for the throbbing in his chest to subside.

"Thank you," Daniel whispered, his eyes moist. "Thank you."

"He is a wonderful young man who loves you and he will be here soon, safe and under our protection." Vega's voice was soothing. "The police don't yet know of his rescue. We thought it best to get him out, avoid the trauma of the interrogation and publicity at this time while gathering information about who is behind the kidnapping."

"How can you avoid police and bring him here?" Bruiser demanded, shocked at the revelation.

"Yesterday, Mr. Bloomingdale," Vega explained in a business-like, patient tone, "I said regular police could not handle this kind of operation. If I had not put a unit of my men in place this morning, Garrett would still be tied up in a cheap apartment in downtown Los Angeles, his life at great risk or already ended. Now he's safe and en route to see his father. I do what is needed. End results often trump procedure." He cocked his head, his voice just shy of smug. "My apologies for disobeying your wishes."

"I'm grateful," Daniel said.

Vega checked his watch. Opened his phone and dialed. He spoke in Italian and handed the phone to Daniel. "Here is

Garrett."

Bruiser watched, emotions raw. Should he be grateful or pissed off at the arrogance of the man? The publisher stepped across the room and notched up the sound on a television, flipping channels. CNN had a report on Garrett's kidnapping. Several student eyewitnesses were interviewed: some of the children hysterical. Other channels were also broadcasting live from Beverly Hills. There were pieces on the gruesome murder of the assassin in Buena Vista Park and one station even showed Daniel's shooting in slow motion. Really disgusting.

Several crime consultants speculated that the attempted assassination was an effort to silence Daniel from disclosing what he knew. They almost sounded disappointed. Anchormen and women, beautifully coifed and their faces lined with heartfelt concern, asked about the fear this created for children and what might be done to console them.

"Pansy ass reporters," Bruiser mumbled. He watched discussions about the missing space scientists and obfuscation by the federal government. Clearly, none had a clue.

"He's safe just like Romaldo told us," Daniel said offering the phone back to Vega. "Seems to be handling it well. Better than me. He said Jurg from Tahoe was one of the rescuers." He shook his head. "Now we know Garrett's a target too."

"I assigned Jurg. He is young but first rate and got to know your son a little at Tahoe. I knew he would be diligent."

"I'm appreciative too," Bruiser said, his voice conveying suspicion even as he offered praise. "I still don't understand how you can operate outside the law."

"I'm not outside the law, Mr. Bloomingdale, I simply augment it and, when possible, work in partnership. Police are invaluable for certain operations. The fallout from *Misago* is not one of them. Their focus is too narrow."

"Inside or outside, Romaldo, I'm grateful," Daniel said.

Vega nodded, "You're welcome. I suggest we put your son and his mother in a hotel penthouse suite where we can provide security. But first they will come here via a back entrance and avoid the media."

Bloomingdale lifted his head, looking suspiciously at the re-fined man across the bed. "I want to go back to another topic you didn't respond to yesterday."

He looked at Daniel. "Let's discuss what happened to your would-be assassin," he said. "I intentionally avoided specifics ear-lier because you were too weak. But Garrett is sure to know so you need to be briefed before he arrives." The publisher explained what had been on television, newspapers, radio and the Internet. The video making the rounds, emailed by millions to friends in every country, showing the assassin pleading for his life claiming he was talking to an angel. Bruiser described speculation in Arabic media as well as English.

He turned to Vega. "Yes, someone caught up with the assas-sin in Buena Vista Park. It was bloody gruesome. Camera crews got a tip and arrived before the police."

Daniel showed no reaction. He rolled his head toward Vega. The Vatican envoy, resplendent in a chocolate suit, white shirt and pink striped tie, was silent.

"The White House is stiffing reporters," Bruiser said. "So's the FBI. The other people you filed with in court are also quiet, Daniel, waiting for your recovery, actually, hiding behind it. Ev-eryone still thinks you're unconscious."

Bruiser flashed on other media storms he had weathered over the years, the Zebra killings, earthquakes, and scandals. This was far bigger. "Instead of real information there's bullshit. The reli-gious chatter is all over the map. All nuts. Some say it's an elabo-rate publicity hoax. The fantasies on talk radio are Oscar wor-thy. There are reports surfacing about an employee murder at the Japanese space agency."

The publisher squinted at Vega. "Yesterday I asked if you were Gabriel. I'm still waiting."

Vega's expression was flat, his voice quiet. "Some things are better left unsaid, my friend."

"You can't do things like that to people!"

"Gentlemen, we are not in a normal world anymore. For the

success of our mission, I will neither confirm nor deny. But I urge you to accept this new reality." He glanced between them; a calm tinged with molten warning. "You chose to unleash the furies, Daniel. I warned you. An example was made of the assassin, immediate and instantaneous. As news of your wounds went public so did the story of the assassin and how God or Satan inflicted immediate, brutal Old Testament justice. Both were in the same news cycle, visual and startling. There must be an immediate connection between a crime and punishment if you want deterrence. Many will be confused, perhaps most, but those who would consider violence against you will understand. This is justice from the Bible and the *Qur'an*. The assassin's colleagues absorbed the message immediately and graphically. And they are afraid. People like them are afraid."

"Do I thank you or attack you?" Bruiser asked with sarcasm. "You don't have the right to take justice into your own hands."

"The forces of religious certainty can lead to destruction and chaos if this isn't handled well," Vega responded with a hint of righteousness. He took a breath and stepped back. "Remember when Israeli Prime Minister Yitzhak Rabin was assassinated? A right-wing radical who opposed the Oslo Accords shot him as he left the stage, surrounded by thousands of Rabin's supporters singing '*Shir Lashalom*,' literally 'Song for Peace.' To many radicals, that killer, that ignorant, evil madman, is a hero even as he sits in a jail cell. There was no justice. Afterward Israeli politics degenerated into an angry charade and periodic wars."

Vega's eyes narrowed; his voice hardened. "The man who shot you may initially be admired by some, but that view is now mixed with fear. They are now uncertain if the same fate, wielded by the sword of Gabriel, awaits them should they make a similar effort. An angel of the Jews, Christians and Muslims inflicts a brutal justice. This they now understand."

Bloomingdale was shaken. The man was unapologetic and exuded physical power. Should he turn him into the police, write this confession into the story, or just plain be grateful?

The Vatican envoy continued. "There will certainly be additional disclosures. Prepare yourselves. If there are other attacks, there will be a merciless response. The forces who are with me are not squeamish in the pursuit of peace nor the kind of justice recommended in *Exodus*."

Daniel started to ask a question, then grimaced as if hit with a stabbing pain in his chest.

Bruiser bent over him. "Are you all right?"

"I'm fine," Daniel said and waited to regain his strength. "But conflicted," he confessed haltingly as he adjusted his position in the bed, Vega reaching down and helping.

Bruiser recalled Daniel talking about how he and Vega took jogs on the beach together and discussed theology and history. Could this truly be the same man?

The publisher inched his good hand across the bed toward Vega. "No time for weakness. Thank you. You take the meaning of a communications plan to a whole new level." They shook hands, firm and genuine. Neither smiled.

"Thank you, Mr. Bloomingdale, for saving Daniel by shielding his body with your own. You are a hero. You took great risk. It confused the assassin and saved our friend's life. That life is crucial in the days ahead." Vega looked down at the patient. "I know my methods seem cruel. But so is assassination, kidnapping and street violence. There are worse horrors. Keeping you and your son alive, containing the fallout, is the goal."

The three were still and silent trying to make sense of it all, looking at each other, listening to the news as sunlight came through the window and brightened the room.

"The conference is tomorrow, Daniel," Bruiser said, trying to sound matter of fact as he pushed other issues aside. "You're not strong enough. We can't take the risk. We need to cancel."

Northern California

Tio was in an interrogation room somewhere, she calculated, close to where she was taken—based on the length of the ride in a military transport. Her head bandaged and aching, she'd been hooded for the trip here, wherever here was. Then another prison cell and the hood removed. She was handcuffed to a chair. One wall was mirror, the others scruffy plasterboard. She had been told she would be shipped out within the hour. No destination was mentioned.

"You're the feisty one, aren't you, bitch?" The scowling FBI agent stood before her with his arms crossed. "You busted an agent's nose."

"Did you never learn to knock?" Tio barked, meeting his sneer. She was not intimidated despite their best efforts and that seemed to make them angrier. "You crashed into my room. What was I supposed to do? I assumed it was a break-in robbery. Who would know this is how police operate in America? You're lucky I didn't break more. What're the charges?"

"Lady, you're a foreign national accused of fomenting terrorism. We don't need reasons. You hurt two of my men. You have no rights here."

Another agent entered the room. "It's time. Move her out!"

55.

Today was the day of the announcement and no one in the administration knew where, how or exactly what. Duboce was unconscious, Wada and Ito in custody. What could they really accomplish without any of the main players? Jake Machin was in his office with Press Secretary Dennis Myers, still stunned by the teaser headlines in the *Times* and *Beacon*.

> **Special Announcement on** *Misago*!
> **8 a.m. PSD and 11 a.m. EST today**

Calls to their contacts at the newspapers were not returned. Every morning talk show was speculating and repeating scenes of the shooting and the dead assassin. A few reported speculation in Japanese media and SETI. The hidden secrets behind *Misago* had captured the national attention. The printed morning *Times* was out with the banner, no explanation amid its regular news stories. The *Beacon* had no morning edition.

Machin re-checked both web sites. The same headline. His pulse was racing, this was heavy foreplay before a nasty fuck. He couldn't believe Bloomingdale could outfox him. Well, he wouldn't bottom on this one. Jake Machin was always the most ruthless, the most devious. But no newspaper had ever done anything remotely so duplicitous. Worse than a reality TV show.

He glanced at his watch: 7:45 a.m. His cell phone whistled. The screen showed "McMillan" and a 415 Area Code.

"What?" Machin bellowed at his political contact in San Francisco before remembering his stature, clearing his throat, and repeating, "Do you have a report?"

"It's crazy here!" the man said. "I'm downtown and hundreds of paperboys are running everywhere in the City screaming about *Misago* and handing out free newspapers. People are pouring out of every shop and office building, even getting out of their cars, even street cars, holding their phones—it's going viral. Here's a video I just shot. Transferring now."

Machin watched in disbelief as Press Secretary Dennis Myers came up beside him. Wholesome boys and girls, maybe early teens, wearing old-fashioned 1900s wool brimmed caps, were passing out papers to people crazed to get copies.

"EXTRA! EXTRA!
Misago Secret Revealed!
Intelligent Entity Created Life and Left a Message!
Government and Religious Leaders Desperate to Hide the Truth!'

"P-p-paperboys?" Machin was dumbfounded. He disconnected. "It's a Ta-Twitter madhouse. Why not put it on the web like they normally do? Why the bizarre headline?"

Myers clicked on the *Beacon's* web site. "Still nothing here but the teaser. Bloomingdale wants it out by newspaper first, a physical record in thousands of hands, a happening." He shook his head, an admiring grin parting his lips. "Someone called the top papers, reporters, and network news directors last night, said they should have crews in the area ready to move when the leaker gives the location. I assume it's Bloomingdale and he may have even given the exact spot to a few. Everyone's tight-lipped. Every network is carrying it live and it'll be global in minutes."

"But Wada's the one with the credibility."

"Is Wada safe?"

"I assume so."

"And Dr. Ito?"

"Probably. Why wouldn't they be?"

"Beauregard has friends."

"Crap!" Machin looked at his watch. "Who do they have?"

"Cleaver said she'd introduce the main speaker," Myers replied. *"Hold on!"*

Myers read a text. "OK, an update. One guy, who may or may not be telling the truth, says three locations have been leaked: at the hospital where Duboce is, a space conference at the Oakland Convention Center and the Chabot Space and Science Center a few miles away." He put his phone on the desk. "Cleaver has religious cred and I've seen Duboce on PBS. If he's the one, the guy is articulate and the cameras love him. Masculine, handsome and sincere. But, of course, he does have to be conscious."

"Yes, there is that," Machin said nervously, a rare emotion for him. "But there're others listed on the Writ of Habeas Corpus. The FBI staked out all of them. I'll call the Director now. Maybe some or all should be taken into custody."

"Don't!" Myers warned. "Let this play out. Check on Wada and Dr. Ito. We don't need another murder on top of everything else."

CPMC Hospital, San Francisco

A patient was wheeled in a gurney through the hallways and into a waiting ambulance. A gauze mask covered most of his face; a sheet and blanket his body. Trudy and Garrett were already inside. The vehicle drove slowly past the encampment of reporters at the front of the Davies campus of the CPMC. No one paid attention.

It pulled onto Castro Street and headed toward the freeway

entrance a half-mile away. A black sedan moved in front of the ambulance; an SUV behind. The caravan drove over the Bay Bridge and into Oakland, going underground at the Convention Center.

56.

HUMANITY'S CREATOR REVEALED

SAN FRANCISCO, CA (*New York Times and San Francisco Beacon*)—*A monumental discovery in space, perhaps the greatest in history, offers physical evidence of how an intelligent entity created life on Earth and contradicts the teachings of several major religions… It is being suppressed by the American and Japanese governments out of fear of offending powerful American Christian leaders… "Most shocking," said one source who has seen the evidence, "is that it may contain a message from the creator."*

West Wing, White House

"I can't believe it!" Machin felt his lungs deflate watching the two newspaper websites as the story popped onto the screen.

"Print it out! Print it out!" he gasped to a secretary as he tried to read it. The story went on for pages. Bylined by Carroll Bloomingdale with a long list of contributing writers and researchers. Could the headline be any bigger? This wasn't the stock market crash of

'29.

A minute later, Machin scurried down the hall, rushing into the president's office and handing him a copy.

"Please excuse me for a moment," the president said to members of the Kansas Hereford Association. He stepped into a side office and began skimming the story.

"We're contacting select publishers," Machin said, "suggesting they treat this with skepticism, Mr. President. Editorials will urge caution."

"What's in the works?"

"The *Washington Journal* will go on the attack and treat it as a hoax. We set that up a few days ago, although we didn't offer any details. Our favorite network and our radio talk jocks will scream it's a sick publicity stunt by liberals. Several well-known talking heads, the usual, are primed, ready to claim fraud. They have scripts." Machin laughed quietly. "Media consolidations and getting rid of the Fairness Doctrine make this so much easier."

The president listened while scanning the *Times*.

Machin continued: "We have the story in the *National Muckraker*, unfortunately it looks a bit silly considering what's now out. We're not sure where the event will be but have three leads." Bloomingdale was good. He waited until Walton finished.

The president folded his arms and looked down, deep in thought. "Some of our in-bed reporters may look like fools."

"Despite my instructions," Machin said, "the dossier on Wada is already in play with some second-tier bloggers. There's also some nasty stuff on Duboce. I've a good idea on the source, someone who violated my direct instructions."

"Michaels?"

"Yes."

"Why am I not surprised? What about Duboce?"

Machin gave a rundown.

"Unacceptable. Let honest reporters know there's a smear underway. Let our friendly ones be warned off."

"It's going viral. Emotions are hard on this as you know and people are and will be hungry for an explanation to discredit

Misago. I'll meet with my staff to plan spin control. The article, as you can see, is pretty accurate which is unfortunate but not important."

"Are you suggesting we try and stop whatever they're about to do?"

"No, that would just add to the story line and offer proof of our efforts to suppress. It's already too widely distributed and our silence has helped make the media frantic. I think at this point we just seek to minimize the story, make people believe it's a hoax."

"Do you think *Misago* is a hoax?"

Machin felt uncomfortable. "I've no idea. That's not my job. I win elections and political battles anyway I can. I have a very good track record."

"No denying your record, Jake. Let me say, I don't think it is."

"It may be true or not, I'm not the one to judge. But it risks upheaval. Whatever you decide, we're prepared. I hope the American people are ready."

"Me too. Find Dr. Ito!"

Myers ran into the office. "Something is about to happen. CNN, CBS, NBC, PBS, a dozen cable channels and streaming video on several web sites."

"I'll watch it in my private quarters upstairs and we can meet afterward."

Convention Center, Oakland

In the grand ballroom of the Marriott Hotel adjacent to the Oakland Convention Center, hundreds pushed through crowded hallways, queuing up before security guards to show credentials, and then into their seats in preparation for the closing plenary session of the American Institute of Aeronautics and Astronautics (AIAA). It was nearly eight a.m. The officially scheduled topic: Space Defense Systems.

Delegates stared and whispered to one another as they saw over fifty television cameras across the back of the room and well-known reporters, even two network anchors, coiffed and tailored, preparing their stand-ups. People started looking at their cell phones for answers but found they had no reception and a notice that it would be restored after 8 a.m. Someone spotted Bloomingdale, his arm still in a sling, and people pointed and took photos. He waved and grinned.

"Five-minute notice," a male voice announced from speakers above the auditorium. "Please settle down. I will give you a notice at one-minute intervals and then a thirty second countdown for those wanting to go live." It was enough to convince people to sit although the noise level seemed to increase.

"Thirty seconds."

At precisely eight a.m., Dr. Steven Combs, one of America's most recognizable scientists with his trademark white handlebar mustache and thick, black-framed glasses, walked out from behind a curtain and stood in the center of the stage. There was no podium; he carried a cordless microphone and waited for the audience to quiet down.

"My name is Steve Combs and I'm one of two speakers set for this morning. The other is Dr. Sally Smithers of Harvard University. We were supposed to talk about the morality of weapons in space. That will not happen this morning by mutual agreement and I suspect you'll be very pleased to be part of what will be presented instead. As I walked out here just now, the block on your cell phones was removed. I suspect there's a hint of what will occur here today. Take half a minute." Within seconds, hundreds of cell phones lit up. He waited, smiling, as people shrieked with "OMG" the most common phrase.

"If I can have your attention, please." All eyes were on their phones. "LADIES AND GENTLEMEN! YOUR ATTENTION PLEASE! *Put down your phones!*"

That seemed to work. "Thank you. Dr. Smithers and I believe that the presentation you're about to hear will be historic. Something extraordinary is in the works, something I suspect you'll be telling and retelling for years to come. You'll brag to friends and colleagues, perhaps even strangers on the subway, that you were here at this conference, on this day, at this hour, where this unscheduled but widely rumored announcement was made to the world."

Everyone in the audience seemed to be whispering, phones recording the moment, many doing selfies with Dr. Combs behind them, perhaps to prove to friends they were here.

"Less than ten minutes ago, the full story of *Misago*—the discovery itself, the attempts by two governments to keep it secret, a threatened military coup, the arrest by the FBI of the chief scientist who made the discovery—was placed on the *New York Times* and *San Francisco Beacon* websites. Around the country millions of copies of a special edition of the papers are hitting the streets. Our focus today, on this stage, will be what was found and its implications."

Combs pointed to Bloomingdale and twisted one end of a mustache that seemed to defy gravity. "In the audience is the lead author of that story, Carroll Bruiser Bloomingdale, a man wounded along with Daniel Duboce in an attempted assassination. Also, in the audience, as you may have noticed, are strategically placed wagons with red plastic tarps. Somehow just seeing the story on a cell phone screen just isn't big enough. We brought you the real thing." He turned to Bruiser.

"Mister Bloomingdale!" he shouted, dragging out the words, sounding like a carnival barker. *"Let the truth be free!"*

Bruiser waved as the entire audience instantly turned to him. He stepped in front of his wagon and yanked off the thin red plastic cover. He picked up his own cordless mike and shouted:

"Paperboys! Unload your wagons!"

Like young toreadors with capes, the boys ripped off the red coverings, twirling them overhead. They energetically skipped and ran to all parts of the auditorium, pulling their wagons and shouting in chorus:

"EXTRA! EXTRA!
Misago COVER-UP Revealed!"

Audience members and reporters were frantic to get a copy. There were gasps when they read the headline and started to scan the article. Holding an actual copy of the newspaper with the story made it more real. The secret that had captured the imagination of the world was page one. On stage, more was to come.

Dr. Combs allowed everyone to get their papers and settle down. "The newspaper article in front of you," he stated, "gives a sense of what is about to be presented. This is a complex story. I suggest you pay close attention. Put your phones down, take part in this reality. Read and text later." Combs felt almost giddy and worked hard to bring back the thoughtful scientist into his voice.

"The discovery is almost overshadowed by the intrigue to suppress it," he said. "You'll need to sort through many issues to ascertain the truth. But I've been involved in studying the secret *Misago* discovery myself for days. Before he was captured by the FBI, an extraordinary Japanese scientist, a man I call my friend and colleague, Dr. Yoshito Wada, shared with me data and granules from the asteroid and urged me to study them. I have done so with my colleagues at SETI and Stanford.

"Our findings are being added to our website as I speak. I know enough to say to my brother and sister scientists of the world—this is likely the most important discovery in modern history! It shall no longer be hidden!" His tone was defiant and carried the ring of truth. People squirmed with excitement; applause was loud, punctuated with nervous whistles.

"I wish Dr. Wada were here today to tell his own story." Combs halted to maintain his composure. "My sense of shame in my government is heavy." The audience stirred, sensing his anger.

"This is for you, Yoshito! A major disinformation campaign is underway, far worse than occurred during J. Edgar Hoover's nasty work on Martin Luther King, Jr., the Trump Administration on Russia and most everything, and, of course, our last presidential election. It's scurrilous and evil, but such is the decay of politics. This may make public understanding more complicated and it challenges us as scientists, and reporters here as well, to help find the truth."

He scanned the room, every eye upon him. "Let me say, I've studied Wada's results and I have personally used Stanford's state-of-the-art labs to examine the granules from space. I've found no inconsistencies with his findings. I suspect and hope that many of you will have the same opportunity to review and reflect. For me at this hour, I believe Dr. Wada's findings are accurate."

The room was silent, all waiting for his next words. He suspected and hoped that millions at home were calling their friends and telling them to turn on the television, much like the morning of 9-11. Now he needed to introduce his friend.

Backstage, Daniel watched a TV monitor. A doctor and two nurses had gently lifted him from the gurney into a motorized wheelchair and checked his vital signs. Bruiser had insisted they come. A full medical team was in an ambulance outside.

Vega had gone one better and arranged for a medical unit to be set up in an adjoining room, just in case. It didn't add to Daniel's confidence. His son was sitting in a front row seat along with Trudy.

The wheelchair was torture, knives in his back, and he was strapped in for stability. His chest ached, a volcano above his heart. He'd refused any painkillers that might dull his senses. This was for Tio and Yoshito. Vega pinned a tiny cordless mike to his lapel. He was grateful Saito was hours into a flight from London to San Francisco. The man was now family and an important new part of his life.

Vega set Wada's silver-handled cane across his lap. "Are you ready, my friend?" Do you have the strength?"

"Whatever my condition," Daniel said, "I'm the only option. The issues are more important than I am."

"I think you're more vital than you realize but that's a topic for another time," Vega said, keeping an eye on the screen. "I've alerted the pope so he will not be surprised. I suspect the ministers, at least some, will be apoplectic."

Vega smiled, giving Daniel energy. Adrenalin was starting to kick in. This was going to happen. He pushed the lever and the chair backed up, then went forward, slow, and silent. He wanted to get in some practice with the controls.

"Please," Vega warned, "do not exert yourself. Save your strength."

"They deserve my loyalty. Is that corny?"

"Your commitment is admirable and Wada, Ito and Saito are extraordinary. A virtuous trio." Vega pushed the wheelchair out of the room and into a dark curtained area on the side of the stage. "Saito will be with you soon. Be positive."

Daniel scanned the phalanx of cameras in the back, hoping he had the strength and inspiration to meet his son's high expectations. It sounded like Combs was getting ready to make the next introduction. Would anyone try and stop him?

West Wing, White House

"Is he their big gun?" Jake Machin mocked the man on the television screen, hopeful and sarcastic all at once. "Who the fuck is he? He looks like Howdy Doody with a mustache. A PBS guy for fuck's sake. He's a joke! Who else do they have? Nobody!"

He laughed at the same time glaring at the press secretary and then down to check messages on his phone looking for confirmation. "Yes! The FBI confirms they arrested all of the petitioners except Elizabeth Cleaver and her group. If this nerd's all they have, maybe we can get through this."

Convention Center, Oakland

"I would now like to turn this microphone over to a woman I've known since college days, Elizabeth Cleaver, head of the Wilkins Institute, a Christian research organization sometimes associated with the Intelligent Design movement and efforts to bring conservative religious teachings into public schools. I've shared information given to me by Dr. Wada and Elizabeth's team has examined it. You may have seen her on the news at an impromptu and almost incendiary press briefing yesterday. Please welcome a woman I deeply admire, Elizabeth Cleaver."

The applause was loud but many people looked confused. This was a scientific conference.

"Thank you, Dr. Combs—Steven—for that generous introduction," Elizabeth said, taking the microphone. "I have the honor of introducing our main speaker. His tale is extraordinary, his insights provocative.

"My friend Steven is a scientist looking for ET, I'm a researcher focused on faith, wanting to assure God a front-row seat in society. Together we've studied *Misago* and, for different reasons, we are stunned, thrilled, excited about the new dimension on faith and science that has now opened to humanity, and willing to consider, *what if?*"

She lowered her microphone and cleared her throat before lifting it back. "Dr. Combs has stated that four brave individuals sought to bring this story public. Dr. Wada and scientist Dr. Tio Ito are being held somewhere to compel their silence. Dr. Hideo Saito, a prominent scientist with an international reputation is spreading the word." She paused. The audience, as one, leaned forward.

"The fourth person is Daniel Duboce, a distinguished historian and author on medieval history and religion. He is also a widely respected journalist and a key figure in the story before you." Elizabeth waited again, tension rising, enjoying the moment.

"Yesterday morning he was shot and nearly killed in an assassination attempt to force his silence on *Misago*, the bullet barely missing his heart. Against the wishes of his doctors, with two emergency medical crews in the wings, a brave man on so many levels risks his life this morning to give you the facts. He is sitting just behind the drapes, tied into a wheelchair, his wound raw, life threatening, refusing pain medication so his mind is clear to explain to the world what was found. He is ready to present the story and how this discovery will forever change the way we look at life, religion, science and God. Please join me in welcoming Daniel Duboce."

West Wing, White House

"Crap!" Machin yelled, pounding his fist on the desktop, then rubbing his wrist. "They lied. He's supposed to be unconscious."

"Far out," Myers responded, unable to keep from grinning. "You never can trust those doctors."

Convention Center, Oakland

The audience erupted, on its feet, applause deafening as Daniel rolled slowly onto the stage. A set of spotlights tracked his movements. Alone in his wheelchair, sharp stabs in his chest, moving with caution, he hoped he wouldn't drive it over the edge. Bruiser had choreographed it all. He saw him nearby, gleeful, worried, grinning.

Hundreds of cell phones were in the air. Television cameras and audio recorders were rolling; those reporting live hurried to wrap up their running commentary.

Daniel moved to the center of the stage and turned toward the audience. He inched the wheelchair to the edge and looked down. Garrett was standing in the front row, applauding wildly, his curly hair flopping, his face all teeth and tears. His handsome young son. Standing next to him was the boy's mother also standing and clapping, looking sophisticated in a yellow suit and green scarf. He pointed at Garrett and gave him a thumbs-up. He nodded at Trudy and smiled. She returned the gesture. It felt good.

Photographers were going crazy trying to get close and capture this moment. Daniel lifted his good arm and the applause gradually died down. As he was about to begin, Garrett yelled, "Go Dad!" Many in the audience laughed. Daniel backed up the chair from the edge just to play it safe.

He held up Wada's black walking stick and turned the Osprey handle to the cameras. "This belongs to Dr. Yoshito Wada," he said, beginning the revelation, "wherever he is, a prisoner of my government. A shameful act. Hopefully he is still alive." He stopped, letting his emotions settle. Breathe, he told himself.

"Dr. Wada's late wife gave him this cane after an accident on the International Space Station decades ago. He had saved a man's life at the risk of his own and lost the partial use of one leg. A hero in so many ways. In Japanese, the white-chested Osprey on the handle of this cane translates into... *Misago*." He thrust the cane in the air and winced in pain. "This day is for you, Yoshito Nathan Wada, and you, Tio Ito, wherever you are. And for Hideo Saito, spreading news of this wonder to those who will be in the vanguard of this revelation. Jails and bullets and murder will not hide this secret." In the days to come, he suspected there would be much speculation about the cane. A symbol was important to a movement: the fierce Osprey of Japan.

"Thank you, Dr. Combs for that dramatic introduction," he said softly, trying to conserve his strength, hoping the mike was strong enough. He saw a man enter from a side door. It was Saito. The man grinned and it gave Daniel added strength. "I hope I will be an acceptable substitute for the scheduled debate on weapons in space." There was a scattering of laughter. The only movement was the blinking lights of the cameras and hundreds of cell phones.

"My tale is one of science that unexpectedly crossed into the realm of faith," he said. "Who thought these two worlds would meet like this, competitors that might someday form a new partnership, new truths from the grains of an asteroid, new communications from a creator, a creator we will learn about in the next hour as we begin a new age of discovery. Today, we are pilgrims beginning our journey to find God." There was a murmur in the audience. "Or, the creator, whoever, or whatever it may be."

As he related the story and slides of the *Misago* discovery flashed on screen, he hoped those present felt they were part of history. Scientists would be skeptical but the findings enumerated here were seriously presented in exquisite detail and Dr. Combs had already put his prestige on the line and mentioned other distinguished scientists doing the same.

At the end of the presentation, Daniel asked for questions. He was met with only stunned silence. A single cube rotated on the screen, the mandala coming briefly into luminous view every three seconds. He thought of his own journey as he checked their faces—doubt, excitement, joy, rapture, anger, confusion. What can you say, what do you think, when your world, believer or skeptic, is pulled inside out?

The stillness was broken by the sound of one person clapping loudly from the back of the auditorium. The handsomest man anyone had ever seen walked down the aisle shouting Daniel's name mixed with "Bravo!" as if this were an opera house and Luciano Pavarotti had just finished *La Boheme*. Vega was amazing. Garrett and Trudy took the cue and jumped-up clapping and whistling. Bruiser pounded his foot into the bottom of an empty wagon and the paperboys screamed and slammed their feet, making as much noise as they could. Others begin to clap; then the audience was on its feet.

Eventually the applause subsided, people lost their inhibitions and wanted details. Portable mikes were passed to questioners so everyone could hear and the cameras could record. Daniel answered technical questions as well as inquiries about the cane, his personal life, the future of faith, his fears, his reaction when he learned his son had been kidnapped.

The back doors of the auditorium slammed open.

Scores of reporters and TV camera crews, on stakeouts at Davies Hospital and the Chabot Planetarium, stormed into the room, some running to the base of the stage, pushing other reporters aside, shouting their questions, determined to earn their bylines. It added to the theatrics. He wondered if Bruiser had planned this too. Daniel watched—exhausted, energized, amazed—as they lobbed their queries.

Thirty minutes later, Daniel held up the palm of his hand.

"No more." The pain was too much; even adrenalin was no longer enough to sustain him.

At the signal, Garrett hurried up a set of steps and walked alone onto the stage as silence enveloped the room. He placed his hands on his father's shoulder and bent over and kissed the side of his face. He whispered but within range of the microphone. "We gotta go, Dad. You need to get well." Tears flooded Garrett's cheeks. Overcome with the emotion of the past few days, having been through so much, he tried to keep from crying, brushing the tears aside with his palms, wiping his nose.

Daniel took his good arm and held the boy. Their foreheads pressed together, eyes closed, a loving, spiritual portrait to the world. The image, Bruiser predicted in setting it up beforehand, would fill the front pages and loop endlessly on cable news. Iconic. But they were just supposed to hug. This was a connection, a moment with his son ingrained forever. Daniel's voice broke. "My son says it's time for me to go."

The applause seemed impossibly loud; many wiped their eyes, others wept, many tried doing selfies.

Garrett gripped the handles of the wheelchair as they moved to the side of the stage and slowly down a ramp. Dozens of arms stretched toward them, trying to connect. "Thank you," Garrett croaked repeatedly, his voice emotional, "I love my dad," his face gleaming wet. Daniel smiled, touched hands, and waved as best he could. Saito, Vega, Bruiser, guards, and a medical team waited at the bottom.

Television cameras, pre-positioned overhead and to the sides, captured the exit as his godfather envisioned, the image instantly available to all networks; people reaching out, screaming the names of the father and the son, the triumphant march of new media icons.

57.

West Wing, White House

Machin and Myers sat in a private office, watching CNN, and taking notes. Four other TV sets flickered in muted silence on the wall.

As Daniel left the stage, Myers turned up the sound on all five, trying to catch wrap-up commentary by different networks, scribbling notes in his reporter's shorthand.

"I think 'historic,' 'shattering,' 'eloquent' are the favorite words," Myers concluded. "This guy's good. The media loves him. Both of them. The public will too." He scanned the Internet while he watched one network do instant highlights. "The boy is fantastic."

He swiveled his chair toward Machin. "The *Times* says the president personally asked the Japanese to quash the discovery. True?"

"If I tell you, will you still follow the official line?"

"I hate these situations!" Myers snapped, pushing to his feet. "If we deny it, a thousand reporters will work to prove us wrong. Did he do it?" This wasn't the first time he'd been left out of the loop. He knew Machin enjoyed power discussions if he was the insider.

"Yes, it's essentially correct," Machin said, "A few points I disagree with but nothing important."

"Is there a reason why I'm only finding out about this now?"

"We were trying to limit information to a handful of people, like any other priority-one item discussed in private by decision makers. Only the president, General Beauregard and I were initially involved."

Myers glanced up at a television screen, catching a giggling interview from one of the conventioneers. "But now the world knows about the story and the accusation that our president was directly involved. Cover-ups don't work when word leaks."

"He's vacillating on this. First, he wanted to protect the public from likely violence. Now that it's out, he feels we, America, need to use our scientific power to study and understand it, not just call it fake. It needs to be managed. He wants to have it both ways. The backlash could be staggering. Maybe not today but in a few weeks or months, certainly in the mid-term elections."

"You mean he might actually put country *ahead* of politics?"

"I don't think you appreciate the danger."

"I won't be another professional deflector and liar." Myers was emphatic, thinking about Nixon's embattled press secretary during Watergate and a dark trail of other swindlers of communication who followed. "President Walton doesn't want to be cornered by a false denial."

"Truth can be subjective, my friend."

"I'm going to talk to the president."

"Go ahead. Do your self-righteous liberal thing and destroy him."

"Why is honesty always the last option?"

Oval Office, White House

This was not just a performance. Walton was certain of that, thinking of Duboce and his son. It had obviously been staged but the man spoke his truth in a way that seemed to transcend politics and religious proselytizing. Did he have a reason to lie? What did he gain by this? In an age where so much was deceit and fake astroturf front groups dominated partisan debate, when truth was fungible, was there such a thing as honesty? Could you take someone at their word? Walton couldn't erase the image of Duboce on stage, wounded, in pain, risking his life to bring forth the story of *Misago*. Some partisans, he knew, would likely deny the shooting really happened or was staged, anything to destroy the messenger and defang his message.

And the boy, the purity of his love and that of his father, hit an emotional nerve, creating a powerful link with every family. It was the most thrilling performance he'd ever seen and it left him in tears when the child embraced his dad.

Was this theatre or real? Was Duboce a messenger, a new John the Baptist, or a fraud or dupe? Refurbished truth, feigned shock, counterattacks, artificial anguish were stock and trade in politics. Even his own election had come on the back of fraud, joyously perpetrated by zealots. Might he have won anyway?

The White House communications team was deadlocked. Walton met for an hour with Myers and Machin, letting them argue face to face. It was bare knuckles, suppressed rage finding voice. He hoped the confrontation would remain private and he listened but declined comment. He had his own ideas. This was his test, his alone, for history and God. And maybe honesty. He had three more tasks to accomplish today.

Hours later, he looked up from his desk as his science advisor, Jeremy Stong, walked into the room. The outgoing former Princeton chemistry professor looked tense. "Is it true?" the president asked, not interested in small talk. He gestured to a seat.

"I've examined the data in Wada's computer and it seems real," Stong said, sounding remarkably collected. He paused before giving his full report.

"Scores of top space scientists have released detailed statements saying they met with Wada or Dr. Ito, examined the data and found it accurate and compelling," he said. "The two did significant outreach before they were taken into custody and those early contacts networked to hundreds of scientists in numerous specialties. Experts from around the globe were primed and ready to step forward as soon as the story broke.

"He also has another scientist colleague, Dr. Hideo Saito, who went to London and briefed an auditorium filled with European scientists at a convention. They in turn have done their own outreach. I've talked with several, the best in the world in their fields, about their examination of the cubes and data. At least ten A-list researchers outside the United States have issued statements of confidence in Wada and JAXA. Here's the clincher. Minutes ago, NASA issued a statement that it re-tested samples from the old *OSIRIS-Rex* mission using Wada's methodology and confirmed the findings. Our own space agency backs him. As a scientist, I'm proud to say that honest scientific discovery has rejected the obfuscation and deceit of politics. A new day. Thank you for not interfering."

"My god!" Walton rubbed fingertips over his eyes and leaned back in his chair.

"All the scientists I've mentioned, NASA included, urge serious research to understand it and condemn any cover-up. This is fast becoming a catalyst for scientists of all specialties to claw back respect for their profession, an enough-BS moment, one biologist called it their Waterloo, anti-science denialists in a standoff with data and research. Wada and his allies also put up his own web site giving extensive data. He set technical specifications so it could handle millions of hits simultaneously. There's an Internet war going on, hackers trying to bring the site down, an army of supporters protecting it. This guy was organized. If this isn't true, it's the most elaborate hoax in history."

"Is it a hoax?" The president wiped his mouth with the back of his hand.

"No, Mr. President. This is the real thing. I stake my career on it."

"You just have. We both have."

One step at a time. Walton moved around his desk and surprised Stong with a hug— "Thank you for your honesty and service"— and stepped through a side door into an adjoining office. He entered and five senior military commanders jumped to their feet, standing at rigid attention.

"Remain standing," the president said sternly to the members of the Joint Chiefs of Staff. "I have questions."

Walton looked carefully at each of the men, as they looked straight ahead, a commander inspecting his troops.

"May I ask what this is about, sir?" Admiral David King asked, his hat tucked under his arm. The white at his temples contrasted with his black hair and deeply tanned face.

"Who am I?" Walton asked, his voice dramatic and harsh.

Despite the order, the men glanced nervously at each other before shouting, their words tumbling over one another:

"The president."

"Commander in Chief."

"Jeremiah Walton."

"President Walton."

"The correct answer," the president said, almost a growl, "is Commander in Chief."

He walked five paces from the men and turned, his arms at his sides. "Please be seated."

The five officers sat simultaneously. They continued to look directly ahead.

"As you undoubtedly know, Carlton Beauregard was arrested in my office just hours ago. The charge is treason, putting his personal beliefs ahead of supporting the Constitution, bragging he would oppose a direct order from me. Then he somehow escaped in a van taking him to a cell at the Pentagon. It is without question that he had help from the military, people under your command. Since his treasonous statements before me were pre-planned, so was the escape."

Walton leaned against a desk in front of the men, voice strong with indignation. "The general claimed the *Misago* discovery is an affront to Christians across America. He told me that some military officers and enlisted men and women believe their loyalty is to Jesus first, not their country nor their Commander in Chief. Do any of you feel that way? Before you answer, let me say if you support his views, I will accept your immediate resignations."

Admiral King stood. "Sir, you are the Commander in Chief. Our loyalty is to you."

"I wish each of you to state your positions."

Each officer stood, affirmed his loyalty, saluted, and sat.

"You have, I assume, seen the *Misago* story in the *Times* and *Beacon* and perhaps the full television coverage from Oakland. Its implications are shattering. I need to know that the people in the military are loyal as we work through this challenge."

He pulled a folded piece of paper from his jacket. "My intelligence operatives tell me that Beauregard is trying to create mischief, perhaps plotting to overthrow the elected government. He has a cabal of military officers supporting him. An hour ago, he gave an interview from a clandestine location claiming he was willing to be a martyr for Jesus."

"Sir," Admiral King said, "Let me…"

The president waived his hand to cut him off. "I have the names of three generals—two Army and one Marine—a Navy admiral, and two Air Force colonels who have privately expressed sympathies with his views. I don't want to make him a martyr but I want to end this now. Taking him out quietly is on the table. Now, your suggestions."

Press Room, White House

Dennis Myers walked to the podium in the White House pressroom at 4:59 p.m. Everyone was silent, hungry for new detail on the biggest story in history.

"We will begin the press conference in sixty seconds. The president has a statement. There will be no questions."

He stepped back from the stage. The rear section was filled with White House staff. At the precise sixty second moment, Myers announced:

"Ladies and gentlemen, the president of the United States."

There was applause from staff and everyone stood. Radio and television network reporters, bloggers, finished their live introductions and cut to the podium mike. All TV and cable networks were carrying the press conference live even though it had been announced less than an hour earlier. Myers had said only that it would be an official comment on the *Misago* discovery and related developments. It was all they needed.

Walton was dressed in a dark blue suit with a white shirt, red tie and an American flag lapel pin, his favorite campaign attire. The podium spots highlighted his silver hair and he looked every inch the most powerful official in the world. His jaw was set; he seemed focused, lips pressed, brow furrowed, fronting a war in his head. He spoke without notes or teleprompter.

"Members of the White House media, my fellow Americans," he said. "This has been an extraordinary week of surprises topped by the dramatic revelations of the *Misago* discovery by a fine journalist, brave in the extreme, who would not be silenced. I speak of Daniel Duboce at an aeronautics conference in Oakland this morning."

Walton looked down, taking control of his emotions, then over to his staff, his head nodding almost indiscernibly, as if making a decision. "This is a story that, *if* true, and I emphasize the *if*, this story is about God and creation. It could change humanity for good or evil. There are details of the *Misago* discovery that could be interpreted as suggesting the hands of an intelligent designer." His style was slow and deliberate, considering every word, care in pronouncing each syllable. He paused, looking out beyond the room, his hands gripping each side of the podium.

The room was silent.

"Some aspects of Misago I comprehend, many I cannot, such is the complexity. It is, literally, an atomic revelation. I've been wrestling with this discovery for several weeks. It's the most profound issue I've ever confronted."

He looked pensive, glancing down, then back at the cameras. "I was not planning on talking to you tonight but issues make this the time to communicate directly. The topic is startling, certainly disturbing and let me say, exhilarating, opening one's mind to new dimensions if we can be receptive to the infinite. I speak to you as your president and as someone who is as confused as you may be.

"I don't know if the *Misago* results are true or not. I believe the discovery is legitimate but we don't know all that it means. NASA has confirmed the findings. I've directed my scientific adviser to convene top scientists to coordinate a Manhattan-style project to study this discovery, working closely with our Japanese allies. I will also ask religious leaders to participate as well, perhaps as an adjunct group, working closely and sharing ideas.

"A few minutes ago, I spoke with the Speaker of the House and the Majority Leader of the Senate and their Democratic counterparts. I will submit a funding request to Congress later this week.

"You may have seen a press conference by the Wilkins Institute leadership yesterday urging me to do just that. I know some religious organizations have condemned the discovery as false. Let me say we have no reason to doubt there is a loving God in heaven. But this is only part of the reason I speak tonight." He took a breath and exhaled slowly.

Effective, Myers thought, the image of a thoughtful man offering honest and deep reflection on profound and incendiary issues. But he knew maturity was not a hallmark of public discourse. Would Walton's performance dampen emotions or set them ablaze by giving credibility? Fake news was popular for a reason.

Walton waited again, wiping fingers over his chin. Myers knew the look; the man was struggling.

"We must remain calm. I understand when faith is threatened some may resort to violence. But it's wrong. Daniel Duboce was shot to silence him. His assassin was butchered by someone unknown, claiming to speak for God. Mr. Duboce's son was kidnapped and rescued by private security forces. My own Director of National Intelligence threatened treason in the name of his faith, trashing the Constitution and his own honor. All this for a discovery he clearly does not understand, does not want to understand, his mind frozen by a belief system that paralyzed his ability to analyze and ponder something this revolutionary and discomfiting. He had allies who allowed him to escape to plot whatever is in his deranged mind. Treason is unacceptable. He will be found and justice served. Murder to silence a discovery will not be tolerated in my Administration, nor should it be in any democracy. It is unacceptable conduct to the American people. What is happening to our American values?"

The president scanned the reporters and staff, then back to the camera, his intent clear; he wanted to calm the public even as he was frightening many of those listening by granting the discovery credibility rather than the comfort of scorn. Myers realized this was like no other press conference in the memory of the reporters in attendance—perhaps in the history of the republic. And the military was being warned.

"This is unacceptable behavior in a free nation," Walton said with controlled fury. "This is unacceptable to anyone who believes in a merciful God. This is unacceptable in a nation of laws. If you say you believe in Jesus Christ, you do not murder or resort to violence of any kind. Jesus would condemn you. This is not about squashing an unpopular message by killing a brave man who sought to bring a scientific discovery public. I know that many, who first learned of the discovery several weeks ago, are afraid. I know that many who are reading news stories about the discovery today are afraid. But if we use the brains God gave us, common sense can prevail."

Myers thought his friend sounded like Franklin Roosevelt in the dark days of World War II or Churchill. This was not about talk show ratings or half-truths or phony news. The stakes were too important.

Walton held out both arms, speaking to millions. "I ask every American tonight to stand and pledge that you will not allow this kind of madness to grow. If you are a Christian, Muslim, Jew, atheist, or anything else, you don't seek revenge or scapegoats for your fear. I ask leaders in all faiths to take the initiative and advocate calm and peaceful discussion. I ask you to step up and make that pledge publicly as we move forward in honest discovery. If we dismiss this, crush it because it's uncomfortable or threatening, what have we accomplished? What if it's true? Mr. Duboce talked about a message from the newly minted creator. Do you want to hear it or block the call? Do you want to marvel at the wonder of stardust or build the ramparts of fear and loathing?"

The president shook his head. "Let me assure you, this is one issue I never imagined when I ran for this office." He smiled disarmingly and shrugged.

On the sidelines, Myers watched some of those around him. One of the president's young aides snorted with excitement then covered his mouth with embarrassment. An intern trembled and had to steady herself; this was the kind of drama she'd hoped to witness during her White House stint. Myers was pleased that his old Army buddy was showing the leadership he had hoped for but until now hadn't seen; spine often disintegrates as one moves up the political ladder. Machin was watching from his office, Myers knew, disappointed and likely bitter from the arguments the two had had in front of the president.

"I take responsibility for much of the chaos. I thought the world wasn't ready for this and I initially sought to suppress the discovery, reaching an agreement with the Japanese government. History will judge that action.

"In my zeal, I allowed the FBI to pursue the head of the *Misago* program when we discovered he was in the United States. We arrested Dr. Yoshito Wada. I'm not proud of how we handled it, treating him as a terrorist rather than a distinguished and thoughtful scientist. I met him when I was first briefed on the findings. Dr. Tio Ito, his close associate and a fine scientist in her own right was also arrested. I'm not proud of my order nor the FBI in its handling of her capture. Let me also state there are scurrilous rumors on the Internet and peddled by some radio talk shows about the private lives of Dr. Wada and Mr. Duboce. *It is nonsense!* Character assassination, even by well-meaning and frightened Christians, is reprehensible. It demeans them and faith itself. With such serious issues before us, let us concentrate on substance not political fantasies designed to deflect honest inquiry."

He paused again, collecting his thoughts, and smiled. "Last evening, when I returned from my Los Angeles trip, I brought back a special guest. We spent hours talking about what was found and what it means. He spent the night in the Lincoln bedroom. His name is Yoshito Wada."

Walton pointed to the doorway beside the stage. "Here he is now."

Reporters gasped. Wada stepped forward, a bit sheepishly, nodded and waved.

A blizzard of shutter clicks and cameramen jostled for position.

"He will be holding a press conference tomorrow, in this room, with my science advisor, Jeremy Stong, to advance the public dialogue. The NASA director will also take part. Dr. Tio Ito, the other Japanese scientist taken into custody by the FBI, will join them and be available for questions. She is being brought here tonight."

The president took a sip of water. "I know the results are terrifying to many of us. I include myself. New evidence suggests that an intelligent hand created us and that some of our religious beliefs, indeed perhaps most of them, may not be exactly as we have thought. Go slow. Take a deep breath and, as a nation, let us study this in peace and with a sense of genuine curiosity. Many have a vested interest in perpetuating what we have believed. I speak of churches, religious leaders, and the communities they serve. Self-protection could lead many to deny what we have been presented with no interest in truth only self-preservation. Obfuscation, angry denunciations, attacking science, political posturing are not what we need now. Thoughtfulness, humility, and a search for truth should be our guiding star."

President Walton signaled Myers that the conference was over.

"Thank you, my fellow Americans. Good night."

He left the stage as reporters shouted questions.

58.

HOLY ASTEROID!

NEW YORK, NY *(The New York Post)*—*One day after disclosure of the Misago discovery, religious leaders are dumbfounded and many irate. Few have taken up the president's request for public statements from the pulpit urging calm. Scientists, meanwhile, are ecstatic about the massive volume of data suddenly available on dozens of websites.*

Apostolic Palace, Vatican

"We've been examining the contents of the pack retrieved from Daniel Duboce's family tomb," Father Alito said, sounding confused. "Some of the asteroid samples smell like a stale cigar."

"Have you ever smelled stardust?"

The priest started to respond then changed the subject. "While I dislike Duboce's message, I respect his honest intent. I admit to rigidity when I first learned of it but watching them at Tahoe seemed to widen my boundaries. Just a little. I remain a man of faith."

"Is that a confession, my friend?" He smiled as the priest looked down, perhaps embarrassed. "Yes, we need to face the issue, now that it's out, with serious purpose."

Sylvia Carini knocked twice and entered the room with a nod to the pope as she gave a note to Alito. He read it and smiled as she exited. "Opus Dei is mounting a major march within sixty days. They hope for 500,000 people in Rome."

"Now we enter the public phase and the fight really begins," the pontiff said, slipping off his gold ring and looking at the cross. The Fisherman's Ring, named for St. Peter, a fisherman before he became a prophet. He kissed it before slipping it back on. "The church has survived much in two thousand years, but does it still have the suppleness to change and adapt when faced with something like this?" He wondered what he could do to help his friend Jeremiah and looked at Alito. "It might be easier if we knew less about the discovery," the pontiff said. "Facts can be so deflating when they support the other side."

"Do you wish to make a statement?" Alito asked. "The press office has been inundated."

"Yes. Indicate I support President Walton in his noble pursuit of the truth. Indicate my deep admiration for his integrity and leadership. And urge calm. I will address it in my Sunday blessing."

Transcendent Communications HQ, Chicago

Mike Michaels was back in his Chicago office late at night reviewing a contract with the Christian Values Association for an anti-*Misago* web site modeled after the Homosexual Urban Legends.

He heard a sound, looked up and jumped to his feet. A figure, dressed in a dark suit, stepped out of the shadow, and walked to his desk, slowly pulling on a pair of ultra-thin surgical gloves.

"V ... Vega?"

The man continued to inspect the fit of his gloves.

"What the fuck are you doing here? How'd you get in?"

Vega took off his suit coat, folding it over the back of a chair, removed his lion head cufflinks, slipping them into a pants pocket, and rolled up his shirtsleeves two turns. "I'm aware of your role and that of Sister Esther in setting up Daniel Duboce for assassination and the kidnapping of his son."

Michaels grabbed the receiver on his desk phone and punched the security code.

"It is non-operational," Vega said in a deep, satisfied voice.

Michaels listened, no sound, and slowly set it back in its cradle.

Vega put one foot on a chair and lifted his pant leg and unsnapped his *navaja*. Standing upright, he flipped it open, examined the ancient square nose blade and looked at the man in front of him. Michaels backed away knowing the closest guard was at the building entrance forty floors below. Vega snapped the knife-edge into the polished mahogany desktop and it cut deep, with the ivory handle up, ready to be retrieved.

"I believe we need a new communications plan from a PR man with your sense of virtue."

59.

CHICAGO, ILLINOIS *(Chicago Tribune)*—
Transcendent Communications CEO Michael Michaels remains under suicide watch. Police today confirmed the executive had his tongue cut out and stuck on the end of a pen on his desk like a note. In an earlier online press release, he confessed that, "I fabricated and am the source for scurrilous Internet rumors about Daniel Duboce and scientist Dr. Yoshito Wada, all part of a smear campaign paid for by the Congress of Conservative Christians (CCC)." He gave names of contacts and a copy of his contract. Two radio talk show hosts have confirmed Michaels was the source of the salacious material they had used. They also announced their immediate retirements.

CCC did not respond to repeated requests for comment.

Charlottesville, Virginia

The program, broadcasting live from the Christian Television Association studio in Charlottesville, opened with a wide shot as Reverend Adam Wright walked onto the stage and joined Reverend James Robinson. The audience applauded enthusiastically, many on their feet, watching the two men embrace, excited to hear their words as the two sat together on a white couch, knowing in their hearts that the *Misago* discover was fake.

The men were cordial even if they were more rivals than friends and, if truthful, neither liked the other. This issue was bigger than politics, it was about the survival of faith, Robinson had explained in making the invitation. Wright couldn't disagree. Twenty million viewers were expected, the largest in CBN history. Sister Esther was in seclusion somewhere, her agent cancelling all future appearances and her silence was a relief in so many ways.

"You've seen the stories," Robinson said stridently as he looked into the camera. He seemed weary, older, and angrier, Wright thought as he looked at him, a marked contrast to his usual genial style, his dream of being named the Prophet of God's Kingdom, likely in ashes.

"You likely watched Daniel Duboce give his theatrical performance designed to hype this *abomination*," Robinson said with a clenched jaw. "I suspect you saw the president announce his plans to give credence to this defamation by studyin' it. I'm deeply disappointed in this man we helped elect. If you heard my podcast sermon last night, you know the dangers we face and how we must unite to protect our faith.

"You've seen the Japanese scientists, you know we are planning our own marches of the faithful, you know people are flocking to their churches all across America. You know about the kidnapping, the attempted assassination and later, a murder. Is it any wonder, is there any doubt that Satan's behind it all, creatin' chaos as we approach the End Times?"

He turned to Wright and the camera cut to a two shot.

"What are your thoughts? We sat together at Tahoe with the Japanese scientists and Duboce. Together we heard about *Misago* and questioned it and damned it. Tell us your thinking."

"Thank you, my friend," Reverend Wright said as he watched his long-time colleague and nodded in a gesture of respect before turning to the camera, directly to millions of viewers. He wondered how many watched other sources and how it might impact their views.

"This is the most difficult and painful issue I've ever confronted," he began in a gravelly voice and a face his wife once said publicly was a pudgy Charlton Heston leading the Israelites to the Promised Land. "I too have wondered about Satan's role or whether this was a test by God."

Wright looked heavenward as if seeking counsel before returning his gaze directly into the camera lens. "But as I listened to the scientists, the journalist and even his son during those fateful days at Tahoe, as I watched them and supped with them, I did not sense Lucifer's foul presence. I also don't believe God would deceive us to test our faith."

Robinson gasped. "Surely, you're not suggestin' you believe it?"

Wright looked at the host but didn't respond. He turned again to the camera. "I have spent many hours with my wife, Mary, and my teenage son, Rolph. We've talked and prayed and argued and laughed and cried. Rolph was with me at Stonehouse Lodge. My quest for truth on *Misago* has brought my family closer together than ever. For the first time, I'm embarrassed to admit, I told my son I loved him. Just as shocking, he said he loved me."

He recalled his cathartic discussion with Rolph after the conference, remembering Duboce's comments about his own bisexual feelings as a teenager, and asking what Jesus might do. It had been just the two of them on the back deck, rocking slowly on the swing set. He asked his son's forgiveness and promised his ministry would change. He didn't care what the CCC might think. This was family. Rolph had cried. He himself cried. And his heart lifted.

Wright raised his head before the cameras, eyes glistening. "The charge that the CCC commissioned a campaign against *Misago* is true although nothing like the viciousness and distortion done in our name by Transcendent Communications. The slander against Daniel Duboce, his son and Dr. Wada is grotesque in the extreme. I denounce it on behalf of the CCC and feel truly ashamed as should all of us who agreed to it. I ask forgiveness."

The camera dollied in more tightly to capture his Moses-like countenance. "I encourage you all to be cautious as we go forward. Be skeptical. You should be. But also keep your minds open. If this is a communication from the creator, we should seek to understand what He is trying to say. If it is God reaching out to us, still a big if, do you want to risk ignoring Him? I encourage you to extend beyond your comfort zone even if it makes your hands sweat. Heaven itself could be at risk."

Robinson looked apoplectic.

"My fellow Christians," Wright went on, "with due respect for Reverend Robinson, a man I love as a brother, I support the president's call for full-scale research on this issue. How can we do less? I've my doubts it's true, at least in the current interpretation of the facts we know so far. But, we ignore it at our peril in this life and the next."

The studio audience was silent then clapped vigorously when the applause signs flashed. The camera cut back to Robinson and zoomed in close. The American Eagle of Christianity stared into the lens, his mouth agape. Clearly, for the first time in his life, he didn't know what to say.

Apostolic Palace, Vatican City

"It's good to hear your voice, Jeremiah," Pope John said, looking into the screen on his desk. "But your face is looking worn. I worry about you. Is it that renegade general still plotting to overthrow your government in the name of Jesus?"

"Yes, one of many challenges since I took a position on *Misago*. General Beauregard is being helped by a well-organized clandestine campaign. A group of military officers are aiding his camouflage and organizing."

"Very third world. Any idea where he is?"

"We've been searching. A handful of military leaders are in detention and remain mute. But finding him is only part of the problem. How do I keep from making him a hero?"

"*Stealth take out.* I saw that term used in a television show."

"The pope watches television?" He laughed.

"Sometimes. It helps provide distraction. But perhaps I can be helpful. I know someone with unusual talents."

"I didn't know your work on heaven included sublunary duties."

"I do from time to time become part of this world. And, no, I just make connections. Give me a name and phone number for your lead agent and tell them to expect a call."

60.

Daniel's Apartment, San Francisco

Sipping coffee at his apartment near Buena Vista Park, Daniel examined a photo of the girl suicide bomber from her school yearbook, now on the front page of his newspaper. It was less than a year since he got involved in this discovery, as it turned out, a bloody discovery. And there would be more. Religious disagreements were historically the most lethal, often leaving armies of the dead. For many, they didn't want to know, they only wanted to believe. And demanded that others believe along with them.

He never saw her face. Just pieces of her in the stairwell. Now he knew what a beautiful little girl she was, knew what she looked like, an innocent, naïve child. It was painful and depressing.

"She was very sweet looking," Woesha Jones, his downstairs neighbor said, setting down her own coffee mug. She was wearing a favorite ensemble, emerald flowing dress, a red and yellow Kente headscarf, and large hoop earrings he focused on now, trying to settle himself. "You gave me these earrings," she said quietly, gazing at him.

"What? I did?"

"Daniel, it wasn't your fault. It was the asshole minister!"

"You have a way with words." He didn't wish death to anyone but wasn't sorry that Reverend McConnell had received swift justice for his recruitment and indoctrination of the dead girl. What he'd done was the work of a coward drunk on his own righteousness. Hours after the girl blew herself up, police had reported that McConnell had been found naked, hanging from a rope high above his pulpit—twisting left, then right—in the empty church. Stuck into his coat pocket on the floor was a note in his own handwriting:

God sent an angel to punish me for my sins.
Hell awaits.

No question who'd done it. The death scene, the retribution matched Vega's maxim that justice needed to be swift and in the same news cycle as the offense, if there was to be deterrence. The bad guys needed to be afraid, Vega had argued in Daniel's hospital room long ago. Hopefully now they would be.

This was ugly; it tore at his gut. It should not have happened.

"I had tea with Mrs. Polenko yesterday," Woesha said of their Russian neighbor who had intervened in that other, nearly successful attempt on his life. "She may be in her late eighties and using a walker but she is one feisty woman."

"Yes, she is. And I love her. I love you."

Woesha grinned, touching his cheek with her fingertips. "Any news on finding a new place to live? I want you here but I know it's not defensible from the crazies."

He nodded. He and his son were not safe here and the target on his back endangered some of his favorite people. Vega had stationed half a dozen military style guards here and near, plus a sophisticated electronic envelope. But it wasn't fair to his neighbors. Last week's incident had confirmed it in blood.

"My book gets released in a few days. If it does well maybe I'll have more options."

"You got an amazing advance if stories are true."

"No one was more surprised than me. But yes."

Reverend McConnell's righteousness was an extreme manifestation of a new breed of angry, righteous religious militants determined to force America back to the way they perceived it was in the 1950s, other views or religions be damned. President Walton was now a target for not following through on gutting democracy.

The newspaper story had also reported that along with the letter in McConnell's pocket was a page ripped from his Bible with one passage highlighted in blue ink:

Put on the whole armour of God, that ye may be able to stand against the wiles of the devil.
– Ephesians 6:11

McConnell believed, as did many, that Satan was active on earth and they alone could see him. Daniel suspected that Satan, if he, she or it existed, was helping the Kingdom movement and opposing Misago as a means of sowing discord and violence. He himself suspected that God, either the old one or the new, likely favored democracy. It seemed like something a loving god would favor.

Garrett jumped to his feet as soon as Rolph and his dad entered the hotel room. The two boys hugged, traded brief pleasantries with the dads and then disappeared into a bedroom suite to talk.

Daniel and three security guards, all pretending to be businessmen, had booked rooms in the luxe ten-story hotel in Chillicothe, Ohio so that the two boys could meet and talk as well as the dads. Rolph and Garrett were anxious to get together in person rather than endless Zoom talks and texts. Both dads thought their boys had benefited from building their friendship.

Garrett was past eleven now and growing into his teen years. Rolph was fifteen, still young for his age. They'd bonded at Lake Tahoe and talked regularly.

"It's so wonderful to see you in person," Rolph gushed to Garrett. "You've such a positive view of the world. I hope becoming a teen doesn't change that." He plopped into a large, upholstered chair, crossed his legs.

The room was divided into two sections, the bed in an alcove and a seating area in a kind of small meeting space. Garrett sat in a sofa, kicked off his tennis shoes and curled his feet up under him. "How is your new school *really*?" he blurted with excitement. "I know you said it was a major improvement. But our dads aren't listening in on us now. Tell me the truth." He grinned at his friend.

Rolph giggled, and blushed. "It's so much better than that Christian school Dad pulled me out of. It's a small private academy. No real bullying and…and…I met someone!"

"Oh!...Really!" Garrett jumped up and ran to him, kneeling on the floor. "I want the dirt! Spill!"

Rolph's face was alight with his grin and sparkling eyes. "His name is Toby. He's my age. A virgin, like me. We're taking it real slow, just like you said. My father's met him and likes him. His family is friendly, nice. At first they were leery of my dad because of his super righteous ministry. But since he's pulled back from *Leviticus* and sin, talking more about Jesus and love, they like him better."

"I can imagine. My dad's played a couple of his new podcast sermons and I listened. A ministry based on love and respect is good." He slapped his shoulder. *"Have you kissed?"*

Rolph suppressed a grin.

"Spill!"

"YES!" the teen shouted, lifting both arms overhead and laughing.

The two hugged. Garrett sat cross-legged on the floor. Rolph joined him and they gossiped. Rolph so excited to give more details. Garrett was sure, or as sure as an eleven-year-old can be, he would be straight. But he had gay friends. And obviously his dad was dating a dude.

Afterward, at lunch, the four sat at a table, enjoying cheeseburgers and fries. The boys were tight together, laughing.

"Reverend," Garrett asked between bites. "I know my dad has talked to you about joining the board of his new non-profit. Will you?"

"My, you are direct, just like your father."

"I hope that's a good thing."

"Yes, it is. I learned to admire your dad at Lake Tahoe. Rolph, do you think I should?"

"Wow. Uhmmm. Yeah. I think it would be nice having your viewpoint represented on what might be a big factor in the debate over *Misago*."

"Thank you for that," Daniel said. "Another young man who speaks his mind."

"Daniel, Garrett, let me consider it. My ministry hit real turbulence when I broke ranks with the CCC. Can I give you an answer later in the year?"

"Will Garrett attend board meetings?" Rolph asked. "And if so, can I go too? He's my friend."

61.

City of Souls, Colma

Daniel stood in his mother's tomb. He didn't want to draw attention to the location and only came at odd hours when the grounds were empty as they were this day at dawn. He put one arm around Saito's waist, the other rested on Garrett's shoulder.

Behind them, Vega stood silently with a guard.

"When I was last here, I had no idea where this would lead." Images flooded his mind—the threats, the attempted assassination, the hiding and secrecy. "The darkness has at times seemed overwhelming."

"Read your book," Saito said, teasing. "Through the darkness, *Misago* brought the light."

He laughed, biting his lower lip. "It also brought us together." Daniel kissed his cheek and squeezed his son closer. "All of us." His new life partner and Garrett had bonded, Saito a great teacher, friend, and baseball coach. Plus, he liked dogs.

Daniel felt fully recovered, energized, re-born, a family man drafted into a religious war like no other in history. He recalled the words of his childhood hero Carl Sagan—*"I would rather know than believe."* As the answers were revealed, truth must not be left to self-proclaimed prophets who could distort and covet and twist for their own gains as they had throughout history. This time it must be different. This would take decades to sort out, if even then, given the ferocious pushback. People did not give up comfort food easily, or cigarettes despite health issues, much less religious faith rooted in long held traditions and part of what defined community for many. Many religious leaders had rejected it without examination. Some agonized, wondering if they would have a place in this new world.

"Mother, so much happened when I was a boy," Daniel said as if she sat nearby.

"The problems with Dad that you never wanted to talk about and my dream to make you proud. I was rash and unforgiving with him, for what he did to you, did to us. You left me when I was a very young man just a little older than Garrett is now. You would love him, mother, this wonderful grandson you never met." He pressed Garrett's shoulder. The boy put his arm around his dad's waist and slipped a thumb through a belt loop.

"I don't know if you can hear me or not," Daniel said. "My religious views are a little confused now but I've often visited you here and there's much to be said for tradition, particularly in these times. I want you to meet Dr. Hideo Saito, his second visit here. Please call him Saito; he prefers it simple. I like to think you would approve of this relationship because you were so open minded, had gay friends, and always wanted the best for me. Saito is the best. I've asked him to marry me and he has agreed. One complication is that it's not yet legal in Japan but it is in California. There is the possibility of another location. NASA has hired him as a liaison with JAXA and an upcoming massive mining operation in deep space, an international project to be managed by our friend Tio Ito. There is even talk Saito may be one of the astronauts. If selected, which seems likely, we're exploring the possibility of me going with him to the International Space Station and getting married there. An estimated billion viewers in the audience. That would be an interesting new record and make a statement to the millions who would approve and disapprove."

He kissed the top of his son's head. "For lots of reasons, Garrett is back in my life full time. I have a family again."

He ran a finger along her name engraved in the marble wall. Garrett did the same. Surprising him, Saito stepped forward and repeated the greeting.

"Nice to meet you, *okaasan*."

The three of them hugged.

Trudy was living in London now with her husband and his two daughters. They wanted safety, away from the danger and notoriety of *Misago*. Daniel had full legal custody of Garrett. Vega's security force, a small army, would keep his son safe. Daniel's book, *Misago & God*, easily fit into the manuscript on faith he'd already written. A signing bonus made him wealthy enough to lease a Pacific Heights mansion built like a fortress, and sales were massive. His days as a reporter were over. He was the news story now, not a storyteller about others. He was now president of a major new non-profit called *Faith Forward*, to fight the charlatans and seek honest discussion. Vega had seeded the fundraising with an astonishing ten billion dollars; contributions from a wide range of other donors had been generous. Wada, now president of JAXA, would be on his board. Reverend Wright had agreed to join as well, thanks to the two son's lobbying. That added an important dimension.

He thought about Jeremiah Walton facing his own problems, including threatened impeachment by frightened, pandering politicians, his base in turmoil and furious. He'd asked for Daniel's help. That surprised him given the hate letters, threats, and blind panic in the president's own party. But Walton claimed Daniel was the most famous man in the world; millions respected him, even if millions more wanted him dead.

"You suck the oxygen out of any room you enter," Walton had told him with a grin. "Many believe you are a new John the Baptist, a saint in Christianity, a prophet in Islam, heralding what is coming. That qualifies you as a superhero." Daniel had laughed at the time but knew the phenomenon was real. He'd agreed to take part in the fight against impeachment under certain conditions, admiring the man's intellect and how he'd handled the issue once his hand was forced. At the top of the list was a public statement opposing the Kingdom Movement and, second, a major initiative by the Department of Justice challenging voter restraints that kept most Americans from voting.

Walton had agreed.

The man could have gone safer at his press conference on the discovery, but curiosity and an open mind had compelled him to back science and exploration. Courage in politics should be encouraged and supported. Science needed to be respected again, particularly in the highest office. Often it seemed the most publicly pious were the least sincere, using faith to exploit for personal gain. Walton had suggested they both make good use of the Gospel of Matthew. In it, Jesus condemned the hypocrites who made an ostentatious display of praying. He could think of many examples. But Daniel thought humility a better course.

As they exited the tomb, the door was pulled shut and locked by a young guard.

Daniel touched Jurg on the elbow, the man who had rescued his son, and smiled. Garrett was beside the man, the two like brothers.

Daniel glanced at Vega, a man who had been on both sides of the *Misago* issue. For now, he was with him. Time for second thoughts later, family first.

They stood in the cool morning air looking over the green hills of the dead. Birds chirped as they often did at dawn and a breeze made noisy passage through the forest. A reassuring melody.

Civilization, even heaven, may splinter but the physical world seemed safe, at least for now. Three armor-plated black SUVs waited and a half-dozen armed guards, three looking combat ready. Saito led Garrett to the middle car, opened the door on the driver's side and his son slipped inside, Saito following. Vega walked to the passenger side and opened the door. The two men faced each other.

"Congratulations," Vega said, "on your upcoming wedding. I think it's a perfect match, two men of destiny uniting and changing the world. There is some irony on gay men playing a pivotal role in the future of faith; haters beware. Garrett seems pleased as he should be. A strong and loving family unit."

"Thank you. I appreciate your support. How do you think this new family of mine will impact public discourse on *Misago*?"

"Those who find purpose in hate will spurt bile no matter what you do or whom you love. Anger can be an addiction, my friend. Politics is often more about theatre and less about honesty. It seems to me they focus on the irrelevant. With heaven at risk, seeking to condemn a segment of society for personal gain is both repugnant and dangerous for them. In the back of the mind of even the most fervent believer is a voice whispering: what if *Misago* is real? Critics should at a minimum hedge their bets given the risk to their souls. And the god, old or new, created you this way."

"Nice. Thank you. You clearly are not a one sentence guy."

"Some issues are more complicated than monosyllables."

He still had so many questions about this man, a stranger, former enemy now an ally, friend and protector. "You said your ancestors moved from the Middle East to Spain. Vega sounds Spanish not Arabic."

"It is Arabic. Have you heard of the star system Vega?"

"Let me think…of course. Carl Sagan wrote a novel about a SETI astronomer detecting a signal from that constellation leading to first contact. The movie starred Jodie Foster."

"Indeed. A fine actress and great story. Vega is derived from an Arabic word and was selected to honor the traditional importance of astronomy in Islam. As the heavens turn, that constellation is the past and future North Star for Earth." His lips spread into a dazzling smile.

Daniel stared at the man and found Vega's intense green eyes looking back. He had to grin. So, Vega. Always mysterious and not without a sense of humor.

"What now, Romaldo? You're a man of history."

"Some thoughts, my friend. When Galileo first looked into his telescope and saw that earth was not the center of the universe, the Catholic Church crushed him. Under the whip he recanted. Different churches have sought your destruction. Yet their bullets made you stronger and birthed a legend. Your army grows, soldiers with open minds who can see the wonder, as Dr. Wada likes to say. Those opposed, and they are vast in number, will become more desperate as their idols prove false. But good guys can sometimes win."

"Just who are they?" Daniel kept smiling even as he absorbed Vega's insights. From anyone else, such words would seem overblown, apocalyptic, even a bit silly. But Vega was not just any man.

"A short list to begin with. You, Drs. Wada, Ito, and Saito, Mr. Bloomingdale, my dear friend Pope John XXIV, your remarkable son, President Walton, Reverend Wright. Then thousands of journalists and scientists," Vega replied, his eyes luminous in the morning light, his voice reassuring. "An American public surprisingly more curious than hateful, as many relieved as disturbed. The numbers will shift your way over time."

"Many good people, people of faith, sincerely believe I'm evil."

"You can be sincere and wrong. Trust me, you did the right thing."

"How do you know?"

Vega's broad grin returned. "Inside information."

Once in the backseat, Daniel draped an arm around his son. His fiancé, on the opposite side did the same, taking a moment to mess up Garrett's hair. The boy pushed his head back and laughed. As the sun broke through the fog, they left the cemetery, headed back to their new home in San Francisco, unsure of their future but united as a family and full of hope.

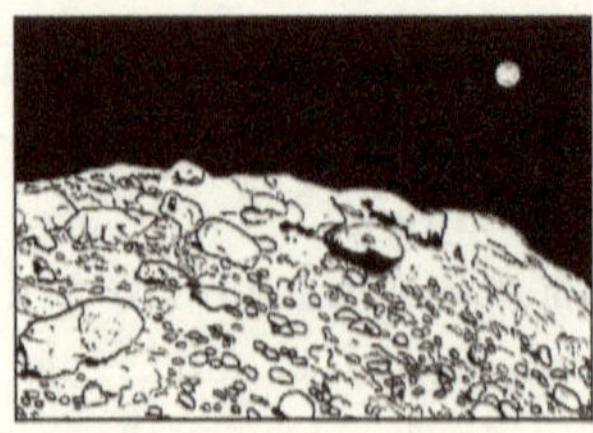

ABOUT THE AUTHOR

Steven A. Coulter writes speculative fiction, exploring issues of consequence embedded in fast-paced action, exotic settings, with nasty bad bays and reluctant heroes. He also likes to feature LGBTQ+ protagonists.

His work is enriched by his varied careers—soldier, teacher, journalist, state legislator, corporate executive, and library commissioner. He was a Lambda Literary Fellow in 2008 and 2013, later spending two years on the Board. He lives in San Francisco with his husband, Greg.

Other books by Steven A. Coulter:

CHRONICLES OF SPARTAK, RISING SON (2015)

The ruling elite see Spartak as a trophy; the people see him as their best hope. By the year 2115, twelve families control all wealth in America, the middle class is myth, democracy a con game and the Supreme Court has just legalized a new entertainment option for the bored elite.

CHRONICLES OF SPARTAK, FREEDOM'S HOPE (2017)

Fighting to restore the America of legend, Spartak Jones becomes one. By 2116, the war between the ruling elites is now full frontal and the seventeen-year-old has become its celebrity warrior and icon for an America that used to be.

COPPERHEAD—STUDENT. SINGER. LOVER. SPY. (2023)

When his family is torn apart, a college freshman uses his charm and looks to infiltrate the world of the rich and powerful risking his life for a greater cause.. .

COPPERHEAD 2—HERO. HEARTTHROB. HUSTLER. PREY. (2024))

Abel Torres is now one of the most famous young men in America, a national hero, a sophomore at San Francisco State on the edge of superstardom. At the same time, white supremacists seethe over his role in the death of their fellow conspirators, ruining dreams of a civil war.

PASSAGEWAY (2024)

Chosen by mystical warriors to protect a parallel Earth from a catastrophic future, a young man must push his mental and physical abilities to the limits if he is to help save mankind.

PASSAGEWAY 2—HOMO SAPIENS FUTURIS (2024)

In the ancient forests of northern California, a mother's final act to protect her child sets off a chain of events that draws Guardians of the Passageway, Darwin McQuaid and Daruk, into a deadly mystery.